PROMISE
OF
WRATH

By Steve McHugh

THE HELLEQUIN CHRONICLES

Crimes Against Magic

Born of Hatred

With Silent Screams

Prison of Hope

Lies Ripped Open

Infamous Reign

PROMISE OF WRATH

STEVE McHUGH

WITHDRAWN

47N●RTH

Text copyright © 2016 Steve McHugh

Published by 47North, Seattle

www.apub.com

Amazon, the Amazon logo, and 47North are trademarks of Amazon.com, Inc., or its affiliates.

ISBN-13: 9781503940062
ISBN-10: 1503940063

Cover design by Eamon O'Donoghue

Printed in the United States of America

For Mum.
Thank you.

LIST OF CHARACTERS

Flashback

Nathaniel (Nathan, Nate) Garrett: Sorcerer. Works for Merlin as the shadowy figure Hellequin.

Mordred: Sorcerer. Traitor of Avalon, and nemesis of Nate.

Nanshe: Sorcerer. Mesopotamian goddess of social justice.

Isabel: Human. Resident of Acre.

Siris: Earth elemental. Mesopotamian goddess of beer.

Irkalla: Necromancer. Mesopotamian goddess of the underworld.

Nabu: Och. Mesopotamian god of wisdom.

Gilgamesh: Giant. Exceptional warrior.

Asag: Utukku. Ekimmu. Monstrous warrior.

Enlil: Utukku. Shedu. Nate's guide to Acre.

Current Timeline

Nathan (Nate) Garrett: Sorcerer. Once worked for Merlin as the shadowy figure, Hellequin.

Erebus (Nightmare): The living embodiment of Nate's magic.

Thomas (Tommy) Carpenter: Werewolf. Nate's best friend. Partner to Olivia. Father of Kasey.

Kasey (Kase) Carpenter: Half-werewolf. Daughter of Tommy and Olivia.

Chloe Range: Witch. Best friend of Kasey Carpenter. Daughter of Mara.

Brutus, Friends and Employees

Brutus: Sorcerer. King of London.

Diane: Half-werebear. Brutus's lieutenant and head of his security.

Licinius: Sorcerer. Brutus's lieutenant.

Avalon Members

Olivia Green: Water elemental. Director of southern England branch of the Law of Avalon (LOA). Partner of Tommy. Mother of Kasey.

Remy Roax: British son of a French aristocrat. Turned into a fox-human hybrid by a witch coven.

Realm of Nidavellir

Zamek Merla: Dwarven warrior-commander.

Birik: Dwarven warrior.

Malib: Dwarven warrior.

Udthulo: Dwarven warrior.

Grundelwy: Dwarven doctor.

Stel: Dwarven rune scribe.

Jurg: Dwarven doctor.

Jinayca Konal: One of the dwarven elders in the city of Sanctuary.

Brigg: Dwarven realm-gate guardian.

Mythanus: Blood elf.

William: Human slave to the blood elves.

Miscellaneous

Sir Kay: Sorcerer. Ex-director of the Shield of Avalon (SOA). Traitor. Brother of King Arthur.

Mordred: Sorcerer. Traitor of Avalon, and nemesis to Nate. Was presumed dead.

Morgan: Sorcerer. Traitor of Avalon, and ally of Mordred.

Irkalla: Necromancer. Mesopotamian goddess of the underworld.

Nabu: Och. Mesopotamian god of wisdom.

Mara: Witch. Chloe's mum. Enemy of Nate.

Jerry: Vampire.

Ivy: Youngest Fate, able to see the future. Daughter of Grace, Granddaughter of Cassandra.

Grace: Middle Fate, able to see the present. Mother of Ivy.

Cassandra: Oldest Fate, able to see the past. Mother of Grace.

CHAPTER 1

September 1195. Kingdom of Jerusalem.

I do not like the feeling of being hunted, of being pursued by some unknown force. I do not like that itch in the back of my shoulders where I can almost feel someone staring at me. It's not a feeling anyone should ever get used to, but I more than most knew not to ignore it.

And I *was* being hunted. I knew that for a certainty. In fact, I'd known it for the better part of the last three days and nights, ever since we'd arrived in the Kingdom of Jerusalem on my way to Acre. I wanted to turn around and confront whoever—or, as was more likely, whatever—happened to be behind us. But my guide pushed me on, forcing me to follow or get lost behind.

"Not far now," my guide said, as the first rays of the morning sun broke over the horizon.

We'd been walking through the night and resting during the day, ever since we'd met four days earlier. He'd explained that the night was when our hunter friend would be active, and that it wasn't capable of following during the day. I still didn't know what "it" was, but it was enough to scare my guide, and I took his concerns seriously. When a demon is scared of something, you damn well listen.

Technically my guide wasn't a demon, although those who used to worship the pantheon he followed certainly thought his kind was. His name was Enlil, and he was one of the *utukku*, a species the ancient Mesopotamians considered to be demonic. Unfortunately, their short, slender appearance, the two small horns that adorned their head, and their long red tails did little to help dissuade otherwise. Still, they were no more demonic than a werewolf or sorcerer.

"We will need to rest," Enlil told me as the sun continued to rise, and with it a respite from having to keep ahead of whatever was coming for us.

"Do you ever plan on telling me what it is?" I asked after we'd found suitable shade in an old building that had seen far better days. One of the walls had all but collapsed, and the sands had taken most of the lower floor, but the upper was mercifully barren from both sand and the multitude of small animals that lived in the area.

"This used to be an outpost," Enlil said as he settled in a corner. "It was destroyed during the last crusade."

"Enlil," I said, keeping my voice calm, "no more changing the subject. What's hunting us?"

Enlil sighed. "It's nothing to worry about."

"Yet you clearly are. So you either tell me, or I'll go back there myself and find out what it is."

Enlil sat upright. "No, you must not do such a thing. It will kill you."

"What is it?" I asked again, keeping the fact that I wasn't exactly easy to kill from my tone. It wouldn't do to mock his concern.

"An utukku."

"You're scared of someone like you?" I asked. "I find that hard to believe."

"There are two types of my people. I am *shedu*. As a rule, the shedu are children of the light; we believe in peace, harmony, and balance within all things. The one hunting us is an *ekimmu*."

I'd heard the word before, but had never come across one of its kind. "And they're not the peace, love, and happiness that the shedu are?"

"They are monsters. Whereas both shedu and ekimmu use elemental power, the ekimmu also use a dark, twisted power—a power you would call blood magic. The one hunting us is named Asag. He is a being of considerable power. A being who has allowed the use of blood magic to turn him into a hideous creature."

"They're blood leeches?" I asked, genuinely interested and wanting to understand more about something that was trying to hunt me.

"No, the utukku are not sorcerers, nor are we elementals. The use of blood magic in our kind has different repercussions from yours. It makes them incredibly powerful, much more so than any shedu could hope to combat. But with that power comes insanity, and a twisted appearance." Enlil looked down at his feet. "I pray you never come across their kind."

"Why is he—" I started.

"It is male, yes."

"Why is he hunting us?"

"*You*. He's hunting *you*, not us. He cares little for my kind—or anyone who isn't him, to be honest. Hellequin's arrival appears to have sparked some interest from people you would rather not deal with."

I looked out across the terrain behind us; the constant hills and rock formations made it easy for someone to stay hidden and out of sight. Why did this monster stalk me? What was his purpose? And how had he discovered my being here? "My arrival was meant to be unknown."

"Then you have a leak that needs plugging. We will reach Acre tonight. Asag will not pursue you into the city." Enlil laid down, his red-tinged skin becoming darker as he fell asleep.

I dozed on and off for a few hours until dusk once again brought a need for Enlil and me to move.

There was more speed now, being so close to our destination, and I felt a surge of relief when the lights of Acre shone in the distance, but after a short while Enlil stopped and looked behind me. "Run."

I didn't need telling twice and the two of us were soon sprinting toward Acre, but there was a low roar that caused me to stop, and freeze while the safety of the city was close in the distance. We weren't going to make it.

"Enlil, stop moving."

Enlil did as I asked, looking at me with a mixture of concern and realization.

"You hear that?" I asked as the low rumble that appeared to come from all around us grew in size.

"Asag is here," he told me.

I risked a look behind me and saw something standing on top of a hill only a few hundred yards away. Its massive shape was masked by the darkness, but I knew it was what had been hunting us.

"Asag, I presume?" I asked.

Enlil looked up at the hill and nodded once. "He must have ignored the pain of daylight traveling."

The earth around our feet exploded and a dozen creatures tore free, standing just out of reach. Each of them was about two feet high, and appeared to be made of solid rock.

"An extension of Asag's power. These creatures are a part of him. Destroy these, and it weakens him." Enlil drew a sword from the sheath on his hip.

I stared at the relatively small creatures. Asag must have been pushing them in front of us while he chased from behind, it was a smart move, and now we were trapped only a short distance from the city.

"Hellequin," the voice of Asag boomed through the night as the monster began walking toward us. "You are not welcome here. None of your kind are."

"My kind?" I asked Enlil.

"Avalon."

I unsheathed the jian, a Chinese sword, and held it toward Asag, ignoring the small creatures between us. "Feel free to come remove me."

Asag screamed in rage and charged toward us as his creatures pounced. I knocked one into another using my air magic, trying to ensure they didn't swarm over us. Enlil stabbed his blade into one of the creatures, and was forced to leave it there, using his natural strength to throw the creatures around, as he made his way toward Asag, where his battle began anew.

I was too preoccupied with keeping the smaller creatures busy to watch them fight, but after a short time the creatures vanished back into the ground, and I turned to Enlil and Asag, moving toward the pair to help my guide.

Enlil was holding his own against the larger Asag, but that soon turned when the small creatures burst from the ground, grasping hold of Enlil. I was flat out sprinting when Asag punched a hole through Enlil's chest, tearing out his heart and tossing it aside as if it were nothing.

Asag picked up Enlil's lifeless body and threw it at me, forcing me to dodge aside, right into the path of his minions, who quickly swarmed over me, dragging me down as I threw magic around, trying to give myself a fighting chance. Asag stalked over until he towered above my kneeling position.

"Hellequin should have stayed at home."

He raised his hand, and I ignited my fire magic, pouring everything into it. The magic forced the creatures off me, and caused Asag to scream out in pain. He staggered back as I got to my feet, ready to tear him apart. But the noise of a horse galloping behind me made Asag's eyes widen with shock. I didn't dare risk a look as the huge monster turned and fled.

The first I saw of the horse or its rider was when it passed me and was brought to a halt. The black warhorse was massive—which was for the best, considering the size of its rider. A mountain swung off the horse and walked over to me. He was close to seven feet tall, with a long beard that touched his chest. His bare, muscle-laden chest looked more like an immovable wall. Frankly he looked like he could have juggled horses, not just ride them.

"Hellequin," the man said, his voice deep and commanding, used to having people do as he said. And for good reason: this man had once been a king, and some things are not easily forgotten.

"Gilgamesh," I said, grasping his forearm. "Thank you for the timely intervention. Unfortunately, Enlil didn't make it."

Gilgamesh picked up Enlil's body, cradling it in his massive arms. He walked over to his horse, and heaved the body up onto the animal's back. "He was a good man—a brave man. We will sing songs about him."

"Asag knew I was coming," I told Gilgamesh as we walked back toward the city.

"Maybe those who requested your presence will know more. I am but a soldier."

As we reached the first guard post just before one of the sets of gates to the city of Acre, I began to wonder if I'd imagined that I'd heard a tone of displeasure in his words.

The guard waved us past the checkpoint and toward a second checkpoint posted just outside the huge gates that signified Acre's entrance proper. The second set of guards consisted of a dozen heavily armed men, all of whom were trying to get people into the city in an orderly fashion. It usually meant shouting at people until they stopped talking, and/or demanding money from them.

Gilgamesh merely walked through the group as if they weren't there. Several of them looked at the body of Enlil, still draped across the horse's back. Some recoiled in horror, while others quickly moved their gaze toward the ground. Gilgamesh didn't speak as we walked down small alleyways and through a courtyard, until we eventually reached a large house overlooking the sea below.

The smell of the fresh sea air was a welcome break from the desert of the last few days and I found myself wishing I'd just taken a ship to arrive here. Gilgamesh opened the door without knocking, leaving the horse and Enlil outside. I used my fire magic to give me night vision, casting everything in an orange hue, but it meant I could see no more than a few yards ahead.

Gilgamesh took me further down the staircase until we came to another door. He opened it with a small key and motioned for us both to enter.

"Where are we?" I asked, as I stepped into what appeared to be a huge cavern beneath the city.

"Old catacombs," Gilgamesh explained. "Been abandoned for a long time. We think they used to belong to smugglers."

I looked around at the ornate columns and rune work on the walls. "Smugglers didn't make these."

"Maybe they did, maybe they didn't," he said, with a wave of his hand. "I'm sure you have probably seen a great many things that rival our *small* efforts."

"Gilgamesh, the last time I saw something as impressive as this, the dwarves had made it. It's stunning."

He stared at me for a moment, before bowing his head in thanks. He took me to the left of the cavern, where a huge iron door had been built, almost as if it were part of the rock that surrounded it. Gilgamesh knocked twice and opened the door, motioning for me to enter.

I had no idea what the room looked like, or who else was in it; all I saw, sat in one corner, was Mordred. He was chained around the wrists and tethered to the ground, a sorcerer's band—a metallic bracelet with runes inscribed into it that removed his ability to use magic—sat on one wrist. He was powerless and I could have killed him without thinking twice about it: a fact he knew exceptionally well. He smiled.

"Glad you could make it," he said. "I'd wave, but my hands are fastened to this seat."

I stepped forward, my hand instinctively dropping to my sword that hung against my waist.

Gilgamesh stepped in between us. "You will not touch him," he told me.

"Gilgamesh—" I protested.

"I said no," he repeated, this time crossing his arms over his chest as if to signify that the conversation was over.

I weighed my odds. Could I get past Gilgamesh toward Mordred before the former killed me? Gilgamesh's maul was leaning up against a wall a few yards away, but I'd also seen the man punch out a troll, and I doubted Asag would have been able to hold off the old king's advances for long. I relaxed and took a step back.

"Good man," Gilgamesh said with a slight smile.

"Someone had better explain why Mordred is here, why he isn't dead, and why I can't kill him. Enlil died to get me here. I've been attacked by a rock monster. I'm in no mood to play games."

"I can explain everything," a woman said from beside me. She looked at Gilgamesh. "Enlil died?"

Gilgamesh nodded. "Asag."

The woman closed her eyes and breathed out slowly. "Damn it. Damn them all for doing this." She turned toward me. "For all of the awfulness that has happened, I'm glad you're here, Hellequin."

I looked at the young woman who regarded me with such warmth, and felt guilty about even considering killing Mordred in her presence. I'd met her a century ago in Camelot, when she was a guest of Elaine's. In Sumerian mythology, she'd been known as a goddess of social justice, prophecy, and fishing. She was loved by her people, and trusted by Elaine. I'd liked her immediately, and found her an interesting and warm person to be around.

"Nanshe," I said, with a bow of my head, "this man sullies your presence."

"Now that's unfair!" Mordred shouted. "She hasn't given me a chance to sully anything yet!"

"Be quiet, Mordred," Nanshe said.

Astonishingly, Mordred actually shut up. "We need his help," she said, regarding me once more. "We need your help too."

"Why?"

"Mordred was involved in a plot to attack Avalon personnel here in Acre."

"That's not a surprise; he's always involved in something. And that tallies with what Asag said about Avalon personnel not being welcome. I assume they're friends?"

"It would appear that any flame of friendship between them is long since extinguished. Unfortunately, we don't know what their plot is. When I told Merlin, he insisted he send you along to help."

I got the feeling she hadn't been too impressed with Merlin sending me, but I ignored her irritation. "Can't you make Mordred talk?"

"He doesn't know the plot itself, just the players involved. And once he learned that you were on your way here, he decided he'd only give those names to you."

I was stunned. "Wait – Mordred asked for *me*?"

Nanshe nodded. "We found him in the city and had him arrested, but he will only talk to you about those involved."

I stared at Mordred. "Why?"

"Why?" he asked. "Because I want to watch your face when you fail. I want to see your expression when thousands die because you couldn't stop it."

I looked back at Nanshe, determined to ensure that Mordred's words didn't come to pass. "Right, let's get started then."

CHAPTER 2

Now. Basingstoke, England.

This really doesn't seem fair," Tommy said, as he landed on his back while his daughter, Kasey, put him in an arm lock.

"I think it's brilliant!" I told him through bouts of laughter. "Seeing you thrown around the room: it's like a dream come true."

"It's not bad for me either," Kasey said as she released the grip on her father's arm and got back to her feet.

Tommy glared at me. "I thought *you* were meant to be the one training her."

"I am! I'm training her to kick your ass."

A year earlier, in front of a large part of Avalon's more powerful players, I'd agreed to become one of Kasey's sentinels. The job requirements were easy. As a sentinel, it was my duty to ensure that Kasey, or "Kase" as she liked to be known, was always ready for whatever life threw at her. On top of that, I'd agreed to train her. She was going to be Hellequin's pupil, and frankly that had brought with it a host of people looking her way with a kind of alarm. Getting someone many considered to be little more than an assassin to train a young woman to follow in his footsteps was hardly going to make everyone happy. Thankfully, Tommy, his partner, Olivia, and Kase were the only people whose opinions I actually cared about, and all of them had been thrilled.

I'd started training Kase within a week of returning from Avalon, and for months Tommy had asked when she was ready to spar with someone. I don't think he had himself in mind, but after seeing him thrown onto the floor for the twentieth time, I felt like I'd made the right choice.

"This isn't as fun as either of you seem to think it is," Tommy said as he climbed back to his feet. "You do realize, I'm not actually fighting back here."

"Well, you have several hundred years, at least a foot in height and a few stone in weight on me," Kase said. "It wouldn't be a fair fight."

"And this is?" he asked.

"No, this is fun," I told him.

"I'm glad to see she's improving so much," Tommy said as he rubbed his arm.

"I'm a machine," Kase said with a laugh and boxed at the air.

"Cocky, too," Tommy told her. "Am I allowed to say the force is strong with this one?"

"No!" Kase and I said together.

Tommy grinned and got back to his feet. "I'm genuinely impressed. Now go shower—you stink."

Kase laughed and ran off.

"Seriously, are you trying to kill me?" Tommy asked when we were alone.

"That's the plan," I admitted. "I figured with you out of the way I could run your empire and keep your riches."

"My empire runs without me already," he pointed out. Tommy had worked for Avalon—specifically for the Shield of

Avalon or SOA—for centuries before leaving and starting his own security firm. The SOA was basically Avalon's MI5 and MI6, and Tommy's experience with Avalon, and his subsequent departure, allowed him a lot of goodwill from people who might not want to go to the SOA to discuss their troubles.

Tommy marketed his business as a place where Avalon politics didn't enter into any work done, and from what I could see, it appeared to be working. He'd had to open two new branches—one in America and the other in Japan—just to keep up with the demand of work from all over the globe. It also allowed him to put people he trusted in charge so he could spend more time doing things he loved. Like eating and watching *Star Wars*.

"What about your riches?" I asked as we left the gym in his building and walked toward his office.

"You can have that. But you'll have to work here for it."

I chuckled. "I think I'm good, thanks. The last time I did work for you it didn't end well."

We were both silent for a few seconds after the humor evaporated. The work I'd done for him had led to us hunting a serial-killing monster: a monster that nearly murdered Tommy, Kase, and me. It wasn't a good memory.

"Well, that killed the mood," I said when we reached his office door.

"Make yourself comfortable. I'm going to shower."

Tommy's office had undergone an overhaul since I had last visited. It still had the mass of windows down one side, giving less-than-incredible views of roads and an industrial estate. Pictures that Kase had drawn as a young child still hung on walls, but Tommy had converted an adjacent room into an office bathroom.

Tommy wandered off to the small bathroom so he could shower, hopefully with the end result of him smelling considerably better. While I was left to my own devices, I perused his bookshelves, finding various fantasy and science fiction books nestled in between a plethora of *Star Wars* comics and novels.

"I'm surprised you didn't have this office redecorated as a Sith temple or something," I called out.

"Considered it," Tommy shouted through the door. "Olivia told me it wasn't overly professional."

I paused. "Smart woman."

"Or spoilsport."

"My answer is more accurate."

Tommy exited the bathroom after a few minutes, wearing an expensive black suit. "I have a board meeting in an hour," he told me, explaining the reason for dressing up before I had the chance to mock him.

"How unbearably exciting."

"Not even a little bit, but they're necessary, and frankly I want to see how the new offices are doing."

"How's Olivia?"

"Neck-deep in Reaver awesomeness, as per usual, for the last year. She stays in contact when she can, but it's not unusual for us to go days without actually seeing one another."

The Reavers were a group of psychopaths who decided that killing me and taking over Avalon was their new life goal. They were working with King Arthur's brother, Kay: a man who had tried to start a coup to overthrow the government of Avalon. It hadn't gone well, and Kay had ended up with most of his allies being killed or arrested. But Kay himself escaped. No one had seen him since, but I was certain he'd resurface soon enough.

There was unfinished business between the two of us, and I was pretty certain I didn't need to hunt for him. He'd find me. And then I'd end his miserable little existence.

After Kay's failed attack, Olivia, who was already the head of a Law of Avalon, or LOA, office—Avalon's police force—and someone who had excelled at the role, despite those above her throwing barriers in her way, had been promoted. She was put in charge of Special Operations, overseeing the capture of any and all Reavers currently operating. It had turned out to be a full-time job. Avalon was meant to be the secret governing power behind everything in the world, but if the Reavers got their way, it would be less secret and a lot more dangerous for everyone. Especially me.

At the moment, Avalon mostly allows humanity to do as they wish, only intervening if things get to a stage where it infringes Avalon's power, or causes concern within the Avalon community. And even then the political nature of the beast means that by the time anything ever gets done, whatever they were worried about is usually over. In this instance, Avalon—and its leader, Elaine Garlot—had decided to act decisively.

"Merlin still want me dead?" I asked.

"I don't think he's taken out an advert in the paper or anything," Tommy said, "but that's the general idea, yes."

I'd been told by multiple people on multiple occasions that after Merlin had removed all protection from me, I should beware incoming attacks. So far, nothing. But I doubted it would stay that way forever. Over the sixteen hundred years of my life, I may have made an enemy or two. Maybe.

I grabbed a newspaper from the table beside me and leafed through it. "You still read these? I thought everyone had gone digital."

"I get a bunch delivered every day. I like to keep up with whatever lies they're peddling. If you read them enough, you can see Avalon's influence in anything important. Reading between the lines in a paper is sometimes quicker than actually contacting Avalon for information."

I continued to flick through the pages and paused at a picture of some old stonework. The article mentioned that several ancient Babylonian artifacts were going to be taken to the British Museum for display and scientific research.

"Has anyone looked into this?" I asked, showing Tommy the page. There had been occasions of old artifacts being discovered that did all kinds of weird stuff, like summoning monsters or containing blood-magic curses: things people don't really want activating in the middle of a museum.

"Yep. It's all safe. There are some rocks with what appeared to be runes carved into them, but Avalon sent some people to look into it."

"What did the runes say?"

"I have no idea. I'm not exactly in the loop for stuff like this. I'm pretty certain it's nothing, though. Olivia would have heard if they'd found something worth worrying over. I can look into it if you want?"

"I'm just curious," I told him as I replaced the paper beside me.

"You've got too much time on your hands, my friend."

"And you have a meeting to go to."

"Thanks for reminding me." Tommy had almost made it to the door when his phone went off. "For crying out loud . . ."

"I'll get it," I told him and pushed the speakerphone button. "Tommy's office."

"Mr. Carpenter," the voice on the other end of the phone said, "there's someone here to see you."

"Who is it?" Tommy asked as he walked back to his desk.

"Just let me up there, for fuck's sake!" an angry voice shouted.

"Remy?" I asked.

"That is the man's name, yes," the voice on the phone said, trying his best to sound professional.

"Is that Nate?" Remy snapped. "Tell him I'm not his fucking delivery boy."

"He sounds happy," Tommy said with a slight smile. "Put him on the phone."

"Who's this?" Remy asked.

"It's Tommy. I'm going to let you up, but first you're going to say sorry to the person you were rude to."

"I don't fucking well see why."

"Because I fucking well told you to," Tommy said.

There was a sigh. "Sorry," Remy said. "Happy?"

"Yeah, come on up."

"I'll arrange his visitor's badge," the person Remy had been rude to said.

"Good. Don't let him give you any shit," Tommy told them and hung up.

"He's thrilled to be here," I said with a smile.

"Sounded like he had something for you. I guess my meeting will have to wait."

Remy came marching into the office a few minutes later, flanked by a massive guard.

"Is this fucking necessary?" Remy asked as the guard left.

"No. I imagine you got that because you pissed off the receptionist," Tommy told him.

Remy opened his mouth to speak and thought better of it. "Okay, I shouldn't have been an asshole, but I've come a long way and I'm tired and cranky."

"You're always cranky," I pointed out.

"Fuck you, Nate," Remy said with something similar to a smile on his face. "You'd be cranky too if you'd been turned into a three-and-a-half-foot fox."

Remy Roux was the result of a pissed-off witch who'd managed to convince her coven to change her cheating lover into a fox. The spell backfired and resulted in the deaths of twelve witches, the souls of whom transferred into their victim. Unfortunately for Remy, the spell partially worked. They turned him into a half-fox, half-man hybrid.

Remy was covered in red fox fur. He walked upright on legs that were more human than fox, and had a red fox muzzle and big bushy tail. He usually wasn't quite as angry at the world as the previous few minutes would suggest, but he was capable of being a giant pain in the ass when pushed.

"Why are you so irritated?" Tommy asked.

"Well, let's see," Remy said. "First of all, I get contacted and told to bring you this." He passed me a small, padded, brown envelope.

"What is it?"

Remy's eyes narrowed. "I don't know, Nate. Maybe you could open it and find out? What a fucking idea that would be."

"You seem more sweary than usual," I said.

"Well, as I was saying. I got given this and asked to bring it to you. Even got to sit in the back of an expensive car while I was driven here. For eight fucking hours I've been in the back of a car so I can bring you your fucking mail."

"Why didn't you just post it to me?" I asked, looking at the envelope. There was no return address: just the cottage Remy lived in—the usual place for any mail to be sent before it was brought to Avalon Island and distributed to the recipients after it had all been checked.

"Because Elaine told me to take it to you personally. Apparently she wants me to check on you—make sure you're okay. So, are you, Nate? Are you okay? No sprains or boo-boos I need to tell her about?"

I shared a glance with Tommy. "Okay, what's going on?"

Remy set his jaw, as if willing his anger to stay in one place, but his shoulders soon sagged. "I'm tired, I haven't eaten, and I've been stuck in a tiny village for the last year with the entirety of my visitors being those who say hello before they run off to Avalon Island. And now I'm delivering mail. None of those things is exactly a demanding job. In fact, they're all downright boring."

"Why don't you go eat something?" I suggested. "Maybe a full belly will cheer you up."

I opened the envelope and tipped out a USB stick onto my hand. "Well, that's not something I get every day."

"I'll show you the way," Tommy said, turning back to me as he reached the door. "Use my laptop; it's on the desk there."

I sat in the comfortable leather chair and opened the laptop, which sprang to life. As I had no idea who had sent the USB stick, or even what it contained, I ran Tommy's antivirus software on it, which said it was safe to proceed.

The USB contained two folders. The first was titled *1. Pictures*, and contained photos of the exterior of a building in

Whitechapel, London. A building that was familiar to me, as it was home to a vampire by the name of Francis who had helped me over a decade ago, when I'd had my memory wiped by an old nemesis of mine: Mordred.

Francis had allowed me to feel like I wasn't so alone in the world. He'd explained that I was a sorcerer, that I was capable of incredible feats of magic, and that I might not like it if I ever discovered who I was. Over the next ten years, I made a good living for myself as a thief and did a lot of jobs for Francis and his nameless clients.

Then, five years ago, Mordred came back into my life, bringing pain and death with him. He forced someone I cared about into such a position that she sacrificed herself to break the blood-magic curse Mordred had given me and give me back my memories. I'd killed Mordred for what he'd done—although what I'd learned only a few months earlier suggested that he'd somehow lived through that ordeal. It was something I was still having trouble coming to terms with. I didn't know many people who could survive a 7.62 x 51mm NATO round to the eye.

A horrible feeling settled in my stomach. I'd told Francis that I owed him three jobs for the help he'd given me—jobs he still hadn't cashed in. But if Mordred was still alive, and wanting revenge on the man who'd shot him, there was every chance he'd go after my friends rather than come at me directly.

I clicked through the rest of the photos, but they were nothing more than external shots of the local area, of the door to Francis's lair: an underground station abandoned long ago.

I exited the folder and clicked on the second: 2. *Video*. The feeling of dread grew inside me as I clicked the icon and a new window popped up showing a black screen. I turned the sound up slightly and clicked play, hoping I was wrong about whatever awful thing someone had decided to send me.

A man unfolded a chair and sat in front of the camera. He was stocky, but I couldn't tell much else. He wore a black jumper, black leather gloves, and a black balaclava that covered all but his eyes.

"Nathan," he said. His voice was deep, and the accent placed him from southern England, but I couldn't tell more than that.

"Don't try to figure out who I am," he continued. "I'm using some voice modulation software. It's quite clever. I'll reveal all at the end, but right now that's not why you're watching this little movie."

I looked at the timer; there were fifteen minutes left to run, so whatever the man had to say, it was going to take a while.

"You're watching because I sent you a USB stick. You'll have to excuse the address; I don't know where you live now. Otherwise I'd have delivered it personally." He sat back in the chair, looking relaxed and comfortable. "You wronged me, Nate. You wronged me exceptionally badly, and I'm here to pay you back for that. I'm here to ensure that the scales are balanced, that you feel the full power of just how much I hate you for what you did to me."

He stood up and reached out of camera shot, returning with a gleaming baseball bat. "Do you know what this is—apart from the obvious? It's an aluminum baseball bat that's been dipped in silver. I had it made especially for you, Nate. I was going to use it to stave in your skull, but I think it would be better to save that for later. To build up to it."

He walked over to the camera and picked it up, taking it over to a man lying prone on the floor. The man's shirt had been torn open, exposing his chest, and someone had used a sharp blade to carve lines across it, bathing him in his own blood. The camera panned down the man's legs, showing that his legs were pinned to the floor by something that had been driven through his shins.

"Silver spikes," the cameraman said. "Had them custom-made. Look, there're some more."

The camera panned up to show more spikes, which had been driven through the prone man's hands after his arms had been stretched out. Essentially they'd crucified their victim while he was lying down.

A black hood sat over the victim's face.

"Are you ready?" the cameraman asked. He grabbed hold of the hood, and tugged it off with a flourish, exposing Francis's battered and bloody face beneath it.

"Say hello to Nate," the cameraman said as he removed the gag that had been placed in Francis's mouth.

"Fuck you," he said and spat at the camera.

"He's not all that pleasant," the cameraman said as he walked away from Francis, placing the camera back on whatever stand it had originally been on.

"Are you listening to me, Nate?" the cameraman asked. "This is because you got in my way. This is because you crossed me." Anger crept into the man's voice for the first time.

He crossed back over to Francis and rested the tip of the baseball bat against his skull. "Any words for our sorcerer friend?"

"I'm sorry, Nate. I'm sorry for everything."

Rage erupted inside of me as the masked man brought the baseball bat up and then down, crushing part of Francis's face. The man rained down blow after blow on the helpless vampire, driving the baseball bat into the skull again and again, turning Francis's head into a mess of pulp and blood.

I don't know how long I sat there and watched the video, but I made sure to remember every single blow of that bat. And when he'd finished turning Francis's head into a bloody mess, he removed a dagger from behind him and slit the vampire's throat before plunging it into his heart.

The man stepped over Francis's corpse, dropping the blood- and gore-drenched bat onto the floor. He wandered out of sight for a moment before returning with the folding chair, which he unfolded before taking a seat on it. He slowly removed the gloves from both hands, letting them drop to the floor beside him.

"Did you enjoy the fun?" he asked, reaching toward the camera and turning the picture black for a second as he got in the way of the lens. "Do you recognize me yet?"

The voice was no longer distorted, and the voice was familiar but I couldn't place it.

He sat back on the chair, grabbed hold of the balaclava and pulled it off, throwing it aside and running his hands over the short, dark hair on his head. He'd grown a beard since I'd last seen him, and gained a fair bit of muscle. He looked like he'd done some training. It wouldn't help him.

"Kay," I whispered, my voice fueled with contempt and anger.

"I'm back, you son-of-a-bitch," Kay said, with a smug smile. He stood up and walked over to the camera again, crouching in front of it so that his face filled the screen. "I'd like the chance to repay you for all you did to me. And if you don't come, I'm sure I can find some more of your friends to play with. I'm in London. I'll leave a note here with the address where you can find me." He placed an envelope on the table beside him, and switched off the camera.

I looked down at the table where my hands had turned red- hot, orange glyphs igniting over my hands and arms. I shut my magic off and saw that my handprints had burned into the desk. I stared at the screen for several seconds. I was going to kill him. I was going to find Kay and do what I should have done years ago. I was going to rip his fucking head off.

CHAPTER 3

I don't really remember leaving the office, the building, or getting into my green Jaguar F-type R and pulling out of the car park. It was only after I'd been driving for a few seconds that I forced myself to take a breath. Driving to London would be a much worse proposition if I wrapped my car around a lamppost.

I drove the remainder of the way in the sort of mood that would have made me explode at the first person who cut me up, or didn't use their indicator, should I have been able to stop the car and get out. Fortunately, I was more interested in getting to my destination than I ever was in getting into an argument with some random shitty driver.

As I reached the outskirts of London, I was grateful that the car I was driving was exempt from the London congestion charge, due to being on a list of vehicles approved by Brutus, the king of London—which meant I could drive through the streets without any concerns other than my destination of Whitechapel. Also because having to pay to drive through London always bugged me.

Ordinarily the journey would have given me ample opportunity to think about what I was going to do when I actually got to Whitechapel, and where I'd go from there if I didn't find anything. But, instead of taking my mind off things, I only thought more about what I'd seen. What Kay had done to someone who had once been a friend of mine.

I parked the car around the corner from the entrance to what had been Francis's home, and took a deep breath, preparing for whatever I was about to find inside. As I walked up the alley to the massive iron door, the whole world appeared to move slower. I thought about whether or not coming here was the right thing to do, but the decision to stay was an easy one. The need for revenge outweighed the uncomfortable feeling in the pit of my stomach.

I grabbed hold of the door and pulled it open with a loud screech as the metal rubbed against the brick floor. Inside, a small room led to a staircase that went down to an old subway station, long abandoned and forgotten about. Francis had probably paid off several people so he could use it as his base of operations and home.

I stepped into the room and closed the door, bathed in the flickering lights that sat on either side of the staircase. Every step down into the subway station echoed around me. It was a good thing I hadn't bothered to try being stealthy; I sounded like a herd of elephants trampling around. By the time I was all the way down to the station platform, anyone who might have been waiting for me would have had plenty of time to prepare for my arrival.

I moved to a wall and made my way along it, taking my time as I walked to the archway that led to where Francis and his people had plied their trade of dealing in information and goods—not all of which were acquired legally. I looked around the corner and found that the room was empty and completely trashed. The lights that sat high above the room flickered in time with those on the staircase, and I wondered whether I'd be better off without them, relying instead on my fire magic to see in the dark. But then I realized I had no idea where the fuse box or light switch or anything else that might control them was, so I decided to put up with it.

A quick search of the room revealed nothing of note, so I carried on to the next, moving from room to room, but finding nothing that might be helpful. Each room brought back memories of my time here. Memories of laughter, friendship, being healed after I was hurt, and of the death of some of the people I had known just before I regained my past.

I walked into the medical room, and, after finding nothing once more, threw a gust of wind toward a collection of rubbish strewn across the floor. My magic scattered the rubbish, taking some of my frustration and anger with it. Most of it slammed into the wall and fell to the floor with nothing more than a clatter, but I watched one piece of paper slide under the wall and disappear behind it.

Kneeling in front of the wall, I cast a small amount of air magic, watching as it seeped under the wall. It could be nothing, but it could also be a door to a hidden room. Francis was big on secrets, and I wouldn't have put it past him to keep his most important things hidden from everyone.

I didn't want to force the wall apart, just in case Francis had booby-trapped anything, so I went searching for a switch or lever to open the door, but found nothing. I was just beginning to think that maybe I'd only been hoping that the wall would lead somewhere, when I re-entered the medical room and noticed that one of the wall tiles was the wrong color. All the other tiles on the wall were dark blue or white. Over time those colors had faded, but the tile I found myself looking at was pale green.

I pressed my hand against the tile and felt it give just a little, but something behind it clicked, and almost immediately the wall beside me also clicked and moved back a bit. I cursed myself for not looking at the walls when I was searching, for not seeing what was right in front of me, but then I guessed that was the whole point of hiding something in plain sight.

The detached part of the wall moved easily enough, sliding to the side and exposing the room behind. I stepped into the pitch-black room and ignited my fire magic, using it to give me night vision as I tried to find a light switch. It didn't take long, and the room was soon bathed in the soft glow of artificial lighting.

The room itself contained a wooden desk opposite the entrance, which stretched the width of the room. A leather swivel chair sat in front of it. On top of the desk were a computer, a small lamp, and about fifty pieces of paper, another fifty of which appeared to have fallen onto the floor at some point. A filing cabinet sat just inside the room.

I opened the cabinet, but found it empty; presumably the contents were now all over the floor and desk. I picked up a few things, but they were just receipts or agreements for work carried out. Mostly the names meant nothing, although a few of the dozen I'd grabbed had my name on them. I wondered if it was for blackmail purposes, but more likely it was in case someone tried to blackmail Francis.

The computer was a bust too. Someone had literally torn the insides out, leaving pieces of wiring hanging from a gaping wound in the side of the desktop. I looked through the drawers on the desk, but found nothing more than some stationery and about thirty packs of sticky notes.

Kay and whoever had helped him take Francis had been

thorough in their destruction of Francis's property. I got down on my hands and knees and looked under the desk, but found nothing of interest. I was about to get back to my feet when I saw something under the filing cabinet. I reached under and took hold of some masking tape, pulling it free, and with it came a small case with a micro-SD card. I pocketed the card and left the room, wanting to go somewhere private to look at whatever was on it.

I left the medical room and soon found myself standing outside of the only room I hadn't been inside of. I placed my hand against the steel door and gave it a slight push, finding the large room to be devoid of everything barring blood, a folding chair, and a table. This was where Francis had died, and before then where those who'd lived here had laughed and worked together. I'd had good memories of being in this room when there had been furniture. The last time I'd seen it, it had been covered in blood, just like now, when a friend of mine, Jerry, had been bleeding to death after having his arm torn off. I wondered what had happened to Jerry. Had Kay killed him too?

I walked over to the blood and found that it was dry: probably a few days old. What had I been doing while Francis was being beaten to death? Laughing, joking with friends? I clenched my fists and counted to ten. There was no one to hit, but there would be soon enough.

I picked up a blood-stained envelope and opened it, removing the small card inside, on which was written:

Tate Modern. 10:30 a.m.

There was no date or anything else: just a place and time. I guessed Kay would have to turn up at the museum every day at

10:00 a.m. until I arrived. He couldn't have screamed *trap* any more than he already had.

I looked at my watch. I had the better part of sixteen hours before I'd be able to find Kay, and that was if he turned up, and then I'd have to get help from others—something I didn't want. I wanted this done without the need for any intervention. Leaving Kay alive was *my* mistake: one *I* intended to correct.

I wasted no time in leaving the station, glad to be out in the fresh air. I'd walked to the end of the short alley when four men blocked my path.

"You need to give us some money," one of the men said. He wore a black hoodie, with blue jeans and had a diamond earring in one ear.

I looked at the other three, who wore similar clothing and were nodding along with their friend.

"I don't have any money," I told him.

"Your phone, then," one of the others said with a slight smirk.

"It's been an unbearably long day," I told them. "I get that you think I'm easy pickings, but if you don't leave, you're going to get hurt."

"You sure?" one of the men asked as he brought out a switchblade, flicking the blade to life and looking quite pleased with himself.

Of the two beside him, one had put some knuckle-dusters on his hand. The one who'd spoken first held a dagger with a six-inch blade. They'd come to hurt someone. I doubted they'd have let me go even if I'd given them the money.

I could remove them as easily as clicking my fingers, using my magic to throw them around with ease, but I was angry and frustrated, and I wanted someone to take that pent-up anger out on. And seeing how Kay wasn't readily available, these four would have to do.

I let one of the thugs move so that he was almost behind me, before burying my elbow in his face, breaking his nose and probably doing some damage to his jaw, too. I sprang forward, driving my foot into the knife-wielder's chest, sending him sprawling to the ground.

The last two men moved toward me as one. The third threw several punches, but they were easily deflected, and I grabbed his arm, dragging him toward me, forcing him off-balance, and slamming my fist into his nose as he fell forward. The knuckle-duster-wearer threw a powerful right that would have done a lot of damage had I not easily been able to avoid it. I stepped to the side and planted a kick on his knee, which dropped him to the ground.

He threw another punch and tried to get back to his feet, but I grabbed his arm and punched him in the face, spilling blood all over the ground from his torn lip. He fell face-first onto the ground, and tried to swat me away. I grabbed his arm again, planted a foot on the back of his neck, and snapped the limb at the elbow. His howls of pain weren't going to be alone for long.

The fourth man was back to his feet, but it was only for a moment before I kicked him between the legs, dropping him back to his knees. I drove my knee into his face, doing more damage to it, and knocking him out. The one I'd punched in the mouth earlier was still where I'd left him: on the ground. He was breathing, though, so either he'd hit his head or had a glass jaw—maybe both. That left the knife-wielder, who was back on his feet, looking pretty angry about everything that had happened.

"I'm going to cut you," he said as he started toward me. He

was confident in his knife skills, although I doubted he was as good as he believed. It takes a lot to learn how to wield a knife with dangerous efficiency, although both experts and novices can kill you just as quickly if they get close enough.

Despite the fact that there were several feet of air between us, he stabbed at nothing, presumably hoping that in my fear I'd run onto the blade and save him the trouble. I took a step toward him, and then another and another until I was close enough that it would be more effort for him to step back than just come at me with the knife. I kept eye contact with him the whole way, hoping he'd step forward and try to finish what he'd started, but he just stood there, clearly terrified of what he'd seen.

"Come on, then," I said. "You wanted to do this when you thought I was just some nobody you could threaten and hurt."

"This isn't worth it." He looked behind him, giving me the opportunity to dash forward and grab his wrist, twisting it until he released the blade.

"You should have taken my advice," I told him, releasing his hand before getting a better hold and throwing him into the wall behind me.

"Get up," I said, my rage bubbling over as the man got back to his feet.

I hit him in the stomach with everything I had, knocking the air out of him and causing him to crumple to the ground. I picked him up and slammed his back against the wall. I hit him in the jaw, snapping his head to the side, but I kept hold of him to stop him from falling to the ground again.

"You picked the wrong person," I told him and hit him again.

"Sorry," he said through his ruined mouth, dribbling blood down his chin.

"Fuck your sorry!" I snapped and smashed my forearm into his nose.

He dropped to his knees, his eyes no longer capable of focusing on me. He needed a hospital—all four of them did—but I was in no hurry to get any of them attended to. They'd decided to hurt me and come off the worse for it, but the fight hadn't made me feel better. Hurting four humans who were unaware of who I was, and were certainly ill-equipped to fight me, was no way for me to release the anger inside.

I picked up a mobile phone that must have fallen from one of my attackers' pockets and dialed 999, telling the operator to send a police car to this address as there was a group with weapons, threatening people. I dropped the phone onto the now-semiconscious man. Let the police decide if they required medical attention. I had better things to do.

I was soon driving through London once again, looking for a suitable place to bed down for the night. I eventually found myself at the Savoy Hotel in Covent Garden, and after checking myself for blood, walked up to the reception and asked for a room with a large bed. They had a few available, so I passed over my credit card and they handed me a room key.

I went back to the car first, removed a spare bag I kept in the boot, and took it up to my room, emptying the contents onto the king-size bed. It contained a change of jeans, some underwear and socks, and several T-shirts. There was also a black hoodie, some deodorant, mouthwash, and soap: everything I might need. A second pair of shoes was still in the car, along with my spare jacket. There were no weapons of any kind in the bag, mostly because on the odd chance the human police pulled me over for something, it's much easier to explain why there's deodorant in the boot than why you have a small arsenal.

I took a shower, which did little for my mood, and once dried and dressed, I switched on my phone, discovering a lot of messages from Remy, Tommy, Kasey, and Olivia, all of whom were concerned about me and wanted to know where I was. I hated not telling them, but I didn't need their help, nor did I want it. I explained to Tommy via text that this was something I needed to do alone and would be in contact soon. Sooner or later Tommy, at the least, would come looking for me, if he wasn't already on the way, but I had a while before they tracked my number plate or credit card, and I hoped the text would give me a few more hours to find Kay.

It took me until the early hours of the morning, but I eventually drifted off in a fitful sleep, and was woken by the vibration of my phone from an alarm I'd set to go off at half nine in the morning. I swung my legs out of the bed and stretched. Time to go to work.

CHAPTER 4

I threw on a pair of jeans, a T-shirt, and my hoodie, putting on my trainers before I left the room, making sure I had the key with me. I jogged the hallway to the lifts, trying not to break immediately into a sprint. It wouldn't do me much good to let my emotions get the better of me.

Once outside the hotel, I took off at a run toward the Southbank. There was a possibility it would have been quicker to drive, but with London traffic, there was also a good chance I'd be no closer to my destination in the short time it would take me to run.

I was at Blackfriars Bridge within a few minutes. I didn't want to use my air magic to increase my speed as I wanted all of my magic available to me. Kay was an evil little sociopath, but he wasn't stupid, and his taunts for me to come after him in London weren't the words of someone without a plan. Either Kay had a way to counter my magic, or he had an ally to do it for him.

I walked across the bridge at a brisk pace, but was only about halfway across when I first wondered what I was going to do when I got hold of Kay. What was my plan for taking him down in broad daylight on a busy summer day? I looked around me and saw kids with families, large groups of schoolchildren, all among those just out for a pleasant day in London. I needed to be able to neutralize Kay quickly, without fuss, and without him being able to hurt anyone else.

By the time I'd reached the end of the bridge I'd decided that the best way was to watch Kay and follow him somewhere less open. I could sate my anger while I waited for my chance. He was clearly going to be expecting my arrival, and I really didn't want to make my presence known until I was ready.

Once off the bridge I followed the path toward the Tate Modern art gallery, blending in with the large crowds until I spotted Kay sitting on a bench by the entrance. I moved down a nearby path, hoping to be able to circle around him and put myself somewhere he wouldn't be able to recognize me. At that exact moment, Kay turned toward me, smiled, and waved.

He took off like a rocket, sprinting toward the Millennium Bridge, barging past anyone in his way. I ran after him, avoiding people as best I could. I was just over halfway across the bridge when I saw Kay only a dozen feet ahead. He grabbed hold of a young girl, picked her up off the ground, and winked at me. I took another step forward, and he tossed her over the side of the bridge as if she were nothing.

The bridge railings were only a few feet high, and were easy to vault, using magic from my outstretched hand to try to slow the fall of the young girl as she screamed in terror.

Using air magic to slow the movement of someone when both people are on solid ground is hard enough; doing it while both of you are falling through the air is exceptionally difficult. More than once I managed to slow her down only to have the magic slip past her. But on the third try, I wrapped tendrils of air around her and a microsecond later I caught her. I immediately stuck out my hand, throwing air toward the bridge railings forty yards above my head. The magic wrapped around one of the supports and I hardened it in an instant, yanking my shoulder out of its socket, and swinging me and the still-screaming girl down closer to the water only a few feet below us. Another quick blast of air magic sped up the swing, until I released the magic and we sailed through the sky, landing on the bridge with a thud.

Dozens of people stood around us as the young girl, who I now saw was no older than five or six, got to her feet.

"Are you okay?" I asked.

"You're like Spiderman!" she said with a mixture of awe and fear.

"Except for the webs and spandex, just like him, yeah," I said with a forced smile.

"Emily! Emily!" a young man and woman shouted as they forced themselves through the crowd, wrapping themselves around their daughter the second they saw her. The woman looked up at me as I got back to my feet. "Thank you," she said softly.

I nodded as the sounds of people asking, "*How did he do that?*" began to reach my ears. It wouldn't be long before people stopped whispering and actually started demanding answers. Answers I had no time or inclination to give.

"Thank you," Emily said as her dad hugged me, causing my arm to hurt again.

"Take care of yourself," I told her and started running up toward St. Paul's Cathedral, tracking Kay's last known movement. My arm was slowing me down. I could wait for my magic to heal me, which it was bound to do soon enough, but I needed my arm now, not in an hour. Healing is always quicker if the bone or joint is set first. I walked over to the nearest solid wall and slammed my shoulder back into its socket. The pain was intense but brief, and I was soon running back toward the cathedral, hoping I hadn't lost Kay's trail.

I stood opposite the cathedral and tried to figure out where he might have gone. I stared past crowded streets in a hope I'd spot him, and was rewarded with a glimpse of him getting into a dark-blue Volkswagen Golf. He saw me and waved before setting off along Cannon Street at a much more leisurely pace. Traffic in London isn't exactly the best for a quick getaway.

I took a step after him and stopped. I was angry—furious—both at Francis's murder, and the fact that Kay was the man responsible, but I was acting like an idiot. I was charging in head-first without a plan other than to crush those who opposed me. It had been something I'd been doing a lot of since I'd decided to bring back the Hellequin name: using brute force and wits to overcome enemy traps I willingly and arrogantly knew might eventually get me killed. I wasn't going to do this with Kay; I couldn't. He wasn't some witch with delusions of grandeur, or a werewolf challenging me to a fight. Kay was someone who had serious power, and he was no slouch in battle.

I put my hand in my pocket as the Volkswagen vanished from view and removed the micro-SD card I'd found at Francis's. I jumped in a taxi and took the cab back to my hotel room. Kay would be incensed that I'd ignored his plan and gone my own way, but that was Kay's problem.

I'd wanted to show everyone that there was nothing I feared, that there was no obstacle too powerful for me to overcome, but that wasn't going to work this time. I wasn't going to be able to walk into Kay's trap with the assurance that I'd walk out again in one piece. He had powerful allies, but so did I.

I called Diane.

"Nate. I heard you're in London," she said upon answering.

"Hello to you too."

"No bullshit, Nate. What's going on? Tommy has been calling every ten minutes looking for you. He's driving up here. Apparently he gave up trying to get hold of you and decided I was the next-best contact."

I explained about Kay, Francis's murder, and my run through London.

"And you didn't come to someone about this because . . . ?" she asked when I was done.

"I'm an idiot?" I suggested.

"Bingo. What do you need and where do you need it?"

"I need to find Kay. He's in London, and I have no idea what his plan is, beyond killing me."

"You think he'll go after someone else?"

"It's possible. Not sure who, though. I doubt it's you, unless he's going up against Brutus."

"I doubt he's lost all of his sanity since you last saw him, so I'm probably out."

"Okay. Who else is in London?"

"Some of the Mesopotamians are in town. They're helping with that exhibit in the British Museum. They got Brutus's okay before they started sending pieces."

"Who?"

"Irkalla and Nabu."

"Where are they staying?"

"In the Aeneid."

The Aeneid was a five-hundred-foot-tall building near the center of London. It was designed to look imposing and inviting at the same time, and it served as Brutus's place to live and work, along with hundreds of others. Diane also lived there as Brutus's head of security, so if Irkalla and Nabu were there, then they were probably safe.

"The Fates?" I suggested, not really believing that even Kay would want to start going up against Brutus, who was responsible for their protection.

The Fates were, in fact, three related psychics who had been forced to undergo a ritual that allowed them to see either a person's past, present, or future. The oldest, Cassandra, was the daughter of King Priam of Troy, and the other two Fates were her daughter, Grace, and granddaughter, Ivy. The latter had once been in Mordred's company for several decades, if not longer, as he tried to harness the power of the Fates for himself.

With the discovery of Mordred's return several months ago, I was worried that he might try to get back to old habits and go after the Fates. The possibility of Mordred being involved in whatever Kay had planned wasn't something I'd wanted to consider, although the sudden thought now made it impossible to consider anything else.

After I'd managed to save the Fates from Mordred's grasp, I'd left them in London, and asked Diane to keep an eye on them. They were powerful beings, and I didn't want them to fall into the hands of someone like Mordred ever again. They mostly lived in the Aeneid, but left a few times a week to tend to their bookstore.

"They're at their bookstore today and yesterday. You think Kay would really go after them?" She sounded as convinced of the idea as I was. "There's a round-the-clock protection detail on them. You'd need an army. I checked in with them an hour ago, and all was fine."

"I'll go check it out anyway. Can you let your people know I'm coming?"

"Can do. You want me to meet you there?"

"Sure. Why not?"

"I've told Tommy to come straight here, to the Aeneid. He's got Kasey and Remy with him at least. I heard them in the background. Remy sounded *thrilled* about your disappearing act. I'll meet you at the Fates' bookstore in an hour."

"I'm going to head right over then. If the Fates are okay, hopefully they can shed some light on what Kay's doing. Either way, it's a worthwhile trip."

"They need to be in proximity to him to do that, don't they?"

"It's not like my ideas are in abundance."

"Obviously. Otherwise you'd never have run off like an impatient toddler."

I winced. "You're not going to let that go, are you?"

"Depends if you stop being an idiot or not."

"I deserved that. I'll see you in an hour. Just make sure your guys know I'm coming. I really don't want to be shot trying to knock on their door."

"That actually might be entertaining."

I knew she was grinning, but I wasn't in the mood for much frivolity. "Diane!"

"Yeah, yeah, I'll make sure. Don't get all pissy with me. Just be careful. If Kay has a plan for the Fates, you'd better believe he won't want you there."

She hung up and I removed the micro-SD card from my pocket, placing it in my phone and opening the video file it contained. For a moment I thought it was going to be another film of Francis being murdered, planted there by Kay to screw with me, but instead it was just Francis in front of a camera.

"Hi, Nate, it's been a while." He ran his hand through his long hair, and adjusted his eye patch. "I'm hoping you got this okay." He paused. "That's stupid, if you hadn't gotten this, you'd never have seen it. Okay, scrap that."

He looked upset, tense, as if something was bothering him but he was unsure how to get the words out.

"There are some things you need to know. And I'm a coward and can't tell you to your face, so it's going to be done like this. I have no idea how you're going to react—angrily, I imagine. But I've kept this for a long time, and I can't keep it to myself anymore.

"When you last saw me, I asked you to do three jobs for me—that they would make us even. Well, I remove that burden from you. We're more even than you can possibly imagine."

I sighed and wondered if Francis was ever going to get to the point.

"I knew who you were—the whole time. I told you I had no idea who you were, but it was a lie. I knew, Hellequin."

The knowledge hit me like a truck. Ten years of lying to my face, of keeping me in the dark.

"You're probably furious with me, and rightly so, but I didn't do it for personal gain. When I found you, I knew that second who you were; I'd seen you before with Brutus. So, I went to him and he told me to keep it silent—to not tell you anything, or tell anyone else that you were there—that you were alive. He was worried that whoever had tried to kill you—Mordred, as it turned out—would continue the search for you, would still try to finish the job. It was a fear that was well founded, as that was exactly what happened. Brutus knew that Ares and Mordred were working for Hera in his city; he'd allowed it, after all, and he wanted to know if Hera was planning on trying to invade London. He was scared of it; terrified, in fact. He was even more terrified of the idea that you were the precursor to it all. So I kept your identity secret, asking you to go on jobs to steal for me, keeping up that pretense while I hoped one day your memory would just come back to you on its own, that it would absolve me of having to worry about it.

"I'm sorry for that, Nate. But there's more. I think Brutus is under attack again: a more subtle attack this time."

Brutus was the king of London. He was in charge of the whole city, and while he allowed humans to go about their daily lives, the nonhumans were bound to treat him with the respect he commanded. He was powerful and dangerous, but his position was not without its own concerns. Chief among those was the idea that someone would want to take his position from him. And if I was honest, I could think of no one more dangerous to have in charge of London than Hera. London would be a very deadly place for anyone she considered an enemy. Me included.

I pushed the thought aside and went back to watching the video.

"I know you must just think 'Screw them all' for what we did to you, but I think Brutus needs your help. Diane and the others are all sure nothing is happening, but Brutus? He's tense, concerned. I've never seen him like it."

Francis closed his eyes and took a deep breath, exhaling slowly.

"I think Jerry is up to something, too. I'm not sure if he's working against me, or whether it's anything more specific than a gut feeling, but something is wrong there. Laurel sees it, but refuses to acknowledge it—refuses to do anything about it. But she's scared of him. I can see it in her eyes. He spends less and less time here. He's gone for days—weeks—with no word, and when he comes back, he's changed. He's more intense. I'm not a powerful vampire, no matter how many I've sired, but I can sense when something is wrong. And he's going through something. He needs help, and won't ask for it. I'm hoping you could come here and talk to him. I know I'm asking a lot for you to come here, to see Brutus too, but I know you, Nate. You always try to do the right thing, even if it's not very nice. And I wouldn't ask if it wasn't important."

"Anything else?" I asked sarcastically, fully aware I wasn't going to get a reply, but needing to say something.

Francis leaned toward the camera as if to switch it off, then paused, sitting back in his chair instead. "One thing before I go. I know you were friends with Arthur, before he got hurt by Mordred. I know that you consider him a good man, a good friend, and a good king. But over the years I've heard things— mostly rumors and innuendo—but these are things that people would never say to someone who works for Avalon. I'm not saying you're wrong about him; I've never met him. But if *any* of these things are true, then you need to be careful of those who consider him an ally. He might not be as spotless and perfect as history makes him out to be. Just a thought. I'm not sure you'd sit and let me bad-mouth him, but if you want to talk about what I heard, let me know."

It wasn't the first time someone had said something negative about Arthur, about those who were closest to him, but I was one of those people and I saw nothing at the time. I wondered how much of it was just Francis buying into people letting off steam, and how much of it was down to Merlin and the way he went about keeping Arthur alive. Taking the souls of the innocent to feed to his comatose body.

"Hopefully, you'll come and help. I think something bad is going to happen in this city, and frankly I'd rather you were there to help stop it." Francis ended the video and I remained seated, staring at the blank screen. It looked like I had more questions than answers, but now that Francis was dead, those answers had died with him. And as for Jerry, I hadn't seen any evidence of him, but if he was still alive, he might be able to tell me more about Francis's murder.

As for Brutus and the possible attack on his position, I wasn't convinced that anyone would be that brazen or insane. Brutus had Avalon's backing, and trying to oust him could cause a civil war if Avalon wasn't happy with his replacement. It was something else to talk to Diane about.

As if on cue, my phone rang, the screen showing Diane's name.

"I've spoken to my people, and they're waiting for you."

"Thanks. Where are your guys stationed?"

"A house across the street. Green door, number sixteen. Go introduce yourself."

"Thanks. I'll see you soon."

"Tommy is here. He's not happy."

I sighed. "Yeah, I figured as much."

"Kasey, Chloe, and Remy aren't happy either. I'm thinking you're going to get kicked in the ass. A *lot*."

"You sound a lot happier about that than you should be."

Diane laughed. "Oh, you have *no* idea!"

I thought about asking Diane about Brutus, but figured that could wait until we were face-to-face, just in case someone was listening in to the calls on her end. Instead, we ended the call and I prepared to—hopefully—get some answers.

CHAPTER 5

I took a taxi to Le Tre Donne, the small bookstore owned by the Fates. I got out of the cab just as the sun was beginning to set. It had been an incredibly long day, but I doubted it was going to be over any time soon.

The Fates had moved the shop after my initial meeting with them several years ago to a small cul-de-sac, which consisted of the shop and three other houses. I wondered how much business they actually did, and realized they probably didn't care too much. They hadn't seemed that interested in actually *selling* any of the books they'd owned when I'd last seen them.

The rest of the street was made up of chain-link fencing, and the promise of work starting "soon." I wondered if that was Diane's doing. Build a few houses, make them look authentic, and have no intention to build more.

I had half an hour until Diane was due to show up, but if she had hand-picked the security team—which, knowing her, was a dead cert—the Fates were probably the safest people in the entire city.

The lights were on inside the shop, but as Diane had asked me to introduce myself to her team, I walked over the road to the house directly opposite. It was three stories tall and probably worth a million quid, based on the area and the size of the place.

If Brutus ever wanted to finish completing these buildings, he could probably make a nice profit.

I walked up the driveway, past the double garage, and knocked on the green door. There was no answer, so I tried the handle and pushed the unlocked door open, calling out once again into the massive hallway and staircase that greeted me.

"Back here," someone called out from the rear of the property.

I closed the door behind me and walked through the barren home. There was nothing to suggest it was occupied at all, which I guessed was the point. I walked under an archway into a huge open-plan room, which contained an old couch pointed at a massive TV set that hung from the wall. An old, tatty chair sat in front of a set of patio doors. In the chair sat Jerry.

"*Jerry?*" I asked, the realization that I'd been set up quickly flicking to the front of my mind. "You're working for Kay?"

Jerry nodded. "You were meant to follow him to a place of our choosing. The fact that you wanted to come here wasn't a problem for us—considering we've been in control of the whole area for a week."

"Diane just spoke to her people. Are they all still in one piece? I assume she's not working with you and Kay. She'd rather tear Kay in half."

"Diane's people were never here. And no, Diane hasn't been *invited* to work with us. As for why she thinks her people were here—" He picked up a phone and showed it to me as if I'd never seen one before. "—all the calls route to this number."

"So, someone in Brutus's operation is involved too. Feel like telling me who?"

"Not really. You're going to be dead before you need to find out."

"Jerry, you're a one-armed vampire. I'm going to tear the other arm off and beat you to death with it." I took a step forward.

"I'd stay there if I was you." He picked up a remote and clicked it on. The TV flickered to life, showing the three Fates sitting on the floor in a room somewhere. The background was some sort of blue cloth, obscuring any details of where they might be hidden. None of the women looked as if they'd been beaten, although they all had bags under their eyes. Jerry had said they'd been in control of the area for a week. A week under Kay's company before I'd arrived. I really wanted to hurt someone.

"They're safe," Jerry told me. "For now. But if you come toward me in any way, those who are with them have orders to kill."

I buried the anger I was feeling; it wouldn't do a lot of good. "So, what are we meant to do? Have a chat?"

"Sure. Why not? How's things, Nate?"

"Well, I'm in a spartanly decorated room with a gaping piss-hole of a man, trying very hard not to tear his head off and use it as a football. You?"

"I get that you're angry, but this is all your fault."

"Let me get this right. You betrayed me, helped Kay murder Francis, kidnapped the Fates, and somehow this is all *my* doing? That's some really impressive way of twisting the facts to your own ends going on. By the way, did you kill Laurel? You remember her: the woman you professed to love?"

"Laurel isn't dead, Nate. I *love* her. She's nice and safe, far away from everything that's happening. I hadn't wanted to kill Francis, but he left me no choice. He was plotting against me, talking to Laurel about my change in personality, asking her if she'd thought about leaving me. I couldn't let that slide. She's mine. You understand why I did what I did, as a man, right?"

"That you helped murder someone just to keep your girl-friend? No, I don't really understand that. I'm pretty certain that most men would think you're fucking insane. You murdered one friend and betrayed how many more?" I wondered if I could get to Jerry before . . . I stopped and looked out of the windows behind him. There was a one-story annex building at the bottom of the garden. It had glass doors, although from this distance there was no way to see through them.

"The Fates are in the annex building at the bottom of the garden, aren't they?" I asked. "And there's someone watching us through the windows."

"Maybe. Maybe not. That's not your concern. Your concern is our conversation."

"Really, we're still doing that? You're a psychopath, working with psychopaths to do psychopath things. Pretty certain that's the end of the conversation."

"You made a promise. You promised me that if I started to do evil things, you'd come kill me. But you didn't, and I just kept on down that dark path. I killed so many people before Laurel found out. She tried to help me, but that didn't work out too well for her. And it certainly didn't work well for poor Francis. He was so surprised when I turned up with Kay."

I opened my mouth to speak and found I just didn't quite grasp the words I needed. Eventually they came, spilling out of my mouth like water from a cracked dam. "Fuck you, you prolapsed badger rectum!" It wasn't exactly poetic, but it got the point across. "You're blaming me for your deeds—for your need to hurt people. That's *nothing* to do with me; that's all on you and your complete lack of self-control. No one *forced* you to murder people, no one *forced* you to kill and betray your friends. So take that statement and shove it right up your ass, you utter coward!"

Anger flared behind Jerry's well-maintained mask, but it was gone an instant later. "Do you want to know why we went after the Fates?"

"I couldn't give a rat's ass," I snapped. "Either kill me or shut up, because we're done here. And if you've hurt them, in any way, I'm going to snap your fingers one by one, which, as you only have one arm, won't take long. Bonus for you, I guess."

Anger flickered once again, and Jerry almost sprang up from the chair.

"You want to come at me, boy?" I mocked. "You want to see what you can do? Go for it: let's see how well a one-armed, cowardly vampire fares against a sorcerer. I'm excited about finding out."

"A little gentle *persuasion* is hardly hurting them." Jerry's voice couldn't have been more controlled if he'd tried. "Kay wanted to cut their fingers off, but I suggested killing innocent people in front of them. Turns out it works. And it only took one innocent death."

"What do you get from this?"

"Power. Money. Respect. Things people like you and Francis never gave me, always keeping me down, always making sure I knew my place, never allowing me to become what I deserve."

"You deserve to have your entire insides scooped out, replaced with straw, and plonked in a field as the world's best scarecrow."

"I *will* have your respect!" Jerry shouted, the mask collapsing as the demon inside of him changed his face to show the vampire replacing the man.

"Come get it," I told him, taking a step forward. "You and

Kay wanted me angry, wanted me to rush to London, to stop him without thinking. I'll admit, it was a good plan; almost worked. But I'm not rushing into things, needing to show everyone how strong Hellequin is. I'm done. I'll admit, I didn't expect you to be here, but you're clearly working with people inside Brutus's organization, and there's no way Kay is the head of that, so why don't you tell me: who's in charge here?"

The vampire vanished once again and Jerry lowered himself into the chair, a smile plastered on his face. "You were meant to follow Kay. You were meant to die in some little shit-hole of a building where you'd never be found. You weren't meant to be here."

"Sucks to be you."

"Not really. It just meant we had to be creative. And I had to stall."

The ceiling above me cracked and exploded as a dozen rock monsters fell through it onto me. I managed to blast several of them away, but more than enough grabbed hold of me, dragging me to the floor, as the remainder of the ceiling above my head was torn apart when Asag dropped through it, destroying the floor beneath him as he landed.

I blasted the small creatures away with air magic, creating a sphere of lightning and plunging it into the ground beneath my feet, tearing the floor apart and throwing everyone away from me, giving me room to think.

I was surrounded on all sides. The rock monsters were more than capable of causing devastation in quick measure, and a vampire is always dangerous, no matter how little I thought of him, but Asag was in another league. And was meant to be dead.

"Remember me?" Asag asked as the small creatures scurried around him, waiting for his order to attack.

"Yeah, I remember. I remember the last time we met, it didn't go so well for you."

"Got better."

"Well, that's going to be short-lived." I threw a bolt of lightning at Asag, but several of his creatures leapt in the way, sacrificing themselves for their master as they exploded from the force.

As pieces of rock filled the air, I darted forward, a second sphere in my hand, ready to take the fight to Asag, when an unseen rock creature dropped from the ceiling onto my shoulders. There was a stabbing pain in my neck and the creature jumped off before I could stop it.

My vision went blurry for a second and I dropped to one knee. I reached around to the back of my neck and found a syringe there. I pulled it out and tossed it aside.

"How are you feeling?" Kay asked as he entered the room, walking over to Asag and touching him on the shoulder. The large rock creature nodded and left the room, walking through the glass doors to the garden as the glass continued to drop and smash on the floor.

"That man just does not care," Kay said, glancing up at the massive hole in the ceiling, before punching me in the jaw, knocking me to the ruined floor.

"What was in it?" I asked, knowing Kay must have been dying to reveal his diabolical plan to me.

"Tranquilizer. A lot of it. Enough to knock out a rhino, I imagine. We figured it wouldn't quite knock you out, just make you a lot easier to deal with." Kay looked over at Jerry. "You got anything you want to say?"

"Enjoy death, Nate. We'll be right here making the world a better place without you in it." He punted me in the ribs, and left through the broken glass door.

"A lot of people hate you, Nate," Kay told me, removing his jacket and tossing it onto the chair that Jerry had occupied. "When we found out you were coming here, I had to rush across the city to get here in time. I had the tranquilizer all ready for you—just had to wait for Asag to create enough of those little bastards. Had to wait for the sun to be completely down. Man, Jerry sure can talk."

"Get on with it," I told him. "I'd rather die than listen to you."

Kay's smile faded and he kicked me in the ribs, breaking at least one when he started stamping on them. "That was fun," he told me as I spat up blood onto the floor.

The tranquilizer made everything swim in front of me, made me sleepy and feel like my whole body was made of lead. It was an effort just to keep my eyes open, although the pain shooting through my torso helped in that regard. I wondered how long I had before Diane arrived, and whether she'd be able to help in the face of Kay *and* Asag.

Kay stood over me and placed his foot on my chest, pushing down. "How does it feel to know you're beaten? How does it feel to be a hundred percent aware that you're not going to survive this?"

I used every ounce of necromancy power at my disposal, every tiny bit of any souls I'd claimed and not used to try to remove the toxins in my body. It caused me to feel the pain in my side more, but I was able to concentrate on what was happening.

"No smart-assed answer?" Kay demanded as he pushed down harder with his boot-covered foot.

I grabbed hold of his trouser leg, which caused him to laugh, until I punched him in the side of his ankle with every piece of strength I possessed. I couldn't risk using my magic until the tranquilizer was gone from my system. I didn't want to exhaust myself by doing too much.

Kay fell away, and I got back to my feet. He looked over at me and then stared out of the door, hoping to see his allies.

"They're gone, Kay. You should have used more tranquilizer." My head was feeling clearer, and I hoped I'd managed to stop the drug from going any further through my body, but it took a maintained level of concentration to ensure it didn't return.

Kay stood up. "I'm still going to kill you."

I dove toward him, any pretense of a well-fought battle replaced with a need to tear his face off. I wrapped my arms around his chest and lifted him up off the ground, over my head, planting him headfirst into the floor behind me.

You can have access to all the magic in the world, but if you get picked up and violently dumped on your head and neck, you're going to need a few seconds to no longer see double. And a few seconds was all I needed.

I turned and kicked Kay's head, snapping it back with incredible force, but he rolled with a second blow and the floor beneath my feet tore apart, flying up toward me. I activated a shield of air magic, deflecting the barrage of wood and stone, but it gave Kay enough time to put some distance between us.

I followed him, creating a sphere of air, spinning it over and over until it was a blur. The second I was close enough, I drove the sphere toward Kay, who blocked it with a hastily created shield of rock. The sphere hit the rock and exploded, the magic tearing it apart, and threw Kay back toward the far wall.

He impacted with a crunch, bringing plaster down with him as he fell to the floor.

But Kay was nothing if not tenacious, and was soon back on his feet as I closed the distance between us. The glyphs on his arms vanished, replaced with ones of darkness, and a tendril of blood magic whipped up toward me, lacing across my chest despite my shield of air, causing me brief but unimaginable pain.

Kay used the opportunity to close the gap, and placed his hand on my chest. The blood magic caused my entire body to feel as if it were on fire. I staggered back, trying to put distance between us, but my body began to weaken. The use of magic had removed the concentration needed to keep the tranquilizer at bay.

I wobbled slightly, and dropped to one knee, using air magic to blast Kay back, hoping to give myself a moment of respite.

"The tranquilizer not quite gone yet, is it?" Kay bragged. "Soon, you'll be weak, and then I'm going to tear you in half."

I was down on both knees at this point, trying to concentrate so I could use my necromancy to slow the effects of the tranquilizer and heal my body, but I couldn't do both in the midst of a battle. And I doubted Kay was going to give me a moment to myself.

He stepped toward me and kicked me in the sternum, knocking me to the floor, causing me to gasp in pain. The bone wasn't broken, but there's no pain quite like an impact on your sternum to make you regret your life choices up to that point. My regrets mostly consisted of not killing Kay a thousand times over.

Kay crouched beside me and placed a hand on my chest. "Hurts, doesn't it?" His blood magic reactivated and pain tore through me once again as he moved his hand across my torso, settling over my broken ribs. His blood magic ensnared me, squeezing across my chest, and my vision began to darken. Kay was going to kill me. *Kay.*

Anger exploded inside of me as the idea of being killed by Kay caused a fury I had rarely felt before. Kay of all people was going to be my murderer. And that just would not stand.

I created a blade of air in my hand and struck out, aware that Kay was nearby, and hoping he wouldn't see it until it was too late. His scream of pain and the sudden lessening of my own agony told me it had worked, and I watched him stagger back, blood soaking the inside of his trousers.

"I guess I got you," I said with a painful laugh. I wasn't certain I could get back to my feet; I wasn't even certain I could *feel* my feet, but I looked around and discovered that I'd half-fallen into the ruined floor, one arm out of sight in the hole that had formed there.

I might not have been able to get to my feet to fight, but that didn't mean I was helpless. With my hand out of sight, I created a sphere of lightning, spinning it faster and faster until I knew it would be a blur. The tranquilizer made it difficult to know just how much magic I was pumping into the sphere, but I didn't care. I threw in as much as my body would take.

Kay's expression of murderous intent as he walked back toward me was clear to see, and I knew he wanted to kill me up close. He took a look at the lit-up glyphs over my arms, and smiled.

"I don't think so. I'm not stupid."

Thunder rolled high above us, and Kay's expression changed to one of ever-so-slight uncertainty. He glanced up and I took the moment, launching myself up and toward him, unleashing the magic inside the sphere right at him.

At the last second, Kay created a sphere of rock and fire to counter my own. The explosion as the two spheres met was powerful enough to throw both Kay and me away in opposite directions. For Kay, that meant a trip up through the top of the ceiling and part of the roof, tearing the building apart as he went. I was thrown back into a wall close to the patio doors, where I hastily created a shield of air as the entire structure began to collapse.

I quickly increased the air shield's power as the room collapsed in on me, raining down huge chunks of wood, brick, and mortar. I kept my air magic flowing freely, keeping the tons of brick a few feet above me as the rest of the roof came down all around me. If I removed my magic, I was dead. A few tons of brick while I slipped into unconsciousness, with no way to escape, would probably do the trick.

That didn't mean I was about to give up. I would fight to the end, and if I could keep the shield up for long enough, hopefully Diane would arrive before I died. I was only a few feet from the door. If I could just get to it, I could be free.

I tried to shuffle forward, but the movement of the shield forced more brick to fall, some of it slamming into my left leg and causing me to yell out.

I don't know how long I was like that. I don't know how long I knelt there, covered in brick dust and filth, as the tranquilizer went to work, as my strength ebbed away, but it felt like a long time. Eventually I heard voices, but couldn't quite make out who was talking. I shouted for help, but only heard a muffled reply.

Suddenly half a dozen golems, the product of a sorcerer using water and earth magics together, crashed through the debris and lifted the rubble above me. My magic vanished, but I didn't have the strength to crawl out through the new hole they'd made.

"Whoever you brought with you, I thank you," I told the person I was certain was Diane, who stood just beyond the ruined building.

"No problem," a man said.

I looked up, horrified as Mordred's face came into view. He had a folding chair in one hand that he placed beside my head before sitting down.

I tried to throw magic at him, but I was too weak as the tranquilizer took its full effect.

"Don't try to fight me, Nathan," Mordred said. "We need to have a good long talk, you and I. And frankly I can think of no better time than when you're helpless and about to be crushed by a falling building."

CHAPTER 6

September 1195. City of Acre.

You want to just tell me the names of everyone involved in the attack on Avalon, or would you prefer I start cutting you first?"

"Ah, Nate, ever the smooth talker," Mordred said with a grin. "You don't need to do anything to me. Just listen and maybe you'll learn something useful."

"Mordred, I've learned a lot from you over the years, mostly about how to betray your friends and murder innocent people. Those are two things you excel at. Oh, and being completely twisted in your head. That's a talent of yours, too."

"We will leave you two alone," Nanshe told me. "Do not kill him. I will not have death committed here."

"I promise," I said, biting down on the frustration. The fact that I was so close to ending Mordred's life meant it took every bit of discipline at my disposal to calm the rage that just being this close to him created.

When we were alone, I turned back to him. "What do you want?"

"Your help." He spoke with the same confidence that he always showed. But there was no taunting, no need to try and get one over on me or anyone else. It was just a statement of fact.

"No. Not now, not ever."

"Then you can go on not knowing who is behind this plot. Nanshe knows torture won't work on me; you cannot force me to tell you anything. All you have to do is aid me, and hope I'm honest."

"I would spit on your honesty if I thought for even one second you had any."

Mordred stared at me, and I knew with all certainty that if he weren't in chains, he'd try to kill me. But I needed his help if we were to figure out who was plotting an attack on Avalon.

"Why did Merlin send you here, I wonder?" Mordred asked. "I mean, I'm sure these fine people could figure this all out on their own. Maybe he doesn't trust them? That would be interesting, wouldn't it? Merlin accepting the Mesopotamians into the fold, but not really trusting them: that's not a good basis for a friendship."

"And you'd know all about friendship," I snapped before I could stop myself. I took a deep breath and forced myself to remain calm. "I'm not doing this, Mordred. I'm not getting into an argument with you. It's what you want, and frankly I can't be bothered to allow you to make me angry right now. Either tell me what you want or you can rot down here."

A smirk spread across Mordred's face, which did little to ease my need to punch it repeatedly. "You're not much fun anymore."

I kept my mouth clamped shut.

Eventually he understood I wasn't going to argue with him. "I need your help," he said at last. "Despite the fact that I hate you and everything you stand for, I know you. I know you won't let innocent people get hurt."

"Since when have you cared about innocent people?"

"I care about this one." Anger leaked into his voice a little.

"Why?"

"None of your business. Her name is Isabel. She's currently being held here in Acre, under guard in a house close to the marina. You will find her and help her escape this place. You will do this, and she will come to no harm. Only then will I tell you what I know."

"Who is she?"

"All you need to know is her name."

"Actually, no, I need a little more than that. I need to know what she looks like, I need to know what she is, I need to know why she's under guard, and I definitely need to know why you want her freed. I'm not in the habit of breaking people out of secure areas on the say-so of a madman."

"She's twenty-six, human; long, dark hair, olive complexion, green eyes, and her name is Isabel. That's all you need. Go find her."

"No." I turned to leave.

"She's under guard because she was caught with me. They tell me it's for her protection. This is despite the fact that she has nothing to do with the plot, nor does she know anything about it. She was here before I arrived; she's training to be a physician. She was just unlucky that I happened to be there when Nanshe and her guard turned up. I'd already decided to go to the authorities by then, but getting caught sped things up a little."

"Why do you want her protection removed? What is she to you?"

Mordred was silent for several seconds. "She helped me. Telling those I was working with that I wouldn't help them got me a lovely silver stab wound. She found my bleeding body and nursed me, even though she didn't have to. She had no way of knowing I'm a sorcerer. I want to repay that kindness. And I don't want her protection removed; I want her out of the city. That's the only way she can be protected."

It didn't sound like the Mordred I knew to repay kindness with anything but pain and suffering, but we needed the information he had. "I'll have to talk to Nanshe about getting her whereabouts."

"The guard must not know," he said. "I don't want her tracked and hounded. I'll repeat myself for those who are hard of hearing: I want her out of the city. Take her to Jerusalem or something. France would be a good idea."

"France? But she lives *here*. I doubt she's going to want to move that far. I can get her out of the city. I'll arrange passage north, maybe to Constantinople."

"Fine, just get it done. And hurry, because if these people carry out whatever they're going to do, Acre is going to be a city you're not going to want to be inside of."

"How can you possibly know that without knowing their plan?"

"When I tell you who's involved, you'll realize just how much danger we're all in."

"I'll let you know."

"Don't take long," Mordred called after me as I walked away. "People's lives are counting on you doing as I ask. And I know how much you care about them."

I found Nanshe outside of the building talking to Gilgamesh. Both of them turned toward me as I got closer, clearly expecting me to give a report.

"Mordred wants a woman by the name of Isabel removed from the city," I told them, and I gave all of the details that Mordred had divulged to me.

"I spoke to the woman when she was arrested. We do not believe she's involved, but we are keeping her guarded for her own protection. Those who Mordred betrayed might want to get to him through her. Siris is with her."

"Who is Siris?" I asked. All I knew of her was that she had been considered the goddess of beer. Why any group of deities needed one for beer, I'd never really understood, but most of the different pantheons had at least one.

"Ah, you haven't met," Gilgamesh said. "We thought it best to have someone there we trusted, just in case it turned out this Isabel was important. Turns out she's not. Except to Mordred, and no one cares what he finds important."

Gilgamesh was a great warrior, a smart man, and had been a benevolent king for the most part, but he was also arrogant, with a fiery temper, and unable to see the quality in people he hadn't personally fought, either beside or against. Everyone else was either unimportant and beneath his concern, or someone he wanted to do battle with. It was one of the many reasons why he wasn't in charge of the Mesopotamians.

"Gilgamesh, can you ensure the city's defenses are good enough? If Mordred thinks we're about to have unwanted visitors—and that would be a good assumption to make—I'd like someone of your caliber checking everything."

Gilgamesh beamed and walked off without saying a word.

"A vain but brilliant man," Nanshe said when he was out of earshot. "I just wish he didn't pick fights to get to know people."

I remembered the first time I'd met Gilgamesh three

centuries earlier. I had bruises on my bruises after that encounter: an encounter I lost. Although to be fair, Gilgamesh never once lorded it over me.

"Something feels wrong about all of this."

Nanshe regarded me for a moment. "Mordred isn't usually someone to aid Avalon. Even in a roundabout sort of way. You think he's involved in something more?"

I nodded. "Maybe this Isabel is all a big distraction. Maybe she's involved without even knowing it. She could have been regarded as a target for something or other. When a particular person leaves the city, it's attacked. It's clutching at straws, but I don't have a lot of other ideas at the moment."

"Maybe we should go see this woman—or rather, *you* should."

"Come with me. I'd like someone else's take on this, and frankly, anything Mordred is involved in clouds my judgment."

She agreed and we were soon walking together through the busy Acre streets. "At least you know it clouds you," she said after a few minutes.

"That doesn't mean I'm able to stop it. For a long time I just wanted to save my friend; I figured no matter what he did, he could be brought back to us. Then he attacked Arthur, almost killing him. After that, I'm not interested in trying to save Mordred anymore."

"You want him dead."

"Yes. He deserves to die for what he's done. He shouldn't be able to hurt anyone else. Too many have already died at his hands."

"He hates you. I've never seen anyone hate as much as he does. The merest mention of your name was enough to confirm to me how much he wants you dead. I've rarely seen a hate as strong as that. It burns at his soul. It consumes him."

"You sound conflicted about it."

"I'm merely wondering where such a hate came from."

I shrugged. "I wish I knew. We were friends. I was away for a few years, traveling, learning, doing Merlin's bidding. When I returned, Mordred was being hunted for murder. He was a fugitive, killing innocent people for no reason. He'd changed into an entirely different person from the one I'd known; he was now full of hate and evil. I'd never have thought such a change possible unless I'd seen it myself."

"It appears he does not like keeping allies, either."

"I don't know who supports him. He turns up with different people, years apart, with no reason to it other than to hurt Avalon, me, or Merlin. Sometimes all three. There's no pattern to it—at least none I can understand. Maybe his addled brain makes more sense of what he does. Somehow I doubt it."

"I searched Isabel's home when we found her; interviewed her, too. I don't believe she's in a relationship with Mordred: at least no more so than the friendship he claims."

"You're certain about that?"

"Hellequin, I have people who work for me who are *very* good at their jobs. And I interviewed her myself, just to be thorough. There's no sexual relationship there. It's a dead end."

We reached the house and I looked up at the three-story white-bricked building while Nanshe walked off and spoke to the two guards at the front door. Both of them walked away a short distance, allowing us entry to the house.

The interior was sparsely decorated, with some seating and a few tables but nothing to suggest that anyone lived here on a permanent basis. There were no personal items, and everything was spotless. Two guards sat on chairs near the rear of the building, playing cards. Both stood to attention when Nanshe walked past.

"We use this building for some of our more . . . important guests," Nanshe told me. "Sometimes you want to put someone in a place without every guard in the city knowing about it."

We climbed the stairs and Nanshe unlocked the door at the top, allowing us onto the floor above. It was considerably more comfortable here, with more furniture in the one massive room. A divider sat at one end, behind which I could spot the end of a bed.

A woman stood up from a chair by the window and walked over to us. For a second I thought she might have been Isabel, as she fitted the rather pitiful description of olive skin and dark hair, but her eyes were brown, and any notion about her identity was thrown aside when she embraced Nanshe.

"Hellequin, this is Siris," Nanshe said, introducing me to the striking woman before me.

"A pleasure," I said with a slight nod of my head.

"You're the fabled Hellequin, shadowy hand to Merlin," Siris said with just a touch of mockery in her voice. There was a power behind her deep-brown eyes that surprised me; it was at odds with the cool, calm exterior she presented.

"I assume you expected me to be taller," I said with a smile.

Siris laughed. "I was going to say that, but I assume you hear it often."

"Taller, broader, able to turn into a dragon. I've heard a few tales, yes."

Siris suddenly appeared a lot more interested. "A dragon?"

"I've heard it a few times. Also a demon, the devil, and a few others. The stories are always bigger than the truth. No dragons, I'm afraid."

"Shame. I've never seen one."

"If you two are quite done, Siris, can you tell us where Isabel is?' Nanshe's voice held only a hint of reproach.

"She's on the roof. Don't worry; she's unable to fly, so getting off there would be quite the trick. I've discovered that people are more likely to talk if you allow them a little freedom. I wanted to know if she knew more than she was letting on."

The three of us continued up to the roof, where Isabel greeted Siris and Nanshe while watching me with caution.

"This is Hellequin," Nanshe told her.

As I was introduced to Isabel, I wondered for a moment if maybe there was something more between her and Mordred. Back when we were friends, Mordred had been with several different women, usually more than one at a time, and usually each relationship had burned brightly until it had extinguished itself and he'd moved on.

"Mordred sent me here," I told her.

"Where is he?" Isabel asked Nanshe, ignoring me completely.

"Safe. He's a dangerous criminal," she assured her.

"He was never dangerous to me, just kind."

"He told me you helped save him after he was attacked."

Isabel appeared confused for a moment. "Yes, of course," she said, and I wondered if that was a lie. "He's my patient, so I would like to see him."

"That's not going to happen," I told her. "Not now, not ever. He's a murderer and all-round vicious bastard. You're lucky he didn't cut you into tiny chunks and feed them to the sharks."

"You have no idea what you're talking about!" Isabel snapped. "Kindly leave."

"What's the connection between Mordred and yourself?" I asked. "Friends? Something more?"

Anger lit up Isabel's face. "How *dare* you imply anything! You know nothing about me."

"I'm not implying anything at all," I explained. "I'm asking a question."

I knew Nanshe wouldn't be impressed with my question, but while it was her job to help lead the Mesopotamian deities, it was mine to ensure that Avalon was safe. And that meant sometimes having to annoy people I might not want to annoy.

"No, we are not lovers. We are friends: something I imagine you've been told several times given that I've been asked that question a dozen times over since becoming involved in this situation."

"I'm not here to make you comfortable," I explained. "I'm here to find answers, and try to make sure no one dies. So if you're unhappy with any questions I might have, then I'll just have to accept that irritation and move on regardless."

Isabel stared at me for several seconds before her obvious anger drained from her. "I helped him, and that kindness was repaid by being locked away. They say I'm no prisoner, but then they have guards follow me everywhere. Feels like a prison to me. It makes me less than inclined to continue helping."

"I thank you for your aid in this matter," I assured her. "I promise it'll be over for you soon."

"I want to see Mordred."

"I wish I could take you, but I can't. Mordred asked me to get you out of the city, so we need to leave."

"I'll not go. My friends and life are here. He would not ask such a thing of me."

"How long have you known him?" I asked, feeling the warmth of anger inside me. "A week? Two?"

"Three years, on and off. Although I don't see what business that is of yours."

Apparently we were going back to being uncooperative again. "I'm surprised to hear that Mordred has been here for so long, even on and off." I was more surprised that he'd managed to live here without trying to kill a lot of people. Normally, he arrived somewhere, caused mayhem and destruction, and left.

"I'm being held in this building, whether you call it a prison or not, all the while Mordred, whom I trust more than any of you, is imprisoned. Why would Mordred ask me to leave? Why should I believe you? Where is it that you're hiding Mordred?" She waved her hand at the city beside her. "I'm not going anywhere until I see him."

I considering knocking her out and taking her from the city by force, but the thing about doing that is it doesn't exactly lead to a lot of trust, and there would be a good chance that she'd just run off the first chance she got. I know I would have.

There was also the possibility that she was lying—that she was involved in whatever scheme Mordred had planned, or maybe she was working for those who Mordred insisted were a danger to the city and the Mesopotamian deities' move toward uniting with Avalon. A move centuries in the making, and one that would change the face of power across a large chunk of the planet.

"I don't have time for this," I said to no one in particular. I turned to Isabel. "I don't know you, I don't trust you, and I damn well don't trust Mordred. But he has information we need, and that information is reliant on your being taken to safety. If I take you to Mordred, and you try anything that jeopardizes why I'm here—and that includes trying to free him—you'll never see him again. Do we have an agreement?"

Isabel looked around at everyone on the roof, as if trying to figure out if my offer was genuine.

"Just say yes, Isabel," Siris said. "Mordred is on the way out of the city, and it's easier than standing here arguing about it."

"I agree," Isabel said, making it sound like she'd gotten exactly what she wanted all along.

"Okay. We'll go say hello to Mordred and he can tell you himself," I told her. "At least that way Mordred knows we're actually doing what he asked. He can't feign ignorance later."

We were soon all walking through the evening sun back toward Mordred, with Siris and Isabel up front, talking to one another.

"Siris seems very friendly with her," I said to Nanshe.

"Siris is friendly with everyone. I've never met anyone who makes friends as quickly as she does. The thing is, she actually wants to know everything about the people she meets. She's not faking the enthusiasm, either: she's genuinely interested in people."

"What is she?"

"Water elemental. A powerful one, too—much more powerful than her position within the old deity system would have suggested. I don't think she was ever thrilled about being the goddess of beer."

"No. I can imagine that is a job that would get boring fast."

"She's invaluable, and I think she's looking for a more

important role during the transfer of our power to Avalon. I don't think she trusts them. No offence."

"None taken. Merlin will do all in his power to ensure that you keep the influence you were promised. And his power is vast. Besides, Elaine Garlot is helping, and I trust her completely."

"Isn't she related to Mordred?"

I nodded. "Mordred's aunt. She's a good person, though. She has given no suggestion that she's in league with, or even supports, Mordred in any way, shape, or form."

"If Mordred has been here for three years, why only now make it known that there's a plot? Why not get Isabel out of here when all of this started? The negotiations for the Mesopotamians to join Avalon started about then. What's changed with regards to his relationship with them, and with Isabel?"

"I assume it has taken them all a long time to actually organize something, whoever *they* are. I am curious as to why Mordred came here so long after the war ended. Usually he can't go anywhere without a body count following him. I'd have expected him to wade in to the middle of the war, but turning up when it's all over? That's a new one."

"I assume you agree with my assessment that Isabel and Mordred are not lovers."

"I'll admit you're right on that one. I'll see them together before confirming my suspicions, but there didn't appear to be any romantic spark when she was talking about him."

"Do you have any theories about what Mordred's plan is? I assume you think he has one."

"He always has one; I just have no idea what it is. Maybe his old partners didn't go far enough and he wants to start a new crusade between the humans to get everyone killed. It's not like humans need much of an excuse. Although neither do we."

"Were you here during the crusade?"

"Thankfully, no. Although I had to remove a few thorns after it was over. Some people committed unforgivable atrocities and needed to be held accountable for their actions. There are a few who escaped punishment, but they won't forever. Merlin doesn't take kindly to people in power abusing his trust."

We reached the building where Mordred was being held and Nanshe took Isabel inside.

"Thanks for your help," I said to Siris.

"Glad to. I'm not a fan of Avalon and us merging, but I don't want Mordred running around causing chaos. Anyway, I need to get going. Take care of yourself."

"You too."

I entered the house as Siris walked away, and descended the stairs to Mordred's holding cell. When I arrived, Isabel asked him why she had to leave the city.

"Why did you bring her here?" Mordred demanded as I entered the room.

"Because she refused to leave, and because I don't have time to play games. Frankly, I trust her about as much as I trust you, and I wanted to see whether or not you're both playing some elaborate game. I don't give two shits if she lives or dies. Hell, if she's involved with you, I'll slit her throat right here and watch her bleed to death. But you seem to care, and I want to know why."

Isabel looked at me with genuine shock on her face. She hadn't expected me to sound so cold and callous about the death of someone else. That was the evidence I needed, and I knew she wasn't linked to whatever Mordred was planning. There was no way to fake the disgust at having someone tell you they'd be fine with killing you.

"Don't you dare threaten her!" Mordred snapped. "I will kill you if you hurt her! I swear it: I will kill you, Nathan." Apart from the usual hate and bile in his voice, there was something else: affection. There was a deep affection for Isabel, and it made me pause.

"We need to leave," I told Isabel, and turned to Mordred. "She'll be taken somewhere safe."

"Not until you tell me why," Isabel snapped.

I was beginning to wonder at what point stubbornness was going to turn into something that would get Isabel killed.

"They are coming soon," Mordred said. "They're going to kill as many people in this city as possible. The streets will run red with blood. You can't be here when that happens."

"I can take care of myself." Tears streamed down Isabel's face, which was flushed with anger.

Mordred shot off his chair, the chains at his wrist stopping him from going further. "Go! Run!"

The sounds of running echoed in the chamber before the door was flung open and Gilgamesh entered. "Hellequin, Lady Nanshe: we're under attack."

Mordred crashed to his knees, his head in his hands. "It's too late. They moved the timetable up. They're already here."

CHAPTER 7

September 1195. City of Acre.

I rushed out of the building with Nanshe just behind me. We'd told the guards to keep an eye on Isabel and Mordred; hopefully they'd be safe.

Night had settled since we'd been inside the building, and as I didn't know the city well enough to lead the way, I followed Nanshe as we rushed through the streets. People were hurrying back to their homes and places of safety. The city had seen warfare not long ago, and many here would still bear the mental scars of what happened. No one wanted to see a repeat of it. No one wanted to be in the middle of a new battleground. I hoped the walls and soldiers would be able to hold off whatever had arrived.

It didn't take too long to reach the first group of soldiers, all of whom were running toward us. They stopped before us, a dozen men-at-arms all ready to fight. It was the one thing I could guarantee they'd get their chance at.

"Nabu had us come find you," the first soldier said, a tall man with terrible burn scars across one side of his face.

"Nabu is here?" I asked.

The soldier nodded. "He's with Gilgamesh and Ereshkigal near the front gate."

"How many enemies?" Nanshe asked as we fell into step beside her. I let her take the lead, knowing the soldiers would find it easier and faster only talking to one person.

"Unknown at this time. Each of the gates into the city were attacked at the same time. We took nineteen casualties, but we've managed to close them all."

"Nineteen dead?"

"Six dead, the rest wounded. The majority of them will be unable to fight tonight."

"How many soldiers do we have here?"

"Two thousand men, six hundred Templars, and two hundred Teutonic Knights. There's also a smattering of the Knights of St John, but they're helping with the influx of anyone who was outside of the gates when the attack took place. They're not exact figures for men, but that's what I was told."

The notion of the Teutonic Knights being part of the battle force made me somewhat happier. They were well-versed in fighting nonhuman opponents, possibly more so than any other branch outside of Avalon.

"Three thousand men in a city with twenty thousand people to protect. Let's hope whoever is out there doesn't like the idea of a lengthy siege." Nanshe stopped walking for a moment, forcing the soldiers to do the same. "Does anyone know what we're fighting here?"

The men glanced at one another, none of them wanting to speak up.

"Now, soldier," Nanshe said, her voice forceful and leaving no doubt that she wanted an answer within the next few seconds.

"I'm sorry, my lady," the tall soldier said, managing to sound part embarrassed, and part terrified. "But the reports of what attacked us are . . . odd."

"I do not care. Tell me. Now."

"They were monsters," another of the soldiers said, his eyes darting to his comrades, as if seeking solace in their own fear. "Monsters made of rock in some cases."

"And with fangs," a third soldier said, his voice barely above a whisper, as if the attackers outside might hear him. "They came out of the darkness. Vampires. Creatures of pure evil."

Nanshe looked over at me. "Vampires and rock monsters."

"This gets better and better," I said.

We recommended walking, and managed to find Nabu ordering several Templar Knights about. Nabu was considered the Mesopotamian god of wisdom, and it was a role that suited him. He was smart, cunning, and more than happy to treat his day-to-day life like a chessboard: a game I refused to play with him. He was a tall man, with long, dark hair that fell over his broad shoulders. His beard touched his chest, and he held himself with regal bearing. He wore chainmail but held no weapon that I could see. I'd met him several times over the years and liked him. He was smart and knew it, but never to the extent that he showed off or lorded it over other people.

"Hellequin, it's good to have you here," Nabu said, his voice was deep, the kind of voice that resonates in your mind long after he's finished talking. "Although I think Gilgamesh will not relish any competition for defeated foes."

"Gilgamesh can win this one," I assured him. "I just want the battle ended without blood being spilled."

"You know that's unlikely," he said. He kissed Nanshe on the cheek. "I'm especially glad you're here. There are too few of our kin in the city."

"This was to be a human city, run by humans," Nanshe said. "I'd hoped that once we'd joined Avalon, they would station their own people here to protect it."

"I'm sure they will," I told them. "But right now, we're all we've got."

"Not all."

I turned at the sound of the female voice and watched as soldiers hurried out of her way. She didn't seem to mind that none of them wished to touch her; she'd cultivated her reputation as someone to be feared over many years—a reputation that was completely true from what I'd heard.

"I am Ereshkigal," she said to me. The torchlight around us showed off her long, dark dress, although the light barely did the intricate embroidery justice. A red and black cloak trailed slightly along the dusty ground. I was pretty certain that she would have been able to hide weapons on her person with little problem. "You may call me Irkalla. Everyone else does these days."

She had been the one leading the negotiations for the Mesopotamians to join Avalon. I'd heard good things from Elaine about her and her skill at the game of politics. That it had taken so long for the two sides to settle on a mutual agreement was apparently down to Irkalla, and the fact that she was not someone to bend her knee to anyone without considerable compensation. It was something that had angered several high-ranking Avalon members like Hera, and made me respect her all the more.

"It would have been more pleasurable to meet under better circumstances," I told her.

"I was just about to leave for Avalon. It's a shame this happened now, although I assume you'll be wanting my help." The last part of that sentence was aimed at Nabu.

"It would be useful."

"Everything I do is useful, Nabu," Irkalla said matter-of-factly. "Tell me who I need to dismember and I'll get it done. I don't really want to be up all night fighting some horrific little monsters. Have the attackers been positively identified as something we need to worry about, or did the humans just panic at the first sign of something they didn't understand?"

I left them to talk and climbed the stairs to the battlements, where I found several soldiers looking out into the darkness beyond. The torches that usually lined the road approaching the city had been extinguished.

"They don't want us to see them coming," Gilgamesh said as he stood beside me. I hadn't heard him approach; he was stealthy for such a large man.

I closed my eyes and activated my fire magic. When they opened, I was able to see despite the darkness. The colors were all variations of orange and red, but it was better than not being able to see at all.

"They're just beyond the ridge," I said. "Several hundred of them. They're in a long line. There's no battle formation that I can see. I get the feeling they're going to run at the city all at once. Otherwise I see no benefit in what they're doing."

"You can see them?" Gilgamesh asked, surprised. "Impressive. What is the enemy we face?"

"I don't know. I can't make out features, but several of them are in armor." I watched as the line broke and something much larger than the other fighters walked through. "That would be

Asag." I didn't even try to keep the anger from my voice. The monster had killed someone I'd considered a friend, and tried to kill me, too. I owed him for both of those actions, although I knew it wouldn't be easy. I needed to be faster and smarter than when we'd last met, but more importantly, I needed to put him down quickly before he could kill anyone else.

"Asag is among them?" one of the soldiers said, his fear carrying to all those around him as several soldiers exchanged concerned glances. "The devil comes for us!"

"The devil?" Gilgamesh laughed. "Asag is a giant rock: a being that used too much power and twisted himself into something evil. But he can be killed. There is a layer of nothing between his rock and skin. If you can break that rock, his skin is just as easy to pierce as yours or mine." He raised his voice. "All of these so-called demons can be killed—" He raised the arm of the near-est soldier, showing everyone the sword he carried. "—with this: with steel. Their heads and hearts are just as fragile as a human's. They are destroyed just as easily once pierced. Yes, these are for-midable opponents, but you are all seasoned warriors: men who have faced death and found it wanting. Come the morning, you can regale your loved ones, your friends, even your next con-quest with tales of your victory." There was slight laughter at that, and he had the full attention of everyone on the battlements and those waiting below by this point.

"You can tell the tale of fighting beside heroes and gods, and you can tell them that for one night, there were no differences. This night, we will drive this evil from our land, and come the sunrise, we who remain will tell our children fearful tales of what happens to those who wish to do us harm. They think they can scare us? Well, let's show them just how afraid we are. We are all soldiers tonight. We are all warriors. We are all brothers." He raised his maul high into the night and a great cheer went up.

"And sisters," Irkalla said from beside me. "I don't want our part to be left out."

I hadn't heard Irkalla climb the stairs close by—I'd been too busy paying attention to what was in front of me—but I was glad to have her on the wall with us. "Any woman who wants to fight and bleed beside me gains the right to be called my brother-in-arms," Gilgamesh told her.

Irkalla rolled her eyes as Gilgamesh walked away to talk to some more of the soldiers.

"He means well," she said when we were alone. "He really does believe that calling us 'brothers' is a great honor. I doubt many would agree. Would the Amazonians have been happy being called brothers? Would any woman?"

"None I know of," I told her.

"Progress. And that is why Avalon will lead the world, and why our little group will be lost to the annals of history, folded into Avalon and forgotten."

"I doubt you'll ever be forgotten."

"Maybe not forgotten, but certainly no longer the first name that comes to mind when thinking of the powerful gods and goddesses of the past. It happened to the Romans, Greeks, Celts, and anyone else who was folded into Avalon. It'll happen to us, too. And frankly, it's for the best. Like I said, progress is the name of the game here. That's why we're fighting tonight: because not everyone can see progress when it's staring them in the face."

"And you're okay with coming into the Avalon fold?"

"We get to keep our power base; we get to keep a lot. And we have influence inside the Avalon power structure. Frankly we'll have more of a say than we do now. And I for one am sick of standing on the sidelines." She leaned on the battlements and bellowed, "Will you all get a bloody move on? We don't have all night!"

I couldn't help but laugh.

"I've spent far too much time in Avalon arranging this deal. I appear to have picked up some of the traits from those there. It's not considered ladylike, but then no one ever accused me of being particularly good at pretending to be a lady before."

As Irkalla stood beside me, ready for battle, I saw exactly why her reputation was so formidable with everyone in Avalon who'd spoken of her. "I've never been against women who fight, swear, drink, or speak their minds. Those who are, are either idiots or terrified they can't out-think, out-fight, or out-drink them."

A sly smile spread across Irkalla's lips. "You missed one."

"I don't think battlements are the best place to discuss women out-fucking men."

Irkalla's laughter turned more than a few heads. "I'm going to like you, Hellequin." She raised her hand, palm out, and closed her eyes. "Vampires. There are vampires out there."

I scanned the scene in front of us. Beyond the city gate was a large wooden bridge, which covered a dry moat. Beyond that was a collection of boulders and rocks strewn across the open plain alongside a few plants and trees. It was some distance before the plain turned into hilly territory, and by then the well-worn road stretched out away from the city, merging with the rest of the landscape. In short, the city wasn't going to be easy for any attackers to take, but these weren't human attackers.

The soldiers had managed to extinguish all of the torches outside of the city, but that just made it easier for the vampires.

They should have left things alone, but hindsight is always a wonderful thing.

"Can you tell how many?" I asked.

"No. It's more than a dozen, certainly. They're too far away for my necromancy to pinpoint them, but I can feel their anger, their hate." She turned to me. "They come."

The alarm went up as shapes in the darkness began to charge at the city. Dozens of creatures ran toward us. I drew my jian and waited for the inevitable.

Archers fired volleys of arrows, but only a few of the creatures were killed outright. Even those with serious injuries managed to drag themselves toward the city. Apparently death at our hands was preferable to being left behind for whatever creatures hadn't joined in the initial attack.

I didn't have long to wait as creatures sprang up onto the city walls and began scaling them. Boiling oil was poured over the sides, splashing over several of them, and the screams of the attackers tore through the night. But those climbing the walls were much faster than the humans manning them, and it didn't take long for the attackers to reach the apex and climb over, killing those who stood before them.

Two attackers hissed at Irkalla, their vampire teeth already bared. She moved her hands forcing them to drop to their knees. She stabbed each of them in the throat with daggers I hadn't seen before, and a few seconds later the bodies of the vampires slumped to the floor. Heat rose off them as they turned to dust.

"These vampires are young. The masters and elders wouldn't have dropped to their knees so easily. Someone out there is making vampires. I would like to talk to them." She didn't make it sound like that would be a pleasant conversation.

I kicked another vampire off the battlements, and cut the head off a second as he dropped beside me. A third screamed in rage as he launched himself at me from several feet away, but a whip of fire from my hand sliced him in two, both halves turning to dust as they fell into the city.

Somewhere in the darkness a horn sounded and the earth began to rumble. I looked over the city walls and reapplied my night vision. Asag was running full-pelt toward the city gates close to us. Next to him were a dozen smaller creatures.

"We have a big problem," I said to Irkalla, who was busy killing more vampires.

"Asag?" she asked.

"And his friends."

"Gilgamesh, we've got ekimmu on the way!" she shouted to the large man, who was currently flinging vampires off the battlements with ease, his huge maul knocking them aside, destroying bone and organ alike.

"We need to protect the gates!" Nanshe shouted up from below. "If they make it through, a lot more people will die."

"I will take the Teutonic Knights to one of the other gates," Nabu said from beside her. "Nanshe, take the Templars to the third gate. Hold it for as long as you can. There are others of our group already there—they will aid you."

Nanshe nodded and ran off into the city.

"Hellequin, can you, Gilgamesh, and Irkalla hold here?"

I looked over the wall again, and found that only Asag remained; the remainder of the attacking force had run to different parts of the city walls. "I really hope so!" I shouted back.

Any archers still capable of firing rained down death on Asag and his creatures, but most of the arrows bounced off his body.

For the most part Asag ignored them, and even ignored the badly wounded but still-alive vampires, who were tossed over the side onto him. He swatted them away with barely a loss in stride before he reared back and struck the gates.

The entire wall shook with the force of the blow.

"Anyone ever fought this thing before?" I asked.

"I will stop him," Gilgamesh said, launching himself over the battlements, down onto Asag.

"Idiot," Irkalla snapped, just as a dozen small rock monsters clambered over the walls and began pulling men to their death over the battlements, or cutting them open with their sharp claws.

Using my wind magic to knock them back seemed to do the trick, and my whips of fire were able to cut through one monster. The others decided that avoiding me to take on easier prey was a better use of their time.

"They're an extension of Asag's power," Irkalla told me. "I'd advise you to destroy as many of them as possible."

The blows against the city gate had ceased while the sounds of battle between Asag and Gilgamesh rang out below.

"What if enough people attacked Asag?" I asked. "Would he be forced to take these little things away?"

"I have no idea. Only one way to find out: I assume you mean you."

"You're more capable at dispatching the vampires quicker, and the little rock bastards seem to ignore anyone with actual power. They're only here for the humans. We can use that to keep them occupied."

"Go. I'll make sure these little things don't cause too much trouble. Maybe some hammers would help even the odds; I doubt they like them. How will you get out of the city without the gate being open?"

I climbed up onto the edge of the battlements in response. "Best of luck."

Irkalla nodded slightly at me before rushing toward the fighting as it spilled off the battlements and down onto the area just in front of the city gates.

My air magic slowed me down enough that I hit the ground outside of the city with an impressive noise and a lot of dust, but no actual injuries. Starting a fight with a broken leg is hardly the best idea.

Gilgamesh was on his knees in front of Asag, who had one massive fist wrapped around his opponent's maul and was trying to wrench it free of his grasp. Gilgamesh was bleeding from a dozen cuts to his face and body, and Asag's face appeared to be chipped and dented. War had been waged between the two.

Asag saw me, released his grasp on Gilgamesh's maul, and kicked the still-kneeling man in the chest, sending him tumbling down the steep bank behind him. It wasn't a long way down, nor overly deep at the bottom, but even so, I couldn't count on Gilgamesh's help for the next few minutes.

At almost seven feet tall and wider than two men, Asag was still every bit as imposing as when I'd fought him before I'd arrived at the city. Rock jutted out of every part of his body, forming plates that overlapped one another, leaving only the inside of his mouth and eyes free from it. His hands more closely resembled claws. He had the appearance of a smaller, but no less deadly, mountain.

"I tracked you for days," Asag said. "Your pathetic coward of a guide wouldn't let you face me."

"He told me you'd kill me."

"I will."

"Come on, then. We don't have all night."

Asag charged toward me, bringing his considerable rocky bulk to attack. I moved aside of his blow and raked my sword along his ribs to test the strength of his rock skin.

I put enough distance between us and sheathed my sword: it was all but useless. I remembered Asag's scream of pain when I'd used my fire magic the last time we'd met, and an instant later, a whip of fire ignited from one of my hands. I flicked it toward Asag, who moved back slightly, but not quickly enough to tell me he was concerned about it.

I walked steadily toward him, the whip trailing along the ground, scorching the earth, until I was close enough, then I flicked it up toward him once again. He stepped back, and at the last second, I removed the whip and threw a ball of flame at him. Asag raised his hand to shield his face from harm, and I darted forward, changing the whip of flame for a blade, which I brought down on his arm.

I hadn't really known what effect it was going to have; I was just trying anything to see what could make it through Asag's tough skin, so I wasn't expecting the monster to scream in pain and anger. His eyes locked with mine as the blade of flame cut through the rock and bit into whatever was beneath, and I knew he knew that I'd confirmed his weakness: magical fire. Asag swung with his good arm, but I removed the blade, darted aside, reignited it, and plunged it into his side. Asag cried out once more as several of the small monsters he controlled jumped from the battlements above me, landing with a crash.

I twisted the blade and pushed it in further, but my attention wasn't wholly on Asag, so I didn't see him swipe back at me with his enormous arm. He caught me in the chest, throwing me aside as if I were nothing. The breath left my body in one go as several of my ribs broke, and my magical night vision flickered on and off for a few seconds. When my sight was steady, I used the wooden bridge beside me to get back to my feet as Asag barreled into me, driving me over the bridge and down the bank where Gilgamesh had fallen. Water and grime filled my nose, eyes, and mouth, and I rolled onto my side, blindly trying to use the reeds and plants that littered the banks to pull myself out. I was trying to get the muck out of my eyes when I was lifted from my feet and thrown aside, colliding with the side of the bank, but thankfully not rolling back into the muck at the bottom.

My chest was on fire, and I was pretty certain I'd done more than just break a few ribs. I needed time to heal. I crawled toward the nearest tree, hoping to use it to get me back to my feet.

"I'm going to crush you, Merlin's little man," Asag said, his face close to mine, his hot breath making me feel sick.

I didn't even see the blow to my stomach, but I doubled up and vomited onto the ground all the same. I couldn't remember the last time something had hit me that hard. Asag picked me up, his claws raking over the flesh on my shoulder, and once more I found myself sailing through the air. I landed roughly, feeling my wrist snap, but used air magic to get the muck off my face. Unfortunately, that just let me watch as Asag walked up the bank toward me.

I scrambled to my feet and looked around. I was outside the main gate once more, but I was not going to go down without a fight. I limped to the other end of the bridge and watched for

Asag to climb the bank. His little monsters had vanished, and as he walked into view, I saw the last of them merge with him, healing him.

"Neat trick," I said through clenched teeth.

"My next one is ripping your head off."

I placed my broken hand against my chest and felt the blood there. Power flowed through me as my blood magic ignited. Asag paused; he'd probably seen Mordred use blood magic, but while I was nowhere near as powerful as he was with it, I was no slouch.

I flexed my fingers and my blood magic began to block out the pain of my broken ribs and other injuries. Using blood magic in such a way that you ignore your own limitations and injuries was incredibly dangerous, but so was being dead. If I didn't do something, the latter was much more likely to happen.

Asag, now seemingly fully healed, walked methodically toward me. "There's nothing you can do to hurt me, little man."

I breathed in, ignoring the pain in my ribs, and held my breath as Asag walked closer and closer, each step reverberating over the wooden bridge. I held my place, blocking out the noise of soldiers yelling at me to run, to move aside.

Asag stopped only a few paces away from me. "You going to use that flame blade on me again, boy?"

I ignored him and used as much blood magic as possible to mix with my fire magic, giving me the power I needed. And I breathed out.

The flame that left my mouth was almost white hot. I was glad I'd used my air magic to coat my throat, lungs, and mouth before trying this trick. The flame hit Asag's face before he even had time to register it. Just as he was about to speak, he screamed in pain as the flame torched the inside of his mouth, along with his eyes, blinding him instantly. It was then that I saw that the rock plates didn't quite overlap by his neck, leaving the skin beneath exposed.

I reignited the flame blade and drove it up into a gap between the rocky plates of Asag's neck before removing it, stepping around to his exposed flank, and driving it back into where his liver would be, cutting through the plates as if they weren't there.

Asag dropped to his knees as a silver tar-like substance flowed out of his wounds. He swiped at me once again, but I'd already removed the blade and stepped around him to his back, where I drove the blade into his spine.

Asag fell to the ground as the gate to the city slowly opened. Irkalla ran out, followed by Nabu, who steadied me as my blood magic shut off and my body roared in pain. He helped lower me to the ground and placed me up against a tree.

"Is he dead?" I asked.

Irkalla shrugged. "I have no idea. He's not trying to kill us, so quite possibly, yes."

"Gilgamesh fell down there." I pointed to where I'd seen him fall and Irkalla ordered the soldiers to go and check.

"The other gates held," Nabu told me, his voice completely neutral, giving nothing away.

"What aren't you telling me? Did Mordred escape?"

"No, Mordred is fine: he's unconscious, but alive. Isabel was taken. Three human guards were killed in the fight."

"Do you know by whom?" I asked, trying to get back to my feet, but Nabu held me in place until I gave up on the idea.

"Siris." Nanshe's tone betrayed the hurt that her expression didn't give away. "We were betrayed by one of our own."

CHAPTER 8

Now. London, England.

I do hope you're comfortable," Mordred said as he sat on the chair beside me.

The half-dozen golems that had stopped me from being crushed by the collapsing building stood there, stoic and emotionless, as if holding up several tons of rubble was nothing to them. Which it probably was, considering they were a magical construct.

The tranquilizer was beginning to wear off, and once it did, I'd be able to free myself and stop Mordred before he did anything to hurt someone.

Mordred reached out and, before I could move, slipped a sorcerer's band onto my wrist. I tried to push him away, but was too weak, and the second the clasp shut I felt my magic vanish from my body.

"Now don't try to take that off; you know what happens. I don't want you being silly."

If I tried to remove the band, the runes inscribed on the metal touching my skin would instantly ignite, setting off the equivalent of a magical napalm bomb. It would be too quick for me to set up any kind of defense, and all I'd be able to do would be to die quickly and painfully. If it were possible, I hated Mordred even more for making me wear one, for removing my magic from me, but I pushed the anger down. I was in no position to make demands. Instead, I stayed still and stared at the man I had once called a friend.

"Why are you here?"

"To talk to you. I brought someone with me." He pointed over to his right.

I turned and saw a woman. Her hair had been cut short since I'd last seen her over a thousand years ago, and was dyed bright green, but I couldn't mistake the woman I'd once loved. The woman who'd betrayed Arthur, betrayed Avalon—betrayed me. Morgan.

"I wouldn't distract her if I was you," Mordred told me. "She's all that's keeping those golems from letting that roof fall onto you. So here's how it's going to go: you're going to stay exceptionally still and answer my questions. I may even answer a few of yours. Because I'm feeling so generous, I'll let you go first. Just to prove it, I'm not going to trick you."

I continued staring past Mordred at Morgan. I always thought I'd feel something when I saw her again, something bigger than myself, something I couldn't contain and would have to scream and rage at her. Ask her why. Ask her how she could betray me. But when it came down to it, I didn't feel anything for her: no anger, no hate; I just pitied her. I pitied her for the fact that she'd aligned herself with such a psychopath as Mordred. A thousand years of distance between people was apparently a good way to deal with something.

"What's the point? You'll only lie."

Mordred raised his hand, palm out, toward me. "You know what this is, don't you?"

I recognized the small mark still drying on his palm. A blood-magic curse, one that forces the wearer to tell the truth. Like all blood-magic curses, this one had a catch, and in this mark's case, one that made it rarely used. The mark could only be activated on someone who'd drawn it on themselves with their own blood, and done so freely. It meant that Mordred could avoid my questions, he could change the subject, but if he lied, he would feel intense pain.

"You're wondering why I would go to such lengths to talk to you," Mordred said, as if reading my thoughts. "I thought it better that we meet face-to-face, and when I watched you fight Kay, I was going to intervene, but I needed to be sure you had no fight left in you."

We maintained eye contact for several seconds before he sighed. He held out his hand again, showing me the mark. "This mark was drawn here by a wandering giraffe." The screams that left Mordred's throat were immediate, and he threw himself from the chair, using his non-marked hand to hold the other against him, like someone would do if they'd broken a limb.

"No," he said and raised his hand toward Morgan, who had taken a step toward her comrade.

"Do you believe now?" Mordred asked, showing me the mark once more, which had turned bright orange.

"Yes," I promised him. There was no way to fake what he'd done. Which left the question: why had Mordred wanted to talk to me?

"Right," Mordred said, smoothing back his hair and reapplying his ponytail before returning to his chair. "Damn it, I've got mud on my trousers. Do you see this?"

I looked at the specks of mud that had stained the black

trousers of the expensive suit he was wearing. "I knew I should have just worn a T-shirt and jeans. These will need to be dry-cleaned. All it needs now is to piss it down with rain and my day will be complete."

"Did you really come here to talk about clothing?" I asked, feeling confused about the sudden conversation change.

"Oh, yes, sorry. Where was I?" He looked around, as if trying to figure out where he was. "Right, why I'm here. And I assume you want to know how I'm still alive."

"The question did come up," I admitted. "I killed you."

"Yes, you did," Mordred said, his eyes narrowing slightly. "Bloody good job you did, too. Sniper round through the eye. Unbelievably painful. And you took my hand." He raised both hands. "But just like dying, losing a hand didn't take, either."

"How are you alive?"

"Lots of reasons, really. I'm not here to get into all of them; they can wait for another time. Essentially, magic, luck, more magic, some more magic, and a fucking shitload of power. I'm not immortal, if that's what you're thinking, and I'm pretty certain if you tried that trick again, I'd be dead for real this time. I sort of thought of it at the time like an extra mushroom."

"A what?"

"A mushroom. You know, a *mush…room*." He repeated the word slowly the second time, as if talking to someone who doesn't quite understand the language.

"I know what a mushroom is. I have no idea what you're talking about."

"*Super Mario*," Mordred said. "Mushrooms make him bigger. There are other things that give him the ability to fly, or shoot fireballs, but they're not mushrooms, although I guess they'd still work in this analogy. But I went with mushroom, so here we are."

He paused for a second. "Anyway, if Mario gets hit he doesn't die; he just shrinks to a smaller Mario. Then if he gets hit again, he dies. That's me. Although in my case, I've gotten a lot more powerful since you killed me. I guess I should thank you for that."

"You play *Super Mario*?"

"I had a lot of free time on my hands while my body and mind repaired itself. I played a lot of *Mario*, and *Final Fantasy*, and something called *Fallout*. That was fun. Oh, and *Lego*. I love *Lego*."

I was beginning to feel like I'd been knocked out and was having some sort of weird hallucination. "Have you lost your mind? Genuinely curious."

"Yes. I got shot in my brain." Mordred's words were said with a mocking tone, as if trying to get me to bite, to argue with him. He paused again. "It makes me go off on a tangent a lot. So I'll be talking about something and then all of a sudden I'll think of something else and off I go. It gets frustrating for those talking to me. I imagine you're pretty annoyed right now."

I sighed. This was turning into an exhausting conversation. "This is the strangest day I've had in a considerably long time. Any chance you could just get on with killing me? This whole thing is beginning to give me a headache."

Mordred smiled and clapped his hands together. "Oh, it's going to get stranger. You see, I'm not here to kill you. Not today, anyway."

"You're not?" My disbelief was easy to hear.

"Nope. We're going to talk, and I'm going to leave."

Despite every part of me knowing that Mordred was an insane murderer, he sounded sincere.

"Have you got *Mario* on pause or something?" I didn't mean to mock him. I just couldn't help it.

"Don't be facetious. I'm being serious. I don't want you dead today. If I did, I wouldn't have had Morgan save you, I wouldn't have checked the rest of the garden for any more surprises. That annex over there is empty, in case you were wondering. I already searched it. Also, Asag, Kay, and Jerry are long gone. You're safe—for now."

"Today?"

"Oh, I am going to kill you. I have to; it's sort of where my destiny lies. In fact, it's more where your destiny lies. But you're not ready; you're certainly not powerful enough. I need you at your peak before you can die. Or at least a lot more ready than you are now. Killing you now would achieve nothing. It would only make things more complicated in the long term, and I don't really want that."

"Do you plan on telling me *when* you're going to kill me?"

Mordred tilted his head slightly and rolled his eyes. "I might be crazy, but I'm not an idiot. No, I'm not going to tell you. But you will die, and by my hands, too."

"So why *are* you here?"

"To talk to you. To let you know I'm back. Oh, and to see how things are going with you. How many of your blood-curse marks are gone now? Be honest."

For as long as I could remember—right the way back to waking up age eight on a field outside of Camelot—I had six blood-curse marks on my torso. For the longest time I had no idea what they did, but then, due to Mordred trying to kill me a few years earlier, they'd started vanishing. Two had gone so far, giving me an increase in power and my necromancy. Four remained. I had no idea what they would do, and frankly I was a little nervous about finding out.

I wondered if Mordred wanted to know so he could figure out any more of my weaknesses, but there was little point in lying. "Two."

"I heard about the necromancy; that's nice. So, that leaves four to go, yes?"

I nodded.

"They're taking their sweet time, aren't they? I mean, I expected another one, maybe two more, to have gone by now. It must be quite frustrating for you."

"Why do you care?"

"Why? Because when you die, you need to be my equal. I want to kill the best of you there is, not someone who has most of their power locked up. I need as many of those marks gone as possible. Also, I'm really curious about what they do. Aren't you?"

"What did yours do?"

Mordred looked shocked for a second before he smiled. "Figured that out, did you?"

"You've always been able to see my marks before. That means you had some yourself, but you can't see them now, which means you no longer have any. So, what did yours do? And where were they? I never saw them."

"Tops of my thighs," he said. "I don't believe we were ever *that* close. And they did vanish, yes. They've given me some interesting talents; a few other things, too. I've spent the last few years trying to figure out who put them there and why."

"Can I assume you didn't discover who put them there?"

Mordred shook his head. "I wish I had. If I knew, maybe I could kill you now. Maybe I could get all of this over with."

"So you came here to say hi and leave. Okay, you can go now, I guess."

Mordred laughed. "Actually, I thought we could talk for a while longer. I certainly don't want you to think I don't care."

"I won't hold it against you."

Mordred got up and sat on the ground next to me. He leaned up against the remains of the wall and sighed. "Can I tell you a secret?"

This whole thing was beginning to make me incredibly confused. The only times Mordred hadn't tried to kill me were when it benefited him somehow. I stared at the man I'd considered my enemy, a man I'd hated for over a thousand years, and thought something was off with him. There was something different. Maybe the shooting had damaged his brain, but it felt like more than that.

"Sure. Why not?" I said eventually.

"I've had a few truths shown to me since my murder. I've undergone a transformation of sorts. Things have changed—I've changed."

"Yet you're still going to kill me."

"Some things will never change. The rain will always be wet, dogs will always be man's best friend, and Mexican food will always be the greatest food on earth." He looked down at me. "Sorry, went off on a tangent again. Anyway, my secret." He leaned close to me until his mouth was almost touching my ear, then whispered, "Your mother was a Valkyrie. Her name was Brynhildr."

I wanted to say something clever to let him know that I wasn't about to be played, but as I opened my mouth, nothing came out. My brain suddenly felt as if it were on fire, and I began shaking, unable to talk, unable to move. While Mordred's words unlocked flashes of memories, I lay there and stared at the darkness and stars above me.

CHAPTER 9

It felt like I'd taken my first breath in minutes. I tried to sit up, but pain laced through my body, causing me to gasp.

"It'll only hurt for a moment," Mordred said. "Just a moment."

For a second I thought he'd poisoned me, or stabbed me with a silver blade while I wasn't capable of defending myself, but as he said, the pain soon faded and I lay on the cold ground, panting and drenched in sweat.

"What the hell was that?" I asked breathlessly.

"What did you see?"

The words spilled out before I could stop them. "My mother and me, in Constantinople. We were eating a picnic of some sort. I was six years old, and she told me we had to leave, to go north. She was scared. I don't know why, though." I fought the jumble in my mind. "Our marks shared some similarities."

"Yes, several of mine were removed due to memories. I thought it might work for you."

"How did you know who my mother was?"

"I did some digging. I found records of her moving to Constantinople with a contingent of bodyguards and servants, and a son. *Nathaniel Garrett* was the name written there. Took me by surprise. I figured she'd have used a fake name, but then, it was centuries ago, and looking things up on the Internet wasn't really a thing back then."

"How did you manage to find something that I couldn't?"

"I had to bribe a few people in the right places, and I had an idea what I was looking for. It was going to happen eventually."

"Why did you look into my past?"

"Ah, I told you. I need you strong, I need you to be the best you can be, and unlocking those marks is the key to that."

There was something more there: something he wasn't telling me. I was certain of that. "If you make me stronger, you'll never be able to kill me."

"That isn't really important right now."

I stared at my ruined top and saw bare chest where a black mark used to be. "Any idea what it does?"

Mordred shrugged. "No idea. The moment I saw the pain you were going through, I knew that a memory was unlocking a mark."

"Do you know where the Fates are?"

"No. Kay has them, I assume. I've been tracking you since you arrived in London."

"Any chance you've been tracking Kay, too?"

"Ah, yes: Kay. He's a vicious little git, isn't he? Never did like him. Always wanted to gut him like a fish. Never did, though." He stared away across the garden. "Never did."

"And?" I asked, prompting Mordred to answer me.

"No. I've only been interested in you."

"How'd you find me?" I asked, as Mordred went back to staring off into space. He started humming to himself.

Mordred's attention returned to me. "It was easy, actually."

"Planning on telling me, how?"

"No."

"Did you bug me somehow?"

Mordred sighed. "No. And if you're going to start asking lots more questions, we could be here a while, and I don't think Morgan can keep this up all night."

"I'm fine," Morgan said. "But if you get Nate out from under that house, it would make my life easier."

"Nate, if I get you out from under that house, are you going to try and kill me?"

I wanted to kill him. I really did. But I certainly couldn't take both Mordred and Morgan while I had a sorcerer's band on my wrist, and probably not even without. I had to find Kay and Jerry. I had to find the Fates.

"I swear I won't attack," I told them.

Mordred dragged me out from under the building using his air magic so he didn't have to get too close. The moment I was free, Morgan dismissed the golems, and the rubble I'd been lying under collapsed into the vacated spot with a loud bang.

"Why haven't any police come?" I asked.

"Told them not to," Mordred explained. "I have a few friends in the right places. Or rather, other people have friends that I can use as I need to."

"Nice to see you really haven't changed."

"Never said I had. Well, actually I did say that, didn't I? Okay, maybe I haven't changed too much." He checked his watch. "I guess we need to be going. Pleasure seeing you, Nate. Glad I could help you with a spot of trouble. Be seeing you again really soon."

"Mordred, one last thing," I said.

He stopped and turned back to me. "What?"

"Since we're being so civilized: what happened to you? We were friends—like brothers. Then you tried to kill me, and everyone I thought you cared about. What happened to you?"

"Life happens, Nate." He put his hand in his pocket and tossed me a small metal key. "It's for the band. You're going to need your magic, I think. I get the impression that Jerry and Kay weren't your only problem."

I thought back to the small rock monsters that attacked me. "Asag is alive. We killed him. He really shouldn't be up and around."

"I remember," Mordred said with a huge grin. "But then, apparently the people you think are dead really don't like to stay that way. Goodbye, Nate."

I unlocked the sorcerer's band, grateful for the wave of power that entered me the second it was released. I raised my hand, trying to use whatever power I'd acquired, but nothing happened.

"It might take a while, Nate," Mordred told me with a smile on his face, but no mockery in his tone. "You always were impatient. Be seeing you soon."

Morgan stayed a moment, locking eyes with me. "I wish things had been different."

I laughed. "You've had over a thousand years to think of what to say to me and that's what you go with?"

"Should I grovel to you for doing the right thing?" she snapped, before taking a breath to calm herself. "I apologize for you getting hurt, Nathaniel—sorry, you go by Nate now, don't you? You were never meant to get hurt."

"Just Arthur. That was meant to happen. You tried to kill your king. Our friend."

"*Your* king. *Your* friend. He was never *my* anything. I'd hoped you'd have seen the truth by now: why we had to kill him."

"Because you and your allies are power-hungry idiots who aligned themselves with a psychopath?"

"Goodbye, Nate." Her words were said with real venom. She turned and followed Mordred, leaving me alone, bathed in the light of spotlights that sat around the garden.

I wondered what the loss of the latest mark would give me. I guessed that, like the previous marks, I would have to wait a while for it to be usable.

I needed to figure out where Kay and Jerry had taken the Fates. And there was the small matter of Asag's survival, which was certainly something I hadn't been expecting.

I got back to my feet. I felt unsteady, but at least I was alive, even if shaken up, and a lot more confused than I'd been before the day had started. I took a few seconds to ensure I wasn't going to fall over at the first step away from where I was propped up, and found I was okay.

I was certain that Kay and his allies knew I was alive, which meant I had to find them quickly, before they could do more damage.

I climbed over the nearby fence and made my way to the front of the house. I really needed a cup of tea. Or a shot of whisky, although if I started drinking, I might not stop until the bottle was finished. No, tea was the better choice. I looked at the house. It had collapsed like a soufflé.

I sat in front of the bookstore and waited for Diane to show up, which didn't take long. Her white BMW X5 screeched to a halt in the middle of the road. Diane was out of the car the second it stopped and running to the collapsed building.

"Hey!" I shouted, getting her attention.

She ran over. "What the hell happened?"

I regaled her with tales of collapsing buildings and Mordred; the latter she was less than pleased to hear was in her city.

"Any chance of a cup of tea?" I asked. "It's been a shit day."

Diane was soon joined by Remy, Kasey, and Chloe, none of whom appeared that thrilled to see me in my disheveled state.

"You're an asshole," Remy snapped. "Running off like that, almost getting yourself killed."

"I'd really like a cup of tea." I was almost at pleading territory.

Diane sighed, walked into the shop, and returned a few minutes later with a cup of the lovely stuff.

"I'd have done it myself, but I honestly don't know where anything is." I explained anything I'd missed a few minutes earlier with Diane, and occasionally sipped my tea. "This is good." I blew on my tea and took a good, long drink, letting the warmth and sweetness of the sugar calm me. It's a weird thing, but a good cup of tea really can help if you're having a crappy day.

"I've never understood the British love of this drink," Diane said. "I prefer coffee."

"And that is because you're a heathen."

Kasey didn't look like she was in a patient mood. "So, Mordred is back. And so are Kay, Jerry, and Asag. All of whom want you dead."

"Nice summary. They also flattened a house on me. And I have no idea what Mordred wants. He was even weirder than usual."

"We need to go back to Brutus's place and get his help," Diane said. "Tommy's waiting there for us. He's not thrilled about what's happening here."

"Yeah, I think going there is a bad idea. They have people working for Brutus on their side. It's how they managed to make you believe you had people here when you don't."

"My own people conspiring against me?" Diane's anger leaked out slightly and she clenched one hand, making the knuckles pop audibly.

"You shouldn't have left without telling anyone," Kasey told me as she sat beside me and gave me a quick hug.

"You didn't kill Mordred." It was Remy's turn to speak, and it was less of a question and more of a statement of disbelief.

"I didn't exactly have the means or opportunity."

Diane walked off with her phone.

"So do you have a plan?" Chloe asked.

"I plan on finding the Fates, and killing everyone else involved. Haven't really gone beyond that as a plan."

"It's a start."

"What's going on with Brutus?" I asked. "I've heard he's having some issues."

"He's convinced someone is out to get him," Diane said, hanging up the phone. "He's been getting more and more paranoid since the whole episode with Pandora a few years ago. There might well be a threat against him, but as he won't let me do my damn job, I can't easily figure out who might cause him trouble. This time, Licinius told him of a threat to his life, because that way Licinius gets the credit when this fictional threat is vanquished." She rubbed her eyes. "Sorry for the rant. To be honest, I'd be grateful of some time away, although I wish it were for a nicer reason."

Licinius was one of Brutus's lieutenants. A capable sorcerer, a dangerous individual, a brilliant mind, and an insufferable wanker. I admit that it was quite a feat being head and shoulders up his own ass and up Brutus's at the same time. I think it's safe to say I didn't like him.

"Well, first things first." I finished my tea and set the cup beside me. "We need help. Someone is moving pieces around, and I'd at least like to know the game they're playing."

"Okay, let's go get Tommy, then," Diane said, and we all followed her back to the car.

Chloe opened the back door and a foot-long package wrapped in brown paper fell out of it, landing on the ground with a clunk.

"What's that?" I asked.

"No idea," Diane told me. "It arrived just as I was leaving to fetch you. It can wait."

Chloe bent down to pick it up. "Ow! What the fuck was that?" she exclaimed. Her hand had a nasty cut on it, and was dripping blood all over the brown paper, which had ripped open when it fell, revealing runes underneath.

There was a humming from what we could now see was a stone tablet, and Chloe stepped back to look down as the runes lit up bright blue. She raised her foot, presumably to kick the tablet as far away from her as possible, but before her foot connected with it, the tablet exploded, bathing us all in brilliant blue and purple light.

CHAPTER 10

"Where the hell are we?" I asked, as I opened my eyes and blinked repeatedly.

"Ouch!" Diane said from nearby. "I smell nature. Why do I smell nature?"

"Well, that was the exact definition of messed up," Kasey joined in. "I do not enjoy landing on my ass in the middle of a forest."

Kasey was right: we did appear to be in the middle of a forest. A smattering of snow littered the ground.

"Any idea where we are?" Diane asked. "And, Nate, if you say, 'Not Kansas' I'm going to throttle you."

"Well, we're not in London. Or England," I said, getting to my feet and brushing myself down. "Trees are a lot higher here than I would have expected. Oh and it's August. Not a lot of snow in England in August."

"It's not cold," Remy said.

"It's quite pleasant," Diane agreed, "despite the snow."

"I don't think my T-shirt and jacket are going to be all that great if it gets colder, though," I said. "We need to get to a phone, figure out where we are, and what the hell is going on."

Diane searched around her feet. "Where's the tablet?"

"I assume that whatever it was, it was a one-way trip," Kasey said. "I've never heard of a tablet with runes allowing people to teleport, though. You?"

Diane shook her head.

"Nate?"

"Yeah, I've heard of something similar. But that was a long time ago, and it was used to open a gate to a realm. I haven't heard of them since, but I assume they'd gone into mythological territory."

"I don't think it's a myth anymore," Diane pointed out.

"A portable realm gate?" Remy asked, shocked.

We all had the same thought at the same time and began to run through the forest. It didn't take long before we reached a cliff edge. Hundreds of feet below us was even more forest, and in the distance a mountain range. There was a town in front of one mountain, with a huge tower hundreds of feet tall between the city and the mountain.

"No, no, no, no, no," said a voice I immediately recognized. "This can't be happening."

I turned to find Mordred. I launched forward, grabbing hold of his lapels and driving him against the nearest tree trunk. "What did you do?" I screamed at him.

"Me? I didn't do this!" he said. "Now let go of me."

I ignored him. "Why? Why did you do this, Mordred?"

"Release me, Nathan," Mordred said, more forcefully.

"Nate, let him go," Morgan said, placing the tip of a blade by my throat.

"Don't you dare," Kasey snapped and dove into Morgan, taking her off her feet and planting her on the ground.

For a few seconds all I heard were the sounds of fighting, while I held Mordred in place.

"*Enough!*" Diane screamed. "Mordred said he didn't do this.

Right now, let's not kill one another until we figure out what's happening."

I didn't move.

"Let go of him, Nate." Diane's voice left no room for argument.

I released him and stepped back, catching a glimpse of Kasey and Morgan, both with bloody lips, glaring at one another with hatred.

"Why would I want to come here?" Mordred asked as he sunk to his knees. "I never wanted to return to this accursed place."

"Where are we?" Remy asked.

Mordred ignored the question and looked up at me. "You know, don't you, Nate?"

I grabbed Mordred's hand and checked the rune. It had been removed, so it was possible he was now lying to me.

"Nate, do you know this place?" Diane asked, as Morgan helped Mordred get back to his feet.

"Yes," I said. "It's the dwarven realm of Nidavellir. Over there is the city of Darim, and beyond that the dwarven city of Thorem. This is the realm where the Norse dwarves originated."

"How far away is Darim?" Kasey asked.

"A day or two's walk," Mordred said. "Two days out here in the wilds. You know what that means, yes?"

I nodded.

"Would you like to tell the rest of the class?" Morgan asked. She walked past Kasey. "Nice right hook, by the way."

Kasey touched her cheek. "Pull a knife on one of us again and I'll tear your arms off."

"Like to see you try, Kid Werewolf."

"Enough!" Diane shouted. "Seriously, I'd quite like to get out of here in one piece, so if that means I need to launch anyone off this cliff now, let me know so I don't have to be worried about you all killing each other."

"I'm good," Kasey promised. "Who are you two, anyway?"

"I'm Mordred. This is Morgan," Mordred told her.

The moment Kasey realized it was Morgan, she dove at her. Diane moved quicker than either Remy or me, and we were both closer to Kasey. She scooped the teenage werewolf up and pinned her against the tree as Kasey snarled and tried to break free.

"Remember what Diane just said about not killing her," I reminded Kasey, while Remy placed his hand on his sword hilt. "Either of you. We need numbers to get out of here in one piece. And while I hate to admit it, killing each other isn't going to get us home."

"But they're murderers—and traitors," Remy said.

"Yes, and I trust them about as much as I'd trust a hungry tiger not to bite me, but right now, we're all in mutual need. Once we get out of here, I'm sure they'll try to do whatever they want. So don't trust them, but don't kill them."

"They're welcome to try," Morgan almost spat, her twin blades already in her hands.

"You're not fucking helping!" I almost shouted, causing her to blink. "Put them away, or I will remove them from you!"

"You can—" she started.

A bolt of lightning left my hand and flew by her ear, slamming into the rock behind her. "Yes. I can."

She put the blades away, her expression of shock one that I might well otherwise have enjoyed.

"Guys, I don't feel so good," Chloe said, collapsing onto the soft earth.

We darted over to Chloe as she tried to get back to a kneeling position, momentarily forgetting about Morgan and Mordred's presence. Kasey wrapped up the deep cut on Chloe's hand as we tried to find out if she was okay.

"It took a lot out of me," Chloe said.

"Nate, kindly explain what kind of things we might find here," Remy asked, clearly keeping his temper in check. I doubt he was thrilled about being in Mordred's company. Everyone in Avalon knew someone who Mordred had killed, either personally or through his games.

"There are a lot of things out here that would probably enjoy eating us. Big things, with big teeth."

"Spiders. There are giant spiders out here," Mordred interrupted.

"Not just spiders," I explained. "Ogres, trolls, things you probably don't want to get too close to. The city is a haven for travelers, though."

"Not anymore it isn't," Mordred said. "Or at least, I doubt it is. Not since the dwarves vanished and left this place in the hands of—" He stopped, as if he'd said too much.

"Hands of what?"

Mordred looked around him. He had the appearance of a man who was incredibly worried about who might overhear him. "I won't say. This place is evil and we need to leave. Now."

"Why are you so scared?" I asked.

Mordred stood and began walking away.

"Mordred? When did you become a coward?"

He turned and immediately sprinted toward me. I readied myself for an attack, but Diane stepped in between us, her hands out to stop anything from happening.

"I do not relish keeping you all apart," she said. "Do not taunt him, Nate."

I put my hands up in surrender. "You're right. Mordred, why are you scared?"

"This place, these people, they broke me. They broke me, Nate. And someone sent us back here. I can't be here again. I can't." Genuine tears filled his eyes. "I can't, Nate. They broke me."

Morgan ran to him, holding him against her.

"What the hell happened here?" Remy whispered to me.

"I have no idea, but I'm pretty certain it wasn't anything good."

"Did someone send you a tablet too?" Diane asked Morgan and Mordred.

"We were watching you," Morgan said, "from on top of the roof of the Fates' house. Maybe thirty feet up, ten feet away."

"So the tablet, whatever it is, has a small range," Remy said, "but it goes up into the air a considerable amount. Could anyone else have been caught up in it?"

"Not unless they were on the roof too," Mordred snapped. "Actually, I don't know. I didn't see how far the light went."

"Let's go check. I don't really want to leave innocent people here to die."

"We need to worry about ourselves, Nathan."

"You're welcome to start walking, Mordred. But since you hate it here, I figure numbers are important to you. Besides, look at that." I pointed over at the mountain range as black clouds rolled in over them, streaks of lightning trailing down to strike some of the peaks. Everyone followed my finger.

"How long before it gets to us?"

Mordred took a deep breath. "Four, five hours. We need shelter."

Morgan didn't look overly impressed with that idea. "We

need to get back. We can't spend days and days away from our realm."

Mordred shook his head. "Days are shorter here, but not by much. A week here is maybe five days in our realm. Someone wanted you all out of the way so that they can do something. What the something is, is a question I don't have the answer to. But I'm going to assume that if Kay is working with people inside of Brutus's organization, then he's at least partly responsible for what happened here. Either way, the quicker we're gone from this accursed place, the better."

"How long did you spend here?" I asked, not really sure I wanted an answer.

Mordred ignored me. "Let's go find shelter."

I watched Mordred retrace our steps back toward the clearing.

"What kind of shelter are we looking for?" Diane asked.

"There are a huge number of caves around here," Mordred said without turning back to her. "The dwarves used to mine this far out of the city, until it became too dangerous for them to travel through the forest below. The caves sometimes get taken over by trolls or ogres, or sometimes something worse, but when I was a guest here, one of the dwarves told me about a set of caves that you could use to keep safe if you were caught out here. That was a few thousand years ago by time here, however, so who knows what we'll find?"

"Has a lot changed since you were last here?" Morgan asked.

"I'd rather not find out."

"What about you, Nate?" Diane questioned.

"I was here once. I was young and didn't stay long—a month or so. I only went to the cities, never this far out. This place is meant to be impossible to get to nowadays. There are no realm gates that go here. After the dwarves vanished, people tried to get to their cities, mostly to hunt for treasure, but no one ever could."

"Well, someone certainly knew how to get here," Morgan said.

Mordred walked around a large boulder and was gone for several seconds before returning, a smile on his face. "Cave found. It's dry and will protect us from the storm."

"Any signs of wildlife there?" Diane asked.

Mordred shook his head. "Not recently. I doubt it's been used for a long time by anything larger than insects."

We followed Mordred to the cave, which was exactly how he'd described it. It was a bit cramped, and the low ceiling in part of it meant we had to stoop to get in and out, but it was dry and warm, and the oncoming storm wouldn't be able to hurt us.

"You get a fire going," Diane told me after we'd inspected our new surroundings. "I'll go get us some food and check around for anyone else who's been dumped here."

"There should be deer around," Mordred said. "Unless they've been wiped out in the last thousand years—which is possible, I guess."

"You're going to stay here," I snapped.

Mordred stood. "We might be able to help."

I stared at him in disbelief. "Help do what? If we go out there, there's a good chance I'll turn around and find you trying to put a knife in my gut."

"Nate, I'll say this again, as you appear to be hard of hearing: I have no intention of killing you."

"Yeah, *yet*," I pointed out.

"We don't have time for this petty crap," Kasey snapped.

"Kase has a point," Remy said. "We need to work together. We have no idea who sent us here, or why, although from what Mordred and Morgan said, it sounds like they were collateral damage in someone else's plan."

I knew Remy and Kasey were right. I knew I should just be mature about it, but damn it if I didn't want to argue anyway. It's hard letting over a thousand years of bad feeling go, even if it's for the benefit of everyone else.

I took a deep breath, and exhaled slowly. "You do what I say, Mordred. No running off, no hurting people. Same goes for you, Morgan."

I saw that Morgan was about to argue, but Mordred rested his hand on her arm and her neck muscles relaxed.

"You're the boss, Nate," he said to me without a hint of anything other than genuine agreement.

Diane walked away with a sparkle in her eyes; hunting was one of her favorite pastimes, although she only killed to eat, and usually with a bow and arrow. The roar from just outside the cave, and the clothes that had been left inside, informed me she'd changed into her bear form to hunt.

The rest of us joined her outside, and once we'd gathered enough supplies and confirmed that we were the only people sent here in the immediate area, we all made our way back to the cave. I started a small fire, and the remaining six of us sat in uncomfortable silence.

"Nate, we have a problem," Kasey whispered to me. She had been with Chloe since we'd re-entered the cave.

"What's wrong?"

"It's Chloe. She fell asleep when we got back to the cave, but she won't wake up."

I rushed over and checked her pulse and breathing, both of which were regular, but she still didn't wake.

"What happened?" Mordred asked from behind me.

"Go away!" I snapped.

Before he could reply, Diane entered the cave, took one look at Chloe and dropped the deer she was carrying, running over to the injured teenager to examine her.

"There's a cut on her hand," Remy reminded her. "But she told us about that earlier. I don't see anything else."

"The cut will fade in time, although it is deep," Diane said as Chloe began to stir, much to everyone's relief. "My guess is she's just exhausted from the jump. She's only human, yes?"

"A witch," Kasey clarified.

Diane nodded. "Okay, she just needs rest. We'll take shifts keeping an eye on her. Once this meat is cooked, everyone eats. I don't care if you have a problem eating meat; you'll have more of a problem passing out, because the next few days are going to be intense."

I didn't think anyone was a vegetarian, but she made a good point. Morals are great and all, but surviving is a bit more important.

It wasn't the greatest night's sleep I'd ever had, what with the wind howling outside and the frequent claps of thunder, but I've slept through worse storms. What made it difficult was knowing that Mordred was only a few feet away. While one of us stayed up at all times—discounting Mordred and Morgan, because no one in their right minds trusted them—I still woke on a regular basis to look over at them both and make sure they hadn't moved.

Daybreak brought a respite from bad weather, and although the smell of wet grass permeated everything, it wasn't the worst thing to wake up to.

"There's some deer left," Diane said once everyone was up. "Everyone should eat something. I've been out already. There's a stream close by; I think the rainfall made it bigger than it usually is, but the water smells okay."

"It should be fine," Mordred agreed. "The rain here is clean and drinkable. Or it was centuries ago."

"Well, I don't feel sick," Diane said. "And I saw animals drinking from it. That's usually a good sign. What isn't a good sign was what those animals were."

"Local carnivores?" Remy suggested.

"Some big ones too."

"Cave bears and saber-toothed panthers," Mordred suggested. "They were both pretty abundant back in the day."

"I saw two bears and a panther," Diane said. "That's not good for us."

"The bears will be fine," Mordred told everyone and grabbed a piece of meat from the fire I'd restarted. "They were hunted by the dwarves, and were a handful from what I remember, but they don't hunt people. Certainly don't eat them unless they're already dead. They're mostly scavengers, not hunters—despite the fact they're the size of a large car."

"And the panthers?" Diane asked.

"That's a big problem. They'll hunt anything that isn't bear. And I do mean *anything*. They're solitary hunters, but that was a long time ago and my memory of them is a little foggy. I know they used to kill townsfolk; took a few dwarves, too. If we have one on our trail, it will hunt us for miles. And they take a lot to put down."

"Between the seven of us, I'm sure we'll be okay," Diane said.

"There are some things you should know about this place.

Some of our magics won't have the same effect on the creatures that live in this realm as it does in ours."

"Meaning what?" I asked.

"Meaning, in the earth realm, you could use your air magic to blow a panther back a hundred feet, but the same amount of magic used here might only cause it to be pushed back a fraction of that. Magic will still be able to hurt anything that attacks us, but you'll need to use *a lot* of it to have even a little of the impact you might expect. Flinging a boulder at something is still going to knock it back, but it might not do any actual damage to it. It might not be a good idea to rely on your magic for fighting. It's something to do with the crystals in the mountains. It doesn't affect the plants, which is why you were able to start a fire on those branches earlier, but it does have an effect on the creatures that live here. And that includes some things that you really don't want to get close to without your magic at your disposal."

"Crystals?" I asked. "Small pink-purple ones?"

Mordred nodded slowly.

"I've seen them before," I told everyone. "They tend to explode when magic is used on them. I once rode a motorbike that was powered by them."

"Why?" Chloe asked. She'd made a good improvement throughout the night, and was eating with everyone else.

"I didn't exactly have a lot of choice at the time. It was mostly that or let an exceptionally bad man get away. Anyway, these things are volatile, to say the least."

"You're talking about Shadow Falls," Mordred said, naming another realm free from the influence of Avalon and its rulers. "It's a bit different there; particles of the stuff get into the air and it makes our magic unstable. A small amount will cause a big explosion. That doesn't happen here; the crystals are more stable, and there's less leaking, less pollution. I can only imagine that over the last few millennia those creatures are even more immune than they were back then. Essentially, don't count on your magic being able to do an awful lot."

I rubbed my temples. "Okay, that makes things more complicated. Anything else we should know?"

"That city you want to go to: Darim. I don't think we're going to find a lot there."

"Why?"

"Bad things happened here, Nate. The dwarves didn't leave for no reason. And their departure left something much worse in charge."

"What things?" I asked, slightly annoyed that he hadn't bothered to mention any of this the night before.

"I call them Evil Bastards, and if we come across them, we will be in trouble."

"Do we actually have a plan?" Remy asked. "I mean, apart from wander through the forest to a city that may—or may not—be overrun by . . . things?"

"There has to be a realm gate there," I said.

"But we don't have a guardian," Remy pointed out.

"There wasn't a guardian who sent us here either," I said. "Maybe we can figure something out. It has to be better than sitting here."

I didn't want to say that I agreed with Remy's assessment, mostly because I didn't want to put a damper on the only hope we had. Realms, like the one we found ourselves in, needed gates for travel. Gates were operated and protected by guardians. No guardian, and the gate won't open. Except that to send us here in the first place, we didn't have a guardian, or even a realm gate. Which meant there really was a way to send people to realms without the use of gates, and apparently that way involved tablets covered in runes, and blood.

CHAPTER 11

The next day we marched through the forest, stopping periodically to drink from one of the many freshwater streams, eat the berries that were safe, and rest. There was an abundance of caves, and most of them contained nothing more than a few birds. Although one cave was home to about a thousand bats, who we left alone and trundled on elsewhere rather than deal with the stench they managed to create.

Apart from being weak during the morning, Chloe managed to improve steadily over the rest of the day. She needed a little more rest, but was otherwise okay. It was just coming up to the evening of the first day when I found her a few hundred yards from the rest of the group, sitting on a rock next to a small stream, dangling her feet into the cool water.

"How are you feeling?"

She shrugged. "Weird. We're basically in paradise—so long as you ignore everything that wants to eat us."

"That small matter." I sat down beside her.

She flicked a small pebble into the stream. "I miss training. I liked the routine."

As well as training Kasey, I'd been giving Chloe lessons too. She probably benefited more from having something to take her mind off her home life, although it certainly seemed to me that she'd all but moved in with Kasey and her family. "I think you can forgo it for a few more days."

"I haven't spoken to my mum in six months," she said out of the blue. "Had barely even thought about her until we got here."

Kasey's mum was a witch, and frankly, one of the most unpleasant people I'd ever met. Not speaking to her for six months—or six years—sounded like my idea of heaven.

"It's weird; she used me, she almost got me killed, and she showed no remorse over either, but she's still my mum, you know?"

I nodded. "Yeah, I know. It took me a long time to get over knowing that Merlin was, in fact, a colossal asshole. But eventually the realization just stopped hurting and I did something about it. Took me a lot longer than it took you, though."

"The last time I spoke to her, we fought. I'd called to give her important news, and she managed to disappoint me yet again."

"I'm sorry she sucks so very, very hard at being there for you."

Chloe shrugged. "I've gotten used to it. I'm seventeen. I've had my naming day at Avalon. I'm a relatively powerful witch. I don't need her or her negativity in my life. But part of me says, 'She's your mum, the only one you've got. Try.' I'm just so fed up of trying. You'd have thought almost getting me killed would have made me give up having anything to do with her."

"Maybe your time here will do you some good. You can relax, enjoy the scenery, run from anything with sharper teeth than you have: good, wholesome fun."

Chloe laughed. "Someone really wanted Diane out of the picture, and didn't care who got taken with her."

"Yep. Kay's grubby little mitts are all over it."

"Could just be a coincidence."

"Could be, but the fact that it all happened on the same day, and that Jerry admitted to having people in Brutus's organization who work for them, makes me think otherwise."

"Maybe they're going after people you care about?"

"If that's the case, there would be a lot more people here. No, this has been kept small for a reason. There's something I'm missing, but I can't put my finger on it."

"Could Mordred be behind it all?"

"No. He couldn't fake how scared he was when he realized where we are. I still catch him looking around. He's nervous, and worried, and that's keeping him pretty subdued. Something is wrong with this place, and he knows it. He either doesn't want to talk about it, or doesn't want us to know. Probably the former, as the latter would mean he'd intentionally try to sabotage his own escape."

Chloe got down from the rock she'd been sitting on and shook her feet dry, using her red hoodie to finish off before putting her socks and trainers back on. "That thing I told my mum," she said without looking back at me as she tied her laces.

"Yeah?"

"I told her I like girls."

"So do I. Welcome to the club. We have cookies."

She looked back at me. "I mean, I'm gay."

"I know what you mean, Chloe. I'm just trying to be funny and failing. Thank you for sharing it with me."

"My mum asked me if I was sure, and then told me it was a phase I'd grow out of."

"Your mum's a dick."

Chloe's laugh was from the belly, full of actual humor. It was nice to hear. There'd been precious little laughter since arriving here. "Yes, yes she is. It would have been nice if she'd given me a better response, though. When I told her that, she flipped out. Haven't spoken to her since."

"If she can't support you, don't worry about it. Did you tell Kase?"

"Kase has known for years. Tommy and Olivia thanked me for telling them and didn't bat an eye. It's weird that they'd have a better reaction than my own blood. Especially to something so important to me."

I put my hand on Chloe's shoulder, squeezing slightly. "When we get back, I'll make sure you have a good punch-bag session. You can pretend it's whoever you like—no judgments from me."

Chloe smiled. "Thanks, Nate. It felt like something I should tell you since you're so important to Kase." She paused. "And to me. You're like an older brother or something."

"I've never been an older anything. Do I need to do anything?"

Chloe shook her head. "Bring me ice cream when I'm upset. Get me alcohol."

"I think I can do both of those things, so long as you like vodka or whiskey, because I'm not buying that swill people your age call beer."

We were both still laughing when we heard the growl coming from the darkness of the woods nearby. I turned slightly and saw a saber-toothed panther pad out of the woods onto a large rock formation a dozen yards upstream, before launching itself into the water below.

The panther was bigger than any cats we had back on our realm, tigers and lions included. Even on all fours, its head probably came up to my shoulder. The cat's fur appeared to be black, but as it moved it seemed to shimmer under the sunlight, turning almost dark blue on occasion. Two gray stripes ran from its nose up over its muzzle and finished just behind both ears, which were twitching as it moved in the water.

"Move slowly," I whispered, and we both took a step away from the stream.

The large cat watched us and took a step forward, mirroring us. I didn't know much about panthers, saber varieties or otherwise, but I vaguely remembered that big cats don't usually like to have their prey watch them as they attack.

I heard a rustle in the leaves, and spun toward it, casting a jet of flame at a second panther that was sneaking up behind us. The animal ran back several yards, its fur slightly singed from the heat, but otherwise unhurt.

"Any chance you have a weapon?" I asked.

"Spells. I have magic. But magic might not do a lot. And witch magic isn't exactly fireballs and lightning."

"Any chance you know something a little more subversive? Like making us disappear?" We continued to back away, until both saber-toothed panthers were directly in front of us.

"Teleporting is a little out of my depth. But I have something that might help." She raised her sleeve on her right arm, revealing the tattoos she'd put there.

Witch magic is different to sorcerers' magic. Whereas we are born with an innate ability to tap into the magic, witches have to read grimoires and tattoo runes onto their bodies to allow them to access magic—magic that is literally powered with their own life energy. Essentially, witches use their own lives to create magic; the more powerful the magic, the more life they ebb away. It's a pretty dangerous way to access some incredible power, and some, like Chloe's mother, want to gain more and more power for themselves, and end up turning to evil to get it.

Mist left Chloe's fingers, traveling out in front of her, putting a dense fog between us and the panthers.

"They can still smell us," I pointed out.

"I know. That's not what I'm doing. When I say go, throw a fireball."

I smiled, aware of what Chloe wanted to happen, and readied a ball of fire in my hand, pouring more and more magic into it until it was white-hot. The soft rumble of a purr from the panthers made me aware that they were now inside the mist that was obscuring our vision as much as theirs.

"Now!" Chloe shouted.

I flung the ball of flame and turned to run, not wanting to be close to the vapor as it ignited. I remembered what Mordred had said about my magic not having as much of an effect on the things that lived here, but I hoped it had enough effect to keep Chloe and me safe.

The vapor exploded like a bomb, making a truly horrific noise and shaking the ground beneath our feet. Something inside the cloud screamed, although whether in pain or confusion I couldn't tell. If witch magic was from a different place to sorcerer magic, then it stood to reason it might well be able to do more harm to the panthers, too.

Chloe and I ran as fast as possible, but I could still hear the great cats coming after us. I caught a glimpse of one of them and pushed Chloe aside as it sailed over where she'd been standing. Unfortunately, this left me in the path of the same panther, who appeared to have a lot less fur on its body and smelled of burning, but considering the amount of magic I'd used, it should have been turned into jerky. Apparently, Mordred hadn't been lying when he'd said magic wasn't as powerful here.

The panther opened its mouth, showing me the sharp teeth inside, none of which I wanted to get anywhere near.

While enough of my magic could hurt the creatures, it wasn't going to be the easiest battle. I had no weapons, and was going up against a master predator in its own environment. It wasn't going to be a fun afternoon.

I heard Chloe say something and a shimmering mass shot up from where she lay, slamming into the panther, taking it off its feet, and throwing it into a nearby tree stump.

"What was that?" I asked, as the panther lay dazed, shaking its head from side to side.

"Jedi magic, according to Tommy," she said with a forced smile. "Something similar to your air magic, but a lot more localized. And a lot more painful for me."

I turned just in time to see the second panther leap toward me. And for a second I thought, *I'm dead.*

And then Chloe and I vanished.

It was as if we sank into the ground itself, coming up several yards away beside a different tree.

"What just happened?" she asked.

I looked down at the gray glyphs that adorned my arms. They were definitely new. "Shadow magic," I said. "Apparently I can do shadow magic."

"Can that help us?"

From what I knew, shadow magic wasn't usually used in an offensive way; it was more for defense, for getting away and manipulating shadows to aid in escape and hiding.

"Hold on to me," I said. "I'm not sure how this works, and I don't want us to get separated."

Chloe hugged me tight and I saw the two panthers turn

toward us and begin running. We vanished from view again, and this time I could feel areas of exit all around me. It was as if I'd stepped into a world exactly mapped over the normal one, but this one was just one large shadow, with the shadows themselves being more gray in color. Instead of moving to one of the shadows, I was able to bring it to me, which took only seconds. We jumped into that gray shadow and found ourselves back in the forest.

The panthers were several dozen yards away, appearing confused as their prey continued to vanish and reappear further and further away.

"You okay?" I asked as Chloe's breathing appeared to be getting shallow.

"It feels like all the air gets sucked out of me when I go in there," she said, her voice raspy. "I'm not sure I can do another one."

Maybe only the person using the magic was immune to those effects, as my breathing appeared to be okay. It was something to figure out another time.

"The camp is close by. Do you think you can make it?"

Chloe nodded.

The panthers continued to pace around the tree they'd last seen us in front of, sniffing the surrounding area. One of them raised their head and turned it toward us.

"Let's go."

I picked Chloe up in my arms and ran back toward the camp, getting there just as a roar escaped the forest behind me. Diane was first out of the cave we'd set up in, helping me lay Chloe down so she could check her over.

"What happened?"

I explained about the magic and panthers, while Chloe's

breathing improved, and by the time I finished, her breathing sounded normal again.

"Saber-toothed panthers?" Remy asked from beside me. "I'll go check. We don't want them tracking us for another day. Kasey, you feel like pissing off some big cats?"

The two of them set out to drive the cats away, hopefully without killing them. The cats weren't doing anything wrong, but if it came down to it, I knew they'd end the problem permanently. We couldn't risk those things coming after us again.

"So, omega magic then?" Mordred said, a slight smile on his face as he leaned against the cave wall.

"Not the time," I told him.

He ignored me. "Shadow magic is rare; much rarer than light. And you used it to escape—that's quite impressive for a first-time use."

"My list of reasons for impressing you is so small you could put it on a pinhead," I informed him. "Now piss off or go help track the panthers, but don't bother me."

Mordred wandered off, humming the same tune I'd heard from him earlier, and I sat with Chloe while she recovered.

"That wasn't fun," she said.

"You feeling okay now?"

"Tired. Wiped out, actually. Like I did when I first got here."

A bad feeling settled inside of my gut. "Can I see your hand again? Nice move with the magic, by the way."

She showed me the hand that had been cut. The wound was scabbing over, but it was still sore and didn't look comfortable.

"Thanks. I've been practicing."

"It shows. Although the fact that you're using your own life force to do those things concerns me."

"I know. Olivia and Tommy said the same thing. I can't practice my magic without using it, though. It's not possible."

"Just be careful."

"I will. Thanks for earlier. And for saving my life and all of that."

"My pleasure. Let's never have to do it again."

"Being chased through a forest by two massive cats is a once-in-a-lifetime thing, I hope."

I left Chloe to rest and found Diane snacking on some leftover rabbit. "There's venom in her blood," she said. "I can smell it in the wound."

"I figured it must be something along those lines," I said.

"My guess is that the tablet was coated in the stuff. She gets cut, and the venom is quickly in her body. Someone really did not want me to be around."

"You think it'll get worse?"

Diane shrugged. "Depends what the venom was. Right now, it's making her tire quickly and giving her breathing difficulties. I assume her going through your shadow magic was exhausting for her, more so than you. Probably exacerbated the effects of the poison."

"We need to get her some help. And then when we get back, I'm going to find out who sent the tablet and feed about a gallon of that poison to them."

"Get in line." Diane looked past me to Chloe. "That girl has been through more than most. Father vanishes, mother a psycho who nearly gets her killed. I'm amazed she's as together as she is."

"I think having Kasey, Tommy, and Olivia in her life helps."

"And you, Nate. I think you underestimate just how much those kids look up to you."

"I am a fountain of knowledge."

"Oh, shut up," Diane said with a chuckle. "They respect you, and value your opinion. I've seen you around Kasey, Chloe, and some of their friends. I think maybe you're closer to having your own little squad of Hellequins than you ever realized."

"I'm training Kasey, and occasionally Chloe. That's it."

"And don't be surprised if that number grows over time. After Brutus, you're probably one of the few people I'd follow into the deepest pits of hell itself if you asked. Just be careful. When you told the Avalon world that you'd train Kasey, that raised a lot of eyebrows. Not many people want two of you, Nate. One is usually enough."

"Yeah, I know. I don't want to paint a bullseye on their heads, but some bad people are going to start making their move. Hell, some bad people have already begun. Kay is still out there. And if he comes for me, it's going to be through the people I care about. I need to make sure people are prepared."

"We drove them off," Remy said as they returned from their hunt.

"They don't like to be threatened," Kasey said. "I tracked them for about half a mile. I doubt they'll be coming back."

"We should still leave, just in case," Remy chimed in.

"How's Chloe?" Kasey asked me, her voice low. "No bullshit."

"She's got venom in her bloodstream," I told her. "It's not life-threatening, but I think that tablet had something on it that was meant to make Diane weak. Unfortunately, Chloe was the recipient. And considering Asag is still alive, it's more than possible that the venom is from him. He's certainly a much easier source of the stuff than trying to acquire it from elsewhere. If it is Asag, I've been affected by the same toxin in the past. She just needs rest and it should flush out of her system in a few days."

"And rest is the one thing we can't give her until we get home," Remy said. "We should get to the city quickly. We'd stand a better chance of fortifying ourselves against whatever is out there."

"I think there's something at the city that Mordred doesn't want to talk about," I told them all, relaying my concern. "He's a lot more skittish and preoccupied than usual. And Morgan won't leave his side for long."

"Anything else you want to share?" Mordred asked as he left the cave. "And to answer your concern, yes, I'm worried about what's up ahead, and no, I can't tell you because I don't know. I only know what was here when I was a resident."

"You want to tell us that, then?" Remy asked. "I know you're evil and all, but getting us all killed is probably going to lower your own rate of survivability."

"Blood elves," he said, the words full of fear.

"What the hell are blood elves?" Kasey asked.

Mordred shook his head and walked away.

"Mordred, you need to tell us," I called after him.

He turned back to me, a smile on his face. "I didn't like *Final Fantasy X*. It was too boring. Nine was good though, wasn't it? So was seven, and there are seven of us. I like the number seven. It's a good number."

I looked at everyone else. "What the hell are you talking about? The blood elves, Mordred. Concentrate on me, not on video games."

"I don't know where they came from," he almost shouted. "I don't know why the dwarves fled from them. I don't know anything about them. All I know is I was tortured by them every single day for a century. I was here, in the realm, for one hundred and thirty-three years, Nate. For a hundred and eighteen years I was in a dark cell, and for a hundred and twelve of those I was broken and healed every day. Without fail.

"I didn't even remember my own name by the time I escaped. And I don't actually know how I did that, either. I don't even know how I survived. I can't remember if they asked me questions, or what they brutalized me for. All I remember is screaming and begging them to stop, and the laughter of those creatures as I did. And if those things—those utter, fucking monsters—are between us and home, then we might as well kill ourselves now, because it'll be a damn sight quicker than what they'll do to us."

CHAPTER 12

After Mordred's fear-filled outburst, it was decided to get to the city of Darim as quickly as possible, so we set off as soon as Chloe felt well enough to do so. Chloe took the news of her poisoning well, especially considering she was in the wrong realm to positively identify the poison or poisoner. She appeared even more determined not to let it stop her.

The plan had been to get to Darim before nightfall, primarily because Mordred informed everyone that if we thought those panthers were bad, they were nothing compared to what hunted in the forest at night. I remembered some of the tales I'd heard when I was last here. I didn't want to find out how true all of that was.

"So how old were you when you were here?" Kasey asked as we reached the apex of a hill that led down to the town. The sun was beginning to set, and it felt like we were making good time, although Chloe was being carried by Diane so that the young witch could rest.

"About thirty-five," I told her. "I came to talk to some of the blacksmiths here; Merlin wanted to use their arms to supply Avalon. Dwarvish steel is stronger than titanium, and only they know how they make it."

"What made them so special?"

"Dwarves? They were alchemists. All of them. But to a level I've never seen in any non-dwarf alchemist. The dwarves didn't just manipulate matter; they improved it, and were able to craft items, imbuing them with magical abilities. Merlin wanted to know how, and we never got an answer. Presumably it's the crystals that allow it to happen."

"Maybe we can find one of them and ask."

I shook my head. "The dwarves vanished en masse about fourteen hundred years ago. They just all upped and left. The realm gates that did work on earth no longer work, or were broken—which isn't even meant to be possible. The guardians vanished, too. No one knows where the dwarves went, or why, or even how. There were at least a million dwarves living in this realm, across seven massive dwarven cities. Being able to move so many people must have taken planning, and a big effort. But it was as if they just disappeared. It's a mystery that a lot of people in Avalon have tried to solve, and no one has ever gotten close to figuring it out."

"Maybe we will," Kasey said with glee. "We could be the first people to truly know what happened."

"Unless some people don't want anyone else to know what happened."

Kasey's brow furrowed. "Yeah, I hadn't thought of that. Maybe the dwarves never left?"

"They definitely left," Mordred said as he walked past us. "Trust me on that."

Mordred had gotten a few more steps in front when Kasey said, "Why do you hate Nate so much? Why do you want him dead?"

"It's a long story," Mordred replied.

"You're never going to be able to kill him. You know that, right?"

Mordred briefly looked back at Kasey and me. "Child, you have no idea. I know you think you're going to protect Nate from me, from whatever I do to him, but you won't. So, don't get hurt, and just stay out of things you don't need to be involved in."

A low growl emanated from Kasey's throat, and I placed a hand on her arm to calm her, while every part of me wanted to grab Mordred and tear his head clean off.

Mordred stopped walking, and turned to Kasey. "You're still young. You don't understand."

"I understand you're a monster."

He nodded. "Yes. That's true. I am a monster—have been for a long time. Will be for a long time to come. Nate and I have done this dance for centuries, one always getting the upper hand on the other, and vice versa. The dance has to finish sometime. We can't go on like this forever. I refuse to allow that to happen. But not now, and not here. So stop trying to bait me, stop trying to get under my skin. Better people than you have tried, trust me. Better people than you have failed."

"I really don't like him," Kasey said as Mordred walked off.

Remy stood beside me. "Trust me, you're not alone in that opinion. The man is the walking, talking equivalent of a gaping dick-hole."

Kasey tried to stop her laughter, but ended up having some sort of mild coughing fit.

"Really?" I said to Remy.

"When the word fits, my friend. When the word fits."

"I think we have a problem," Diane said as she left the trees surrounding us to join the path we were walking on.

"What is it?" Mordred asked, having stopped walking and turned back to us.

"I didn't see anyone in the town."

"As expected." Mordred began walking off again.

"As expected?" I asked as I caught him up, with everyone else behind me.

"Did you think that whatever drove the dwarves away wouldn't attack other cities and settlements?"

"Blood elves?"

Mordred looked at each person in the group before settling his gaze back on me. "Yes."

"Can you tell us anything else about them? Do they fly? Do they shoot lightning bolts? Anything?"

"Don't mock me, Nathan. This is neither the time nor the place for it."

"You should tell us when the time and place is," Remy said, "because we'd quite like to write it down so we remember."

Mordred gave Remy a look of pure malevolence before starting his journey down the hill.

"You shouldn't mock him," Morgan chastised. "You don't know what he's gone through."

"He's murdered thousands, probably tens of thousands of people over his lifetime," I said. "I couldn't give two shits what he's gone through. He kills and tortures innocent people, sometimes because they're in his way, sometimes because he needs to, sometimes just because it's a Wednesday and he's got fuck all else to do. You allied yourself with a monster. I don't know which one of you is worse."

Morgan blinked once, and I wasn't sure if she was going to throw a punch my way. "You're nothing but an arrogant little man who has no idea what he's talking about."

I watched her walk off after Mordred, and waited until enough distance was between us before I set off again.

"You okay?" Diane asked as she placed a hand on my shoulder.

"Been a long few days."

"Going to be a long few more," Remy said. "I really hope we don't run into any of these elves. Whatever they are."

"A figment of his imagination?" Kasey asked. "Do you think he's responsible for what happened to the dwarves?"

I shook my head. "Mordred is a lot of things, but there's no way he's a match for even half a dozen dwarves in open combat, let alone a million. And you can only kill so many people from the shadows before they actively start to hunt you. No, whatever they are, they're real."

"And they scare a man who once struck down Arthur," Diane said. "That does not bode well."

Unfortunately, I had to agree with her. Whatever had Mordred so spooked that he'd essentially left all of us alone for the entirety of our time here wasn't something to take lightly. I'd seen him fight. I'd fought against him, and he was no slouch in that department. On top of that, he was never shy about getting involved when violence was required.

"Let's just find a way out of here." I set off after Mordred, but didn't catch up with him until we'd reached the city limits, where I found him and Morgan crouched behind a white stone wall.

"This city once held five thousand people," he said softly. "Be on the lookout; there's no telling if anything settled in their place."

I knelt beside him, with the rest of the group doing the same. I risked a peek over the wall and saw a street that cut straight through the center of the city, bisecting it. I pointed at Mordred and Morgan. "If there is anything in there, smaller teams will be able to evade easier than all seven of us walking through the middle of town. You two take the right; Kasey, Diane and Chloe the left. Remy and I will go up the center. If you come across anything, come get the rest of us. Do not engage; we have no idea exactly what might be in this town."

"Where should we meet up?" Kasey asked.

Mordred kept his voice low as he spoke. "While it's been a thousand years since I was last here, it doesn't look like much has changed. No electricity, or running water. The town doesn't look much different in way of size, either. Same types of houses, same streets. If I remember correctly, there was a well in the center of the city. They placed a huge statue of one of the dwarven kings on it; I can't remember which one. It's made of solid gold. If it's still there, you'll see it, and if not, you'll easily find the well."

"A thousand years and we're going on maybe?" Remy asked.

"It's better than anyone else's plan," Morgan pointed out.

"No arguments," I interjected. "We meet in the center of town. If the well is still functional and the area clear, we'll find somewhere to rest up for the night. I reiterate, though: fast but steady. Let's not wake anything up that is best left asleep."

"Yes, sir," Mordred said as he snapped off a salute.

"Shove it firmly up your ass," I said with a smile. "You want to go steaming in there and piss off these blood elves, you be my guest."

The rebellious humor in his eyes vanished in an instant. "We'll do it your way. Quick and quiet."

Mordred and Morgan slunk off into the city as the sun's final rays vanished over the horizon. Kasey, Diane, and Chloe were about to leave when I stopped them.

"Chloe, you know what I said earlier about using your magic less? I really don't want you to use your own life force to do anything, but if you need to use it, don't hesitate. You can worry later on about dying a day or two earlier. Right now, we need to get out of here and do it all in one piece. I'm not losing anyone here. Okay?"

Chloe nodded and the three of them moved into the city.

"I have a bad feeling about this," Remy said. "I can smell things in there, Nate. They smell of death and decay. Neither of those are good things to smell."

We were about to climb over the wall into the city when Mordred and Morgan returned. Mordred crouched beside me. "There's no way along there. Lots of cobwebs, lots of collapsed buildings. It would take days to climb over it all."

"You're with us then," I said, not exactly thrilled about the prospect.

We climbed over the wall and began walking along the stone-cobbled street, my gaze kept straight ahead, while Remy, Morgan, and Mordred took turns looking to the left and right. We made it roughly halfway along the street when a large shadow passed over the moonlit path about a hundred feet ahead of us.

"What did you see?" Morgan whispered.

"Something big. Moving fast."

"You think those panthers came back?" Mordred asked, a slightly nervous edge to his words.

"I sure as hell hope not." I certainly agreed with the unspoken sentiment. Panthers in the daytime were bad enough, but trying to fight them during nightfall would give us a serious disadvantage.

Remy sniffed the air. "I don't like that. It isn't panther, and I still smell death."

"Let's just get to the center of the city and find somewhere safe," Morgan said. "I don't think this city has been inhabited for centuries."

"Although it's strange that part of it has collapsed and this is still well maintained," Remy said. "Almost as if they purposely want people to come this way."

"Keeps everything tidy. The city isn't overrun with vines and trees. There's nothing but a few months of growth here. So who's keeping it neat?" Morgan asked.

"You think blood elves like gardening?" I suggested.

"Blood elves might like crochet for all I know," Remy said. "Let's not find out."

The journey continued in silence until we reached the area where I'd spotted the moving shadow. Strands of web had been stretched out across the ground, with the doors to the houses on either side of the road completely removed, replaced with strands of web that moved into the house. The moonlight lit them up, and it would have been quite beautiful, if it hadn't been so mind-numbingly terrifying.

"Well, I think I know what I saw," I said, trying not to turn around and look about for anything crawling up to me.

"Giant spider?" Morgan asked. "That's just perfect."

"They might not be," Remy said hopefully. "Might be giant silkworms."

I didn't even bother to give a response to the idea that massive silkworms were crawling over the city. "Magic-resistant giant spider," I whispered after a few seconds. I sighed. When it rains, it pours. "We're going to need to take a detour."

I took a step back as a piece of rock dropped from the top of the nearest building across the cobbles about two feet from where I stood, rolling over several strands of web, pulling them as it went.

"Run!" I shouted as the first giant brown spider burst from its lair, running toward the stone.

All three of us turned and sprinted away, but after a few yards it had become obvious that Morgan hadn't been as fast as we were. I stopped and turned back to her as she threw a huge block of magically created ice at the spider, which was easily the size of a large car. It was thrown back into the web of another spider, which had no qualms about attacking its neighbor, sinking forearm-long fangs into the tangled beast.

Morgan scrambled to her feet as I used fire to cut through the webs that had snared her. "That wasn't what I expected. Got a plan?"

"Can you freeze up the entrances to those houses?" I asked.

"And then what?" Remy asked. "Just run past those monsters?"

"I was going to go with sprint, but essentially, yeah."

"That spider could change its mind and come after us."

He had a point.

"Morgan—" I began.

"On it," she stated and began using her magic to cover the half a dozen doorways close by in thick sheets of ice, while the now-dead spider in the center of the street was slowly wrapped in silk by its murderer.

When the doorways were clear, Morgan blasted a jet of freezing air on the ground, turning it into an ice rink, making the victorious spider slip off to the side of the road with a large thud.

"Run!" Mordred shouted, scooping Morgan up in his arms and running with her.

I didn't need telling twice, and used my air magic to make me faster as I ran toward the ice rink. Remy hit it before me, dropping onto his back and allowing the momentum he'd built up to carry him past the spider carcass and to the other side of the ice. I landed a few seconds later, just as the spider that had been knocked off the road climbed unsteadily back to it and saw me. I slammed my hands onto the ice, cracking it as every ounce of air magic I had poured into the ground, using it to propel me into the air at high speed. I avoided the spider, which lost its footing once again and landed face first in its doorway.

I landed just beyond Remy, Morgan, and Mordred, scuffing my knees, elbows, and palms, but alive. And soon after the four of us were sprinting off toward the center of the city, hoping the spiders were done for the night.

We continued on in silence, until we reached the center of the city, a ring of buildings all looking in on a large, ornate fountain in the shape of an anvil. Water glistened in the fountain. Like Mordred had said, at some point there had been a golden statue atop it, although it now lay on the ground as if cast aside; time or vandalism hadn't been kind to it. A large part of the statue's limbs had been destroyed, and the king's head was missing entirely.

"Someone didn't like their monarch," Morgan said.

"His son was king when I was here," Mordred said.

"Do you think those blood elves destroyed it?" I asked.

"I have no idea. A lot has changed since my last visit."

"So, where to now?" Remy asked.

"We need to get into the mountain, into the dwarven city. It's the only way we'll be able to figure out how to get home. There should be a realm gate, and if there isn't, the library will hopefully give us clues. So long as it wasn't destroyed."

"The blood elves?" Morgan asked.

Mordred nodded. "They hated the dwarves and anything associated with them, but I can't imagine the dwarves would have let the library fall into elven hands without a considerable fight. Hopefully some of it will remain."

"Heard some commotion," Diane said as she, along with Kasey and Chloe, joined us. She turned to me. "I assume that was your doing?"

"Big spiders," I said as nonchalantly as possible.

"This place is beginning to turn into the worst tourist destination ever," Chloe said.

"How do we get into the mountain?" I asked, wanting to get the conversation back on track.

"Two ways," Mordred said, picking up a stick from the ground and using it to draw a circle in the layer of dirt beneath our feet. "The first is we leave the city, which is this circle, and walk around to the right. There's a bridge there; we cross it to the entrance to the city of Thorem. The big problem there is how exposed we will be. The bridge is over a gorge that is probably a few hundred feet in height, and the bridge itself stretches for the better part of a quarter of a mile. If there're any problems once we're there, we're stuck. There's nowhere to go."

"Second option, please," Remy said.

"There's an entrance in the mountains just up ahead." Mordred drew a second, smaller circle just above the first. "It means descending into the gorge much further along the trail where it's shallower. It'll be several miles of trekking through woods with who-knows-what inside, before we reach a part of the gorge that's only about a dozen feet deep. Unfortunately, it then means a climb up the mountain. There used to be a pathway there, but considering what's now inhabiting this city, it might not be the empty path it used to be."

"So both of our options suck," Kasey summarized. "Excellent."

"There is a third option," a voice said from the shadows.

Morgan drew her twin blades, while I noticed Kasey's fingernails grow longer, the hair on the back of her hands beginning to sprout.

"I'm not a threat," the voice said. A man stepped out of the shadows of one of the buildings. His skeletal appearance made it difficult to age him, especially with a bald head and leather armor that looked to be slightly too large for his frame. "I can take you into the mountain."

"Who are you?" Diane asked.

"My name is William," he told us. "I live under the mountain, close to what remains of the dwarven city."

"You're human," Remy stated. "What happened to the people in this city?"

"Wiped out, or taken as slaves," William said, taking another step toward us. "Fourteen-hundred years of slavery and death. There's a small resistance movement, but we're not powerful enough to overthrow the blood elves."

Mordred looked like he'd been hit when the word *slave* was used. I almost asked him if he was okay, but managed to stop myself. I didn't want to give a crap about what he felt, but it's hard to maintain hatred when you need one another to survive.

"Is there a realm gate in Thorem?" I asked, no less thrilled to hear that the blood elves had taken slaves. To discover that there were untold numbers of humans in servitude to monsters who terrified even Mordred sent a shiver up my spine.

"At least two that I know of," William confirmed. "I haven't been close enough to either to say whether they work or not."

"Any dwarves still remain the city?" I continued, trying to ascertain whether our newcomer was on our side or whether he had ulterior motives.

"A few hundred last I heard; we have little communication with them. They spend most of their time running and hiding from the elves."

"How do you get us into Thorem?" Kasey asked.

"There's a set of passageways under here. It goes into the lowest parts of Thorem, away from the blood elves, who don't like to go down that far. They tend to occupy the furthest left side of the mountain, where the crystals and richer parts of the city used to be. It's safe, I promise."

"We don't have a lot of choices here," Diane whispered. "I don't trust him, though."

"Me neither," I agreed.

"Take us into the city," Mordred said, surprising me with how quickly he'd agreed to go back into a place he'd been professing to hate since we'd arrived in the realm. "The sooner we're there, the sooner we can figure out a way to leave."

Well, at least that explained why he was suddenly so keen to get into Thorem.

"We should leave quickly," William said, and turned to go.

"What do you get out of it?" I asked.

William didn't turn back to the group. "I'm hoping you'll help me. The blood elves have my father. I can't find him alone."

"We'll help," Mordred told William, surprising me even more. "Lead the way."

William led us all into a large building on the opposite side of the city center, which, from the size and number of benches inside, had probably been some sort of political building or a town hall. He stopped at the rear of the large room and knelt, moving a rug from the floor and exposing several dwarven runes.

"What do they say?" I asked.

"*Hidden*," he told me, placing his hand on one, which lit up bright blue, the others around it doing the same as a huge groan escaped the wooden floor beneath my feet. I stepped back slightly when the floor began to lift and move, exposing a set of stairs beneath it that led down beneath the city.

"It's okay; it's torch-lit," William promised. "It's a giant cavern, but it's safe. I already checked it on the way to meet you. I need to go last to ensure it's closed. Sometimes the predators in town like to come in here after they smell us."

I looked down at the flickering light several dozen feet beneath us. "If there's something I don't like down here, if this is some elaborate trap, I'm going to kill you, William."

"I promise it's safe."

"We'll see." And I descended the stairs into the unknown beneath me.

CHAPTER 13

The cave system under the city was expansive, and more than once there were crossroads and closed doors of silver and gold that could have led to a whole separate system for all I knew.

"How do you know where to go?" Chloe asked after half an hour of walking along an identical path, with barely indistinguishable walls and ceilings. Her voice echoed around the massive area.

"Small marks on the walls," William told us. He walked over to one and showed a small green rune next to a white crystal that emitted enough light to see all around us. "Each rune goes to a different part of the system. This whole place was designed by the dwarves to get in and out of the city with minimal problems."

"It's stood the test of time," I said, feeling somewhat in awe of the huge amount of work that must have gone into creating something as impressive as this.

"The dwarves knew how to build things," William said. "But most of this was done after the blood elves came. It was done in haste, so there's none of the impressive finery that was in other parts of the city."

"The blood elves were responsible for the dwarves vanishing?" Diane asked.

I wasn't sure in the light, but it looked like William shrugged.

"That's what the blood elves say: that they came and the dwarves fled."

"That doesn't sound like any dwarves I've ever met," Diane said. "Most of them liked to fight, liked to test their abilities in battle. They were artisans, craftsmen and -women with no peer, but they were warriors, too. Good ones. They wouldn't have left here without a fight."

"That's only what we get told. The blood elves like to limit human reading and we're not allowed to discuss the dwarves in their company. The great library is off limits to all slaves—even those of us who secretly resist them won't go there."

Mordred's eyes appeared to light up. "The library is still intact?"

William looked back, and I could see the uncertainty in his eyes. Had he said too much? Had he revealed something he shouldn't have? He nodded slowly. "Last I heard, yes. Some of the blood elves like to read; there's a lot of knowledge there. They get angry that they can't recreate the dwarves' abilities with alchemy. That and they can't read the runes—not properly. There's a machine that's meant to teach people how to read dwarvish, but it's guarded by the dwarves. The blood elves have lost many trying to get to it, and now they don't bother."

"That machine might help us recreate one of those tablets," Morgan whispered to Mordred.

I wanted to tell her to watch what she said, but it appeared that William hadn't heard. "More importantly, are any dwarves still here?" I asked.

William looked uncertain, but nodded. "Mostly in a city they call Sanctuary."

"How many?"

"Several hundred, maybe more. Neither the elves nor the resistance know for sure."

"So could the dwarves help us? Or at least help lead us to someone who can?" Remy continued. "Someone outside of this realm knows how to make those tablets, which means they must have come here to do so. Or they're a dwarf, and have stayed hidden for centuries, if not longer."

William didn't engage in any more conversation with anyone in the group, although what the tablets were, who created them, and how was all anyone wanted to discuss.

The dividing line between the caves made with haste and those done with love and care was quite literally one stride wide. One second we were walking through an exit from one cave system, and the next we were in a whole new world. Columns of the finest stone stood all along both sides of the huge room. The rock walls had been carved into ornate patterns, the colors of red, gold, and silver shining through. There were members of royalty in the human world who had castles and great halls, but none of them could have held a candle to this. The ceiling was decorated with jewels, showing a huge mural of a battle. Part of it cascaded down onto the walls, as if the dwarves had simply run out of room but were determined to finish anyway.

"What is that depicting?" I stared at one part where two groups of dwarves were fighting what looked like a huge dragon.

"I don't know," William said without looking up. To be fair, he'd probably seen it hundreds of times, and had it committed to memory. "The dwarves had a lot of myths and stories, each one more exaggerated than the last."

"I've been wondering something," Diane said. "How is it you speak English so well?"

"My father taught me English as a child," he said quickly. "The blood elves force us to talk in their language, though, so we keep any human languages secret. Unfortunately, my parents didn't escape with me to the resistance. It's why I need your help."

"To find your dad?" I asked. "What about your mum?"

"She died just after I left."

"I'm sorry for your loss."

"It was long ago. Death is a normal thing here: an expected thing. There's no such thing as living in the city of Thorem. There's only surviving or death."

"Sounds depressing," Kasey said.

"It's all I know," William assured her. "We don't have far to go."

We followed him for a few more minutes until we reached a set of silver double doors. A huge carving of a stag sat on one door, and what I assumed was a panther on the other; in the center, crossing between the two doors, was a tree. It was a stunning piece of work for something as simple as a door.

"Once this door is open, you'll need to follow me exactly. No talking, just in case there are blood elves around. We don't want a fight."

He pushed the doors open and crept inside. We followed until we reached the bright open hallway beyond, then down and around a corner, where the hallway opened out into an expansive cavern. More columns littered the side and there were several doors against one wall. Like other parts of the mountain we'd walked past, crystals were embedded in the walls and ceiling, giving off enough light to see by. The ceiling was at least seventy feet above our heads, leaving a gap of darkness between the light on the wall and ceiling. At one point it had probably been a place of beauty, but over time it had just grown ominous, like much of the blood-elf-controlled mountain.

The wall opposite the one with the crystals had breaks in it that allowed you to look out into the dark chasm just beyond. If I stared for just a few seconds, I was certain I could make out the faint glow of something purple in the distance.

We were on a dwarven street, several miles beneath the top of the mountain. I hadn't been back to the city since I was much younger. It was a strange sensation. I looked up at where the sky should be, and saw nothing but twinkling lights in the rock high above my head.

"We need to keep moving," William whispered to me, suddenly nervous and concerned about everything around us.

We continued on through the city, until we came to a ramp leading down to several buildings.

"This is it: this is the entrance to the resistance," William told us. "Here you'll find help. You'll find what you're looking for—I hope, anyway. I'll go in first, tell them you're here, then I'll have you enter. We'll go in a few at a time. Maybe one group of four and another of three. These people are skittish. They're not used to trusting anyone. I don't want them to not trust you. Is this okay?"

No one had any problems they voiced, although I certainly wasn't okay about splitting up the group again—not here. Even so, I followed William down the ramp and the whole group stayed in the small space between two buildings, the darkness keeping us completely hidden from the street and anyone who happened to come by. Thankfully, and despite the fact that every noise I heard made me wonder what was out there in the city, the darkness wasn't needed and we were left alone from prying eyes for the duration of William's meeting inside the building.

William soon reappeared, standing in the mouth of the alley. "Four of you come with me, I'll be back for the others in a few minutes."

"You know this could be a trap, yes?" Diane whispered in my ear.

I nodded. "Give it sixty seconds. If you don't hear anything, break the door down. Remy, Kasey, Mordred, with me."

"No chance," Morgan said. "He's not going with you."

"Look, I'm not thrilled about it," I whispered, "but if that's a trap—and I'd like to explain how much this pains me to say it—Mordred's ruthless streak will come in handy. And frankly, I don't trust you two together with my friends. I do trust that if you try to hurt anyone that Diane will tear your head off. Also, Chloe is hurt, and I'd rather she stayed out of harm's way."

"If Mordred gets hurt—" Morgan threatened, seemingly ignoring my own threat.

"I'll be fine," Mordred assured her. "Nathan might hate me, but we need one another. And he's right: we're the less threatening of the seven of us. And the poison in Chloe's body makes her weaker than the others. She needs protecting. Diane is much more capable of doing that. And if anything does go wrong, I know you'll tear this place apart to search for me."

"Would you two like to hug it out?" Remy asked. "Because I'd really like to get on with it now."

Without another word, Mordred left the alley, with Kasey and Remy following close behind and me bringing up the rear. William took us to the building's door and paused. "Don't make any sudden movements in there; the people are nervous enough as it is. We get a lot of slaves trying to infiltrate us to feed information back to the blood elves."

He pushed open the door and we all walked inside, while my hand itched for a weapon to hold. The interior of the building was sparse, with nothing on the floor, not even a rug. Only torches hung on the walls, their flame the only thing lighting the dingy room. Someone stood in the corner, wrapped in dark cloth. I couldn't tell what species it was, let alone their age or sex.

"You come to the resistance." The voice was muffled by the cloth over the figure's face.

"Apparently," Remy said, a slight edge to the word.

"How do we know you're not a spy?" the muffled voice continued.

"You don't," Mordred snapped. "We need to get out of this realm. We were told you could help."

"Maybe," the voice said, with a slight chuckle. "Maybe not."

"I have no time for games," Mordred said. Then he turned toward the door, only to pause.

I looked back and saw William, a broadsword in his hand pointed toward Mordred.

"A silver sword?" I said. "Isn't that a bit much? I thought you were the resistance."

"In the center of the room," William commanded.

"They're not with the resistance," Remy said.

"Yeah, I got that," I conceded. "Kasey, calm, please."

Her soft growls ceased and she nodded once, but her eyes never left the sword. Silver could kill any of us in that room, but if Kasey got stabbed there was a lot more chance of it than the rest of us. Even a small cut from a silver blade could be deadly to a werewolf.

"So what happens now?" I asked. "Because you really should have thought this through."

William moved around to stand beside the cloth-wrapped person, who began to laugh. "Nonhuman filth," the figure said. "It's been a while since your kind was here." William placed his hand on the wall beside him and runes lit up all across the floor, which began to move.

"You'll make great fun for us. It's rare we have something more interesting than dwarf or human to keep us occupied. You weren't meant to arrive so far out of town; apparently the tablets weren't specific enough. You will come with us, or die."

"Blood elf," Mordred said, his words filled with enough venom to kill a herd of elephants.

The figure began to methodically unwrap the cloth from around his face, revealing a gray skin stretched tight against pronounced facial bones. Several scars, some old and some new, crisscrossed his face. At some point his nose had been badly broken and never properly re-set.

The floor started sliding under the far wall, jerking suddenly and throwing us all to the ground. Mordred was on his feet in a heartbeat, sprinting toward the blood elf with murderous fury. William tried to step between them, but a blast of air from my hand threw him aside, into the far wall with a clout. The silver sword dropped from his hands and tumbled down into the darkness that filled the space where the floor used to be.

"Oh, shit," Kasey said. "We probably don't want to go down there."

Mordred and the blood elf were engaged in combat in the corner, with Mordred forgoing all sense of fighting intelligently, and just raining down blows on the elf, who avoided or blocked most of them, all the while continuing to laugh. He struck Mordred once in the chest and sent him to his knees, tearing off the remains of his wrapping to reveal runes tattooed on his bare chest. "You'll have to do better than that, little man."

The floor continued to move, exposing more and more of whatever was beneath us. I created a lightning bolt in my hand and threw it at the building's door, which exploded from the impact. Hopefully that would be enough noise to get Diane and the others to come running.

"We need to get out of here!" I shouted as William jumped back onto the floor, another sword in hand. I avoided him, using my air magic to keep him off-balance, while Mordred continued to fight the blood elf, and Remy leapt across to the doorway.

"Let's go!" Remy shouted.

Kasey followed suit and jumped, but after knocking Mordred aside once more, the blood elf used a whip to catch hold of Kasey's foot, dragging her away from the safety of the doorway and into the darkness beneath us.

"Mordred, let's go!" I shouted, and grabbed hold of William, taking him with me as I launched myself into the unknown.

CHAPTER 14

September 1195. City of Acre.

You bastard!" Mordred screamed at me as I entered his cell. His face was drenched in blood, although that didn't seem to be bothering him. "They took her! They took Isabel. And what did you do, you fucking asshole? You did nothing. *Nothing!*" He spat at the floor by my feet.

"Why did they take her, Mordred?" I asked.

"Fuck you, Nathaniel. Fuck. You."

"Mordred, let's get something straight. You're still chained to a wall; you still have a sorcerer's band on. And you're still in a room underground, surrounded by guards. You have no escape, no way of hurting me or anyone else, and this woman you wanted me to help has been snatched away by some awful people." I sighed. This game we'd played for so long was exhausting. "Let's stop with the constant chest-puffing and get on with it. We both have something the other needs. I need answers; you need Isabel found safe and sound. How about we actually work together here?"

Mordred stared at me for several seconds, the veins in his neck bulging as anger permeated every part of him. Then it was gone and he relaxed, picking up his chair and taking a seat. "Siris has her. Siris the goddess of beer has Isabel."

"I know who she is, Mordred. I want to know *why* she took Isabel."

"To get to me." His voice was soft, and there was real feeling there: something I was unused to.

"Who is she? Really?"

"She's the daughter of an old friend: a human friend. Her father died when she was a child, and I knew her mother well. I only found out about her mother's death a few years ago, so I came here to keep an eye on Isabel. I promised her mother I would always keep an eye on her. I told her that Isabel would be safe."

"You loved her mother."

"That's none of your concern. All you need to know is that her mother was a wonderful person, and someone better than most I've met over my life. She died from some disease I barely knew about until it was too late. I stayed in the city to make sure that Isabel was taken care of, that no one tried to take advantage of the young woman. A promise, it appears, you've broken for me. Congratulations, Nathaniel."

"I don't understand why kidnapping Isabel puts pressure on you. I don't understand why *anyone* would go to such efforts to grab one human woman, even one you care about. This doesn't make sense to me. Are they trying to get you to stop helping us? Are they trying to punish you *for* helping us? Help me out here, Mordred."

"I came here to kill Siris. My reasons for that act are my own, and I won't share them with you. I infiltrated her organization under the assumption that I was going to help them break the negotiations between Avalon and the Mesopotamians, something in reality I care little for. But she knew: she knew I was there to kill her, and she knows why I want her dead. The latter I was unaware of until it was too late."

"That's why they didn't share their plan with you?"

"Yes. Taking Isabel has nothing to do with their plan. It's to do with hurting me, and that's all it is. The second I decided to go after Siris was a mistake. I didn't realize she knew my true intentions. When the time was right, she told me about her plan to take Isabel, and gave me the option of trying to kill her, or save Isabel. I ran to Isabel's side, and found several members of Nanshe's security force waiting for me. They'd been tipped off."

"By Siris?"

"I assume so."

"So, do you know anything more about Siris and her group's plan?"

"She's in charge—at least she was in charge of those I met. There was Asag and a vampire, who I found quite unpleasant. He liked to kill young men and women; he liked to turn them. I wanted to tear his tongue out. If he's hurt Isabel, I'll do a lot worse."

"Anyone else in the little group?" I really didn't want to get Mordred off track.

"Lots of people, but they were the upper echelon. I wasn't permitted to talk to any of them. One of them was named Nergal. People spoke to him like he was important."

The shock on Nanshe's face was easy to read. "You're sure? Nergal? That's what he called himself?"

Mordred nodded. "He wasn't around much. He was always leaving to work with other groups. This anti-Avalon movement is made up of more than one group in Acre; it has spread out across the world. At least that was the impression I got. I don't think Avalon is all that popular."

"Where did you meet?" Nanshe asked, her tone hard for the first time.

"Siris's house. I assume you know where it is?"

I looked over at Nanshe, awaiting confirmation.

"It's over by the west entrance. It's a moderately sized building, on a slight hill. It has views of the ocean away from the port."

"It's lovely," Mordred said with a laugh. "You must be really angry with Siris right now. Plotting and planning right under your nose."

"She has your friend," I said, regaining Mordred's glare. "I don't think mocking anyone else is going to do her a lot of good."

"Let me out of here, and we'll find her together. Like old times. You remember, yes? Those murdered farmers we found back when we were young: you remember us hunting down their killers? That Merlin didn't want us to go, he was worried I'd get hurt, or that we'd be walking into a bigger problem than we could handle. But me, you, Galahad, and Morgan, we found those murderous bastards and made them pay. We were like brothers, you and I."

"Yes, Cain and Abel. You tried to murder me, Mordred. You've wanted me dead for a long time. Whatever friendship we had died long ago." I raised my hand before he could say more. "Don't bother threatening me; it's not going to do any good. Just let me do my job."

I turned to Nanshe. "We need to talk. Now."

Nanshe and I left the room and walked upstairs, where, once outside, I took a deep breath. We walked away from the soldiers stationed outside of Mordred's prison, past the guard at the front of the city and across the wooden bridge, stopping in the shade of a large boulder close to where Asag and I had fought.

"Avalon has not stationed troops here because we wanted to show that there was a mutual trust. Acre was meant to be under Mesopotamian control, and we didn't want to screw around with that. Part of the agreement in the joining of yourselves and Avalon was that we would station SOA agents here to protect the city, but they're going to be several weeks away. And until then we're alone in this. If I contact Merlin or Elaine and tell either of them what happened here, they'll send enough Blade of Avalon soldiers that it will appear as if we're taking the city by force.

"I would rather that not happen. I would rather we were able to deal with this ourselves. But our entire thought process was that Isabel was important to Siris because of her plan; that has just been destroyed as a theory. Isabel is important because Siris wants to hurt Mordred. No idea why, although I'm not sure it's important. Siris, however, is important. And judging from your expression, so is Nergal. An explanation would be excellent. As would an honest appraisal of whether or not I need to turn this city into an Avalon military exercise."

"I don't want anything to jeopardize the union between our powers," Nanshe said. "There have been enough foreign powers trying to take control of this city and I don't wish to add to it. Isabel was a ruse, a ruse that Mordred helped along because of his fear for her well-being. Siris, however, is not a ruse. She's incredibly powerful, and apparently has a grudge against the rest of the pantheon."

"And Nergal?"

"Nergal is terrifying. He's also Irkalla's husband—or was until he tried to kill her for disobeying him. As you might have guessed, Irkalla didn't take well to being ordered about."

"Who is he?"

"He's a half fire elemental, half siphon. A few thousand years ago we managed to fight off an invading force, a group who wanted to take control of the area, and remove our names from the history books. Nergal siphons life force; he uses it to make himself physically stronger. The power makes those affected appear as if they've caught some kind of plague, spreading fear throughout the rest of the population. It works best on humans. As I'm sure you know, fear quickly leads to violence.

"During the war, he walked into a civilian city that was under enemy control and infected hundreds, draining their life force to the point of death, making him even more powerful in the process. He watched as the fear took that city by force, and then he made them an offer. Kill the infected and the rest will be spared. Except he kept infecting more, making it look like a disease, until the streets ran slick with blood. Nergal is the single most terrifying person I've ever met. He enjoys warfare. It's what he's good at. You can't defeat him. Not even Gilgamesh can do that."

That was surprising news. "He beat Gilgamesh?"

"Gilgamesh's last encounter with Nergal left him almost completely broken. Nergal had beaten him half to death, broken both his legs, his arms, ribs, nose, jaw, and damaged several internal organs. Gilgamesh healed, but I don't think he was ever the same. That was thirty-six years ago. No one has heard from Nergal since."

"Well, Mordred and Siris have. But, Mordred said Nergal has left to do something else. I assume that's some good news."

Nanshe waited several seconds before nodding. "I hope so."

"Okay, we leave Nergal to one side until we need to deal with him, which hopefully isn't any time soon. That leaves Siris as the most immediate problem. Her home needs to be searched, and—no offence—but I don't want someone who once considered her a friend to do it. I assume that counts you out."

Nanshe nodded. "Siris has been angry at us for a long time, but I never assumed she'd go against us like this."

"Why is she angry with you?"

"She was given the title goddess of beer as a joke. I can't even remember who said it first. I just remember it sticking, and her hating it. People worshipped her for their ability to get drunk. A few thousand years of that, and I think she resented those of us who were given more important roles in the pantheon."

"Not to sound cruel, but your pantheon hasn't been worshipped in hundreds, if not thousands, of years. Why still hold a grudge? Why do something about it now?"

"Only she can answer that. When you go to Siris's house take Irkalla with you. They didn't get along. If anyone would be happy to find something that ties Siris to all of this, it's Irkalla."

"Why didn't they get along?"

"Petty arguments built up over time. Things that were never resolved, and so grew. Also, Siris killed one of Irkalla's attendants for being disrespectful. It happened a long time ago, but Irkalla has never given up trying to punish Siris for that injustice."

"I'd like a half-dozen Teutonic Knights with me too. Can that be arranged?"

Nanshe nodded. "Anything else?"

"Mordred will try to escape. I'd really rather he didn't manage it."

"He's not going anywhere."

"You don't know Mordred. He'll break out eventually; he always does. And then he'll kill people, innocent or otherwise, to get to his goal. If there's one thing you can say about Mordred, it's that when he's focused on something, he doesn't change his mind."

"That sounds like you admire him a little bit."

"I hate him, Nanshe. I hate who he's become, I hate that I lost a brother, I hate that I'm never getting him back. And above all, I hate that I have to be the one to kill him. He's my burden to destroy."

She turned to look at me. She appeared concerned, although I couldn't tell if it was for me or the situation. "Why?"

"Because I was the one who confronted him just before he almost killed Arthur. He'd been murdering people, Avalon members, for years. I hunted him down, begged him to stop, tried to figure out what was going on. We fought, and I had a chance to kill him. I didn't take it. I couldn't accept that my friend of so long was gone. And when it came right down to it, I just couldn't take his life."

"It's hard to kill those we love, Nathaniel."

A slight smile creased my lips, although it wasn't one of joy. "That might be true, but Mordred is no longer worthy of mercy. His continued existence is a blight on this and all other realms. I'll take his life, and then I'll hopefully see the friend I grew up with. I hope his death will break whatever happened to him. He's left me with no other options."

Nanshe placed her hand on my shoulder. "I'm sorry for you. For that burden."

I shook my head. "Like I said, it's *my* burden. And he knows it. But I won't go against your wishes, and I won't kill him while he's under your care. I want your joining with Avalon to be peaceful, the transition easy. I don't want it to be marred by blood and death. That's why we need to find Siris, and anyone else involved, and stop them. Because the attack tonight was only the beginning."

I paused. "The attack," I said, mostly to myself.

"What about it?"

"Well, it was done precisely to get to Isabel, who we've established was only taken to get to Mordred. The whole attack was a ruse. It was to see how well prepared we were. I found it strange that they put so few people against the whole city. If they'd wanted to overrun us, they went about it a strange way. They lost maybe thirty vampires last night, and how many soldiers did we lose?"

"About a hundred and fifty from all divisions, last I heard."

"So we lost a lot more, despite having a greater advantage in numbers. If they'd sent a few hundred vampires they'd have destroyed us. Which means they don't have that many. Or they didn't want to commit."

"It was a test. A chance to abduct Isabel and see how strong we really were. Nothing more. Siris wasn't privy to any sort of details regarding the strength of the defenders of the city. She thought she'd do two things at once, and maybe thin our numbers a little."

I nodded. "Which means, more *will* be coming. We need to be prepared. Siris's plan hasn't truly started yet, but I can't imagine her wanting to wait around while we prepare for whatever it is."

"I'll go talk to the soldiers, get them ready for another attack."

I walked away, needing some time to myself, and wanting to think about what had transpired since I'd arrived in the city. It had been a long few hours, and I doubted it was going to get better soon.

"You know, if you keep looking like your mind is elsewhere,

there's a good chance someone is going to try to take advantage of you."

I stopped and nodded a greeting to Irkalla. I'd walked half the length of the city and found myself close to a small patch of grass, bordered by colorful flowers I didn't know the names of. Children played on the grass without a care in the world. I envied them that.

"Nanshe said I should come find you," Irkalla told me. "I heard Siris was behind the attack."

I nodded. "Not sure how behind it she was, but definitely involved. Nanshe says you don't get on."

"I think she's a manipulative, murdering shrew. She disagrees."

We started to walk together toward Siris's house. The morning sun was just beginning to warm up the city and it wouldn't be long before the heat would be unbearable.

"She killed someone under your protection."

"I think she's killed a lot of people if it helps her. There's no proof, and Nabu and Nanshe refused recompense for the killing. A few days later someone turned up confessing to the crime and was executed before I could question them. Sound suspicious to you?"

"That's one way of putting it. Nothing since then?"

"She got more careful after that. My former husband is involved, too."

"It looks that way, yes."

"Marrying him was a mistake. He got more and more angry over the years, involving himself with human wars until he killed indiscriminately just because he could. He felt we should be ruling them all, that they should still be bowing down to us and worshipping at our feet. Others, like myself, felt differently. Our union was dissolved. It was that or they'd find his body nailed to a wall."

"You wanted to kill him?"

"Every. Single. Day."

"Why didn't you?"

Irkalla stopped walking. "Let's say I kill Nergal. His allies then try to kill me. It leaves Nergal's allies down one person, but it leaves those of us who want change down one too. So we lived for centuries in this sort of stalemate, no one willing to do anything to move things forward because of the fear of repercussions. That was until Elaine arrived and made us an offer to join Avalon. Then those who reveled in the status quo got upset. I couldn't kill Nergal then; I couldn't jeopardize the peace we'd created. Besides, not long after, Nergal went missing and stayed that way for a long time. I'm not surprised he's involved. I just wish he'd stayed missing."

We turned the corner and found ourselves outside of Siris's house. "This is it?" I asked, confused about the one-story house on top of a slight slope.

"She asked for this house specifically."

"How big is your home?"

"Taller than this, although hers is a lot wider and goes quite far back."

"It's just somewhat smaller than I was expecting." I pushed open the wooden door and six Templar knights inside turned to look at me.

"I know I asked for some knights to be sent here, but you're the wrong type, and a lot quicker than I was expecting."

One of the knights drew a knife.

"Going to guess they're not on our side," Irkalla said.

"Which one of you is in charge?" I asked. Several of the knights couldn't help but stare at one large man in the rear of the room. "Keep that one alive."

Irkalla stepped back from the dagger strike, then grabbed the man's arm and broke it. She quickly defeated the knight, attacking a second and third, while the remaining three stared at me.

"Do any of you plan on doing something, or are you all going to attack her?"

One of the knights screamed when she hit him in the face so hard she probably broke most of the bones: nose, cheek, and jaw. I saw him stagger off, his face a ruined mess.

"Let me start," I said and threw a ball of fire at the nearest knight, who dove aside, giving me a clear run at the next one. A blast of air smashed him into the wall and he dropped to the floor, unmoving.

The one I wanted alive came at me with a large hammer, swinging it toward my ribs. A shield of air blocked the blow, and I spun toward the knight, driving my foot into his chest and knocking him back. He tried to get up, but a knee to his face sent him back to the floor. He still refused to lay down and accept defeat, so I grabbed the back of his head with one hand and drove my knee into his jaw, knocking him out, but hopefully not breaking bones.

The first of my opponents was back on his feet and running for the door. I wrapped air around his legs and tripped him, causing him to fall headfirst into the door itself.

"Are you quite done?" Irkalla asked, her three opponents on the floor. At least two were dead, with the third seriously injured but still breathing. "I'm just wondering if I should go find something to drink while I wait?"

"These weren't knights—not of any kind I've ever seen. They were sloppy, disorganized, and fought like thugs down at the docks."

Irkalla pulled up the sleeve on one of the dead men and showed me his arm, where there was a crude tattoo of a ship. "Sailors, I would guess. Maybe pirates. Either way, they were hired to find something and stop anyone coming. Maybe Siris didn't do as good a job of cleaning up after herself as she thought."

The thug whose jaw I'd introduced to my knee stirred. When he opened his eyes, he saw the tip of the short sword I'd taken from one of his dead friends.

"We have questions," I said. "You're the only one in a position to talk."

He spoke in a language I didn't understand.

Irkalla came and stood beside me before talking to him for several minutes. "He's speaking Sumerian," she told me.

"That's still taught?"

She shook her head. "These men were just thugs, hired to perform menial jobs. This man here, he's different. He calls himself an *etlu*—a warrior. He was taught the language as a child. They live in another realm. They are five thousand strong, and they've been brought here to wage war on this city."

"Why?"

"Because that's what he's been told to do. He wants to please Siris and his masters, and considering the fanatical stuff spewing out of his mouth, I'm going to guess he'd be okay dying for the cause."

"What's the name of the realm?" I asked.

Irkalla asked him.

"Phalanx," he said.

"Now that I understood."

Irkalla spoke to him again. "He says he'll answer questions because you can't stop the flood that is coming. We can't stop them from razing this city to the ground and killing all who live here. They want to unleash a monster of some sort: a serpent."

"A serpent?" I repeated. "Why?"

"He says it will end us all and allow their masters to remake the world. He's saying a lot of crazy things."

"Where's the realm gate?"

Irkalla asked him, and when he'd finished, she turned to me. "All he knows is that it's at least a day to the east of here, in an old, abandoned village. He was blindfolded when he left his realm, then taken to a small dock and ordered to sail here. He sailed to the harbor as the attack took place under cover of night. Once here, he met with the men who are now scattered on the floor around us. They were meant to destroy any evidence left here, and then assassinate Nanshe and myself." Irkalla's eyes narrowed at the mention of her name.

"What were you trying to destroy? What did Siris leave behind?"

Irkalla asked him, and even I could tell that his answer wasn't any kind of pleasantry. I got the feeling he was done talking.

"I do not believe he will answer us."

"Anything else useful?" I asked.

"No," Irkalla told me and then she snapped the man's neck. She paused and kept her hand on his chest, her eyes closed. "Everything he said is true. He didn't come alone to infiltrate the city. Three more started with him, but two died in the attack last night, killed by vampires who didn't know who they were."

"And the last?"

"She was with Siris when Isabel was taken. I think this confirms that Mordred was telling you the truth: apparently Siris was always planning on taking Isabel."

"He didn't happen to say why, did he?"

"He said that Siris really doesn't like Mordred. At all. No idea why, though."

We gave the place one last search and found several charred pieces of a scroll that had been set alight and then stamped out on the floor. I picked a piece up and turned it over. "This is part of a map." I passed it to Irkalla. "Recognize it?"

"I can't actually tell what this is; it's too small," she said, turning it over in her hand. "Looks old, though."

"We need to talk to Nanshe and Nabu," I said as I placed the piece of scroll onto a nearby table. It was too fragile to take with me, and it might be useful. "And Mordred. But let's do the one that won't make me feel nauseous afterwards first."

CHAPTER 15

September 1195. City of Acre.

The Teutonic Knights arrived just after Irkalla and I finished the search of the house. We asked them to search the premises for anything they could find, and to take special care of the map pieces, before Irkalla and I ran through the baking city streets to find Nanshe and tell her about what we'd discovered. Attacks were imminent.

After asking several soldiers, we found Nanshe in a large building close to where Isabel had lived. Nabu was with her, and they were discussing the plans for the defense of the city in the event of further attacks. Gilgamesh stood in the corner, staring out of the window. He didn't appear to be all that pleased to be there.

Nanshe's reaction to being told her life was in danger was a slight shrug. I'd expected a proportionally larger response.

"My life has been in danger before, and will be again," she said. "All those who came before are dead. Whoever Siris sends—she won't try herself—will join them. We have a more pressing issue."

"And that would be . . . ?" I asked, realizing that the topic of someone trying to kill her had been well and truly ended.

"Out there is a village with an unknown realm gate, somewhere several hours from here. It's likely that five thousand trained men and women have already left the realm gate with a plan to attack this city. Along with their vampires, and anything else Siris has on her side, this is going to cause a lot of trouble. I can't see them razing the city, though. It would take a lot more than that."

"What could the serpent be? Tiamat?" Irkalla asked.

"She is sealed somewhere with no realm gate. There's no way to get to her."

"Wait, you mean *the* Tiamat?" I inquired. "The dragon?"

Nanshe nodded. "If she were released, death and destruction would follow. The last time she was free, men and women worshipped her like a god. Even we were not immune to her murderous whims, and several of our kin were killed by Tiamat and her children. Even if they were able to find Tiamat, Siris and her allies would have little control over her. No, they'll want something more controllable, but just as deadly: one of her children, maybe."

"And where would they be?" I asked, knowing full well that I wasn't going to like the answer.

"We don't know exactly," Irkalla told me. "They're in several different realms. The person who placed them in their new homes underwent a mind-wipe as soon as it was finished. They could be anywhere within a thousand miles of here, but they'll be remote, and no one will have the means of opening them."

"So, we have a realm where thousands of attackers are coming from. And there's another realm somewhere hiding the children of a dragon." I rubbed my temples to try to alleviate the pressure I suddenly felt. "Siris and her people certainly believe they can open this realm to Tiamat's children. If they can find, or make, a guardian to do it, then I don't see any reason why not.

Maybe that's why they took Isabel: to force her to be the guardian to open the realm gate."

"Did you get anything about the schedule being changed when they discovered that Hellequin would be here?" Nabu asked.

"No," Irkalla informed him. "The plan was always to attack last night. The man I interrogated knew nothing about any changes to incorporate Nathaniel."

"It's why Asag was sent after me; he was meant to stop me getting here. Almost did, too." My words gained Gilgamesh's attention. It was good to see him up and about again.

"That makes sense. Unfortunately, Asag is dead, so asking him anything would be impossible."

"He didn't die that long ago," Irkalla pointed out. "I could try to take his soul. See if I can learn anything."

As far as ideas went, it wasn't a bad one.

"He's curse-marked," Gilgamesh told her. "Blood curses. You take his soul, all kinds of awful stuff could happen to you and anyone near you. It's not worth the risk."

"Did you find anything at Siris's home?" Nabu asked.

"They were searching for something," Irkalla said. "They destroyed part of a map. No idea why."

"Too heavy or large to move?" Nabu suggested.

Irkalla shrugged. "Maybe they just didn't want it falling into anyone else's hands."

I left the three of them to discuss things, and walked over to Gilgamesh. "What's on your mind?"

"I'm sorry I was not more help last night. That monster blind-sided me, and I was unable to continue the fight at your side. I feel foolish that such a whelp as that managed to best me." Gilgamesh didn't appear to be happy with himself over what he saw as a failure. Never mind that Asag would have killed me too if not for his magical weakness. Gilgamesh was a proud man, and the loss against any opponent was going to stay with him for some time.

"I got lucky myself," I assured him. "Asag wasn't a pushover."

"No, but it's a shame he had to die. We could have gotten answers from him. I doubt he'd have been forthcoming, however. He was always a cruel, nasty little demon."

"Were you friends with Siris?"

Gilgamesh nodded. "She's a great warrior. A dangerous opponent, with a smart mind. Hates her drink, though, so she's not exactly good to go out celebrating with." He gave a slight smile. "Probably why she got the goddess of beer name. Did you know she hated it?"

"Nanshe told me."

"She is a proud woman, and to have her mocked like that . . . I don't think she ever recovered from it."

"Did you know Isabel?"

He shook his head. "Never even heard of her until Mordred mentioned her name. Still don't know anything about her. Where she came from, who her parents are . . . nothing."

"Mordred said her mother was someone who lived in the city. She died a few years ago? Mordred said he's lived here on and off ever since." I rubbed my eyes. It had been a long few days, and I was beginning to get tired.

"You need some rest, my friend," Gilgamesh said with a hearty slap on my back.

I nodded. "You're right. There's not going to be an attack in broad daylight, but they might still try again tonight. I'd rather be there for that. Can someone recommend me a place to sleep?"

"There's an inn not far from here," Nabu said. "Go, rest. We'll see you tonight."

I said my farewells and set off for the inn, which was easy to find. Rooms were free to friends of Nanshe and Gilgamesh. My room was at the top of the three-story building, and I almost fell asleep opening the door.

I couldn't keep my eyes open—something was wrong—and staying awake was a literal battle, but I was too tired to fight it. I managed to drag myself toward the bed, and didn't even feel my head hit the pillow as I slid into sleep.

"Wake up."

I tried to open my eyes, but couldn't quite manage it. Pain tore through my shoulder and I jolted awake, to be met with darkness.

"It's not late yet. No one is going to come for you for a while."

"Siris, I presume," I said to the darkness of the room.

A moment later a candle came alive, revealing Siris sitting on a chair several feet away, a dagger on her lap.

"I wouldn't try anything," she warned. "The venom in your blood will not kill you, but this dagger will, should you feel the need to be heroic."

I remained lying on the bed trying to figure out when I'd been poisoned. I thought back over the last few hours, and realized it must have been during the fight with Asag. "So, Asag's venom makes people tired?"

"Mostly. I assumed it would have hit you earlier, but I suppose all that running around fought off the reaction. Asag is furious with you."

"He's not dead?"

"No. You should have taken his head, which would have done it. I don't think he's going to fall for your tricks twice, though."

"Why are you here?" I asked, sitting up and yawning as I leaned against the wall behind me. Apart from a fuzzy head and a general ache that appeared to reverberate through my entire body, I didn't feel too bad. I thought about testing my magic, just to make sure it was useable, but I didn't want to cause Siris to attack, and the simple knowledge that I could feel my power inside of me was enough to calm any thoughts of having lost its use.

"We need to talk."

"Talk? You tried to kill me, and a lot of other people, and you also sent a small army of vampires to murder a lot of people. I don't think talking is going to change anything. You want to destroy the relationship your kin and Avalon have developed. You're hoping that by disrupting it or stopping it, Avalon will just vanish. Well, I've got news for you: Avalon isn't going anywhere, and you're not strong enough to stop all of it."

"You've got it all wrong." She sounded incredibly smug. "Avalon is a festering, corrupt cesspool. It needs to be destroyed, torn down, and rebuilt. The deities who joined it—those I used to call my kin—are willing to accept a small share of the power. We are not. They want to remain in the shadows, twisting the human world as needed. We believe that humans should be our servants, and that we should be worshipped for our power. Humans are lesser beings. It's our rightful place to stand above them as they kneel to us."

"So you want a fairer Avalon, but one that's willing to wipe out a large chunk of humanity should they become a problem?"

Her eyes narrowed. "We are better than humans. Elaine is in control of Avalon. Arthur is dead, Merlin is weak. None of these things should be."

"You sound an awful lot like Mordred." It made me wonder about his motives. His whole reason for being had been to disrupt and destroy Avalon at every opportunity. Yet on this occasion, he infiltrated Siris's organization with the purpose of killing her. A question occurred to me. "Why does Mordred hate you so much? And it must be a lot, because it would take a huge amount of hate for him to put killing you over destroying Avalon."

"We're old acquaintances," she said with a grin. "You should ask him about the time we spent together."

"That sounds a lot less pleasant than it should."

"It was pleasant for me. Probably not so much for him."

"The whole Isabel thing. It was just personal for you, right? Nothing to do with what you have planned for the city?"

"Very good. I just really wanted to screw with Mordred. I don't care about her, or what happens to her."

"You're not going to make her a guardian then?"

The confusion on Siris's face lasted only a second, but it was enough to let me know I was on the wrong lines. I tried a different approach.

"How else are you going to open the realm to wherever Tiamat's children are?"

Siris smiled, and clapped slightly, patronizing me. "Very clever. You figured out what the plan is. Well, you still can't stop it. As for how we're going to open the realm, we don't need a guardian. There are more ways to get there than the ones Avalon likes to feed you."

"You've lost your mind. There's no way that Merlin or Elaine or anyone else is going to allow you to tear Avalon down. You're a group of misfits and power-crazed idiots. You're going to die here. You're going to die painfully, and if, by some small chance, you succeed here, Avalon will crush you and anyone you call a friend. They'll wipe you from whatever realms you call home. You can't win."

"We're in this for the long game, Nathaniel. Our aims here aren't about winning or losing, they're about hurting you. Hurting you and your friends. Hurting this city, taking away one more jewel in Avalon's crown."

There was no use in trying to talk to her; she was fanatical, and fanatics are rarely rational people. "So is this the part where you kill me?" I was still feeling achy, and probably not a hundred percent capable, but I was pretty sure I could give Siris a good fight, if that was the direction she wanted to go in.

"I'm here because I've been asked to give you a message. And this was as good an opportunity as I've had since you arrived."

"A lot of effort to get me a message."

"It's an important message. And the man who told me to give it to you isn't used to disappointments."

"Nergal?" I guessed.

"You've learned quite a bit since you've been here. I'm almost impressed."

I ignored the taunt. "Let me guess: you're going to tell me to leave the city. To let you take it, and to tell my Avalon masters that this whole area is off limits. Maybe you'll threaten a few people too." I leaned as close to Siris as I dared. "Not sure if you know this, but I don't respond well to threats."

Siris chuckled. "Nergal doesn't want you to leave. He wants you to stay and watch as everything burns down around you. He wants you to see the bodies litter the streets as you try in an impotent attempt to stop us. He wants you to witness the beginning of the end of your world. His only regret is that he couldn't be here to watch as we break your spirit. Then you'll be our message to the world. The Hellequin, broken and beaten. Merlin's pet destroyed."

"That's a big message."

Siris pushed herself onto her feet and threw the chair aside, which collapsed from the impact against the wall. "You should take us seriously."

"I do. I take all threats against people I care about seriously. I just like making you angry. I find it entertaining that you would come here to tell me nothing. You've literally told me nothing, and you've risked yourself to do it. So, why are you really here, in the city? What are you here for?"

Siris looked out of the window. "To deliver a gift." She turned to me. "Your friends are coming." She pushed the window open and jumped out. I walked over and watched as she vanished into the ground, making any attempt to follow her impossible.

Six Teutonic Knights were running up the street. They stopped below my window, and I launched myself out, using my air magic to slow my descent.

"Siris paid me a visit," I told them after landing on the ground.

Irkalla came a short while later, while the knights threatened the screaming innkeeper with obstruction. I felt sorry for the man, but I had neither the time nor energy to intervene, so I left the knights to deal with him.

"Sorry. This shouldn't have happened," Irkalla said to me as I washed the remains of sleep from my face in a bowl of water.

"Not your fault. No one expected her to come *back* to the city. She said she'd brought a gift."

"Like what?"

I shrugged. "She didn't give me anything. And she came back

here to give me a warning from your ex-husband. Apparently I'm to be used as a cautionary tale for those who would oppose him and his group. I don't plan on letting that happen."

"Hellequin!" a soldier shouted as he sprinted up the street toward me. "Hellequin!"

"Over here," I called with a wave of my arm. "What's happened?"

He paused and took a deep breath. "Nothing, everyone is fine. Better than fine, actually."

Irkalla and I shared a confused expression.

"The woman, Isabel. They found her outside the city gate. She's alive, but asleep, or something."

We followed the soldier back through the city to the building where I'd first met Isabel when arriving in the city.

I entered the building alone, but instead of going up, I followed a set of stairs down into a room beneath the earth. A large cell had been built at the far end. Runes had been carved into the stone where the bars had been set.

"Nice cell," I said to Nanshe and the two guards, none of whom were facing me.

All three turned around, and I got my first glimpse of Isabel, who was alone in the cell, sleeping. Her hair had been pulled up and tied on top of her head, the bite marks on her neck easy to see.

"Vampire," I almost whispered.

"Yes," Nanshe agreed. She rubbed her eyes with the heels of her palms. "Isabel has been bitten by a vampire. This whole situation gets stranger by the day."

Isabel opened her eyes, but remained still. "Food." It was not a request.

"I think it's going to get worse before it gets better," I told Nanshe.

"Food," Isabel repeated.

"You're going to want to get her something," I told everyone. "And you'd best hurry it up, too."

Nanshe ordered her knights to find a chicken or other small animal that wouldn't be easily missed.

"She needs a person," I said before they could leave. "She needs the blood of a person."

"We have prisoners," one of the knights said.

"Bring the most evil bastard you've got. *Human* bastard. Someone already scheduled for execution."

"You're going to let her kill someone?" Nanshe asked.

"It's that or have her go insane in there." I turned to the knight, who hadn't moved. "Now."

I returned my attention to Isabel, who had rolled onto her side, watching us. Her pupils were bright red, and I knew that if those bars weren't there, she'd have attacked us. Newly awakened vampires don't have a lot of patience, and most lack the ability to tell friend from food.

"I assume no one saw who dropped her off?" I asked.

"No," Nanshe confirmed. "It was done not long after nightfall."

"It's possible the Siris visit was a diversion."

"When did Siris visit you?"

I'd forgotten that Nanshe hadn't been told about the visit, so I filled her in on what Siris had told me.

"Nergal knows about you. That can't be good."

"He might know about me, but he doesn't seem to care that I'm here. He's still off somewhere else. No, Siris came back into the city for something else. I was just on the way, and Isabel is a diversion."

Nanshe's sigh was one of a person having reached the end of a very short fuse. "This is not becoming a good day."

"Also, Asag is still alive. That's not great news."

"Cut his head off next time," Irkalla said as she descended the stairs behind me. "His body vanished from where we'd placed it, in a locked cell at the other side of the city. He killed two guards there. We only learned about it just before I came to see you. I was actually on the way to warn you of his escape."

"Did he do anything? Open any gates? Steal anything?"

Irkalla shook her head. "Nothing. He got up, broke the cell, killed the guards, and left. We don't know where he went, but no one has reported him leaving the city."

The knight returned shortly after with a prisoner in tow. The man was covered in dirt, and scars adorned his hands and arms. He'd been in the dungeon for a while.

"You were sentenced to die?" I asked him.

"I betrayed my knight brothers during a battle. Stabbed my commander in the back, and tried to kill two more."

"And the rest," the knight said, shoving the prisoner slightly.

"Killed a man and women as I was trying to escape. They were in the wrong place at the wrong time."

"And the same could be said for you," I told him. "Everyone else, out."

"Everyone?" Irkalla asked.

"It's probably best. The fewer targets she has, the better."

Everyone filed out without another comment, leaving me alone with the prisoner and Isabel, who'd now sat up.

"Isabel," I said, and she looked in my direction, licking her lips. "Here's your food. You try to come for me, and I will kill you."

"Wait, what?" the prisoner asked. "*She's* going to eat me? She's just a little thing."

He laughed as I opened the cell door and shoved him inside,

closing the door and keeping my eyes on Isabel. His laughter stopped when Isabel's face changed, showing the monster beneath, and she leapt toward the prisoner, taking him to the floor with a show of exceptional strength. The prisoner screamed, and I felt a tiny sliver of sorrow for him as she sank her teeth into his neck and tore out his throat, drinking the pulsing blood as it flowed freely from the gaping hole.

I sat silently for several minutes until Isabel had finished, until she'd dropped the prisoner and stared at what she'd done. And then she started to cry. Crying or vomiting was the usual response from what I'd heard, or at least it was if you weren't insane and actually enjoyed feeding on the blood of others.

I picked up the blanket from her cell bed, a scratchy brown thing that probably offered little in the way of comfort or warmth, and draped it over her blood-drenched shoulders.

"I'm sorry for that," I whispered.

"I killed him."

"You weren't you. You were the monster inside of you, an animal that only thinks of food. The animal is probably still there, but hopefully quieter."

"I can feel the need for blood still. It's like a tiny voice way back in my mind."

I nodded. "I'm sorry for bringing him to you, but you'd have killed an innocent person if not him. All new vampires have to kill. Most, from what I know, try to find prisoners, or get someone to prey on them, and turn the tables. A few hunt the first thing they see."

Isabel looked up at me, her eyes full of fear, regret, and more than a little anger. "They took me. Made me into *this*."

"I know. They did it because, for some reason, Siris really

hates Mordred, and I don't know why. I'm hoping maybe you have some idea."

Isabel closed her eyes. "I don't know. I don't know why I'm involved in this, and I don't know why Mordred decided to come into my life. So maybe, just maybe, you should go and ask him. Because they turned me into a monster and I deserve the answers he can give."

I for one agreed with everything she said. "Let's go see Mordred."

CHAPTER 16

Now. Dwarven city of Thorem.

After what felt like an eternity of sliding down into the darkness all around me, I stopped worrying about the fall and began to concentrate on the landing. I dumped as much air magic as I possibly could in front of me in an effort to slow myself down, but it didn't seem to do a lot of good.

Fortunately for me, the ride didn't last much longer. Unfortunately for me, it ended with me going feet first into freezing cold water. The ice-cold deluge took every bit of breath away. It was as if the air in my lungs evaporated instantly, causing me to panic a little as my head went under the water.

Once above the surface, I immediately ignited my fire magic, warming my body and turning the water to steam, which rained back down as ice, forcing me to stop. I'd done enough to catch my breath, and I regained the use of my body long enough to start swimming toward Kasey, who, in her werewolf form, shouted at me from land.

The same crystals I'd seen being used as lights on the way to the trap we'd walked into, adorned the walls and pillars. They let everyone see without the use of magic or torches.

"Are you okay?" Kasey asked as I dragged my dilapidated

carcass out of the water and flopped down on the dry, and slightly warmer, land. My fire magic ignited immediately, drying my clothes and warming me completely.

"Did you see William?" I asked. "He went first, and I'd like the chance to ask him some very interesting questions."

"He's cowering behind that rock over there." Kasey nodded toward William, who was crouched behind several large pieces of stone, which at some point had probably been a statue of some kind.

"Where are we?" I shouted to him, but he just hugged his knees and rocked back and forth. "That's helpful, thanks."

"Stop shouting at him," Kasey said. Her fur was still wet, but most of the water had been shaken off. A werewolf's coat is designed to be waterproof and insulated from the cold. "I don't think it's going to work. I threatened to tear his face off and all he did was burst into tears. And start talking about someone who's going to punish him."

Another splash behind me signified that Mordred had finally arrived, and I turned to let him know we were there. I may have hated the little bastard, but I wasn't going to give anyone else the joy of killing him and mounting his head over their fireplace. Not that I wanted it; I've always found the stuffed-dead-thing a weird concept.

As I opened my mouth to shout, I spotted a second figure falling out of the tube. The blood elf.

"Get out of the fucking water!" Kasey screamed as Mordred reappeared, looking momentarily dazed and in shock from how cold it was.

He saw us and raised his hand to wave, before deciding not to bother. It would have been funny if it wasn't for the blood elf coming back to the surface and setting his sights on the back of Mordred's head. My old nemesis began swimming, unaware of the nearby danger, as the elf followed in hot pursuit. I had never heard of blood elves before, but they were really fast in the water.

The blood elf caught up to Mordred before he was even halfway toward us, pulling him under the water. Mordred emerged with a large splash moments later.

"Move your ass, Mordred!" I shouted, and he began swimming in earnest while I hoped that Bruce the blood elf didn't complete his homage to the opening sequence of *Jaws*.

Mordred reached us before he was attacked again, and Kasey almost hauled him out of the water single-handed, throwing him behind us without a word, while she kept her eyes on the water, ready for Bruce's attack.

I motioned for Kasey to take a few steps away from the water's edge, which she did without taking her eyes off the glass-like stillness in front of us.

"Where is he?" she whispered.

I was about to answer when the water erupted and the blood elf launched himself out of it, several feet from where Kasey and I were looking. He sprinted toward Kasey, ducked under her massive arms and drew a blade from his belt.

Kasey saw the danger and leapt away. The elf crouched down and looked between Kasey and me, presumably deciding which one of us was the least threatening. He was slightly taller than I was, and thin, with long, dirty, black hair that cascaded over bare, muscular shoulders. His skin was mostly mauve in color, although there were blotches of lighter or darker skin across the torso. The elf smiled, showing sharp teeth like a piranha's, although his were a light red.

He blinked twice, his bright red eyes containing nothing close to emotions I wanted to know about. He was a killer—a monster—and he enjoyed it. Eventually, his gaze settled on me, and he attacked, brandishing his curved dagger. A plume of flame left my fingers. I hoped it might slow the elf down, but as the flame died, only his bandages were on fire. He smiled—an evil, wicked grin. Apparently uninjured, he lunged at me.

I dodged the blade and rammed my fist into his kidney, causing him to gasp and dodge back, but he swiped with the blade at the same time, cutting my tricep.

Kasey darted toward the elf and caught him in the ribs with a punch that lifted him off his feet and dumped him on his ass. She growled at him, a low, menacing noise that set the hairs on the back of my neck upright.

"I wonder," I said, as a shimmering battle-ax appeared in my hand, "whether you're as good at stopping necromancy as you are at stopping fire magic." I tested my soul weapon, feeling the weight of it in my hand.

"You got this?" Kasey asked.

I nodded. "Make sure that William doesn't run away. I'd like to talk to him when I'm done with Bruce the elf."

"Blood elf," the elf corrected, his voice deep and full of arrogance. "Better than elves. Better than you, sorcerer. Maybe you'd like a nice stay with us? We could ask you questions. Peel the skin from your face, make you watch while we eat it."

"Sounds like fun," I said. "Why don't you come get me? Unless you're afraid of a little old sorcerer like me?"

The elf screamed and charged forward. I avoided the first swing of his blade, and he avoided the battle-ax, although only just, and I thought I saw a look of concern cross his face. He turned his head slightly, but saw that between him and any escape was Kasey, and a seated Mordred, who appeared to be watching the contest with interest.

The blood elf screamed something I didn't understand and charged at me once more. He didn't even get the chance to strike. I swung the battle-ax, stepped around him and buried it in his shoulder. The elf cried out and dropped to his knees. I spun the ax and brought it down with every ounce of strength I had onto the creature's skull.

He was dead before his face hit the ground, and I kicked his dagger aside before placing my hand just above him, looking for his soul. Soul weapons hurt the spirit, killing the opponent without ever leaving a mark. A few years ago, when the first of my blood-curse marks vanished, so did my ability to use blood magic. It was replaced with necromancy, a powerful, but for me, limited ability. Most necromancers can disrupt the souls of living things, moving the soul inside the person just enough that it sort of shorts out. It causes the victim to collapse. It's a dangerous and difficult trick to learn, so most necromancers just stick to absorbing the soul to make them more powerful. Some can track people by feeling their soul, using it like a dog would a scent. It was another trick I'd never been able to do. I could use my soul weapons, but I could only absorb the souls of those who'd died fighting, which made sense, considering my mother had turned out to be a Valkyrie. It meant I was capable of bolstering my magic with the souls I'd taken: a rare and powerful talent in its own right.

There was a problem with absorbing the souls of the departed, however: I got their memories—all of them. No matter how evil or depraved that person had been, I got to see it. On more than one occasion, I had wished I hadn't been forced to take the soul and see the things they'd done. Unfortunately, with our current predicament, taking the blood elf's soul would give me more information than blindly stomping around. And I doubted that William, in whatever subservient position he held for the elves, knew anything.

The second the first sliver of soul reached me, I knew I'd made the wrong decision. It burned as images of death and destruction tore through my head, showing me acts of depravity and violence that made my stomach lurch. I saw the blood elf murder humans and dwarves, feed on their flesh and drink their blood, all the while laughing with his blood-elf kin. I saw battles with hundreds of elves fighting against dwarves, and I watched helplessly as he butchered innocent people. He loved being able to inflict pain and death on those who were different from him.

Information about the other blood elves, the layout of the city, and the underground lake location flashed through my mind. And just as I thought it was over, there was a picture of Mordred in a dungeon, chained and beaten, while unseen faces laughed and threw things at him.

When my mind was once again my own, I threw up. It's not enough that I got to see everything that the person had done; it was as if I had lived it, and those memories, those thoughts and feelings, stayed with me forever. Taking a soul was not something I did lightly, and I felt as if I should bleach my brain in case I'd been tainted.

"Nate?" Kasey asked, standing a good few steps away from me. It was a bad idea to touch someone who'd taken a soul. Sometimes we lashed out at something that was no longer there.

"Nate, are you okay?" she asked again.

I raised a hand asking for a moment while my mind settled down.

"Who's Bruce?" she asked after a second.

"Shark from *Jaws*," Mordred explained. "And *Finding Nemo*."

"You're a Disney fan?" Kasey asked, astonished.

"Who isn't?"

"That wasn't fun," I said and spat on the ground, trying to get the taste out of my mouth.

"What did you discover?" Mordred asked, pulling William along by the scruff of his neck.

"He's a Judas goat," I said, nodding toward the terrified human.

Kasey looked between Mordred and me for a few seconds. "Um . . . a what?"

"You get a goat that leads sheep somewhere, then one day that goat leads those sheep into a slaughterhouse while the goat is spared that same fate. Judas goat."

"So he leads people to the room above, and they drop them down into this lake?" Kasey said, disgusted. "How can you kill your own people?"

"He doesn't have a choice. Do you, William?" I said. "I saw what they do. I saw you being chosen."

William stared at me, his eyes all but consumed with fear. "What are you?"

"A sorcerer." I got back to my feet. "And a few other things. How many people have you led here?"

"I don't know. Dozens. They come through into the city, which has enough dangers in it to force them to stay near the fountain."

"Who brings them to the realm?"

"Different people. They live in your realm and send the victims through. People no one will miss, or—" He stopped.

"Or what?" Kasey asked.

"Or people who have crossed those in our realm who need to be removed," I finished.

"Yes," William admitted. "There are some people who come here because people in this realm wish to deal with them personally. Or because they've angered the wrong person in your realm. At the end of the day, it's all the same. People from your realm come here and die."

"Who sent us here?"

"No idea. We were told to wait for a group to arrive in the city and bring them down here for collection. Originally a larger number of blood elves were stationed here: dozens of them. But you were late, and blood elves aren't very good at waiting, so they were taken away to keep them busy. They'll return soon. I doubt you'd be able to defeat them all."

Mordred released William, but spoke before walking away. "If a smile crosses your lips at any point as you talk about what happened here, I'll slit your face open from ear to ear, and I'll leave you for whatever vermin comes to find your screams. You hear?"

William nodded.

"Your life is one of pain, suffering, and threats," I said. "It's all you understand. I'm sorry for that. I'm sorry they took your parents when they chose you. I'm sorry you get to live a good life, a life where you'll die of old age rather than on the whim of some monster. I'm sorry all of this happened to you. But you *choose* to do this. You could stop."

"They'd kill me, kill my parents. Make me watch."

"Didn't you already say your mother was dead?"

William forced back a smile.

"Either way, I get the feeling you don't mind," Mordred said. "I can always spot someone with a fucked-up mind-set. And I think you're pretty close to it, William. You like the feeling of power you have over these people. You enjoy knowing they're going to die slow and hard."

"So?" William asked, his eyes never leaving mine.

A low growl emanated from behind me. "Calm, Kasey. Like you said, hurting him won't do anything. He gets hurt enough by people who enjoy it a lot more than you ever would."

"What's with the water then?" she asked.

William looked past me to Kasey as he spoke. "Humans come down that tube and into the freezing water. The shock usually knocks them silly. Sometimes it kills them, but most of the time they make it to the edge: wet, freezing, disoriented, and terrified. And then the elves hunt them, take most of them back to the pens. They're using them for something."

"What?" I asked.

"They have these scrolls that they make people read. I don't know what happens after that."

I searched the blood elf's memories but found nothing to corroborate what William was saying. But then there was nothing to say he was lying, either.

"We can't take him with us," Mordred said. "He'll betray us first chance he gets."

"I know," I said. "I'm not entirely sure it would make much of a difference to him if he lived or died."

William shrugged. "If you'd been human, we wouldn't be having this conversation; you'd be prey, or slaves for the elves. They always pick some out of the group to hunt."

"I saw," I told him, feeling my stomach churn at the memory. "What are these blood elves, really?"

He shrugged. "Don't know much else. I know my family have always been slaves to them. My father, his father, his father's father . . . all of them. The elves need us. They don't like to kill too many of us; we taste like those crystals, so they say. We're as immune to magic as they are. Occasionally one of us is picked to work with the elves, either as an escort like me, or serving them. Mostly, the humans build, clean, and cultivate those crystals into something workable. The elves don't like doing it. Kill me, don't kill me, it doesn't matter. If you don't, the elves will for making a mistake. You need me, though. You can't get under the archway without me."

"Um . . . what?" Kasey asked.

I searched the memories of the blood elf. "There's an archway about two miles to the north of here. We need to go through it, but it's guarded by a cave troll. It's blind, but it'll let certain people through: elves, slaves, and the like. I don't really know how it works; the elf certainly didn't, nor did he care, but it's the only way past the troll. The blood elves take prisoners that way, and the humans are left alone by the trolls so long as they're with the elves."

I punched William in the jaw so hard it lifted him from his feet and dumped him on the cold ground. He was unconscious, but hopefully not too injured.

"Why aren't we killing him?" Mordred asked.

"I know where the dwarves are," I told him. "I have a partial map of this place in my head. I know we have to get through elven territory to get there, and we have to go under that arch. It's the quickest way from here to the elves. Everything else takes days. There are tens of thousands of elves between us and the dwarves. Find something to gag him with and tie his hands, because he's going to help us whether he wants to or not."

"And how is he going to help us stop the troll?" Mordred asked, sounding unconvinced.

I raised one of the sleeves on William's arm, showing the scarred tissue where someone had carved a rune into his bicep. "His flesh has been marked with a rune. It's a slave mark, like a cattle brand. It allowed him to walk around without being constantly attacked by elves who come across him, and it tells others who owns him. Besides, no matter how helpful the elf's memory is, I'm going to guess that William knows all of the little shortcuts and ways to get around without being spotted. We might need him to get around the patrols and past the citadel."

"The *citadel*?" Mordred asked. "Are you insane?"

"It's the fastest way, and the longer we're out here, the more chance we have of being caught by a patrol."

"What's the citadel?" Kasey asked.

"The place of absolute power in this city," Mordred said. "It used to be the dwarven palace where the kings, queens, princes, and anyone with an ounce of importance lived. When these monsters took over, anyone left inside was killed. It's probably the most dangerous place in this entire realm."

"We're not going in," I assured them both. "We're taking a detour around it. About half a mile away from it is a small collection of buildings; they're abandoned, according to the memories in my brain. Dwarves used to regularly go there to hunt elves, and they used to set traps and ambushes, so the elves stopped sending patrols."

"Why wouldn't the elves just swamp the place and crush all opposition?" Kasey asked.

"The dwarves know this place better than anything else here, even after a thousand years, and they can make new tunnels in minutes or hours, where it would take the elves weeks, if not longer.

"Besides, capturing a dwarf isn't easy. They're trained to go down swinging. They literally won't stop until you or they are incapable of fighting. Five elves will bring down a dwarf, but you'd better believe that those five elves are going to have their work cut out for them. And elves are in finite supply; they can't just make more."

"They're sterile?"

I searched the memories again. "It looks that way, yes. There are untold numbers of them, but if the dwarves chip away a few every time they fight, that's only helping the dwarves."

"Anything else?" Mordred asked.

"The part of the city we're going to has streets that aren't wide enough for more than two at a time. The dwarves, or elves, would be destroyed before they could even get halfway through it, but the roads are windy and there are a lot of places to hide. They've essentially left it as a no man's land because neither side could take it easily."

"You want us to run into a dwarven ambush?" Mordred asked.

"Not quite. I'm hoping they'll see we're not elves, or insane, and let us talk."

"And if they don't?" Kasey asked as she used some rope she'd found on the dead blood elf to tie up William, gagging him with part of the blood elf's clothing.

"Then we'll have two groups who want to kill us. But let's try to stay positive and just have the elves who want our heads on spikes."

"Can we not draw the rune on ourselves?" Kasey asked.

"I don't know how it works," I explained. "You need to know the way in which the rune is drawn before you can use it. If you get it wrong, it might create an incredibly permanent solution to our problems. Besides, I don't know if it needs to be carved into flesh, or just drawn on."

"Let me guess: we get that wrong and it's bad too," Kasey said, rolling her eyes.

"The dwarven runes are complicated," I explained. "Put one on the wrong way, or on the wrong species, and all of a sudden it has a completely different effect to what you wanted. And that's not including the original, much more powerful runes, which this isn't one of. Basically dwarven runes give me a headache, and I'd rather not take the risk of messing about with them."

Mordred hoisted a semiconscious William to his feet. "Fine, but the second he betrays us and we no longer need him, I slit his throat."

I stared at Mordred for a few seconds, but could think of no reason to argue against his statement. "Did you hear that, William?"

He tried to speak, realized his mouth was gagged with some of the bandages from the dead elf, and nodded slowly instead.

"Excellent," Kasey said. "Mordred and Nate, you're going to have to work together here. No little jabs, no biting comments; let's just get through this. Agreed?"

Mordred and I told her we agreed, and he pushed William forward, with Kasey taking point, and me following behind. I watched Mordred as he shoved William ahead.

Since Mordred arrived to save me from the collapsing building, I hadn't wanted to see that there was something different about him. I couldn't put my finger on it, but over time there had been a growing certainty that the Mordred by my side was not the same person I'd been trying to kill for over a thousand years. Unfortunately, I couldn't decide if that made him even more dangerous.

CHAPTER 17

I'm really not loving this," Kasey whispered.

The four of us were crouched behind a low stone wall, directly above a blood-elf patrol who had paused to eat and drink their provisions. I'd hoped they'd move on after a few minutes, but they seemed to be taking forever. I wished I had the sun or moon to tell me the time.

Occasionally I looked up. Far above me, maybe even miles away, I could see a small twinkle. For a split-second, I thought that somehow the stars had found a way through. But I knew it could only be a light from a presumably massive crystal or jewel. There were probably millions of precious stones just a few miles above my head.

"Nate?" Mordred whispered. "I'm feeling less than thrilled about being this close to these monsters. And our gagged friend is getting anxious."

I looked over at William, who was rubbing his feet in circles in the loose dirt. His face was sweaty, and he kept twitching and looking around as if expecting something to grab him at any moment.

I motioned for Kasey—pushing William ahead of her—and Mordred to follow me to a nearby building. William went in first and sat in the far corner, his eyes closed and his head against the wall.

"We need to get out of here and find out what they gave to him," I said, no longer needing to whisper.

"How do we get the elves out of the way?" Kasey asked.

"I know what they gave him," Mordred said a second later. "They give their prisoners elven blood to drink. They do something to it before it's mixed into the food. Makes you stronger, faster, heal quicker, and also more susceptible to their torture, to wanting to help them, to wanting to hurt people. It's addictive, too. The more they give you, the more you want it, the easier it is for them to control you. A never-ending cycle."

"He's going through *withdrawal*?" Kasey asked.

Mordred nodded.

"What happens when you come off it?" It was my turn to ask questions.

"You'll want to kill elves to get it. You'll be pretty desperate."

"They gave it to you." I said, astounded by the knowledge of just how much Mordred had gone through during his time in blood elf hands. "How'd you get yourself off it?"

Mordred looked over at William. "I forced myself off it. Took two months before I was completely clean. And another three years before the cravings went away."

"*Three years?*" Kasey asked.

"I was here for a long time, even after my escape from their dungeons," was Mordred's only answer. "He's going to start gaining their attention soon. I'm hoping that archway is close by."

I searched the memories of the blood elf. "It's not far. Once past there, we'll release William, or tie him up somewhere."

"When he goes back to his masters, they will kill his parents," Kasey pointed out.

"They were killed the second he was chosen," I told her.

"They're just used as a threat to keep their slaves in line, but they've been dead a long time. The elf who was with him was his handler of sorts. It was his duty to train him, and kill all of those who would have been a link to his past. He has no one."

William made a muffled noise and Mordred removed his gag after a warning to be quiet. I hadn't seen him retrieve the elven dagger, but while I was loath to allow Mordred anything more than a letter opener, he didn't have anything but his magic to rely on, and that was pretty much useless. He placed the dagger's blade against the man's neck, just to emphasize his point.

"It smells the blood," William chuckled to himself, making my skin crawl. "The troll smells elf blood. And it's not as strong inside of me as it should be. The smell of elven blood seems to subdue the troll. I really don't know the ins and outs of it; it's not really my problem. *Your* problem is getting me some elven blood." He smiled, showing his blackened teeth. "I'll get you past the troll, then I'm gone. I heard what you said about my parents. Those elves lied to me."

"I get the feeling they do that a lot," I told him. "I'm sorry for your loss."

"I don't know anything else. Why should I be sorry for my life?" He laughed slightly. "No one in your realm even knows we exist. I only hope that one day, the elves finally figure out how to use those tablets and flood the earth realm with death."

"I think you'll find that the earth realm is a little harder to take than you think," Kasey said.

"Do you just drink the blood?" Mordred asked, taking the conversation back to more immediate matters.

William nodded.

"Nate and I will find you some."

"I'll wait right here. If you like, have the wolf-girl look after me."

"I will tear your head clean off your shoulders," Kasey said. "No exaggeration."

William's smile faltered, but his gaze didn't leave Kasey.

"If he tries anything, kill him," I said. "We'll get past the troll."

"Not without making a lot of noise and attracting a lot of attention you won't," William told us.

"Fine. If he tries anything, break all the bones in his arms. He doesn't need those."

William's glare at me was one of pure, unadulterated hatred, and I suppressed the need to smile back at him.

Mordred took a step back from William and stared at me, before looking back at our captive. "We will get you your blood, but if you do anything to misplace our trust in you being here, or annoy Kasey in any way, I will personally feed you to that troll."

William laughed, so Mordred bounced his head off the wall. "Nate and Kasey are good people—or at least that's what others tell me. Ask Kasey if she's heard tales of my deeds. Ask her if *I'm* a good person."

William touched a small cut on his forehead.

"Mordred, enough," I said. "Let's get him the blood he needs."

Mordred dragged William over to a nearby metal bar at the foot of a staircase and tied him to it. "Do. Not. Move."

We left a few seconds later, keeping low and moving as quickly as we dared, until we reached the wall we'd been crouched behind earlier and peered through the broken stonework at three elves below.

"They appear to have disbanded," Mordred said.

"Where are the others?" I looked around the rest of the ruins that had once been a residential area. Many of the buildings had long since been destroyed, although many more of the structures remained sound, and would be so for thousands of years. Dwarves didn't build things that fell down easily.

"There," Mordred said, pointing in front of him.

I stared through a crack in the wall and saw a small band of elves making their way toward one of the tunnels built into the rock. They were easy to spot, even from a distance.

"As soon as they go into that tunnel, we'll attack the ones below," Mordred said.

I nodded. We'd have to be fast. "No, wait," I said, placing a hand on Mordred's arm.

"Why?" Mordred asked through clenched teeth.

It was my turn to point.

Mordred looked through the crack in the wall at a creature the height of a single-decker bus, probably weighing as much as a car. Its gray-and-purple skin was covered in brightly shining armor, and the sword that hung from his back looked like something out of one of the fantasy Japanese video games that Kasey played. It didn't even look possible to pick up, let alone swing with any degree of accuracy or speed.

"What in the name of shit is that?" Mordred asked, turning slowly to me. "I didn't see any of those when I was last here."

"One big elf," I said.

"It's a mountain more than an elf. He looks like a boss fight."

I sighed. The weird tangent thing was going to drive me nuts.

The elves below us all stood to attention, looking more alert and just a tiny bit terrified as their new comrade joined them.

As the mountainous elf got closer, I saw that the armor was dwarven in design, with several marks that looked like finger-drawn lines of blood. Dozens of scars ran down each huge arm, and he had hair—dark and long—dropping over his shoulders. He was not something I wanted to fight, even with all of my magic working at full-power.

"What are they saying?" Mordred asked after listening to the group of elves talk for a few minutes. "I know you took that soul. I know you can understand them."

"Then let me listen."

Mordred shut up, and I paid attention to the conversation below.

"*Where are those who fell into the water?*" The giant elf asked.

"*We were not given the search as an order, commander,*" one of the elves said. "*We were to secure this position and await further instructions.*"

"*On whose orders?*"

"*A high priest's, commander,*" a second elf told him.

"*We were meant to subdue and capture all seven of the interlopers for questioning. Our failure in this will not shine a good light on us. Three of them went into the water, the rest escaped into the mountain. We have not found any of them. Do you think this is good enough?*"

"*Forgive us, commander. Mythanus and two hundred elves were meant to bring the captured to the citadel. The interlopers were sent too far away from the city; it took them too long to get here. Mythanus had to disband the blood elves with him. They were anxious to feast. He didn't want to start fights between groups.*"

"*Mythanus is dead,*" the huge elf said. "*Slain by one of those we seek. I will talk to your commander, and have you all placed somewhere more helpful. I think you have rested long enough.*"

"*Yes, commander,*" the elves said in unison. "*Thank you, commander.*"

"*One last thing,*" the commander said just as he was about to turn away. "*We have been informed that one of the sorcerers is Mordred. He is mine to kill, and mine alone. His escape from this place brought great displeasure to the Exalted One and I've waited a very long time to show Mordred the error of his ways.*"

"*He killed many in his escape,*" one of the elves said. It quickly realized it was the wrong thing when a huge hand wrapped around his throat and lifted him up to the commander's eye level, the elf struggling the whole time.

"*He murdered a high priest. That is a stain our kind has never scrubbed free. Not even the dwarves have managed such an affront.*"

I could tell that the commander was squeezing hard, and the elf began to stop struggling, but after another second, the commander released his grip and allowed the elf to fall to the ground.

"*Do not make me return here. Find these escaped prisoners. Do it now.*"

"*Commander,*" one of the elves asked, while his comrade was helped back to his feet. "*Is it true that the wrong people were sent here?*"

The commander didn't look angry at the question, but he didn't exactly look thrilled, either. "*Our allies sent them. We have no control over their inept actions. We all serve the same masters. They will be punished for their mistake. The high priests are happy that we have the children of our enemies. That we have Mordred here in this realm. There is another though: Hellequin.*"

The elves looked at one another.

"*Yes, we have all heard the name. He is but a man, a man whose power is all but useless against us. He was meant to die in the earth realm, and instead he'll die here, among his friends. And no one will ever know what happened.*"

The commander walked back the way he'd arrived, while the three elves appeared very happy to have escaped lightly. I recounted the conversation to Mordred.

"How do they know I'm here?" Mordred whispered. "It's not like they have photographs. And no one could have foreseen that I'd be close by when you were all zapped here. And they know you're not dead, but that you're meant to be. That thing said so."

"Someone has been relaying information to this realm. Someone who didn't want to fight all of us in the open. It's someone who knows I'm here, knows I was meant to die in London, and knows what you look like. That's a slight concern, and probably a very short list of people." It also confirmed my suspicion that Jerry, Kay, and Asag were working with whomever sent the tablet to Diane.

"My money is on Kay and his friends," Mordred said, as if reading my mind.

"Mine, too. You ready to get rid of these elves?"

The three elves started walking away. All of them carried swords on their hips. One had a hammer.

Mordred started after them, slowly, the grip on the dagger intensifying, his knuckles white. I wondered just how much he was looking forward to killing these elves, but then it was probably best not to think about it.

Mordred paused at the corner of a building and raised his hand, signaling for me to remain still. He looked back at me, raised two fingers and pointed to his left, before slowly creeping back. I stayed low, and walked to the corner, peeking around it. The shadows of the building kept me hidden.

Mordred had been right. About fifty feet in front of us were two of the three elves. Both stood outside the entrance to a building, and both were holding their weapons out in front of them.

It was the first time I'd been able to get a good look at the swords they carried. They appeared to be dwarven in design, but as if they had been made by someone who hadn't quite figured out how a dwarven sword should look. While dwarven swords were elegant, these were rough and ragged, as if the blood elves' own appearance had been recreated in sword form. The edge still looked sharp, though, and the unusual design of the blade probably spoke to the chaotic side of these monsters.

"The third must be inside," I whispered.

Mordred pointed to the roof of the building. "I can get up there."

"You take the one inside and I take the other two?" I asked.

Mordred nodded.

"I'll go first. I need to get their attention so you can climb up there. You go around the back of these buildings and across the street further down."

Mordred remained quiet as he looked back and forth across the roof. "Done. Won't be long." He set off along the back of the buildings.

I sprinted across the street, just as one of the elves looked my way. I stopped and waved, before continuing to the side of the building. The elf shouted something—I couldn't quite catch the words—and made off toward me, while the second stayed at the doorway, talking to someone inside, apparently believing that I wasn't worth his time or effort.

I ran around to the rear of the building and waited until the blood elf ran past me, then leapt out, barreling into the elf, and took him off his feet. We were out of sight of the others and I needed this to be quick so that I could deal with his friend before Mordred could get into the building. I rolled to my side, kicking the sword out of the elf's grip.

Ignoring the sword, the elf swung a punch, which I blocked. I grabbed the leather armor on his chest, spun him around, and threw him into the wall. He hit it headfirst, putting a considerable hole in the stone with a crunch that usually meant a person wasn't getting back up.

Apparently elves were made of stronger stuff, because, despite the gash on his head and the massive amount of blood streaming down his face, he still wanted to fight. But my necromancy allowed me to use the blood-elf soul I'd taken to increase my power and strength. The blood elf in front of me had no chance of winning; he just didn't know it yet.

I kicked him in the knee, dislocating the joint. He grunted, but otherwise gave no outward sign that he felt pain. Before he could do anything else, I picked up the sword from the floor, drove it into his throat, and decapitated him.

A second later, I heard a commotion inside. With the sword in my hand, I ran toward an elf who was just about to walk into the building. I threw the sword like a javelin, using my air magic to keep it moving in a straight line while maintaining its speed. The elves might be able to shrug off my magic, but I doubted they could shrug this off.

The elf couldn't do a damn thing but turn at the last moment and watch the sword go into his chest. It lifted him off the ground and pinned him to the wall behind. He snarled and tried to pull out the blade, but I was in front of him in a moment. I pushed the sword in further, turning it slightly before pulling it out and driving it back into his chest. The second elf died a moment later, just as the third crashed through a window above me, landing in the dirty street. Cuts laced its face and arms; one hand was partially severed, blood still pumping from the wound as he tried to get back to his feet.

"These things don't like to die," Mordred said as he appeared beside me and threw the knife, which caught the elf between the eyes, dropping it to the floor.

I looked from the dead elf to Mordred, who was bloody and looked exhausted.

"That was not as much fun as I was hoping," he said, leaving the dagger in the elf's head and taking the sword from his hip. "I managed to go from roof to roof around the top of the street. Unfortunately, the bastard was right there when I dropped into this building. Luckily, I didn't give him time to draw this or I might not be here right now."

I turned away and picked up the sword I'd used to kill the other elf. "So, which one do we take back?"

Mordred picked up the elf he'd killed and slung it over his shoulder. "We should hide the other two."

"The other one is around the corner. He's missing his head, but the darkness around there makes it difficult to see." I grabbed the elf by his feet and dragged him into the building, which, like all the other buildings around here, had presumably been someone's home at some point. Now it was just full of dust and dirt; any possessions had been long since looted or destroyed by the elves.

I went back outside and saw that Mordred was standing in the middle of the road, the dead elf still on his back.

"You took your time," he said. "This thing is heavy."

"Probably shouldn't have waited then," I pointed out. Somewhere in the distance the sound of a horn blared. "Let's get it back to William so we can get going. Sooner or later more elves will come, and I'd rather not be here when that happens."

CHAPTER 18

William hadn't ingratiated himself with Kasey. When we returned, her foot was on his throat and he was trying to breathe while also trying to apologize.

"What did this idiot do?" I asked.

"Doesn't matter," Kasey said, glancing down at him. "I didn't like it. Or him. In fact, the longer my shoe touches his bare skin, the longer I feel like I'm being tainted."

Mordred dropped the corpse on the floor beside William, and cut through his bindings with a blade of air magic. William stared at the dead blood elf, his eyes opening wide in need.

Kasey removed her foot and walked out of the building, saying, "I don't need to see or hear that."

"You staying?" I asked Mordred, who shook his head, and followed Kasey and me out of the building as another horn sounded.

"They're still hunting us," Mordred said. He walked away to be by himself in a secluded little spot where he could see anyone coming but was invisible from the roads or houses around us.

I sat beside Kasey in front of the wall we'd been crouched behind earlier. "Would it be really stupid to ask how you're doing?" I asked.

Kasey smiled. "I'm okay—honestly. This is all weird, and fucking horrible, but it's one of the many weird, horrible, and frankly messed-up things I've seen in the last few years. I would have thought that being a half-werewolf would be the weirdest thing to happen to me before I turned eighteen. It's not even in the top ten."

"Chloe told me she's gay," I said, wanting to change the subject to more pleasant topics.

Kasey smiled. "I know. I've known for a long time. It's nice that she can out herself, and it's nice she's comfortable enough with people to be herself. Not her mum, though."

"How does her mum feel about Chloe living with you, Tommy, and Olivia?"

"I don't think Mara is thrilled. She threatened my mum with lawyers once because she wasn't allowed to see Chloe, who had told her she didn't want to see her. Mara backed down when Avalon arrived and explained what would happen if she threatened a director of the LOA again." She turned to me. "What about you? Morgan here? That's gotta be weird."

"That is one way of putting it, I guess. I loved Morgan, but she has no bearing on my life now, or anything in it."

"What's going on with him, then?" Kasey asked, meaning Mordred.

"I don't know," I admitted. "He's different. That look of rage and anger has gone, replaced with something I don't understand. He says he's still going to kill me, though, so who knows what's going on in his head?"

"I've been thinking. Someone wanted to get rid of Diane so they could attack Brutus. Why? Brutus has a lot of power, and security. Could someone really do that: hit Brutus?"

"Anyone can be gotten to with enough patience, backing, and skill. Why Brutus, though? His removal would have no effect on the day-to-day running of London. Most Londoners don't know he exists, and he delegates a lot of the important matters to other people. Someone else would just step in, and there's no way Avalon would accept someone like Hera or one of her friends taking the job. It seems like a lot of effort for not a lot of payoff."

Kasey was quiet for a few seconds. "Do you think the others are okay?"

I nodded. "Hopefully the dwarves can help us find them, but there's no way Diane or Remy would allow anything bad to happen. They're probably in a better place than we are."

"I hope so. They could be anywhere in this city."

"If they've gone into the catacombs far below us, we could be searching indefinitely," Mordred told us as he walked over.

"You're such a ray of sunshine," Kasey said.

"I was merely telling the truth," Mordred said. He paused. "I'd really like some enchiladas."

Kasey and I shared a glance.

"Sorry. Like I told Nate, my brain sometimes goes off on tangents. Even so, an enchilada would be great right about now. And nachos. I love nachos."

"I don't think anyone delivers here," Kasey told him.

Mordred looked sad. "Probably. Like I said, my brain sometimes goes off on a tangent." He walked away without another word.

"So, how do you go from loving someone like a brother to wanting to murder him every time you get within spitting distance?" Kasey asked.

"I don't know. I wish I did, but Mordred has never been one to explain that. I don't even know if he knows anymore. Maybe his reasons got lost in time, and now we just hate one another out of habit. It's become a Pavlovian reflex—we see one another and want to fight."

Mordred re-entered the building and came out a moment later. "He's finished, apparently. Also, I take back what I said. I really don't want any food right now."

Kasey and I got to our feet, and while I felt no interest in re-entering that house, I did it anyway. Kasey followed.

The smell was my first clue: the stench of blood and death. And as I entered the building and my eyes adjusted to the lack of light, I saw the horror of what William had done.

"I feel full now," William said with a belch. His face, hands, and pretty much every other part of him were stained black with the blood of the elf. I looked at the corpse and immediately wished I hadn't. William had eaten a large portion of its face, almost to the bone in some cases. I maintained my composure and left the building, followed by Kasey and Mordred.

"What the hell was that?" she asked. "That was fucked up."

"He did it for show," I told her. "He wanted to see our reactions."

"He's not exactly a well man," Mordred said. "In fact, I do believe he thinks this is funny. Even the old me would have found little humor in eating someone's eyes, lips, and tongue."

"Thanks for that," Kasey said and sat down.

"Would it help if I told you seeing things like this gets easier?" Mordred asked.

"How the hell does *that* help? So eventually I'll become so desensitized to this sort of sick crap that I'll just shrug and move on?"

"Not really," I said. "You remember what I told you about taking things and putting them aside in your head: not seeing the dead as people, but as just things? It takes a long time to learn, but it does help. That's one of the more disturbing things I've seen someone do, however."

"So what do we do now?" Kasey asked. "We can't drag him like that through the city. He needs to ingest their blood, not bathe in it."

"Mordred, we need water. Any chance you could use your water magic on him? Clean him up a bit?"

Mordred glanced back at the house; he didn't look keen to go back inside. I couldn't say I blamed him. "I can hose him down. I assume you'll be accompanying me."

I nodded. "Shame there's no water on tap. I could use a drink." I dug around my memories. "Actually, the pipes are still there. The elf I killed, Mythanus, remembers drinking water. It comes straight from outside, a lake about fifty miles to the east of the mountain. The elves sent people up there to check the supply. Mythanus has been a few times, and the lake is essentially an ocean from what the memory shows me, so I doubt it's dried up. I wonder if it's drinkable, though? We should take a look while we're here."

"The pipes will come in from the roof; we'll have to go up there."

"You can't drink magical water?" Kasey asked.

"You probably can, but I have no idea what effect it would have on you. Some things you're just better off not knowing."

Mordred smiled. "On the plus side, water-element users never get dehydrated."

"Okay, so what do I do?" Kasey asked.

"Stay here and keep a lookout. Those elves are hunting, and they will be here soon enough. Just let me know if anything comes along."

Mordred and I went back into the house of horrors to find William drinking the elf's blood from a cup. "Tastes so good. Thanks for this."

We ignored him and walked upstairs, continuing upward until we found the exit to the roof, which we climbed onto.

"With no rain under the earth, dwarven buildings have flat roofs," Mordred said, like he was narrating some weird nature documentary. "It allowed them to use the extra floor space."

I stared at Mordred while he found one of several pipes sticking out from a nearby rock formation, one of which was joined to the roof of the house. White glyphs ignited over his arms, showing that he was using air magic, although the reason behind it eluded me.

"What are you doing?" I asked after a few seconds of watching him concentrate.

He didn't turn around as he spoke. "Using my air magic to place a bubble inside this pipe. There's no water coming, which means a blockage somewhere. I'm trying to find it."

"Maybe there's no water full stop?" I suggested.

"If that were the case, this whole process would be irrelevant," he snapped, before taking a breath. "I am having difficulties being in this place. My mind keeps showing me what happened the last time I was here. It is—I do not know how to deal with it."

The words left my mouth before I could stop them. "You want to talk?" I could not believe I'd said it.

"You hate me, remember."

"Because you tried to kill me. A lot. And you murdered innocent people. A lot. Including children."

He stopped and turned back to me. "I never killed a child. Not one."

"You tried to kill the children in the tower," I reminded him. "And what about when you were working for Mars Warfare, and you were putting children through the Harbinger Trials? How many of them died?"

The glyphs on his arm faded. "You stopping me from killing the princes was probably the best thing you ever did for me. And I was never part of those trials. Never. That was all Ares. I went to work there to get close to Hera. I wanted information—information I never got, as it turned out. So, yes, I did awful things while I was there. I turned the other way, and allowed the worst of our kind to have free rein, but I have to live with those decisions. Even if they were not really mine."

Mordred ignored me and the glyphs reignited. Unfortunately, that also ignited my temper. "What does that mean?"

"It doesn't matter. We need to leave this place."

"Right. I'm sure you want some time to come up with a good excuse as to why you allowed the murder of innocent children, and why you tried to kill the princes in the tower. You can make a list of other people you blame for your own actions." I said it before I could stop myself. "I'm sorry. I know you're not *him* anymore. It's just difficult: seeing you, remembering everything that happened over those centuries."

"I was an evil man, Nate. I know that, and I will have to live with that every single day for as long as I live. I can't blame you for being wary, or for having anger at me inside of you. I never thought seeing you again would be easy—for either of us. But I am glad I got to see you. I'm glad I got to say sorry. I don't ever want to forget the horrific things I've done. I just want to try and somehow make them better."

I walked over and stood beside him. "We need water. Let's work together."

We both used our air magics to probe the pipes for a blockage, but it took a nervous few minutes before we found something.

"There's a crack in the pipe," Mordred said. "The water is seeping out into the rock. If we can crack the stone the water should come out. We only need a small crack through."

We put air bubbles inside the rock, expanding them as the sound of cracking mountain filled the air around us.

"I think this is a bad idea," we said almost in unison.

There was an almighty crack and before either of us could do anything, the rock gave way as thousands of gallons of water tore forth.

The water burst out of the rock as if it had been building up for years, the power behind it throwing Mordred and me back across the roof. It pounded the roof, tearing large parts off and pushing us both over the side, despite our magical shields. Huge pieces of masonry and rock fell all around the building as Mordred and I smashed into the street below, followed by even more water, which continued to pour over us.

We eventually managed to crawl off to the side, away from the waterfall, just as William ran out of the house, slipped, and was carried away toward the end of the street. Kasey turned into wolf-beast form, ran through the water, caught William with one hand, and threw him to safety. She slipped, but her momentum got her through the worst of the flood. By the time they made it back to us, the water had turned the street into a lake, and the building we'd been on was collapsing under the weight of the water on the roof.

"What happened?" Kasey asked as Mordred and I coughed up our lungs.

"Miscalculation," Mordred said. "On the plus side, William looks clean."

Kasey looked between Mordred and me.

"We didn't count on the rock being so brittle," I told her. "The second we tried to force it apart to let water out, it just crumbled to dust. Hence the sudden bath."

I was upright, leaning against a nearby house when the sound of a horn tore through the noise of the water and collapsing buildings.

"We need to leave," I said. "Now."

Kasey hoisted William to his feet and pushed him along. She paused beside Mordred and me. "You okay?"

We both nodded as a horn sounded again. Closer, more urgent.

"Let's go," Kasey said. "We've lost a lot of time, and I don't want to find out firsthand what those blood elves do to their captives."

CHAPTER 19

For the next few hours we made haste through what used to be a bustling hub of dwarvish life, but was now all but abandoned. We came across several elven patrols, usually in groups of at least six, and managed to avoid most of them without incident.

On those occasions when violence was necessary, it was short and sharp, and the elven bodies were hidden as best as possible to cover any obvious trail.

We stopped rarely, usually only for a few minutes at a time, so that we could drink something from one of the many sources of water, without almost killing ourselves. It hadn't taken long for our clothes to dry, especially with a little fire magic thrown into the mix, but no one wanted to stop for long.

It wasn't until we got past the patchy patrols and further into the city that we first saw the citadel. Even from a half-mile away, it still loomed over everything, stretching up high into the mountain above us to a place I couldn't see.

"Wow," Kasey whispered from our hiding spot in the shadows of a large building.

"We do not want to go in there," Mordred said, his voice surprisingly calm.

"I'm not planning on it," I assured him.

Kasey looked up, following the citadel for as far as it went.

"Does that place have a giant eye floating on top of it? Because it really looks like it should."

The dark brick that had been used to build the citadel was lit by torchlight, casting eerie shadows over even the most benign of places on it. Dozens of elves patrolled a massive bridge that connected the citadel to the rest of the city. I wondered how many hundreds, if not thousands, more lived in the camps that sat around it.

"We shouldn't linger," Mordred said.

I nodded, but continued to stare at the feat of architecture in front of me. It was a fearsome sight, made even more so with the makeshift spikes that had been placed on the many windows all over the structure. It was not impenetrable—nothing was—but it talked a damn convincing game at saying it was.

We moved off, keeping to the wall, and let the rock overhang shield us from the eyes of the blood-elf empire.

"Even this distance is too close," Mordred said.

It was harder going through this more inhabited part of the city. Blood elves were everywhere, and more than once we had to dart into the nearest building—on the assurance from Mordred that they'd be empty—and wait for them to leave.

"Why are all of these buildings empty?" Kasey eventually asked.

"Blood elves don't want to live where the dwarves lived," Mordred explained. "They don't like being enclosed. They have camps in the levels below this one, where they're closer to the heart of the mountain."

We slipped back into silence after that while we continued through the city. By the time we'd reached the archway where the troll was, I was beginning to wonder what we were going to do with William once we were past the traps incorporated into it.

"Any chance we can't just walk around it?" Kasey asked as we crouched behind a large boulder close to the archway. "The rock up there appears to be climbable."

I dug through the elf's memories once more. "No. There are more trolls, spiders, and other things living in the holes that litter the rock around us. This is the safest way that doesn't involve hours, if not days, of walking to get around it. And that walk will take us through heavily populated areas. We've managed to get lucky so far. I'd rather not push it further."

"So what's beyond the arch?"

I peered around the corner at the arch. It was huge. Maybe fifty yards long and high enough to fit a double-decker bus under. Dozens of dwarven runes covered the archway, the black of the runes a stark contrast to the gold and red of the stone used to build it. One building sat on the other side of the arch, but I couldn't see beyond it.

"The main living quarters for some of the dwarves," Mordred said before I could. "Those who lived here were government officials. Beyond there is where the dwarf artisans lived and worked. The arch used to be manned by dwarven soldiers, and you had to show documents to be allowed in. Basically it was a way to separate the various districts of the dwarves: separating the rich from the poor."

"So everyone in the city went under one arch?" Kasey asked, astounded.

"No, there are over two dozen of them in a sort of ring around this area. I don't know if they all still work, or if they're booby-trapped. They never used to be; just manned."

I continued to watch the large hut just beyond the arch. "The blood elves clearly don't like visitors."

"Seeing how none of us can read dwarven runes, any chance that William can?" I wondered aloud.

Mordred unfastened William's cloth gag. "I'd answer the man."

William wiped his mouth and rubbed his jaw. "No idea. I just know that if someone walks through there without a rune inscribed on them, you won't feel very good. Oh, and the troll."

"You'd better work, then," I told him. "Let's go."

The four of us dropped down from our vantage point, and, after checking that no one was around, walked toward the arch. I looked up at the runes as we approached the archway, expecting them to do something, but they remained dark and seemingly inert as we got closer.

"Can you see the troll?" Kasey asked. "Because I can't see it anywhere. I can smell something pretty awful, though."

I searched the area around us. "Nope. Is that good or bad?"

"It stays hidden until it needs to come out," William assured us.

"Even so, keep an eye out," I said.

"If this doesn't work, I'm going to kill William," Mordred said, just loud enough for the human to hear. "Painfully."

As we were about to step under the arch, William paused and turned to us. "I told you I wouldn't let you down." He took a step and the runes above us shone a deep blue, but otherwise nothing happened. We stepped after him and still no negative reaction.

"There's something I forgot to tell you about that archway," William said. "I guess I do know what those runes do. They're linked to similar runes in that hut over there."

The door to the hut in front of us burst open and a cave troll stepped out.

"They're a bell," I whispered.

"There used to be several more buildings here," Mordred said, glancing around at the rubble.

"They didn't need them," I said. "The elves destroyed a lot when they took over here. They left the buildings further on, though."

"Just walk with me and you'll be fine," William said, sounding incredibly confident about his current predicament.

The cave troll was at least eight feet tall, and his brown-and-green skin was covered in armor that wouldn't have looked out of place on a tank. Huge spikes adorned his silver pauldrons, and he wore spiked gloves. He was bald, his head a mass of scar tissue, and I wondered what had been done to him before he'd been chained up inside the hut. The chain itself was as thick as my leg, and trailed off back into the hut.

The troll sniffed the air, and then appeared to relax, his hands dropping to his side and his head lolling forward.

"What happened?" Mordred whispered.

"You don't need to be quiet," William said. "It can smell the elven blood. Makes it docile. It'll be like that for a while, certainly long enough for us to get away."

"Let's leave quickly anyway," I said. I'd fought trolls in my life, killing more than a few, but cave trolls were vicious and cruel, and I really didn't want to see if anything in the tunnels carved into the rock on either side of us contained even more of his kind. One cave troll is bad enough.

We'd walked past the troll and around to the side of the hut when William took off at a flat sprint. Mordred launched himself forward to give chase, but I called after him to stop, and to my immense surprise, he did.

"He might be trying to lead you into a group of blood elves," I told him. "He can tell them what he likes. They'll never find us before we reach the dwarf stronghold."

I was more than a little surprised when William didn't run down the slope toward the rest of the city, but turned and sprinted around the nearest pile of rubble that used to be a building.

We soon caught up to where we'd last seen William and checked the area, spotting him running back up toward the hut, using the rubble to keep himself hidden from the main path.

"He's running back to his masters," Mordred said with a sneer.

"Let him be," Kasey said. "You can't force him to be free of them."

We continued on our path until a roar of pain stopped us. It came from behind us, and we turned to look back at the hut.

"You think the troll got him?" Kasey asked.

We were about a hundred yards away from the hut and I didn't see anyone. There wasn't anywhere for pursuers to hide. "That didn't sound like a human cry. And we're sitting ducks out here. Let's get moving."

We paused at another roar of pain. Part of the hut collapsed in on itself, and then something sailed over the hut and bounced a dozen or so yards from us.

"That's the troll's head," Kasey said. "What can tear off the head of a troll?"

"I think the boy was hiding something from us," Mordred said as we watched William kick through the back of the hut, razing it to the ground. He was twirling part of the chain in his hands as he strolled slowly toward us.

"We should run," I said, and no one disagreed. William had

doubled in size and the smile on his face was as bloody as the rest of his body. We ran in search of hiding places.

"I'll find you all!" he shouted, as his laughter echoed around us. "I think the elves would like it if I brought back your heads."

"What is he?" Mordred asked when we finally stopped running and had hidden behind a large wall next to a disused street.

"No idea," I said. "He said something about making the humans read scrolls. Maybe this is the effect."

"It turns him into the Hulk?" Kasey asked.

"He's human, I'm certain of it; the elf I killed was certain of it. I have no idea what the hell is letting him kick a troll's head around like a rugby ball."

Mordred peered around the corner. "We need to keep moving. I don't think he's giving up."

I took a look for myself and watched William walk down the ramp and into the workers' part of town. He appeared to be even larger than before and just as determined to find us.

We slipped away into the side streets, where buildings remained intact and there were fewer crystals lighting the way, but kept running, stopping every now and again to listen for elven patrols, even though this part of the city appeared to be devoid of anything remotely elven.

An almighty crash behind us stopped us all in our tracks.

"What the hell was that?" Mordred asked.

"Maybe he kicked in another building," Kasey suggested.

I ran to the end of a nearby alley and looked back at where I'd last seen William. Five dwarves had surrounded him and were trying to bring him down, but he was fighting back, and had thrown one of them into a nearby building, which had collapsed from the impact.

"They're going to die," Kasey said from beside me.

"And we might, too," Mordred pointed out.

"You two, see if you can get to the dwarves to attack from the rear. I'm going to keep William busy. Don't be long; I'd rather not be punted all over this city." I stepped out of the shadows and onto the street, where I was easily visible.

"Come on, William!" I called, my hands cupped around my mouth. "Why don't you come and fight me instead? Don't you prefer the unarmed type?"

William shoved a dwarf into a nearby wall and began running toward me. It didn't take long for his massive frame to reach full speed, which made the street beneath my feet judder with every one of his steps.

Fortunately for me, the size increase hadn't improved his maneuverability or intelligence. I dove aside, and allowed the now nine feet, four-hundred pounds of William to crash into the building behind me. I sprinted past him until I was a good few dozen yards away before I stopped and waited for him to remove the roof that was currently on his head.

Huge pieces of masonry flew in my direction, but a quick blast of air magic sent them tumbling harmlessly to either side of me. I threw a ball of flame that hit him with no effect whatsoever. Apparently my magic wasn't going to work on *him*, either. Great. I was really beginning to hate this realm and everything that lived in it.

Once William was back on his feet, he roared at me, and I ignited my soul weapon, spinning the battle-ax in my hand as if I were currently in the most casual of settings. My nerves and fear were shoved aside; I'd beaten bigger and badder things than whatever the hell William was, but I'd done that with my magic—with my power. Not being able to use that was a severe blow, and I had no idea what kind of effect my necromancy would have on the monster before me. While I'd absorbed the blood elf's soul, making me faster, stronger, and quicker to heal, that didn't really mean much when going up against . . . well, for want of a better term, Hulk-lite.

William stepped out of the rubble, kicking a large piece of it toward me. "Little sorcerer!" he screamed.

I motioned for him to get on with it.

William rushed toward me and threw a huge, deceptively fast punch. I dodged and raised my battle-ax, cutting through his arm. It left no mark, but he screamed in pain.

"What did you do to me?" he screamed.

"It'll wear off in a few seconds. But this won't." Kasey ran right into William as if she were a freight train. She grabbed hold of whatever she could and used her considerable strength to take him off his feet, dumping him on the ground, his head bouncing off the street.

William tried to grab Kasey, but she was too fast for him and easily avoided his attack. William got to his knees as a short sword thrown by one of the dwarves slammed into his chest. He caught one of the dwarves that got too close and threw him aside, the small, stocky, figure sailing over the nearest building.

"Stay back," I told Kasey when she stepped toward William again. Kasey could tear a car door off, but only moments earlier William was much, much stronger than she was. She nodded and stepped back again, joining the dwarves and Mordred circling around him.

He swiped at us, but we were out of reach. Snarling, he stayed where he was, turning his head so he could see when any of us made our next move. He wasn't about to leave himself open to attack.

"We are at a stalemate," William said with a chuckle.

Kasey inhaled and there was a sound like the cracking of ice on a frozen river. An instant later, a blast of ice left her mouth and crashed into William with terrifying force. The ice drove him back toward the building behind him, and then as quickly as the ice had started it stopped, leaving William's arms pinned to the wall.

I had no idea Kasey was even able to use her mother's elemental powers, and seeing her in full wolf-beast form as ice exploded from her open mouth was a staggering, and scary, experience. I wondered for a second just how powerful a werewolf-elemental could actually become.

"This won't stop me!" he shouted at her.

"That will," she said, and she pointed up.

William looked up at a dwarf leaping off the roof, a broad sword in each hand. William roared in defiance, struggling to free himself from the ice, but he wasn't fast enough. The dwarf drove both swords into his skull, right up to their hilts.

The dwarf perched on top of William's head until the monster pitched forward, then leapt off and landed softly on the ground, rolling to his feet and walking toward me as if nothing had happened.

He said something I didn't understand.

"I don't speak enough dwarvish to be able to communicate with him," I said, hoping one of the other dwarves might know one of the earth-realm languages. "Last time I was here, I had a translator. I know a bit, but not enough to converse."

The dwarf chuckled, grabbed hold of my hand and shook it before saying something else I didn't quite catch.

"He said 'pleased to meet you,'" Mordred told me before replying to the dwarf, who laughed.

"I told him that we were pleased to have his help."

One of the other dwarves left the group, returning a few minutes later with a grave expression on his face.

"Can you translate?" I asked Mordred, who nodded.

"*Balithis is dead,*" the returning dwarf said. "*Crushed by rubble.*"

"*She was a good warrior and friend,*" the dwarf who'd shaken my hand said.

"Can you say we're sorry for his loss?" I asked Mordred, who nodded and relayed my words before telling me what the dwarf said.

"*Thank you for your kindness, but she was old, and sick. This was to be her last battle. If she was going to die here, she'd be glad to know she played a part in bringing down that beast. The name is Zamek Merla. We're going back to camp. You're more than welcome to join us.*"

"Thank you," I told him. "I'm Nate. That's Kasey and this is—"

Mordred gave him a name that certainly wasn't his.

"*Let's get going then. We've got a funeral to arrange, and we need to be out of here before anyone comes looking for their friend. Besides, we've got more of you tall buggers back at the stronghold. They arrived not too long ago. I've no doubt you know them.*"

"Hopefully it's Chloe and the rest of the group," Kasey said once Mordred had finished translating.

"You want to tell me why you lied about your name?" I asked Mordred after we'd started following the dwarves. One carried his dead friend over his shoulder.

"Not really," he told me. "But let's just get to the stronghold before I make things a lot more complicated."

Excellent, because things weren't shitty enough.

CHAPTER 20

No one bothered us on our way to the dwarven stronghold, although the dwarves stuck to the side streets and more than once changed direction to avoid large bands of blood elves. As the dwarves told it, they were quite happy to kill as many elves as they could, but there weren't enough of them to start doing anything reckless.

It was a fairly short walk, maybe a mile at the most, before we reached two massive doors, each one twenty feet high and equally as wide. The doors sat in the middle of a large wall that stretched from each side of the mountain—about three hundred feet. The wall was fifty feet tall, with a gap at the apex separating it from the mountain above. A host of runes had been carved into the dark stone in various places, several just around the door. I didn't want to find out what they did.

Zamek placed his hand on the side of the door and spoke softly. Several of the runes ignited in silver and gold, and a few heartbeats passed before there was an almighty noise from behind the doors. Zamek motioned for us to take a step back, and we avoided the slow, but unstoppable swing of the doors as they opened.

"*Welcome to the stronghold,*" Mordred translated for Zamek. "*Welcome to Sanctuary.*"

Zamek spoke to the dwarf who was carrying the body of their friend, and they shook hands. Zamek waited while the other dwarves entered the city before he entered last, nodding to and saluting those who greeted them.

The dwarf carrying the body stopped and bowed his head in front of someone before lowering the body to the ground. Several dwarves around him wept openly.

"*They are her family,*" Mordred translated, and it took me a moment to realize that Zamek had even spoken.

"If you want to go and speak to them, we can wait," I told him as he ushered us into Sanctuary, the huge doors closing behind us with a thud that made the air flow over me.

Zamek shook his head. "*Later. First, they grieve. They don't want to talk to me right now; it is not proper for a commander to see a family in the midst of grief, just as it's not proper for the family to see the commander grieve. Once I have spent some time reflecting on her passing, I will go to them. Before the feast tonight, before we celebrate her life. It will be an event you are more than welcome to join.*"

I bowed my head in thanks.

"*But first, we need you to see the elders. They're going to want to know why more of your kind—outsiders—are here. And it would probably be wise for you to learn the language. I'll see if the rune scribes can be made ready. Seeing them would make your time here much easier.*"

"You can put a rune on me that will make me understand the language?" Kasey asked, slightly awed. "That would have made every single foreign language lesson at school a lot easier."

Zamek laughed once Mordred had finished translating.

"*The elders will explain better than I can. I'm just a warrior.*"

He turned to face Kasey. *"And you are wolf-kin. I have not seen one of your kind since we closed our borders. I assume your kind hasn't evolved the ability to freeze things with their mouths?"*

Kasey chuckled and shook her head.

"Then you have been given a rare gift. Although I'd keep it to yourself while you're here. Wolf-kin are welcome; elementals are not so warmly met. They bypass the natural magic dampeners of this realm. Personally, I'm glad you're on our side, but not everyone will be so accommodating."

"Thank you for the warning."

"No problem, wolf—sorry, Kasey. Let's get you to the council chambers. You can meet the other tall ones, and a short hairy one who won't shut up."

"Remy," Kasey and I said at the same time.

We followed Zamek through Sanctuary, and found that it was much larger than I'd been expecting. Just finding out from William that there were still dwarves in the city had been a revelation, but to see the city was astonishing. People went about their lives close to an army of creatures who would like nothing more than to kill them all. That kind of proximity to an enemy for so long would make the dwarves tough. Those who lived here were not to be underestimated.

"Just after the main gate is the processing area," he said as we walked over a small bridge under which ran a stream. *"Lots of people get clogged up there mostly because they're waiting to go out on a mission. The only reason Balithis's family were there was because they knew it was to be her last quest. She was sixteen hundred years old—not ancient by our standards, but getting there, certainly. She'd have been given a nice job training or some such if she'd have made*

it back. We can always use good trainers, although it's not the way a warrior wants to go.

"This is the first of six residential areas. They're spread out all over the . . . well, I guess it's a city, although I've rarely sat down to think about how much it has grown. In between each residential area are different sections for different crafts, be they weapon-making, armor, artistry, combat, and the like. At the rear of the city is the council, and beyond that are the dwellers."

"'The dwellers?'" I asked.

"Those who live inside the tunnels, always mining, always making more room and finding us more materials. This place was always on the list of places to mine before . . . before . . . before the world fell. We've been digging there since most of my kin left."

"What happened here?" Kasey asked.

"That's best left to the elders to explain. My feelings about it go against the grain. Mostly I'd like to find the dwarves that betrayed us and tear their heads off." Zamek stopped walking. *"Forget I said that last bit. I get into enough arguments with the council as it is."*

He continued walking, although his pace had increased, as if he realized he'd continue to say unpopular things the longer he was with us.

"You should know something. The dwarves have been here for a long time. We've been trying to fight the elves, taking pieces of them where we can. Until they found some of the spirit scrolls, and then it all went to shit. But we still go out there and cause trouble. Unfortunately, there are not enough of us left to mount much of an offense."

"Why do you stay, then?" I asked.

"Lots of reasons. Some will say because we have the library. We took a lot of the interesting stuff when we found ourselves stuck out here, but we have to keep it safe. Others will tell you we stay out of

pride, or anger, or hate, or because we're stubborn buggers. Most will say we stay because this is our home, and we want one day to take it back. I tend to believe it's a mix of it all. Like I said, I'm just a warrior. My days of ever being more are long gone."

There was no resentment or anger in his voice as he stated the last sentence. He'd seemingly accepted his new role from whatever he used to be. And after seeing him in combat, I was pretty certain that a lot of people were very happy that Zamek was fighting for them.

The tour continued unabated with Zamek showing us various interesting buildings, or saying hello to the dwarves we passed. If nothing else, he appeared to be popular among his people.

We reached a sizable building with a large garden growing in front of it. It was the first time I'd seen flowers since I'd entered the mountain. The patch of garden stretched for as long as I could see, curving around toward the rear of the building.

"We grow food here," Zamek explained. "Most of what we grow doesn't require natural sunlight, but those plants that do are helped by the crystals above."

I stared up at the multitude of crystals in the ceiling high above us. If it weren't for the hordes of blood elves and other monsters trying to kill us, this might have been a place I'd liked to have stayed longer. But being hunted by murderous bastards tends to put a damper on relaxation and sightseeing.

Thoughts of relaxation came to an even more abrupt end when I heard someone shout to Zamek. I turned to watch as Zamek walked over to a nearby building, slightly away from the gardens, where the newcomer had exited. The two dwarves got into a heated debate.

"What's happening?" Kasey asked.

Mordred listened for a few more seconds before answering. "It appears the newcomer is unhappy at our presence. He's also unhappy at Zamek's presence. And generally appears to be a very pissed-off dwarf. They're talking too fast; I can't keep up with what they're saying."

The argument got more and more intense until several guards stepped between the two, separating them. The newcomer stormed off, waving his hands, while Zamek returned to us.

"If you'll follow me, I'll take you all to the main chamber."

He offered no explanation for the argument with the other dwarf, and we probably wouldn't have gotten one even if we'd asked.

Zamek led us to a pair of guards, who nodded a greeting and pushed open the door, while a third stood to one side, watching us intently.

The building inside was no different to any other building or structure I'd seen since arriving in the realm, except that it wasn't covered in dust. The style and architecture was the same, and suggested that the dwarves preferred to make their buildings impressive, no matter who occupied it. Pillars sat every few feet, each one carved with intricate line work. Several of the carvings depicted scenes of battle, and I wanted to spend more time walking around each of the dozens we passed, studying the details. The dwarves might have fled from their homes and made Sanctuary out of necessity, but they'd made it their own, and all appearances suggested they continued to live on their terms. There were also dozens of guards in the massive building, each of them wearing dwarven armor dyed red and gold.

We entered an expansive hall with doors spaced along one wall every few feet. The balcony above suggested even more rooms. Eventually Zamek stopped outside a pair of black and silver doors flanked by four guards. He spoke to the dwarf I assumed was in charge, and they nodded and pushed open the door, revealing some sort of meeting chamber inside.

A rectangular table made of gleaming rock sat in the middle of the room, running almost its entire length. Chairs lined up all around the table, with the largest at one end on a raised portion of floor. The dwarven woman occupying it got down from the chair and walked over to Zamek, embracing him.

"You are from the earth realm," she said in perfect English. She was considerably thinner than Zamek, her face gaunt, and looked much older. She wore her black hair tied up on top her head with a red ribbon, and several bangles of different colors adorned her wrists.

I introduced myself and Kasey, but the dwarf looked at Mordred before I could say his name.

"Mordred of Camelot," she said.

Mordred blinked. "A long time ago. Now, just Mordred."

"You were imprisoned here, long ago, for a crime you did not commit. No apology was ever given, no reason ever explained. It has been long overdue, but I apologize for what you went through. Unfortunately, your jailers are no longer with us, but if there is anything that I can do to make up for the wickedness you went through, I will be happy to do it. That is as close to justice as I can give you."

Mordred blinked. "I . . ." He stopped and bowed his head. "Thank you. Would it be okay if I left the room for a while? I need some air."

The dwarf placed her hand on Mordred's shoulder. "Go. You have the freedom of the city."

"I was informed that, at one time, he was a great evil," she said after Mordred had hurried from the room, "but I sense no evil in him now. Before you ask, his tale of what happened to him here is not for me to tell."

"You can sense these things?" I asked, a little curious. I'd never heard about dwarves being able to do such things, but it felt good to know that my assumption of Mordred was right. *No evil.* Those two words made me smile.

"Part empath," she said with a smile. "My mother was an empath: very rare among dwarves, and not highly regarded. It's not widely discussed, either. A dwarf without the ability to do dwarven things like create? It's not exactly accepted as the norm. Dwarves are many things, Mr. Garrett, but most of all, they are slow to change. Presumably because most of them spend all day with rocks and crystals, which aren't well known for their forward-thinking properties. To many, a dwarf who can't create, can't mold things to a whim, isn't much of a dwarf, no matter how well they carry a sword, or bloody the nose of everyone who mocks them. My mother was not one to let her lack of alchemy get in the way of beating the shit out of anyone who mocked her."

She turned to Zamek. "Can you bring the others who were found here? I believe these two would like to be reunited with their friends."

Zamek bowed, and nodded in my direction before leaving.

"I should introduce myself. It's a great oversight that I haven't already done so. I've had to do it more in the last few days than in several hundred years, so you'll have to excuse me and my poor manners. I am Jinayca Konal, lead elder of Sanctuary."

"Thank you for having us here."

"Nathaniel Garrett?" she asked, squinting her eyes slightly. "I recognize that name. You've been here before."

"A long time ago, as a young man."

She stared at me for a few seconds. "Yes, that must be it. I remember names of those who aren't dwarven. It's why no one wants to try and replace me; I doubt they'd have as much joy remembering those blood-elf bastards."

"What are they?" I asked.

Jinayca waved me away. "Explanations all in time. First, we will have to convene an elder meet. That will take a few hours, and then we can discuss how we're going to get you all home. Tonight will be a feast for Balithis; after that few will be in a position to discuss anything much. Best to get it all resolved before then." She opened the door and bellowed, "Get the other elders here! Now!"

I smiled. Jinayca was not what I'd been expecting from a dwarven elder. I'd thought of someone more suited to pondering, and stuffy. I got the feeling that Jinayca could be a formidable political opponent—and probably not someone to cross.

"That'll take a good bit of time," she said as she closed the door. "When your friends arrive, we'll arrange for the rune scribes to put you through the machine."

"That sounds ominous," Kasey pointed out.

"Oh, it's nothing awful. It just puts runes on people. It'll let you both understand and speak the language. Your friends all went through it, or are in the process of, depending on when they arrived."

"Do you know their names?" I asked, hopeful that those who'd arrived were the missing members of our group.

"Diane, and a few I don't know. It was nice seeing Diane

again. I remember hunting the forest above with her. She was always an interesting woman. She was keen to find you; they all were. Unfortunately, that's where the good news ends. Your witch friend, Chloe: she's not well."

"She was poisoned," I told her, worried about what had happened to Chloe. "It looks like the venom belonged to a monster by the name of Asag. I've had the same venom in my blood. I'd hoped with rest it would've dissipated."

Jinayca shook her head. "Chloe is currently undergoing tests, but she's getting worse, not better. We'll take you to her once you've all seen the rune scribe."

"I need to see her now," Kasey demanded.

"I know you feel like that. I'd be the same in your shoes. But you need to wait. She's currently being tended to by the finest physicians we have. You can't do anything for her while that's going on. And if you don't speak the language, you won't understand a thing they tell you. Very few people here speak anything other than dwarvish; maybe some elvish. Until then, you'll just be in the way of people trying to do their jobs."

Kasey didn't look happy about it, but she nodded curtly in response.

"Thank you," Jinayca said as the double doors swung open to reveal the rest of the group, who burst into the room talking at once.

"Where is Mordred?" Morgan demanded.

"He left," I told her.

"If you've done anything to—"

"I didn't *do* anything," I interrupted. "He needed some time alone. I don't think you need to go find him right now. We need to get to these rune scribes and figure out what everyone is saying here so we can help Chloe. Everything else comes second, including us getting out of this realm. Anyone disagree?"

No one did.

"We can head over when you're ready," Jinayca told us.

"You all go. I'll fetch Mordred."

My words gained me a glare from Morgan, who stepped in front of me after everyone else had followed Jinayca out of the room.

"I'm coming with you."

"Morgan, I'm not going to hurt him. I'm not going to do anything, but right now, I have a question for him, and I think he's likely to be more open and honest with me when you're not there. So whatever you think is happening, isn't. Go get seen to. We need to figure out how to help Chloe."

"I won't repeat myself."

My temper flared. "Move aside, Morgan. I have better things to do than whatever the hell you think is happening here. Now either take a swing, or fuck off and make yourself useful."

Morgan's nostrils flared slightly, and for a second I thought she might actually take the swing, but instead she turned on her heel and stormed off, leaving me alone in the room.

It didn't take me long to find Mordred, who was outside sitting on a small bench next to several trees, the smell of sweet fruit in the air.

"We're getting the runes," I told him. "I think it would be a good idea for you to get them too. I don't want anyone left behind."

He nodded, but remained staring at the ground in front of him.

"When we're done with that," I continued, "and we know what's going on with Chloe, I want answers from you. About how you lived, about why you insist you have to kill me, despite the fact you're clearly not the same Mordred I've been fighting for so long."

"I might not be able to give them. And those I can give, you probably won't believe."

"You can try. Come catch us up."

I was a few steps away when I heard Mordred speak again.

"What did the dwarf say to you when I was gone?"

I paused and turned back to him. "There was no evil in you."

Tears fell from his eyes, and I didn't know what to say.

"I'm not evil. Sorry. It's just weird to have someone else confirm it."

"No need to be sorry, Mordred." I told him. "You're not the man you used to be. That's all that matters now."

He nodded. "I guess so. Let's make sure Chloe is okay."

We walked together in silence toward the nearest guard, who pointed us in the right direction, and eventually we found Jinayca and the rest of our friends outside a small building tucked away from everything else.

There were several minutes of hugging and being grateful that we were all in one piece, before Jinayca motioned for us to follow her into the building.

Once inside, Jinayca spoke to a dwarf behind a shop counter. Dozens of rune-inscribed pieces of rock and crystal hung behind him. Jinayca spoke to him and he nodded and lifted up part of the counter, revealing a set of stairs going down under the shop.

We followed them down, torches and crystals lighting the way, until we reached a large cavern several dozen feet beneath the city of Sanctuary.

"What is this place?" I asked.

"Old ruins," Jinayca explained leading us down another set of stairs carved into the rock until we reached a gigantic cavern. Stalactites the size of cars dropped down from the ceiling, and a small stream of water ran along one side.

"Where are we?" Remy asked. "This is essentially the strangest few days of my life. And my life has always been pretty weird."

"This is an old religious temple," Jinayca told us. "Over the centuries, religion mattered less and less to us, so we converted it into somewhere the rune scribes could work in peace. For the most part they transcribed old works we saved from the library, hoping to find a way to locate our lost kin, or remove the blight of the blood elves."

"And sometimes tattoo people, apparently," Kasey said.

"That's also true," Jinayca said with a smile.

We had to walk for a little while before we turned a corner and a temple loomed over us. Seven stories tall, and made from a white brick, the temple was stunning. Dwarves milled about outside it, and there were several balconies where dwarves had stashed large amounts of paper, some of which occasionally fluttered down from high above. At some point, someone had piled it all together outside of the temple. Apparently it wasn't that important, and a closer inspection showed it to be blank.

"We only write on paper or scrolls what we consider to be important," Jinayca told me as I dropped a piece of paper back onto the pile. "Carving into brick or steel is one thing, but paper is too easily transportable, too easy to lose or have taken by someone who shouldn't have it. It's why the library is so important; it has everything we have ever written down. At least, everything before the blood elves came."

"The library: is it still around?" I asked. "The human slave we found, William, said the elves want to get hold of what's inside. But then he tried to kill us, so I'm not really sure what to believe."

"The library still stands. Fortunately, the blood elves can't read the runes."

"So is the library just piles and piles of paper and scrolls?" Remy asked.

"I haven't been there in a long time, but yes, essentially. Different parts of it hold different subjects of varying importance. Unfortunately, we have no idea what else we've left behind. It's why we have so many expeditions—sorry, *had* so many expeditions."

"Why did you stop?" I asked.

"Jinayca!" shouted a dwarf as he left the temple. He was smaller than Jinayca, and with a raggedy ginger beard. He also had the look of someone who was exceptionally tired and really needed a good night's sleep.

"Are these the people for the treatment?" he continued in English. "My name is Stel."

"Treatment?" Remy asked, looking around worriedly.

"My apologies; I've used the wrong word," Stel managed to stammer out, appalled at his mistake.

"It's fine," Diane said, resting a hand on his shoulder. "Just tell us all what we need to do."

Stel nodded. "You'll be taken in one at a time, placed in a chair with your eyes closed. There's a machine in there that will etch a rune into the skin."

"Like a tattoo?" Kasey asked.

Stel frowned, but Jinayca said something in dwarvish, and he nodded enthusiastically. "Yes, just like a tattoo. These aren't permanent, and will come off over time, but while you're here, you'll be able to talk and read the language. You might not be able to read some of the runes; the twenty-one original runes are not included in the machine's ability—for safety reasons."

"How does the machinery work?" I asked as the first in the group, Remy and Diane, went in.

"We don't know," Stel admitted. "It's maybe tens of thousands of years old. We can add the runes we want it to use, and we can sit and watch it work. That's it. No one knows how to actually *get* it to work. It's theorized that the old dwarves, those who came up with the original twenty-one runes, were capable of alchemy that no one else has been able to match. They died long ago, but we've managed to get some of their inventions to work. The crystals that help plants to grow? That was one of theirs. We were able to modify it and use it as we need."

"If it helps, there are things that the Romans and other cultures did that the humans still can't figure out how. Sometimes it just takes one person to spot something."

"Well, we have a lot of time on our hands," Stel said. "We're hoping the great library might hold some secrets, but there are millions of scrolls there: millions upon millions. And some are locked with magic, which should be impossible. There are secrets there we simply can't ever get to. Not now."

The other members of the group got their tattoos and Jinayca took them outside of the temple to wait for the rest. They all said they barely felt anything. As the last two, Kasey and I followed one of the dwarves into the temple and down a hallway until we reached a large room that held what looked like an empty swimming pool. We descended the steps to the floor of the pool and found the machine.

The machine was a block of black stone that reminded me of

an MRI machine. Gears and leavers on either side mystified me, and a golden slab of rock jutted from the front that looked a lot like a seat.

"Please remove your shirt and take a seat," one of three dwarves in the room told me.

I did as I was told, passing my filthy T-shirt to Kasey before climbing onto the golden seat. I lay down with my head just inside the black stone. I heard levers being pulled, and gears whirled as a portion of the black stone opened and slowly lowered until it covered my eyes. Another lever was pulled, and the block moved apart, giving me back my vision. A few seconds later, both sides moved down to my shoulders, the cold stone making me shiver as it touched my skin.

"Can you look up at the rune above the doorway?"

Once again, I followed the orders without pause, and the second I caught a glimpse of the rune in the doorway, my brain was flooded with images and I began to shake.

"What's happening?" I heard Kasey shout.

"We don't know," someone shouted back. "It's not switched on."

I stopped hearing anything as memories tore into my brain with abandon.

CHAPTER 21

416 AD. Dwarven city of Thorem.

I walked into the temple and found it full of people I'd never met. Several adults and more than a dozen dwarves towered over me, discussing secret adult things, but all of them quieted when they saw me. My mother, Brynhildr, and our head bodyguard, Asger, walked on either side of me. My mother's hand on my shoulder squeezed gently when I stopped moving.

I looked at her and smiled. She was radiant—everyone always said so—although there was a tinge of sadness to her, which caused me to be afraid.

"It's going to be alright," she told me with a smile.

I stared down at the pool of red liquid in the center of the room. It appeared to be deep and not at all pleasant.

"That's blood," I said. "Why is there so much of it?"

My mother knelt in front of me and opened her mouth to speak when a large man walked over. She looked up at him, clearly annoyed by the interruption.

"This your boy?" he asked, which was stupid. Of course I was her child, but I said nothing.

"Nathaniel, meet Thor."

Thor got on his knees and offered me his hand, which I shook without pause.

"Nice handshake," he said with a smile. "It's a pleasure to finally meet you, Nathaniel. Can I ask you a question?"

"Be quick," my mother snapped. She looked over to Asger, who walked off to talk to several other adults.

"Did you ever meet your father?" Thor asked, unbothered by my mother's irritation.

"No," I said honestly. "He died when I was born. He was a great warrior, and a good man."

Thor appeared sad. "Yes, he was. Can I give you some advice?"

I nodded again.

"Not everyone here is your friend. Remember that for as long as you can."

I studied all of the people around me, trying to recall any of their faces, but I knew no one except for my mother and Asger.

Thor stood and whispered something to my mother before walking away.

The memory changed, and I began to see everything from outside of my child's body. I looked down and found myself wearing clothes I didn't recognize. I watched the child-me talk to my mother and felt an ache in my chest. I had no idea what had happened to my mother after this meeting. I so wanted to be able to talk to her as the man I'd become, but it wasn't possible. I almost envied the child-me, a notion that quickly made me feel stupid.

"I felt it prudent you watch this from a detached point of view," Erebus said as he stood beside me.

Erebus was the living embodiment of my magic. For all intents and purposes, he *was* me, and he was meant to be evil.

The magic inside of me wanted to be used, to grow in power. It was the same for all sorcerers, but if a sorcerer used too much, too fast, that magic would manifest itself as a living entity inside a sorcerer's mind—a nightmare. The nightmare would use a sorcerer's magic in a way the sorcerer could only dream of, showing him just how powerful he could become if he allowed the nightmare to take complete control. Many had accepted the offer, and then they'd been hunted down and killed for it.

From a young age I'd been told to be terrified of the nightmare, but the blood-magic curse-marks on my chest had stopped the creature from taking control. Over the centuries, I'd allowed the nightmare, Erebus, to take control of my magic. I was playing a dangerous game by even allowing my nightmare to converse with me. The nightmare could gain control of the sorcerer, removing control from the sorcerer over his own body. But something was different about Erebus; he'd saved my life, given me information I needed. Still, I couldn't let my guard down. I wouldn't become a puppet.

"So . . . this is all real?" I asked him. He wore thick furs and held a goblet of drink in one hand. "You look a little out of place."

"They can't see us. You know better than most that you can't affect a memory without repercussions. We're outside of this memory, looking in. I didn't want you to have to go through this as if it were happening for the first time."

"So that's Thor?"

"Yes, Thor. The great warrior, and a danger to those who stand against the Norse gods. I know little of him, because you know little of him. I do know this is the one and only time you meet him."

"These memories were locked from me."

"Everything that happened before this day is locked from you. I assume the walls they'd put up to protect you will begin to crumble."

I searched the room for familiar faces, finding one with ease. "Merlin," I whispered as I watched the young me come face-to-face with the old sorcerer, who laughed and smiled as I spoke to him.

"I told him he wasn't as scary as the stories made out," I said, mostly to myself. Or literally to myself, because Erebus was a part of my mind; it's complicated and makes my head hurt, so I don't like to think about it. "He looks happy. What happened to you, Merlin? When did you become a tyrannical monster?"

"Notice anyone else?"

I looked around for more faces and recognized two more. "Hera and Zeus."

Zeus was talking to a large man whose back was toward me, so I couldn't see what they were discussing, but occasionally I saw Zeus look over to the child-me and smile. He was a broad, tall man, with a visible scar that ran across his throat.

"Legend has it Hera gave him that scar," Erebus said.

"I know," I told him. "I've heard the same thing."

"Sorry, just making conversation. You've been quiet for a while."

"Why was he looking at me? And why is Hera looking so angry?" She looked over to the child-me as he was taken around the room to several dwarves in the corner. "Fear. Why is she afraid of an eight-year-old boy?"

"She's not afraid of you so much as what you represent. What you could become."

"And that is?"

"Why you're here today. Power, Nate: you represent total, undisciplined power. A power she will never be able to corrupt to her needs, and she knows it. And hates you for it. She hates an eight-year-old boy simply because you are too innocent to understand what you could become."

As Erebus spoke the words, I knew automatically that they were true. Hera's expression told me everything I needed to know. "And what is that, exactly? What could I become?"

"Her better."

I was grateful that the child-me had spent so much time looking around at everyone. There were a lot of faces that were dark and clouded over, and the detail on the room wasn't perfect, but I was eight, so I forgave myself pretty easily.

The view changed and we were suddenly beside my mother. "Where did the blood come from?" my mother asked.

I stared at Brynhildr for several seconds, and wished she could know I was there. I had her eyes, especially when they were narrowed in anger. What had they done to remove my memories? What had they done to make my first-ever memory be of waking outside Camelot, beside death and destruction?

"Do you really want to know?" An elderly dwarf asked, his one-time dark beard now peppered with gray.

"Yes. How many did you have to slaughter for this to take place?"

"Hundreds, maybe thousands. The deaths took place in the earth realm. It took a long time to arrange for the two sides to go to war. Even longer to put the runes in place that would transfer the souls of the dead into the soul jars around the room."

Brynhildr rubbed her eyes as I looked around the room and noticed the jars for the first time.

"And the blood?" she asked.

"Animals. The souls are enough to ensure the curse marks will work. Human, dwarf, or cow blood, it really doesn't matter."

"This is unfair."

"I know you're angry," the dwarf snapped, "but you knew this day might come. War is coming, Brynhildr. A war that will not stop until your boy, and those like him, are dead. We need to hide him away from this realm—from any realm. We will give him the power he needs, and then mark his body to keep the rest of his power hidden. There's no other way. Without the marks he will be a beacon for everyone searching for him. Giving him to Merlin to raise is the only way to keep him safe. Avalon can keep your son safe. You cannot."

The words seemed to physically strike my mother, and a tear fell from one of her blue eyes, quickly wiped away before it was too noticeable. "If my son is ever hurt, I will hunt Merlin and you dwarves down. I will find you, and I will feed you your own entrails."

The child-me listened to this with all of the intense concentration an eight-year-old could muster. I remembered not really understanding the problem, although I didn't like the idea of being separated from my mother.

"Say what you need to," the dwarf said, ignoring her threats.

My mother hugged me close as everyone around us departed. "You're a good boy: a strong boy, like your father." She stared across the pool beside us. "I hope one day you get to meet him."

"But he's dead," I pointed out.

My mother smiled. "So he is. Sorry, Nathaniel, my mind is playing tricks. It's been a long few months."

"Do I have to stay with Merlin for long?"

Brynhildr shook her head. "No, not long. But you'll be safe there, and he's going to teach you about your magic, and how to become a soldier. There are lots of other children there your age too. There's a boy called Mordred; he's going to rule Avalon one day. You're going to be staying in the castle with him. I hear he's a nice boy. He sounds a lot like you."

"I'll make sure to say hello," I assured her.

"Good." She hugged me tight and I remembered the feeling of wetness on the back of my neck. "You're such a good boy. I'm so sorry to have to do this to you."

I touched the tear-stained cheeks of my mother. "I promise I'll be brave. I promise I'll make you proud."

She kissed me on the forehead. "You make me proud every single day, Nathaniel. You are the single greatest thing I have ever accomplished, and you will grow up to be a great man, and do great things. And we'll see one another again."

I nodded, and then recalled what she'd said earlier. "You said I wouldn't be there long."

"I know, but just in case."

I nodded, although I didn't really understand, and when my mother kissed the child-me's forehead, I found my hand touching my own in response.

I continued to watch as the child-me was stripped and the blood in the pool was used to draw runes all over my body.

The rest of the ritual was hazy, my child's mind flickering back and forth, ignoring the words being spoken as I was led into the blood bath. I remember being dunked under and told to drink some of it, which I did, although it made me cough and gag. After that it got hazy, the words making the child-me sleepy, but I remember the pain, the agony that coursed through my body as the curse marks burned themselves into my skin. I remember hearing a voice scream out in rage, and thought it was my mother, but I couldn't be certain.

Eventually the room began to darken as chanting and speaking all merged into one, until there was only me lying in a pool of blood, surrounded by an empty void. I remember shaking and panicking as pieces of my memory were obliterated from me, and I fought to hold onto an image of my mother, but it, too, vanished, until there was nothing but darkness.

"What happened here?" I asked.

"They took your memories," Erebus told me. "All of them before the age of eight. You were then placed in a transport with Asger, who took you to Camelot."

"We were attacked on the way; only I survived. Merlin found me outside of the city." A memory of my waking moments flashed into my mind. "Asger was beside me when I woke. He died defending me from . . . I don't know what. He loved my mother, and she loved him. He deserved better than he got."

Erebus nodded. "You remained in the temple for several days after the ritual. You can probably see those memories if you like, although you were barely conscious for nearly all of it."

"Why did they do this to me? Why did my mother?"

"I only know what you know," Erebus said.

"That's beginning to sound like a catchphrase."

"It's true, though. I do not know why they did this, except that there was a war coming, and it was done to protect you."

"I want answers."

"I'm sure you'll get them, although they might not be the ones you want."

"They rarely are."

"You sound angry."

"Merlin knew my mother. He knew her, and he kept her from me. He knew why the marks were on me, and he kept that from me, too. I can't get to him; I can't get answers from him. He'd have me killed. But one day he'll no longer be able to hide in his realm, and I'll get the answers I want."

"I see you gained shadow magic. And now another mark is gone. You're going to lose all of your marks soon."

I looked down to find myself bare-chested, missing yet another black mark. Only two remained. "Now is not the time for the discussion about taking over my body, Erebus. There are still two there."

"Three."

I turned to him. "Where is the third?"

"What do you think keeps you from accessing your child-hood memories? They put a block on them, making you unable to revisit those memories without the right stimulus. When your memories are whole again, when you can recall everything; only then will you truly be the man you were born to be. And only then will I be able to fulfill my role in your life."

"To take control of me? To use me as your puppet? I don't think so."

"You have no idea what I am, what all of us really are. You still believe that the magic inside of sorcerers is there to corrupt and destroy its user. You do not believe me when I tell you otherwise." He paused for a second. "It appears constraints on me have been removed. The loss of those marks is making my connection to your subconscious more powerful."

"What does that mean?" I asked, slightly concerned.

"It means I can tell you that you've been lied to, your whole life. Every sorcerer born in the last two thousand years has been lied to. I don't know the reason why. I don't know when it first started, but the magic inside of you is not your ruin. It's not your damnation. It is your birthright. It is the only way for you to be truly whole."

CHAPTER 22

September 1195. City of Acre.

I punched Mordred in the face. I'd asked a simple question about why Isabel had been turned into a vampire, and why they'd then sent her back to us, and all Mordred did was snarl and threaten me. It had gotten old, and frankly I was bored with it.

Gilgamesh wrapped his massive arms around me and dragged me away to the far corner of the room. "Stay here." It wasn't a suggestion.

I thought about disobeying him, but in the long run it would only cause more trouble, and I needed answers more than I needed to pummel Mordred into a fine paste. I left the room, allowing Gilgamesh, Irkalla, and Nabu to complete their questions, and walked over to Nanshe, who was sat alone.

"You okay?" I asked.

"Asag is in the city," she told me. "He escaped and killed his guards. He fled into the city. More death and destruction. I'm getting exceptionally tired of it. Tired of listening to Mordred's babbling, too."

"He's hard work, isn't he?"

"Was he like that when you were friends?"

I shook my head. "Nothing about the current man is the same as he was when we were friends."

"He still asked to see you when he was captured, though. He was quite insistent, and wouldn't talk to anyone else."

I got up and walked back into Mordred's prison, just as Gilgamesh was leaving. "Did you know that Isabel wasn't going to be killed?" I asked Mordred.

"No," Mordred admitted. "I didn't know they would turn her instead. I believe that was probably the plan all along. I doubt they wanted you to find her so quickly, though. Putting a newly awakened vampire in the city would have resulted in carnage."

"Yes, it would have," I agreed. "I think that was the plan. We split our troops into those manning the walls, dealing with a vampire, dealing with Siris, and dealing with Asag, not to mention those who still guard you, and anyone cleaning up the fake knights and their mess. That's a lot for the guard to undertake."

"They're stretching us thin," Nabu said.

"Yes. While our resources are all over the place, they'll attack. I wouldn't be surprised if they do something else to take our attention away from the defense of the city."

"Tiamat's children," Nanshe said. "That's what you told us those knights were after. Unleashing her children."

"They're safety locked away in another realm," Nabu said. "Been that way for a long time."

"So what does Acre have in its boundaries that they think would allow them to bring her children into this realm?" I asked.

"The catacombs," Nanshe said. "There are lots of old relics down there—maybe something that might help them. Or help us."

"How far beneath the city are the catacombs?" I asked, as I saw Mordred smirk.

"Quite far," Nanshe confirmed. "And it would take a lot of effort to find anything they were searching for. Those things go on forever. It's a maze of corridors and rooms, and it's been abandoned for centuries."

"Any chance there's a realm gate down there?"

Nabu nodded. "It's possible. It's been a long time since anyone used those catacombs."

"What *were* they used for?" I asked.

"All sorts of things," Nanshe continued. "Certainly nothing that suggests—wait. The map that you said Siris had destroyed: what did it look like? Be exact."

I explained it as best I could. "See, there was nothing much," I said when I'd finished. "The knights who went there should have it, though."

Nanshe ran off, seemingly concerned about what we'd found.

"Anyone else think Siris had a map to the catacombs, raise your hand," Mordred said, and put his hand in the air.

I looked over at Mordred. "You're coming with Irkalla and me. We're going to go to the catacombs."

"Nabu, you're going to have to reinforce the defenses. That attack is probably coming tonight."

Mordred raised his hand in my direction. "You planning on removing my sorcerer's band?"

Nabu removed a key from his person and unlocked it. "Ah, that feels good," Mordred said. "Say, here's a thought. Where's Gilgamesh?"

"He went back to Isabel," Nabu said to me, refusing even to acknowledge Mordred.

"Oh, Nabu, come on. Just because I wanted to kill you and everyone you loved, that's no reason for you to be rude."

"Mordred, if you do anything to jeopardize this city, or our lives, I will end you," I said.

"Nate, your threats are worthless. We've done this dance. You're no more likely to kill me now than you were the second we met. You remember that? You didn't know who you were, and you were eight: all scared and pathetic."

I swallowed my reply. "Where's the catacomb entrance?"

"The best way to get there is from a building close to the marina," Nabu said. "The guard have discovered a few people in the city who apparently see it as a . . . a place away from visible eyes."

"People go there to fuck, Nathan," Mordred said, raising his hands in mock surrender when everyone glared at him. "Just explaining things in case you didn't get it."

I ignored him. "Can you lead the way?"

Irkalla nodded.

Mordred stood and stretched. "I need to give something back to Siris, and frankly, I don't trust you to get the job done properly. You didn't exactly do a great job with Asag."

"I'm beginning to regret saying you can come," I told Mordred.

"I know the catacombs. I know the way around. Without me, and without a map, you'll be running around in circles."

I sighed. "My patience is not infinite, Mordred. Do anything to push it, and—"

"What? You'll kill me?" he said with a laugh.

"I'll ensure that Isabel is in the front line of the fighting when it starts."

Mordred's smile dropped. "Don't threaten her."

"If you behave, you'll give me no reason to, understand?"

He nodded, but continued to glare at me.

"Will you and Irkalla be needing time together?" Mordred asked as we left his prison, and got back into the open air—something I was grateful for. "I'm sure I can give you a little moment together."

"Yes, Mordred, we've all stopped listening to you," Irkalla said.

We'd just turned the corner when Nanshe came running toward us, several Templar knights in tow. "That map: it's of the catacombs," she said, confirming our theory. "Better still, I had to go through lots of burned scroll, but unfortunately I found a few pieces that were almost intact."

"Why 'unfortunately?'"

She handed it to me; it had writing on it. "I don't understand it."

"It says 'Tiamat,'" Nabu said from beside me. "So, they're not after her children. They really believe that Tiamat is under this city?"

"That doesn't sound like good news," Mordred said.

"She's dead," Nabu insisted. "I saw her die. Her corpse was turned to ash and scattered to the wind in another realm. The guardian who opened the realm died four thousand years ago. He walked away from the protection and allowed himself to grow old and die. Whatever they're after down there, it's not Tiamat."

"Either way, we need to figure it out."

"Several more Teutonic Knights are waiting for you at the entrance," Nanshe said. "I assume you were going to use the one by the marina?"

"Everyone knows about the love den," Mordred said with a laugh.

I was about to wish everyone good luck when an explosion rocked the ground. Smoke and flame could be seen in the distance, followed by a second and third explosion.

"They're coming as soon as the sun sets," I told Nanshe. I looked up at the setting sun. "Be ready."

"We won't let them win," she assured me.

"I don't think you have a lot of choice," Mordred said. "But if you could make sure *we* don't die, that would be grand."

"I get why you want him dead," Irkalla told me before we began running.

"What will you do with Isabel once this is over?" Mordred asked as we reached our destination. The entrance to the catacombs was a wooden door in the side of a hill, close to the ocean. It had been overgrown at one point, although it was obvious that people had trimmed it all away and just placed dozens of branches in front of it, branches that currently sat scattered across the sand.

"Nothing. She's free to do as she wishes." I had nothing against her, and she'd committed no crimes that I could see. "She's a vampire. That isn't an offense."

I pushed open the door and found ten knights inside a huge room that had been built into the hill. There was a faint aroma of perfumes that lingered in the air. The evidence of several small fires dotted around the room, long since extinguished, but ready at a moment's notice for anyone who wished to take someone to a secluded spot.

"Gentlemen, I believe we have a hunt on our hands," I said. "We're after a rock monster by the name of Asag. If you find him, cut his head off, because this time I'd like him to stay dead."

They said, "Yes, sir!" in unison. It was somewhat unnerving in such a confined place.

"Also, Siris is probably down there, too. I'd like her alive. I have questions."

"I, on the other hand would like to tear her eyes out," Mordred said, "so either or, really."

"Mordred is not in any way part of your command," I told the knights. "If he does anything to jeopardize this mission, kill him. Otherwise, he takes the lead and shows us the way."

"Is this a good idea?" Irkalla asked.

"Not even slightly," I admitted as Mordred walked over to the far end of the room and opened a hatch in the floor, revealing stairs leading down. "But it's all we have right now."

As the city began to burn and my allies prepared for a battle that was all but certain to happen, I descended the staircase with Mordred in the lead. I hadn't trusted him in centuries, and had been trying to kill him for most of those, but now I had no choice. Yet once it was done, once this threat had been ended, I would end Mordred, too. He was simply too dangerous to leave alive. And I was certain he was planning to do the same to me.

We'd been in the catacombs for several hours, finding nothing more than some very large rats and the occasional skeleton, when we came across the first vampire. He'd sat in the darkness, in complete stillness and silence, watching us approach. I'd long since changed my vision to be able to see in the dark, but most of the knights and even Mordred and Irkalla were seeing things only by the light of the torches they held.

No one had seen the vampire, not even after the hiss had left his mouth, and he'd begun walking toward us. The slight movement in the shadows was my first indication that something was coming and I responded accordingly. The vampire ran headfirst into a plume of flame that cooked it. It dropped to the ground, rolling and screaming before Mordred drew a sword from the belt of a knight and decapitated it.

Mordred gave the sword back to the knight, not even bothering to wipe the blood from the blade, and shrugged at me.

"We probably don't want to make a lot of noise," he said and we resumed our search.

I couldn't really argue with what had happened, because I'd have done the same. The very fact that I agreed with Mordred's violent act didn't make me feel good.

We turned corner after corner and fought another half-dozen vampires. We couldn't help the noise. We'd lost no one, though; the Teutonic Knights had killed a lot of vampires in their lives, probably with more enthusiasm than some would have liked, but they were a boon to have alongside us.

We opened the doors to several rooms, and gave them a cursory search, but most contained nothing more than skeletons, old pottery, tools long past useful condition, and dirt.

"Do you know the way or not?" Irkalla asked Mordred, irritated after we'd opened the door to the fifth empty room.

"Yes, I just thought that you'd like to see some of your people again. You probably know a few of them. Any relations?"

Irkalla balled her hands into fists. "Get on with it."

Mordred nodded and we resumed our search. Eventually, the sounds of voices grew louder, and we began to see the flickering of lights, probably torches.

We had to stay far back in the darkness, around a corner, so that the vampires patrolling the area couldn't see us.

"They can't be very old," I said. "Those vampires can't smell us."

"How do we remove them before they alert whoever is down there?"

I peered around the corner. "I count five." They were patrolling the mouth of the corridor, and after a slight drop, a large open area beyond. I continued watching for a few more seconds until I saw Asag walk across the middle of the large room.

"Asag is in there," I reported.

"Then we need to go kill him," Mordred said. "Now."

Before anyone could stop him, Mordred sprinted down the tunnel, screaming something that I was certain to him sounded like a war cry. He collided with the first vampire, using a blade of air to remove its head, before blasting a second in the chest with enough force to almost tear the creature apart. The rest of the group ran after him, and soon the knights and remaining vampires were engaged in battle, while Mordred killed whatever was in front of him in his quest to get to Asag.

I dropped down from the tunnel into the large area and found that the gold and silver brick and stone looked a lot more dwarven than the rest of the catacombs. The area sat on two levels, with pillars—most two or three times higher than a man—at regular intervals on both levels.

"The dwarves made this," Siris told me as she walked out of a nearby door, closing it behind her just as I caught a glimpse of a small stone tablet on the floor, but I saw no realm gate. She held a spear in one hand. "I could see you were curious."

Mordred, who was almost at Asag, saw Siris and changed direction, diving toward her. Forced back, Siris retreated into the shadows, vanished into the soil, and reappeared behind Asag a few seconds later.

"Did you really think I didn't know why you were here, Mordred?"

"I don't really care," Mordred almost snarled.

"You have no idea what we're going to achieve here, but you will. Kill them all."

Vampires flooded the cavern from the floor above, dozens and dozens of them, while Siris ran into a nearby room, slamming the door shut behind her.

"Time for you and me to go again," Asag said to me, as the vampires and knights continued to fight. The undead now vastly outnumbered the knights, but Irkalla joined in, helping the odds.

"Mordred, Asag first, then Siris. Do you understand?" I really hoped he did.

Mordred repeatedly stabbed a vampire in the face, decapitated it then kicked the body aside. He shrugged. "I'll kill what I have to. Try not to get too close to me. I'm not exactly sure I'll be able to judge foe from different foe."

"Two sorcerers at once?" Asag laughed. "This will be fun."

Mordred darted forward first, trying to cut through the rocky exterior with his blade of air, but it was never going to work, and he narrowly avoided a blow to the head, which instead destroyed part of one of the pillars.

I took Asag's diverted attention to try a similar trick, but with a blade of fire, hoping to cut through the gaps in the rock like I'd done last time, but he shifted his weight and lashed out at me.

"No more fire magic like last time," he said to me.

"You don't have your little friends to help," I replied, after rolling aside to put plenty of distance between us.

Mordred attacked once again, this time wrapping a tendril of blood magic around Asag's chest. The large rock monster began to yell, and I rushed to join the attack, wrapping my fist in dense air and striking Asag in the face. It sent him reeling, but he kicked me in the chest and I soared into the far wall.

I scrambled back to my feet in time to watch Asag take hold of Mordred and head-butt him. Mordred's face turned into a geyser of blood, and he, too, was tossed aside as if we were both nothing more than a minor inconvenience.

"This isn't working too well," Mordred said after landing beside me, spitting blood onto the dirt.

"I have a plan," I said, "but I'm not sure how much you'll like it."

"If it lets me bathe in his tears, I'll be pretty happy, thanks."

Asag slowly walked toward us. He didn't appear to be all that concerned.

"How cold can you make your water magic?" I asked.

"Pretty damn cold."

I stared at Mordred for a heartbeat. It had been a long time since we'd fought side by side. It was an odd but familiar feeling. "When I'm ready, pour everything you have into the bastard, and let's see if we can't crack him open."

I began using my air magic to swirl the dirt around Asag's feet.

"That's it?" He laughed. "A light breeze?"

He looked over at the fighting between the vampires and knights, which had moved back into the tunnel, their shouts and screams occasionally echoing around. I couldn't see Irkalla, but I was certain she was in no more danger than Mordred and I were.

I moved around to the side of the room, keeping the air swirling around Asag's feet. When he got too close to Mordred, I blasted his side with air, forcing him to step back, regaining his attention, and allowing Mordred enough time to get away.

"You're not dying over there, are you?" I asked.

"I'm good," Mordred snapped. "I only had the sorcerer's band removed a short time ago, and getting head-butted by that sack of rocks hurts like the blazes."

I increased the ferocity of the wind, picking up loose pieces of brick and debris, and flung them at Asag, angering him. As the winds increased in speed, Asag slowed down, so I continued to pour on the pressure. He took another step, and I changed my attack, creating tornadoes all around him, not just around his legs.

"Now!" I yelled. Mordred blasted water from his hands into my maelstrom encircling Asag. I cooled the air, lower and lower, almost to the point of freezing.

"Do you have a plan after this?" Mordred asked as Asag stopped walking.

Not even slightly. "Of course."

"You feel like sharing? Because I'm not sure that making rocks colder makes them easier to break."

"Good thing that was never the plan, then," I told him. "I need you to freeze him in place."

"You're going to remove your air magic?" Mordred asked, his voice rising as the sound of the magic being poured out of us became louder and louder.

"Yes, the air and water were to keep him in one place. The water magic should be stretched all over him. Hopefully it'll freeze those cracks between the rocks. His skin has to feel that."

"And then what are you going to do?"

"You'll see."

Mordred took over the magic duties as I removed my air magic and began concentrating. Orange glyphs burned across my skin as I created the power of my fire magic, but the second I heard the ice cracking as Asag took a step, I knew I didn't have time.

Mordred grabbed hold of my hand, wiping his blood onto it. "Use that. I'll keep him off you."

I immediately used the blood to access my blood magic, pouring the excess power into the fire glyphs, and created a small ball of flame. It grew in size again and again, becoming hotter and hotter until it was so bright I could barely stand to look at it.

Mordred flew over my head, bloody and beaten, and crashed into the wall behind me as Asag laughed. I looked up and our eyes met only for a second, but he paused.

I shot up from the floor, increasing the size of the ball of flame and releasing it. The fire hit Asag, a blinding inferno that momentarily engulfed him. I stepped into the flame, turning my hands white-hot, and planted them on Asag's chest. The rock around my hands turned to magma, oozing to the side and exposing a bit of the flesh beneath. I gathered the fire roaring around us, and in one motion smashed it into his exposed torso.

Asag's screams were horrific. He clawed at himself trying to get to the fire that I'd put under the layer of rock armor, against his skin, melting it like a candle. I dropped to my knees, stopping my magic for a moment before Mordred threw more air magic at the monster, making it trip into a column which collapsed onto its head.

Asag roared with pain and anger, tossing aside pieces of brick as he clawed his way along the ground, toward the door that Siris had run through. I'd forgotten about Siris, and sighed while getting back to my feet, ready for another fight—one I probably couldn't win, even with Mordred's help. We needed Irkalla, and I was thankful to see her drop down from the mouth of the tunnel, her clothes covered in blood.

"It's not mine," she said by way of explanation. "The vampires are dead. They were newly turned, not very powerful. We lost most of the knights, though. Where is Asag?" She followed the noise of him hammering against the door, trying to get Siris to open it.

"Why is he still alive?" she asked.

"We were getting to that." I got back to my feet. "He's not exactly a pushover."

"Nor is he going anywhere," Mordred said as he staggered past us. "He's mine."

Mordred had made it halfway to Asag when the door exploded open, and a giant snake's head, easily the height of my entire body, grabbed hold of Asag, dragging him back into the room. A second snake's head crashed through the wall. It hissed at us before slithering up toward the ceiling.

"Not Tiamat!" I shouted. "What is that?"

"That is an exceptionally bad time for everyone in the city," Irkalla told me. "Keep it busy. We'll need help."

She ran toward the tunnel, leaving Mordred and me alone as the first snake re-appeared. I ignited hooks of air as the serpent moved past me up toward the hole his friend was making. I hooked the snake and held on with all I had as it smashed through everything between us and the city above, finally exploding out of the ground and shrieking its arrival for all to hear.

I looked down at Mordred, who, with his air magic, had anchored himself to the black and white scales of the huge beast.

"Do you have a plan?" Mordred shouted as the snake fell

onto a nearby building, flattening it without so much as a concern as it continued to slither out of the hole it had made.

"Kill the snakes! Don't die!" I shouted back, finally able to see the whole snake. It was huge, longer than a galley ship, and could probably eat one in only a few bites.

"I like the second bit more," Mordred said, and he dropped from the snake onto the ground, fleeing into the darkness. He would have to wait.

I removed the air magic in one hand and created a blade of fire, plunging it into the snake, which it did not appreciate. It turned to me and opened its mouth, striking forward with incredible speed. Its fangs, almost my equal in height, were inches from me as I jumped off the snake and sprinted toward the marina, hoping to find somewhere I might get an advantage, or at least find it Mordred to eat.

I turned onto a cobbled street along the water's edge, running past boats that bobbed up and down in the waves. The snake destroyed a building, the screams of the occupants silenced as quickly as they'd started.

I vaulted over overturned barrels and tables, dodging people as they scrambled away for their lives, many risking the rough, cold water and diving straight in. But the snake only had eyes for me, and occasionally I would annoy it further by throwing balls of fire at it.

After several minutes of avoiding being eaten, I was beginning to run out of street, but as I looked toward the water, I noticed one of several war galleys anchored at the far end of the marina. Then the reappearance of the snake took all of my attention.

Several pots hit the snake, and it took me a few seconds

to realize they were filled with oil. They covered the head and ground surrounding the snake. A ball of flame came in soon after, hitting the snake, and the whole area went up like kindling.

I stopped running and watched the snake thrash about, bringing down more buildings as it fought to extinguish the flames. The snake's screams made my skin crawl, but they were silenced as it threw itself across a small fishing boat and into the water.

"That should keep her busy," Mordred said as he ran over to me. "You got my plan then, to bring the snake to the ship?"

"You never mentioned any kind of plan or a ship," I snapped. "I thought you were running away."

"Not while Siris still lives."

He ran off without another word, and I followed a moment later, wondering how long we had before the burned one returned, looking for revenge.

CHAPTER 23

September 1195. City of Acre.

After managing to at least subdue the first giant snake, Mordred and I ran through the city streets toward the noise of the second.

"Do you have a plan?" he shouted to me.

I shook my head in response. I had no idea how to kill a giant snake. I'd never even seen one, but apparently setting one on fire does little more than really annoy it and make it go for a swim.

By the time we reached the second snake, rubble surrounded it. It had crashed through several buildings, tearing them apart and scattering the contents over a wide area. Every time a new building got hit, tremors went through the ground, as if from an earthquake. The smell of dust and blood mixed in the air, and the closer we got to the snake, the more dead we saw littering the ground. The people who'd been in those buildings when the snake had attacked had no chance of escaping.

Nanshe and Irkalla were fighting the snake, trying to get close enough to hurt it. Nanshe tore a chunk of rock from the ground and threw it at the creature's head, but the rock disintegrated on impact. The snake acted mildly irritated. It swayed from side to side, before shooting forward at Nanshe, but she was too fast and ducked under its chin, stabbing her sword up into the snake's mouth. Several vampires had dropped from the battlements to try to stop Nanshe, but Irkalla was killing them before they could get close enough to do damage.

When half a dozen of the vampires were dead, Irkalla shuddered, then turned toward the snake and unleashed the souls she'd absorbed as pure energy. The snake's head vanished in a plume of blood and gore. Its body fell to the ground and, after a brief twitch, remained still.

Nanshe, covered head to toe in snake blood, picked her sword off the floor. "That could have gone easier. A lot of people lost their lives to this insanity."

"Any ideas where she's gone?"

She shook her head, and the first snake, which I'd mentally nicknamed Cinder, took that moment to make its presence known once again by crashing through several buildings closer to the water. Its massive bulk was easy to see, even from the distance we were from it.

"Stay here, and help stop anyone from coming through," I said. "Mordred and I will go after the snake."

"First, Isabel," he said as he ran off in the direction of her cell.

"Damn it, Mordred!" I shouted as I followed. "We don't have time for this!"

"We need help; she's a vampire. She can help."

It was obvious something was very wrong the moment we reached the building where Isabel was being held. Mordred destroyed the door with a blast of air and descended the steps without pause. I followed close behind and found Isabel kneeling in front of Siris, facing us, Siris's blade held to her throat.

"Oh, you're early," Siris said. "I was going to leave this one here for you to find. If you managed to live long enough that is. You killed Mušhuššu, but you won't kill Bašmu."

"Ah, I called him Cinder," I told her. "That's because we set him on fire. So, I'm thinking that Cinder, or Bašmu, or whatever you want to call him, can die just like Mušhuššu. It's a shame. You went through all that effort to bring Tiamat's creations here just to have them die."

"She didn't create them outright, but she certainly helped. They have dragon blood in their veins. Did you know that combining dragon blood with various dark magics will create monstrous versions of beasts?"

"I do now."

"If you harm her, I will tear you apart," Mordred said.

"Ah, yes, your favorite. Did you really think I didn't know why you agreed to help, Mordred? I've known you for so long, even before you became the man you were."

"I know you visited me, hurt me."

I had no idea what either of them were talking about, but that giant snake wasn't about to kill itself. "There's nowhere for you to run, Siris."

"There's always somewhere, Hellequin. Always."

"Too late now," I told her. "Put the blade down and leave here quietly."

"Or I can do this," she said, and she slit Isabel's throat, before plunging the weapon into her heart. Blood poured from the wound in her neck and Mordred rushed to her, trying to stop the bleeding. Siris used her earth-elemental ability to run toward the wall beside her, vanishing into the soil a moment later.

"Help me!" Mordred pleaded.

I looked down at Isabel and knew she was dead. "No one can help her now."

"*Liar!*" Mordred screamed at me. "You could have stopped Siris! You could have made sure this didn't happen!"

I removed the blade from Isabel's chest; it was made of silver, so there really was no hope. A silver blade in the heart of a vampire meant death.

"Mordred—" I started, but a blast of air threw me against the wall. Mordred picked up the blade and ran up the stairs.

I ran after him, and watched him run into the city, away from Bašmu, who was tearing apart several buildings. I left Mordred; the snake was the more immediate problem. I ran toward the monster, using my blood magic to power the fire inside of me. When I was close enough, I entered the nearest building and ascended to the roof.

I aimed a ball of flame at the snake and threw it, hoping it would notice. The second the flame hit, the snake looked my way. I got the impression that it recognized me, because it barreled toward me, knocking dozens of soldiers aside as they tried to slow it down.

"That's right, you big scaly bastard: come fight me!"

The snake reared up taller than the three-story building I was on. I was forced to look up at its opening mouth, its long tongue tasting the air. It struck with incredible speed, and I used my air magic to propel me up above its head. The snake was smart, and tried to move out of the way, but I adjusted my trajectory and landed on top of its head. I ignited a blade of fire, and using the power I'd built up with the blood magic, plunged it down into the brain of the snake. I released the fire blade and did it again, pouring more and more white-hot flame into the wound as the snake bucked and twisted, before collapsing onto the rooftop, crushing the building beneath its weight.

I lay on top of the snake for some time, before finally sliding off onto the rubble just as Irkalla arrived.

"You cooked it," she said, tapping the snake's mouth. "It's warm."

"It's dead, too," I said. "So is Isabel."

"Yes, I heard. I'm not entirely sure this worked out the way Siris wanted."

"She wanted you all dead, so I'm guessing not so much."

"We have the lead vampire under our control: the one who turned so many of those who attacked us. He's nothing special, not even a master. We'll interrogate him and find out what he knows. Siris isn't going to give up; she'll come back at some point. But we annoyed her today, and today is what counts."

She offered me her hand, and I took it as I got back to my feet. We walked back to Nanshe and Nabu, who were busy helping the injured.

I spent the next few hours helping those who needed it, which meant first and foremost making sure those who were hurt but alive didn't succumb to their wounds. After watching more people die, it didn't really feel like much of a victory, and when I finally got to my bed that night, I mourned for those who had lost their lives. Siris would be found and she would be punished, but it was something Nanshe and her people needed to do, not Avalon. It was something I was certain they'd want to handle themselves.

"The snakes weren't as powerful as I'd expected," I said to Nanshe the next morning when I entered her home.

"Good morning to you too," she said with a smile. Nabu and Irkalla were already seated at the table, each of them eating a plate of fruit and meat.

Nanshe offered me a plate and I gratefully accepted. I was famished, and quickly made my way through a vast amount of food.

"The snakes were fresh out of their prison realm," Nabu said. "I honestly thought they were dead. Apparently, merely hibernating."

There was a small stone tablet inside his robe, and he caught me looking at it, pushing it into an inside pocket.

"Could they have used something other than a realm gate?" I asked.

"No such thing exists," Nabu said. "From what I can gather, the gate was destroyed by the snakes' emergence. There's nothing left of it."

I got the feeling there was something he wasn't telling me, but it had been a long few days for everyone, and maybe it was just that everyone was exhausted.

"How many casualties?" I asked Nanshe.

"No idea at the moment. Lots. Hundreds, if not thousands, dead."

"I'm sorry about what happened here. And now Mordred has escaped. This is not the finest job I've ever undertaken."

"More survived than died," Nabu said. "Gilgamesh has taken it upon himself to hunt down Siris. She will be caught and punished."

"Not by Avalon," I said, giving voice to my previous thoughts. "It's too early in the alliance. It needs to be seen that Avalon will allow you all to continue with your own governance. If Avalon came in and killed her, it will look like you can't take care of your own problems, and that Avalon will interfere the second we disagree with an ally's method of dealing with their issues."

Irkalla placed a hand on my arm. "There are no traces of Mordred. He's lost to the wind."

"He'll turn up; he always does. Sooner or later, he'll want to come after me, or someone else. Right now, Isabel's murder has given him a new purpose: killing Siris and those backing her."

"People like Nergal?" Nabu asked. "We know he was involved, but he was never here. We wouldn't have won if he had been."

"No one gets this far in a plot like this without help—a lot more help than one person can offer. Too many things could have gone wrong. There's another realm, a lot of people willing to die for her cause, training, money, and above all, power. Someone helped her: someone with influence. I don't know their motives, but I expect they'll turn up again, so be on the lookout."

"Are you going to stay in the city?" Irkalla asked.

I shook my head. "I'm going back to Avalon. I want to make sure no one tries to disrupt anything when you arrive."

"I'll be going myself in the next few days," Irkalla said. "I would appreciate the company."

"It would be my pleasure. First, I wish to pay my respects to those who died."

"The burial will be tonight," Nabu told me. "You're welcome to come."

I stood. "Thank you. Until then, I'll take my leave."

I left the three of them to their breakfast and went out into the city. Those responsible for what had happened were still out there. Mordred was still out there, and I wasn't sure exactly why Isabel had been killed, other than to piss him off. Siris had a lot to answer for, and I really hoped I'd never lay eyes on her again.

But if I did, I'd make sure she didn't get away; some people don't deserve a second chance. Some people deserve to be removed as a blight on this world, and Siris had nailed herself to the top of that list.

I hoped Gilgamesh was up to the task of finding her. I doubted she'd make it easy, but more than that, I doubted she would quit.

CHAPTER 24

Now. Dwarven city of Thorem.

I woke up in a white room, looking up at the ceiling. There was no machine or temple anywhere to be found, and for the briefest of moments I wondered where the hell I'd been taken.

I forced myself upright and swung my legs off the bed. Two runes were inscribed in the room's door, which was certainly dwarven in design, so I couldn't have been taken too far. The runes said *silence* and *monitor,* and both were glowing a faint blue color.

"I can read runes," I said to myself, although it came out as a whisper. The room seemed somehow to muffle sound. "Gotta say, that's a bit weird."

"It's a dampener," Jinayca said as she opened the door. "The monitor rune is so we can hear you speak and check on your vitals without having to come in and out. Also, you're not speaking English."

"Yeah, I figured that bit out," I admitted, and lifted my T-shirt to see that another of my blood-curse marks had vanished. "How long was I out?"

"Long enough for several of your friends to argue with our doctors about not wanting to leave you, and then argue with them some more about Chloe."

"How is she?"

"Aren't you going to ask how you are first?"

"Don't much care how I am, Jinayca. I'm alive, and can apparently read and understand dwarven runes, along with being able to speak your language without trouble. We'll figure me out later. Chloe first."

"We got you some fresh clothes, if you'd like to change?"

I shook my head. "Chloe."

Jinayca led me through a hallway and into a large room with several chairs and two doors.

"Where are we?"

"Away from the temple, back up on the main level of Sanctuary. We weren't really sure what to do with you."

"Where are my friends?"

"I'll contact them and let them know you're awake. I advise you to change your clothes once you're done here, and come meet me at the elders' building. We have things we need to discuss."

You have no idea, I thought to myself. I wanted to ask about the temple, about my memory, my mother, and anything else that came to mind, the second I'd seen Jinayca. But Chloe was more important. She was the only one of us who was hurt, and there was no way I was leaving anyone behind when we left. If she was getting worse, or if the dwarves needed something to help her, I wanted to know. I needed to know how to make her better before I worried about myself.

I sat alone in the room, my anxiety rising with every second no one came to speak to me, and just as I was about to go find someone who might hurry things along, two dwarves walked in. The first was male, his beard trimmed short and his head shaved;

the second was a female with long, red, plaited hair. Both carried no visible weapons and wore simple tunics and trousers.

"Nate Garrett?" the female dwarf asked.

I nodded.

"My name is Grundelwy," she told me. "And this is Jurg. We're the physicians who have been attending to your friend Chloe."

"How is she doing?" I asked, feeling the lump in my chest move toward my throat.

"Not good, Mr. Garrett," Jurg told me.

"As you know Chloe has been poisoned," Grundelwy began. "The venom itself would be quite mild in someone who had a healing ability above and beyond that of a normal human. But Chloe, for all her witch magic, is human. This venom is attacking her body, and she's getting worse. The venom will keep attacking her until she dies."

"Is there a cure?"

The two dwarves glanced at one another. "There is, yes," Jurg said, "but not in the way you think. Her only chance is to use magic to increase her healing ability."

"What about runes on her skin?" I asked.

"That might work if she were conscious long enough for them to take effect, and she was able to activate them herself, but with her being in and out of consciousness, placing them on her skin would make things a lot worse. The activation would have to be done by an external person, and that, too, could have dire consequences. Basically, drawing powerful enough runes on Chloe in her current state could kill her. On top of that, her witch magic means she can't be healed by normal magical means. They're not compatible."

"What's your plan?" I really hoped the plan had something concrete. I'd be okay if it was something I could hit repeatedly until it gave up what Chloe needed.

"Spirit scrolls," Jurg said.

"What?" The words suddenly jolted something loose. "Wait, Zamek said something about those. What are they?"

"Jinayca can explain better. She was with the detachment of people who were tasked to recover them from the blood elves. Until we lost them, very few dwarves were allowed to know of their creation. But essentially, they're rune-scribed scrolls that have been infused with the power of spirits."

"When someone bleeds on it, it creates a contract between the person and the spirits inside the scroll," Grundelwy said. "From that moment on the spirits and the user are bonded until the user dies, for however long that might be. But in the short term those spirits would give enough power to Chloe so that she could heal herself."

"This all sounds very vague," I pointed out.

"It is," Jurg admitted. "Jinayca will want to talk to you about them."

"Can I see Chloe?"

They nodded in unison and led me into a smaller room like the one I'd woken up in. Chloe lay in bed with runes inscribed all around the base. One of them pulsated in red, in time with her heartbeat.

"I thought you said runes would kill her," I whispered.

"Runes on her body. They're healing runes, but only in the sense that they are slowing the progression of the venom and keeping Chloe stable. They're stopping the pain, too."

"Thank you both," I said and they left the room.

"Hey," I said to Chloe as I sat beside her.

She opened her eyes and smiled. "Kasey came in earlier," she said, her voice weak. "Said I looked like shit."

"That depends on how you view *zombie* as a skin color."

Chloe chuckled. "I'm not feeling so great, Nate."

I took her hand in mine, and she squeezed. "We're going to get you some help, and then we're going to get you home. All you have to do is stay here and let these people wait on you hand and foot. We'll be back before you know it."

Chloe smiled and closed her eyes. I panicked for a second, before realizing she was falling asleep. I laid her hand down and ignited my fire magic, turning my finger hotter and hotter, until the fire that surrounded it burned white. I held it against the end of the bed, pressing it into the stone until it burned a pattern there.

It was only when I'd finished that the physicians ran into the room asking me what I was doing.

"Your stone doesn't stop magic here," I said, "so I helped out."

Jurg walked over to the end of the bed and stared at the burned rune I'd carved there, his mouth dropped open in shock.

"What is it?" Grundelwy asked as I walked toward her.

"It's—"

"It's one of the twenty-one original runes," I told her. "It says *power*. It'll increase what the runes on the bed can do. I hope it's enough."

"How do you know our runes?" Jurg demanded. He sounded both irritated that I knew them, and more than a little shocked.

"Apparently the dwarves put them in my head," I told him.

"It was a long time ago, and I've just learned that I know your entire language. Unfortunately, that's the only rune that might actually help. Do you have any more serious patients?"

They both shook their heads and, after one last glance at Chloe, I left. I went back to my own room and changed into the black and dark-blue leather armor they'd left for me. There were small overlocking scales on the inside, and while it looked heavy, it appeared to weigh no more than a T-shirt and trousers would. Dwarven armor was regarded as the finest ever created. I'd heard tell of it stopping an arrow and spear, and of it taking a blow from a mace. I was happy to be wearing the leather breastplate, jacket, and the boots. I got the feeling this was more than just a gift of a clean set of clothes. No doubt I'd need these protective qualities soon enough.

I left the hospital and walked through the city, receiving stares from those I passed by, with the occasional nod from others. So many dwarves just going about their business, living day by day, even with the very real fear of a blood-elf attack. If nothing else, dwarven resilience was impressive to behold.

The guards allowed me admittance to the elders' building, and I soon remembered the way to the chamber where we'd first met Jinayca. One of three guards opened the door for me with a curt nod, and I found myself smiling at a room full of friends.

"We were worried about you," Kasey said, embracing me as I entered the room.

"I'm fine. Just worried about Chloe," I told everyone, stopping questions about my condition before they started.

The silence lasted for only a few seconds before Mordred said, "Lost another curse mark?"

"Yes," I told him. "Apparently I can read runes now. It's very exciting."

"Where did you get that knowledge?" a familiar voice asked from the side of the room.

I turned in the direction of the voice and saw Irkalla. She looked identical to the last time I saw her, and wore a dark-blue sleeveless tunic, showing several scars on her upper arm: a lasting testament to what had happened in Acre.

She hugged me. "Good to see you after so many centuries. It's a shame our paths have not crossed in such a long time."

"You too. But why are you here?"

"Apparently your friends were not the only ones to receive a tainted tablet."

"Anyone else we might know?" Remy asked.

"A few," Irkalla said. She pointed behind me as Nabu entered the room carrying a multitude of scrolls, which he placed on the table.

"We were in London," Nabu told us all. "We were to have talks with Brutus about security for the exhibits at the London Museum. There were rare artifacts that we were allowing to be shown: weapons and the like. It was just a formality, but we received one of those tablets."

"I've never seen them before," Irkalla said, "although I imagine I'd recognize them anywhere now."

Nabu offered me his hand, which I took. "Nathaniel, I'd say it was good to see you, but, um, I'm not entirely sure it is." He turned to Zamek, who was seated at the end of the table. "Anyone else coming?"

"Not that I'm aware of," Zamek said. He put his feet up on the table, visibly relaxing.

"Thank you all for coming," Jinayca said as she entered the room and motioned for the three women with her to take a seat around the table.

"Nate," the oldest of the three, Cassandra, said, while her daughter, Grace, and granddaughter, Ivy, sat at the table, both nodding a greeting in my direction.

My mouth dropped open in shock. The Fates were here, in Sanctuary. The last I'd seen of them, they were Kay's prisoners.

"Let me guess: bad tablet?" Remy asked, narrowly avoiding a playful cuff on the ear from Diane.

"Of a sort," Cassandra said, as her gaze settled on Mordred.

"I had nothing to do with it," Mordred said, standing. His hands were shaking as he placed them on the table. "If you'd prefer I wasn't here, I understand."

"Sit down, Mordred," Ivy told him, her voice held no hint of the hatred she'd once felt for him. "We're aware you weren't involved, and you are just as important here as anyone else."

Mordred thanked her and returned to his seat.

"How are you here? I saw you on the TV screen. I saw you as captives."

"We were prisoners for several days," Ivy explained. "Until we told Kay what he wanted to know. I assume you're aware of Kay's involvement?"

"Yeah, it came up," I told her. "Kay and I are going to have words when we next meet."

"Then you know that Kay was the one behind our kidnapping," Grace said. "He wanted to know where you'd be at certain times. Once he realized you'd managed to escape the trap in London, he sent us to this realm, to be kept quiet by the blood elves, but Zamek and his dwarven warriors ambushed the patrol and brought us here."

"Okay, I now have more questions about everything that has happened in the last few days than I'm comfortable with."

"All will be explained in time," Cassandra told me. "First, I believe Jinayca needs to explain things."

CHAPTER **25**

The trouble started four thousand years ago," Jinayca began, "and it began with the elves. The elves were originally very much against cooperating with other species. They were insular, distrustful. They were powerful sorcerers, and despite many pantheons coming to their door to try and forge an alliance, they refused.

"That changed over time. A contingent of elves thought that keeping to themselves was only going to hurt the species as a whole—at least in the long run. Those who wished to integrate with other species petitioned their elders to grant an alliance with the Norse gods and ourselves. The elven elders refused to allow any kind of integration with other species, and those who had requested it were imprisoned for their beliefs. The elven civil war started then. Two sides: the sun elves, who wanted to be left alone, to have no outside contact, versus the shadow elves, who wanted to engage with other nations, with other species. They wanted to share what they'd learned."

"I assume it didn't work out well," Remy said.

"No. The war lasted for a thousand years, with countless dead, and countless more leaving the elven realms and vowing never to return. But in the end, the sun elves were the victors. Most shadow elves fled into various realms, splitting up to avoid capture, but those the sun elves managed to take were brought to us."

"A mistake that cost us dearly," Zamek said.

Jinayca placed her hand on the dwarven warrior's forearm. "Yes. You see, we were in the process of creating a new weapon: spirit scrolls. Scrolls imbued with the spirits from another realm. You are aware of Pandora, yes? The girl who had a demon from a spirit realm forced into her? This was a similar idea, but the demon would be placed into the scroll, granting the user incredible, but hopefully controllable, powers."

A horrible thought dawned on me. "Bet that worked well."

"No, not exactly," Jinayca admitted. "There was a catch—several. Firstly, as a security precaution, only humans could activate a scroll. Humans were rare in the realms at the time, and it was thought that they would be a good method to ensure that there were no problems with any extra powers or abilities the nonhumans might have."

"Humans were the control part of the experiment," I said, managing not to call anyone bad names for their stupidity.

Jinayca nodded. "In hindsight, it wasn't the best idea, but we didn't want to allow these spirits to bond with sorcerers or anything more powerful, so humans were a good test subject. Although, I'd like to stress that the only humans involved were ones who *volunteered*. We didn't force anyone to do anything."

"You sure that everyone was as nice about it as you?" Mordred asked, a doubt in his tone.

"No. That I can't say. I can only attest for what I was aware of." Jinayca appeared to be troubled by the idea that not all of the humans were as willing as she'd suggested. It was probably something she'd thought about a lot over the centuries. "Secondly, the price for a person bonding with the scroll is that the spirit of its user will remain with the scroll after their death. It was done so that new users could gain the knowledge and power of those who had activated the same scroll. It meant that if someone was the fifth to activate the scroll, they would have four spirits to guide them through the process, share their strength, speed, and the like. It made those who bonded with the scroll, after several others had already used it, considerably more powerful.

"Apart from increasing various attributes of the user, each scroll also imbued the user with one unique power. William's was to become that abomination. But others can control the weather, or turn to water, or manipulate metal itself. Each one is different. Each power is personalized for the user."

"All sounds nice so far," Diane said. "But I fought Pandora. I know there has to be a bigger catch to all of this."

"The biggest catch was the demon inside the scroll. When the user first bonds, the demon isn't in control; that aspect is completely successful. Unfortunately, over time, the user had to accept *all* of the spirits within the scroll to have access to the full power the scroll could bestow. That means they had to accept the demon."

"What do you mean 'accept?'" I asked.

"The user of the scroll has to accept their transformation completely, the power they would have access to, and the spirits within the scroll. They can't pick and choose; it's all or nothing. The demon begins locked in a mental cage inside the user's mind, but the user has to unlock it and accept the demon within. If they don't, if they resist taking any of the spirits or the demon into themselves, the demon will gain more and more power and influence over the scroll-user, eventually turning them insane.

"Even water dropping onto stone eventually wears it down. And the demon is relentless. It might take days or months, and it's completely dependent on the user's current mental state, but the more emotional or mentally fragile they are, the quicker the demon takes control."

"What happens once the demon takes control?" Kasey asked.

"In a normal situation, where the user has accepted the demon, the demon is still there, but it's no longer capable of taking control using normal means."

"It can huff and puff, but never blow the house down?" Remy asked.

"If you mean that when its power isn't in use, it can say what it likes and can be ignored, then yes, you're correct. Once the spirits and demon have been accepted as part of the user, they can tap into that extra power the demon offers, allowing the demon to essentially become a vast dam of energy inside of them. But when the demon and human minds merge, when the demon takes control, the user loses whatever conscience they once had. They'll kill for fun, for sport, or just because. We didn't discover this until it was too late, and people died because of our mistake."

"What does 'normal' mean?" I asked.

"Those who accept the demon can use its power, as I said. But use too much, or allow your emotions to control your use, and the person will become a demon-human hybrid. In this guise, the demon is much closer to the surface of the human's personality. Essentially, it's the only time an accepted demon is a real threat."

"So, the human always has to be on their toes, just in case?" I said. As far as news went, it wasn't brilliant, but it wasn't a death sentence either.

"So why don't the users just accept the demon?" Diane asked.

"I wish it were so simple. The demons are darkness personified. You can tell someone over and over to just accept the darkness, but how many do you think really want to? How many people really believe that they won't be changed by that acceptance? It takes a strong mind to blindly accept something as fact. And when we tell someone to accept it, and then a demon, a creature of power and malevolence tells them the same, they doubt themselves."

"The demon wants out? Why?" I asked. "Surely it's better for it if the demon stays locked away, driving the person insane so it can be freed to kill."

"Whether the demon merges or not, it can never be truly free. It will forever be part of the human: two souls locked together until the human dies. It's not much of a life. But a demon that manages to crack the user's psyche and drive them insane has a big chance of taking control of that person. If the demon is accepted, it's no longer caged, but its power is limited. A demon not accepted just begins to take over the user's mind in total. Either way, the user is in danger of the demon controlling their mind and body."

"You merged a human and a demon, and it all went terribly wrong," Nabu snapped. "Not exactly a shock to anyone else here."

"What do these scrolls have to do with the blood elves?" I asked. "I assume the blood elves and shadow elves are the same thing?"

Jinayca nodded sadly. "After the war, the prisoners were brought here. Their captors decided to banish them from the other elf realms instead of executing them en masse. We agreed to allow the shadow elves to live here, providing they would mine the crystals in the lower parts of the mountain. They'd be allowed to live in peace, to do as they wished, but in exchange they'd have to work for it."

"Why the crystals?" Diane asked.

"The elves are immune to the crystallized magic," Zamek said. "Dwarves get tired and sick after a few weeks being around them. It's why we use them only in forging; it's safer."

"I assume that immunity didn't work out too well," Morgan snapped.

"No. It did the exact opposite," Jinayca admitted. "It took hundreds of years for the crystals to corrupt the shadow elves into those beings you see out there. Hundreds of years where many of them lived beside us, forming friendships, forming bonds. All the while they were reaching out to our enemies and forming an alliance with them. It only took one week for them to rise up and attack us when we were at our lowest point."

"What does that mean?" Nabu asked.

"Our king was assassinated, and Mordred was framed for it. He was a newcomer in the realm and a natural target for suspicious activities. We discovered Mordred's innocence too late, and by then, the dwarves who had betrayed us to the blood elves had already put their plan into motion. Thousands were slaughtered in that first hour as the outer parts of the city of Thorem were taken. Tens of thousands died within the first week. It took two weeks for us to mobilize and arrange a counter-attack.

"Our people fled through the few realm gates we have here. A few stayed behind to destroy them so that the blood elves couldn't follow. Unfortunately, we don't believe the gates were completely destroyed. At least one, inside the citadel, still remains. Hundreds of thousands fled from this mountain over the course of a few days. The citadel was under siege within days, and many tried to keep it from falling into elven hands. But as the last of our kind escaped, the citadel was overrun, and those inside were forced to flee.

"Fortunately, the guardians managed to flee through the realm gates, taking their links to the world our dwarven kin had fled to. Dwarven guardians are not like those in other realms, where a guardian away from a gate becomes mortal, but otherwise there are no changes. Dwarven guardians have their lifeblood linked to the gates, and time away from them leads them all to die within a few years.

"Those of us who escaped that slaughter were supposed to destroy the library. We decided to build Sanctuary instead, and bring with us what we could so we could find a way to stop the blood elves."

"Why not just burn the library and leave?" Irkalla asked.

"If that realm gate is still operational, then destroying the library means destroying the possibility of ever finding information on how to get it working again, on ever getting free, or having our people return home."

"I fought those blood elves," Zamek said. "I stayed behind in that citadel because it was my duty to do so, and I fled rather than die there. I feel no shame for fleeing. I helped many to escape, but I swore that one day I would get back there and finish the job—that I would help our people come home. Destroying the library: that would feel like we were destroying a part of ourselves, of who we were. I'm not sure we can do that."

"Okay, so what can you tell us about the spirit scrolls?" Remy asked.

"They can't be burned, or torn, or broken," Zamek began. "They're immune to magic, too. Which means that even if we'd burned the whole place down, those scrolls would still be there, still available for the blood elves to find. It's another reason for keeping the library intact, and it's also why we need to bring them here."

"How do you tell which scrolls are spirit ones, and which one's aren't?" I asked.

Jinayca answered this one. "The spirit scrolls have markings on the outside of them. It's the dwarven word for spirit, which is a bit of a giveaway, but we had no idea we were ever going to be in this situation."

"How many spirit scrolls have you found since the elves attacked?" Remy asked.

"None," Zamek admitted. "The blood elves managed to ransack the place shortly after arriving and took any spirit scrolls that were outside of a secure location."

"I thought you'd stopped working on them?" Irkalla asked. She'd been quiet ever since she'd arrived. "Why not put them all in a secure location?"

"The dwarves who were working on them were trying to find a way to dismantle the scrolls. Most of them only had the demon attached as they'd never been used."

"Wait, didn't you say that only humans can use these? Why would the blood elves give the spirit scrolls to humans? Wouldn't they be somewhat concerned about a really powerful human running around?" Kasey asked, making a good point.

"From what we understand, most of the humans they use are like William: willing participants for their masters. Any humans sent here are usually hunted, or tested in rune-marked rooms—similar to what we did when we first started creating them."

"How many scrolls do the blood elves have?" I asked.

"Not all of them," Jinayca said. "Several hundred at last guess. We used to go to the library every few months, but the last trip was several years ago, when a contingent of dwarves went there to look in the rooms we hadn't charted. The library is massive. Several floors, millions of scrolls, hundreds of rooms. You couldn't search it all in a human lifetime."

"These people are still there, yes?" Nabu asked.

"Yes," Jinayca said. "We know some are alive. They were all rune-scribed before they went; we do this for all of our warriors. The runes work as tracking beacons. We can monitor vitals and locations from here. Of the dwarves who went only a few survived." Jinayca unfurled a scroll on the table, which contained some sort of map. There were several dark dots on it, moving slowly around. "This is one of a hundred maps for the library. This shows that they're in the southern, highest tip. It's assumed they banded there because of what happened below."

Zamek lifted his tunic to reveal a mark on his stomach. "Their marks are still working. We just can't get to them."

"What happened below?" several people asked at once.

"The blood elves attacked en masse," Zamek explained. "Thousands of them, all led by a hooded figure. One dwarf from the group was sent back to warn us of their advancement."

"Great, a hooded figure," Remy mocked. "That's not fucking ominous or anything."

I looked over at Mordred and wondered if he'd encountered anyone like that while he was here. A hooded figure leading the blood elves could be anyone. Hell, it could just be another blood elf, but I wasn't thrilled about the idea of having someone leading unknown thousands of raving psychopaths hell-bent on the destruction of everything that wasn't them.

"The elves are in the lower levels and have taken control of what used to be the scholars and elders housing," Jinayca continued, ignoring Remy's outburst. "A small group can bypass them."

"Why haven't you done it?" I asked. My words were slightly harsher than I'd intended. Frankly, the whole thing made me feel angry that any group of people could have been so blinded and insular to not see what was happening to them. But that was then, and the now was more important. We needed to help the dwarves to help Chloe, although even if Chloe wasn't hurt, I'd have still offered to help. When someone takes you into their home instead of letting you die, then asks for help, it's usually a good idea to do it. So long as it's not a suicide run: then it's usually a good idea to leave. I hadn't decided how suicidal going up against thousands of blood elves was going to be. Probably very.

"The elders will not allow a big enough troop of dwarves to go. We estimate that it would need most of our warriors to retake the lower levels, but a smaller group could get there."

"By smaller group, you mean us," I said.

"Not all of you," Zamek stated. "Three or four of you, and me and my warriors. The elders don't care if we die, but I couldn't do this alone. I won't die for nothing."

"You were part of the royal family," Mordred said, completely changing the subject. "It's not a question."

"I was in line to the throne, yes. It's why I have a surname. Only those in positions of power have one, like royalty, or the elders. But that's a moot point now. I gave up that right the second the throne was taken from us. I keep the surname to honor my family, but I'd rather die with my people than tower over them."

A thought occurred to me. "Is that why you and that dwarf argued? The one when we first arrived?"

"Several of the elders expect me to overthrow them the second I get the chance. They'd really like me dead."

Jinayca looked shocked. "That's not true."

"Don't. We both know that there are dwarves here who would have been much happier if I'd never made it back. I'm not royalty anymore, but our people have long memories, and most here remember me from when I helped lead the defense of the citadel."

"So, your plan is to have us get into the library, find these people, find the scrolls, and get back here?" I asked, making sure I was up-to-date with the insanity.

"If we can get her one of the scrolls, Chloe's ability to heal will be tenfold what a human's is. But she will have to learn how to deal with the spirits inside the scroll, and master the demon and whatever new powers she's given. And if she doesn't do it, she will go insane, and become a monster."

"We'll help her," Remy said. "We'll make sure that doesn't happen."

"Once the scrolls are here, we have a chance of saving Chloe," Jinayca said. "And you have a chance to get home."

"What does that mean?" Diane asked.

"The dwarf you're looking for is called Brigg. He was one of main reasons so many of our kind got out of the citadel alive. He knows the hidden tunnels into the citadel—the only warrior left alive in Sanctuary to do so. He can take you to the citadel, into the realm-gate room."

"And he's in the library?"

Jinayca nodded. "Once you locate the team in the library, you'll need to talk to Brigg. He can help you find the spirit scrolls, and hopefully the way to get the realm gate activated."

"I thought you said it needed a guardian to do it?" I said.

"Brigg worked with the guardians back when we had any," Zamek said. "That's why he knows the entrance. Only he can get through the locked doors in the tunnel. We need him. *You* need him. Otherwise, you get to stay here forever."

Something didn't make sense to me. "Wait: how can the realm gate go to multiple places? One gate, one exit and entrance."

"The gates in this realm are different than those in others. We created these as a way to travel between realms, so each gate has a set number of a dozen or so destinations. It's why not all of the dwarves are in one place. They're scattered across multiple realms. We kept away from the Norse and elven realms, the former because of their civil war, and the latter because they caused all of this. And we stayed away from Earth, because we don't trust Avalon or its people."

"Why?" I asked.

"The blood elves had help from that realm. We're certain of it."

"What Norse civil war?" Nabu asked.

"We don't know more," Zamek explained. "The Norse realms cut off all contact with the outside. Last we heard they were at war with one another, then nothing else."

Well, that explained where all the Norse pantheon went. "I assume you know the way to the library?" I asked Zamek.

"I do, and we have maps to find Brigg and his people. Hopefully, we'll be there and back within a day. I don't relish the idea of being in that library longer than we need to."

I turned to the Fates. "Any of you three like to say anything? You've all been awfully quiet."

"The future is cloudy," Ivy said. "I don't know what will happen. But I do know this is your best chance."

"Let's get to it, then."

Mordred was up first. "I won't be going. My brain . . . the idea of being near so many of those things." He left without another word, Morgan following behind.

"He was broken by these creatures," Ivy said.

"You forgive him?" I asked, surprised at the disbelief in my voice, something I instantly regretted. He'd done awful things to the Fates, but he wasn't that man anymore.

"He is not the same man."

"I noticed." I sighed. "Anyone who wants to come with me, stay here. Everyone else can go, if you wish."

The three Fates stood. "We are more helpful here," Cassandra said hugging me.

"I know."

To be honest, I was thankful they weren't going to be in harm's way. I knew they could handle themselves; I'd fought beside Ivy before. But I also knew that the blood elves would very much like to capture them again. I didn't want to put them in that position.

I waited until they'd left before I spoke again. "Diane, Remy, Irkalla: you feel like going after these dwarves?"

"I thought you'd never ask," Irkalla said with a smile.

"Only if I get a dwarven sword," Remy said with what I assumed was a grin. "And an ax, and a set of armor. Oh and something that goes boom. I really think that would help us out."

"Explosives will help us out?" Diane asked.

"Sure. Why not?" Remy asked, as if the very possibility of them doing otherwise was insane.

"Okay," Zamek said. "We leave here as soon as we're ready."

"You're leaving me here? Why?" Kasey asked as most of the others had left the room.

"Because you're seventeen, and your best friend is in a hospital bed, dying. Your head is here, not out there, so stay and keep an eye on Chloe."

"I want to be able to do something!" she snapped jumping to her feet and throwing a chair across the room.

"You can't. Not this time, Kase."

"You know, at some point those blood elves are going to realize this is where the Fates are," Diane said, unmoved by Kasey's outburst.

I nodded. "I assume as much, yes."

Kasey looked over at me. "You think they're going to come here?"

"Yes."

"I need you here, Kase, because I need you to help defend these people, and it would be better for you to know that Chloe was here than several hours away while you sneaked around a library. That's why you're staying."

"The Fates already mentioned there was a possibility of an attack," Jinayca admitted. "I've already got the warriors on look out. We'll be ready."

"And now you'll have Kase to help you," I told her. "And Mordred is still here."

"He was in the blood elves' company for over a hundred years," Jinayca said. "I'm not sure how much they broke him."

"Completely," I said, before leaving the room.

CHAPTER 26

I didn't go looking for Mordred, but I found him anyway, sitting alone beside the stream.

"I don't think you'll catch much," I said as I approached, letting him know I was there.

"You must think me a coward."

I sat a little distance away; after all, he had told me that he was going to kill me, even if he'd given no indication that he was planning it any time soon.

"Who told you that killing me was your destiny?" I asked, pretty certain I already knew the answer.

"The Fates."

I nodded to myself. That was the answer I'd been expecting. "When?"

"I went to see them about a year ago. I wanted to . . . find some semblance of forgiveness or something. I don't really know. They told me they were expecting me, and I spent a few hours trying to atone for my past."

"And they told you that you had to kill me?"

"They said that there are lots of paths forward for me. But that killing you, and only when you were powerful enough, would change the world. That if you lived, a lot of people would die. And that it has to be by my hand at the right time."

"You believed them?"

Mordred turned to look at me. "I wanted to show you that I wasn't the person you thought I was. I wanted to show you that apart from the craziness, I'm a different person. But I am also apparently destined to kill you. I thought you should know. I didn't want it to come from someone else, or have you accept the me I've become, only to realize I'd try and kill you. It felt a little disingenuous."

"You probably could have told me in a different way."

"Possibly, but it's not like you're just going to let it happen, and Ivy explained that she doesn't see anything more for me. Either I kill you and save lives, or I fail, and a lot of really bad shit happens. Or maybe it doesn't. Who the fuck knows? The future is fluid, right?"

"Something like that." I picked up a pebble and tossed it into the stream. "You know, this is one of the weirdest conversations I've had in a long time."

"When I woke up after you shot me, I had a conversation with Morgan about the place of nachos in the world league table of foods. That was a bit stranger. I think I suggested that you could use them as weapons. To be fair, it was a weird time for me."

"What did these people do to you, Mordred? The blood elves?"

Mordred remained silent for a long time, and I began to wonder if he planned on talking at all. But eventually he said, "When the dwarves realized I wasn't their king's killer, they let me go. I was almost to the citadel exit when the blood elves attacked. They dragged me back to my cell as they slaughtered everyone else.

"They tortured me, every single day. They broke bones and tore ligaments. They let me heal, only to do it all again. They brought me in for questioning, and would ask the same things over and over, in a language I didn't understand. But despite the blood elves' torture, despite them making me lose my mind, it wasn't them who fucked with my head the most. It was Avalon."

"I don't understand."

"It doesn't matter. You won't believe me."

"Try me," I said. "I want to hear what happened. I want to understand."

Mordred stared at me. "People would come through the realm gate. Not elves, or dwarves, but sorcerers, werewolves, a few other types, too. They'd help the elves hurt me, and ask me questions. There were big names in Avalon who turned up to watch me be broken, who had allied themselves with the blood elves. But then there was this one man who came through. I'll never forget his face; it's permanently etched in my mind. He used mind magic on me, broke me down, made me want to destroy, and hurt, and kill. They gave me a list of names to hunt down and kill. It had names like Elaine, Galahad, Mac, a bunch of others. He made me want to murder them, to drink their blood, to feast on their flesh. To do *anything* I could to complete that list, no matter how many people I had to kill to get to them.

"That went on for a few years, until I no longer knew friend from foe. But that conditioning didn't quite take, and eventually I escaped. I turned the conditioning around, removing the list of people they gave me, and replacing it with Avalon. Merlin, Arthur, and anyone else in a high enough position. Everyone who had helped hurt me."

"Like whom?"

"Hera was there a few times; she wanted answers about Avalon—about you. About various other people, some I'd never heard of. Kay liked to get his hands dirty himself. Siris—you remember her?—she wore a hood, so she didn't think I'd recognize her. It's why I left back in Acre. She figured out I was only going to kill her, that I knew she had been there during those long days in blood-elf confinement."

"So that's why you went after Avalon: because of what they did to you?"

"Some of it, yes. I had other . . . personal reasons. But it started off with me skulking around this realm, killing blood elves after being tortured by them for over a century. I spent over a decade here, trying to find a way out, only to discover that the only way out was through a realm gate. But I found another way. One of the Avalon people who had arrived to talk to the blood elves had tablets with runes etched on them. I thought it strange, so I stole one and managed to free myself, ending up in the middle of Scotland during the winter, wearing only thin, tattered clothing and no shoes. It wasn't a great time for me."

"So you went after me for all of these years, because these people told you to destroy a list of names, and you changed it to those working for Avalon. That's why you went after Arthur and Merlin and me?"

Mordred shook his head. "Merlin was personal. I went to him about what I'd seen, and he didn't believe me. He called me a liar, and a coward, and a murderer, so I escaped the city, and the realm. Arthur is . . . actually I don't know what Arthur is."

I got the feeling there was more to be said on the subject, but didn't push it. I didn't want to start an argument about my old friend.

"And me?"

"Well, you were more complicated. When you tried to stop me over and over, my mind stopped seeing you as a friend and saw you as an enemy. In fact, it saw you as the reason for everything that had happened to me."

"Why would it do that?"

"Because on the list of names the blood elves and their Avalon friends wanted me to kill, you were right at the top. I started murdering Avalon people because I couldn't bring myself to kill you, and Galahad, and Mac, and anyone else I cared for. And when you sided with them, I just snapped again."

We were both silent for several minutes as the news sunk in. "I don't know what to say," I eventually admitted.

"You don't need to say anything. None of this was your fault, but I made it yours anyway. But I will say one thing, Nate. Hera, and Siris, and a bunch of other people who profess to be enemies of one another, or allies with Avalon; they *all* wanted you dead. Siris, when she tried to destroy Acre, was working with Hera and her cronies to pull it off. The enemies of Avalon have been undermining Avalon's power for centuries, and they've wanted you dead for just as long."

"Why do they want me dead?"

"They fear you, Nate—fear us. You went through a blood-curse ritual, yes?"

I nodded. "Did you?"

"Yes. Don't know when, or even who was there, but we were both put through the same ritual, albeit for different reasons, I think. Mine was to just limit my power and remove my memories of my time there. They didn't do much else, memory-wise."

"Mine was to limit my power and hide me from a war. They

took me from my mother, and wiped my mind. On top of that, Merlin put me through the Harbinger trials when I was only thirteen."

The Harbinger trials consist of putting a person who is at least a hundred years old into a deep psychic-enabled sleep, where the person lives their life and learns without ever having to do anything physically. The trials are exceptionally danger-ous and several candidates have died over the centuries they've been carried out. To do it to a thirteen-year-old who had just come into his magic is both unheard of and unthinkable. It's akin to torture.

"I heard about the trials from some people in Avalon," Mordred said. "What war?"

"I have no idea," I said. "Zeus was at the ritual with Merlin; Hera, too. But if she wanted me dead, why not just kill me?"

"Ask her the next time you see her."

"I think I might just do that. I'm getting the impression that people have been playing with our lives for a long time, and we don't actually know why."

"I certainly don't know anyone else with blood-curse marks like ours. Elaine is doing great things with Avalon, but I don't think too many people want her to continue. I think those who want Avalon's power for themselves are beginning to align. I don't think it'll be long before it gets a lot worse."

"Hera, Kay, Siris, and all of their allies working together—that's a scary thought."

"That's the thing: none of those would work for any of the others. You heard all of that 'my liege' crap?"

For a few years whenever someone who worked with this group had been cornered and questioned, all they could talk about was *my liege*; there were no names or other details. It had been discovered that all of these people had had their minds tampered with, removing the names of whoever the liege was. "Yeah, who is 'my liege'? Any ideas?"

"A few. I don't think it's a who. I think it's a them."

I had to admit the idea had merit. "What makes you think that?"

"I've come across a few people over the years who say the same thing. There's no way all of them worked for the same person."

"I had a similar theory," I concurred. "So, more than one person. Probably a cabal of some kind."

"Well, it's almost certain that Hera, Siris, and Kay are all members. Anyone else? The blood elves are clearly all stuck here, but from what you say, it's not hard to believe that the 'my liege' group managed to get things started with them."

"I don't know. It's hard to think of a hierarchy when you have no idea of their aims and objectives. Beyond destroying Avalon, and killing anyone who gets in their way, I mean. After what I've heard today, I think it's all but confirmed that this group actively plotted with the blood elves. There's no way the dwarves would have missed so much preparation for so long. That means some of the dwarves were helping. There's no other way they could have pulled it off."

"Maybe when you're in the library, you can try and figure out who this hooded person is?"

"The thought had crossed my mind. I'm curious about the blood elves' allies."

"And their allies are this cabal's allies."

"Did you find out who killed the dwarf king?"

Mordred shook his head. "Wasn't a dwarf; that's about as far as I got. Could have been anyone but me. Which isn't a sentence I'm used to saying. I don't know why they'd go to all the trouble of framing me, unless they didn't and I was just a good excuse for a patsy while they continued to arrange for the blood elves to fight."

"What were you here to discuss?"

"Some dwarven weapons had made their way to a bunch of raiders in England. A bad group."

"I remember them. They sacked several villages along the south coast, but Merlin had me sent to France before we could figure out who was responsible." I frowned. If Merlin hadn't sent me away, would I have been stuck here with Mordred? Would I have been broken like him? Or maybe I could have helped stop it.

"After you left I found one of those spirit scrolls, fought the man who was using it, although I had no idea what it was at the time. I went to Merlin about it, and he sent me to the dwarven realms to discuss the crimes and try to figure out how the weapons were being smuggled out of this realm."

"Is that why you think Merlin was behind it all?"

"No. He had no idea what was happening, or what was going to happen. Merlin's descent into . . . whatever he is now happened a long time after I was sent here. When I finally returned to Camelot after all of those years here, I begged him to believe me about what had happened to me. I saw the change in him then. That was also when he told me Arthur was to be the new king of Avalon, not me. All that pain and suffering, all of those times I comforted myself with the knowledge that when I got back to Avalon, I would have the realm freed and the blood elves wiped out . . . all of it was for nothing."

"It helped give you hope, kept you alive. It wasn't for nothing."

We were silent again for several seconds, and I stood up to leave.

"You know why I have to stay here, right?" Mordred asked. "Why I can't come with you to the library?"

"You don't need to convince me of anything, Mordred."

"I know, but I also know that those bastards are going to come here. They're going to attack this compound. They want the Fates back. And I want to stay here, because if I go with you, if I see all of those elven bastards, I might lose control and destroy your mission. I don't want that girl to die because I can't keep my emotions in check. But here, when those elves come, I'm going to fuck their shit up." He looked up at me, and smiled. "I'm really looking forward to it."

"Keep safe. I don't want to miss our appointment for you to kill me."

"You jest, but I don't want to kill you, Nate. It just seems to be the way it's going to go. Two friends, they reconnect after spending a lifetime trying to murder one another, and as they become friends again, one kills the other. If there were a woman in between us, it would be a Hollywood movie."

"That would be a really weird movie."

"Yeah, but I like weird movies."

"You haven't said anything about video games for a few hours."

"Been busy concentrating on the blood elves. They've given me something else to focus on. I still go off on tangents, but not as often." He started humming something and stopped himself with a smile.

"Video game music?"

"*Zelda* theme. I had a real Nintendo thing going on while I was rehabilitating. The games helped me to live outside of myself. They gave me something else to concentrate on while my mind healed. I found them relaxing. You should try it."

"I think I'd end up completing something while the world burned if I did that," I said with a laugh.

"Sometimes you can't stop the world from burning. It's like barbecue food: sometimes a little charcoal is a good thing. Gives it extra flavor."

I stared at him. "Really?"

"No. I'm just hungry and I couldn't figure out where my analogy was going."

I left Mordred alone and walked off toward the arranged meeting point.

"He's not the man you think he is," Morgan called to me as I got far enough away from Mordred to hear.

I found her sitting on a small rock formation at the side of a building.

"You were watching us." It wasn't a question.

"Of course. I can't trust you not to hurt him. He's different."

I looked back at Mordred. "I know he's different. I've accepted that. You see enough weird and awful shit happen, and then you see someone you've hated for so long turn back into something close to the friend you knew. You don't dwell; you're just happy for him. But he's not the problem; it's *you* I don't trust. You worked with him. You helped him when he was murdering people. That just makes you a bigger monster, doesn't it?"

"I wasn't helping him *kill*. I was trying to stop him."

"Bang-up job you did. Well done."

"Shove it up your ass, Nate," Morgan snapped. "I did a damn sight more for him than you did. Do you think we just let him run around, doing whatever he liked? We imprisoned him, for centuries at a time. And then he would escape and kill, and we'd have to hunt him down again. We weren't his cohorts; we were his jailers."

I wasn't really sure how to respond to that. It was something I'd never even considered before. "We?"

"I'm not going to tell you who helped. We moved Mordred from realm to realm, always keeping him locked up, until he escaped and we'd have to do the whole thing again. Except last time, you killed him before we could get to him." The anger in her voice was barely contained, and I'd noticed her ball her hands into fists.

"Going to take a swing?" I asked.

She stared at her fists, and unfolded them. "No. I just want you to understand there was more to Mordred than just a bunch of people helping him kill to his heart's desire."

"Not everyone will forgive him. Not everyone will be able to look past the exterior. He did a lot of awful things, and he's going to have to deal with that."

"He knows that. Everything he did was to get to those who had hurt him, to get to those who were part of Avalon. He cared little about damaging others. He's trying to make amends for that—for all of his mistakes."

"When Mordred joined Mars Warfare, when he started working for Ares, why didn't Mordred kill him, or those who worked for him?"

"He joined them to kill Hera. She was one of those who had tortured him when he was prisoner here."

"He said as much. Why would Hera allow Mordred to get close to her?"

"She wouldn't. She wants him dead as much as you did. So, either Ares didn't know and employed Mordred anyway, or did know and wanted to see what would happen."

"That sounds like Ares."

"No one ever accused him of being smart. But then you turned up, and it all went to shit, because Mordred was so focused on killing you, he ignored everything else. He worked there for ten years, knowing you were still alive, and never once tried to get close to Hera. He told me all of this the day he woke up from his coma. You were the name at the top of the list of people his enemies wanted dead, and he could do nothing but try to complete that list. He's been their slave for over a thousand years, and I'm pretty certain that they don't even know. Or care."

I chose my words carefully. "Mordred is as much a victim as anyone else."

I looked over toward Mordred again, who was joined by several dwarven children and their parents. The children played in the stream while Mordred spoke to the parents. One of the men hugged him and shook his hand.

"He was my brother in all but blood. I would have sacrificed my life for him."

"He wants revenge on the blood elves. And I'm terrified he'll die for it."

"No one here is going to die if I have anything to say about it." I found myself meaning those words. Mordred had changed—really changed—and I wasn't about to let him just throw his life away.

"He wants to prove to you that he's not a monster. He won't accept it himself: not without your approval."

"Jinayca told everyone there was no evil in Mordred. And he's had the chance to kill me a dozen times over. I accepted it already, and I've told him as much."

"It had to be said. You mean a lot to Mordred. He wants to make up for all of the things he did to wrong you—to wrong everyone."

"You know, there's just one thing, Morgan. Despite all of Mordred's craziness, you still helped him try and kill Arthur. You were there. You helped. So you can stand there and say that you weren't helping him kill people, but you helped him almost destroy Avalon. Arthur has been in a coma for centuries because of you and your friends. So maybe it's not Mordred I shouldn't trust. Maybe it's *you* I shouldn't trust with *him*."

"Arthur had to die," Morgan snapped as I went to walk away. "You have no idea what he is. What he means. He had to be removed from the picture."

"Explain it to me."

"We discovered that Arthur was pushed into Mordred's place as the king of Avalon by people who wanted to use him, to create a ruler for them. Merlin wouldn't listen—no one would—but we knew it to be true. Hera, Siris, Kay, and anyone else who was involved in the plot to put Arthur as king, to rule from the shadows, they had to be stopped. Removing Arthur was the only way. And it worked. It destroyed their plans, and for centuries they've tried to re-establish a base of power, with little success."

"Even if that's true, there would have been a better way. Arthur would have listened."

"We went to him, and he told us to leave and never bother him with such stories again. And then our friends began to die. We had to move, because his puppet masters were moving on us. And now they're coming back again. And this time they don't have anyone to use, to corrupt."

"No. This time, they're going to destroy everyone who opposes them. They'll take Avalon over the corpses of those who I consider my friends. They learned the lesson you taught them, and they've been building up for a long time to implement their new plan. That's why we were sent here. That's why all of us were removed from the earth realm, because we could have helped stop them."

"You think they're going after Avalon?"

"After Brutus, yes. I think their long-term goal has always been the destruction of Avalon and anyone who opposes them. I think we're almost at the first stage of centuries of planning. And then we'll be at war, and a lot more people are going to die."

CHAPTER 27

Several dwarves directed me toward the building that had been earmarked as our accommodation for the duration of our visit. I went around to each room in the three-story building, asking them to come down to the open first floor as I had things I needed to share.

Back downstairs, I found a seat and waited for everyone to gather. I wasn't going to start until they were all here. I didn't want to have to repeat myself three or four times.

"Okay, everyone is here," Diane said, her arms crossed as she leaned against the wall closest to me. "What is it?"

"Nabu," I said, "you and Irkalla were both talking to Brutus about some artifacts you'd given to the British Museum, yes?"

Nabu nodded. "They were from my personal collection."

"I remember reading a news article about it," I told him, "just before we got zapped here. Any chance that someone could sneak something into your items?"

"Like what?" Irkalla asked.

"A tablet," I said. "Specifically one that could bring people from one realm to here."

"You think that while we're here, an insurrection is taking place in London?"

I shrugged. "I'm just thinking of possibilities. You remember Acre, yes?"

Nabu was silent as he stared at me.

"You told me there was a realm gate in the catacombs; well I never saw one. I did see a small stone tablet on the floor of the room Siris tried to keep me from looking in. I didn't think anything of it at the time, but only a few minutes later those snakes burst forth. How did Siris open a realm gate without an actual gate?"

Everyone turned to Nabu, who remained cool and calm under whatever pressure my question might have placed on him.

"I remember," he told me. "And you now know how she opened that realm?"

"She used a tablet, but when I saw you the next day, you hid it from me. Probably about the size and shape of the one that sent us here?"

Nabu nodded.

"So, you took the tablet for examining, yes?"

Nabu nodded again.

"So, it's possible that a tablet could work its way into your personal stash at the museum. Someone goes there, activates it, and brings forth an army?"

"It's completely possible, yes."

Irkalla punched Nabu in the jaw, and was immediately separated by half of the group while Nabu picked himself off the floor. "You contemptible asshole!" Irkalla snapped. "All this time you knew! I opened that package and got us sent here, and the whole time, you pretended like you had no fucking clue about what it was."

"I've spent a thousand years, longer, hunting down those

tablets. I didn't think for one second that anyone could figure out how they're created *and* use them against us. I didn't say anything because I wanted to figure out *how* Kay and his allies had managed to recreate these items."

"I'm going to guess Siris or Nergal," Irkalla snapped, still angry. "I assume they knew about them?"

"They're old magic," he said, rubbing his jaw. "I worked on their creation with the dwarves and Avalon. But they were too difficult to create, and it was decided we should shelve the project. They required blood to work. And there were other issues, such as the tablet vanishing the second you stepped through the portal, and the fact that it couldn't be created by anyone with any sort of natural power."

"What does that mean?" I asked.

"Humans have to make the tablets. We discovered that the only nonhumans that can create the tablets are witches, and we assumed this was because their magic isn't an innate power, but something learned. They have to willingly decide to use that power through external means. In this case, runes. Those witches also need to understand the language that was created for it, a mixture of Norse, elvish, and Babylonian. Without it, they'd have no way of realizing exactly when people would be sent."

"So, if humans are being sent here," Diane began, "does that mean they're being used to create these tablets? Wouldn't that allow the blood elves to swarm over everything?"

Nabu shook his head. "There are fail-safes in them. Without knowing the precise words to describe the exact destination they want to go, they may as well be carving doodles into the stone— it will have an identical effect. At no point in my life did I ever think these tablets would be used again. Humans can't just copy everything down; they need to know the words themselves. That takes *a lot* of time: time most humans simply don't want to have."

"How about if someone rune-scribed a human to be able to understand those languages? Would they be able to make a tablet then?" Kasey asked.

Nabu nodded. "That would work."

"I have a question," Remy said. "If we need the exact location to be able to create our own tablet, and therefore escape without having to go anywhere near that citadel, I'm all for it. But I'm also going to guess that the descriptions are in the dwarven library, yes?"

"They were destroyed," Nabu explained, deflating everyone in the room. "A large swathe of these 'addresses' were burned to nothing before the war, along with explanations on how to read the language."

"Well, someone knows them; otherwise how did we end up here?" Remy asked.

"Except, dwarves really hate destroying words," Irkalla said, sounding no less calm than she had when she'd punched Nabu. "So they kept it all there—in their library. And a big chunk of it is still there."

"That's what the blood elves are after," Diane said. "The spirit scrolls might be important in the long term, too, but if the blood elves could make those tablets, they could leave this realm. And I'm pretty sure we all think that would be bad."

"I always thought that dwarves didn't write much down," I said, "that they only wrote down what they considered to be important, because dwarvish runes used in writing put too much power into the words."

"Who told you that nonsense?" Zamek asked.

"Merlin," I said, almost sounding apologetic.

"It's true that we only write down what's important, but we consider *everything* to be important. And our written language has no more power than yours. Only the original twenty-one runes, and magic- or alchemy-imbued runes. And we don't put those in books about agriculture. It's why finding the powerful scrolls is so much harder than expected."

I didn't really know what to say to that, so I kept quiet. It was another in a long list of lies I'd been fed over my lifetime. But then something dawned on me. "That's why people like Hera and Kay are working with the blood elves, and probably have been since they began turning into those creatures. They want access to the information the dwarves have."

I received a few blank expressions, so I filled everyone in on what Mordred had told me about Hera and Kay and their involvement with his torture and imprisonment.

"So there's a good chance that we're actually here because we could stop Hera from taking over London?" Diane said. "Because her in charge would be bad—really, really bad. As in people-would-go-missing-if-they-disagreed-with-her bad."

"Ah, Hera: where else can you find all the crazy in one head?" Remy said. "We should probably stop that from happening."

"We don't *know* that's what's happening," Kasey said. "Right now it's just a hypothesis."

Everyone else joined in the conversation, discussing the possibility of Hera or one of her allies taking control from Brutus.

"Why did Brutus allow Ares to put his Mars Warfare company in Canary Wharf?" Kasey asked.

"Brutus and Ares made a deal," Diane explained. "Brutus was advised by Licinius to take the deal—keeping your enemies closer and all that. Brutus hoped to figure out exactly what Hera's plans were by allowing Ares to be stationed there. Didn't really work, though, primarily because you partially destroyed the building, most of its research, and killed a large chunk of employees."

I shrugged. "They were murderous psychopaths."

"Well, your foray into restructuring their business led them to leave London altogether. Apparently Hera wasn't thrilled that you weren't punished for your actions there, but didn't want to take it further because that would have been admitting their crimes against magic, and she would have been arrested."

"If Hera is behind this, it certainly fits with her need to get revenge," Diane said. "And she can hold a grudge like no one I've ever met."

"Why would Hera want London, though?" Nabu asked. "That part doesn't make sense."

Before the conversation went around again, I stood up and stretched, catching the eye of Jinayca, who still stood by the door.

"We're going to need weapons," I told her.

Jinayca nodded. "We've got some just outside for you to choose from."

Remy left the building first, almost barging past everyone else in his hurry to get his pick of the weapons.

"They probably don't have anything that explodes!" I shouted after him, but he ignored me and was soon outside, while the rest of us followed in his considerably bushy wake.

A wooden cart, littered with weapons ranging from swords to spears and daggers to maces, seemed to hold something to suit every style of killing. All of them were made from dwarven steel, and marked with runes.

"So, what's so good about these, then?" Kasey whispered to me.

"Dwarven steel is said to be unbreakable," I told her. "It doesn't dull; it doesn't break, And the only armor that can withstand it is dwarven, and even then not for long."

"That's not quite true," Jinayca said. "Elven weapons and armor are just as well-made, just as dangerous. They use magic to temper their steel; we use alchemy. Some of ours also contain runes that allow sorcerers and elementals to wield their power through the blade."

"I don't really need any," Kasey said. "Werewolf."

Diane grabbed a pair of dwarven knives and passed them to her. "Don't argue. Claws work wonders, until they don't." Diane picked up a bow and a quiver of arrows, holding them gently, as if she might break them.

"Are you okay?" I asked.

"I was given a set like this, a long time ago," she told me, "from a dwarven king. I've missed it since being here."

Once everyone had selected their weapons they all wandered back into the building, leaving me alone with Remy, who was currently giggling about the fact that he had picked up a small sword and twin daggers that sat on a belt around his waist.

"You done?" I asked him.

"I have wanted dwarven steel since as far back as I can remember it existing. It's my holy grail of swords. I would quite literally live here—you know, apart from the never-being-able-to-leave-and-constant-fear-of-death thing."

"Yeah, apart from that."

"Oh, and the lack of sunlight, or moonlight, or anything but rock. When we leave here, I'm going to be really happy if I never have to go underground again."

I looked in the cart and saw a few daggers, and a nice-looking spear, but I didn't want anything too bulky. I picked up one of the daggers and tried it for weight. It felt good: a solid, but well-balanced weapon.

"I have something else for you," Jinayca told me. She pulled out a black-cloth-wrapped object from under the cart. She passed it to me, and I removed the cloth, revealing two swords of equal design and length. I admired the intricate work that had been completed on the scabbards and hilts. The reds and blacks were not something you usually saw in dwarven weaponry.

"What are these?" I asked, removing one of the swords from its scabbard and testing the blade. It was stunning, and the dark-gray color of it shimmered slightly as I moved it around. It was a one-handed, double-edged, sword about the length of a gladius, but more like a claymore in appearance: essentially a one-handed smaller version of the human sword. I'd never really seen anything quite like it.

"They were made for Zamek," she said. "These are the swords of a prince."

I replaced the blade in the scabbard and passed it back to Jinayca. "I can't accept this. It's Zamek's."

"He wants you to have them, although he doesn't want to give them to you himself. Something to do with people seeing a prince carrying those swords about. I think he's worried it would give the wrong impression." She handed it back to me.

"I don't know what to say. They're stunning weapons."

"If you don't want them, I'll take them," Remy said from beside me.

Jinayca passed me a back scabbard to carry the swords, which I quickly put on, placing the two swords in the slots designed for them. It was surprisingly comfortable, and I hadn't really expected that.

"The back scabbard was made especially for you," Jinayca told me, apparently sensing my surprise. "Zamek requested it be made once you returned from your time in the machine. And our people work fast when needed."

"I still don't understand why," I explained.

"That's for Zamek to tell you. I know no more than I've said."

I looked down at Remy. "So, you ready to go pick a fight on our terms?"

Remy's smile bared all of his teeth, making him look more ferocious than he probably anticipated. "I've been waiting since the moment we landed in the godforsaken realm." He turned to Jinayca. "No offense."

Jinayca laughed, and waved away Remy's badly timed outburst. "When you are ready, Zamek and his people will meet you at the city gates. I wish you luck—all of you. But be careful. I do not wish to have to mourn the loss of even more people."

Diane left the building and stood beside me. "Yeah, I'm pretty certain the blood elves aren't going to know what hit them."

CHAPTER

There's going to be no fighting if we can help it," Zamek said as he prepared us for the march through blood-elf territory to the library.

It had been only an hour since the meeting had finished and we'd all filed out of the elders' building, but it felt a lot longer. I was eager to get going, but Zamek wanted to walk us through the pitfalls and perils of what we'd be facing. It might have been necessary, but it sure wasn't something I wanted to hear.

Irkalla, Remy, Diane, and I listened as Zamek explained that we would be going closer to the elf-occupied territory. Any fighting would need to be done quickly and efficiently: no messing about, no giving the elves time to escape or regroup. Kill and move on.

Zamek had brought three dwarves with him; two I recognized from when we'd met during the fight with William, and both were male, called Birik and Malib. The third was a relative of the dwarf who'd been killed during the fight, and her name was Udthulo. She was slightly shorter than the other dwarves, but had tattoos all over her face, something I'd seen on a few dwarves in the city.

Once the introductions were out of the way, the massive gates to the city were opened and the eight of us were allowed out into the rest of the mountain. The gates closed shut behind us, and I spotted several dwarves atop the battlements watching us as we walked away from the safety of the city. I did a double take when I noticed that Mordred was up there, waiting for a battle that was sure to come. I just hoped we'd be back in time before the blood elves attacked.

Talking was kept to a bare minimum as Zamek led us through abandoned parts of the mountain. We met the occasional blood-elf patrol, which was quickly dispatched before we continued on.

Udthulo was the quietest of the four dwarves and appeared to be the most keen in battle. The blood elves we found quickly met her double-headed battle-ax, and more than once I thought I saw a smile on her face as she dispatched her enemies with ruthless efficiently.

"She scares me," Remy said as we all sat to take a break, eating some of the delicious meats and fruits the dwarves had prepared. We found ourselves in a small building; the interior had been gutted long ago, leaving only broken wood and stone among the dust and dirt.

Zamek, who sat beside Remy, laughed. "She is very passionate in her duty."

"And what duty is that?" Diane asked. "I assume it's something to do with those red face tattoos."

Zamek nodded. "After her mother's death, Udthulo pledged her life to end as many blood elves as she can. It's called the cleansing. A relation of someone who has died chooses to go out and search for vengeance. If she can find the person who killed her mother, then she will be immediately cleansed. Otherwise, she'll need to keep killing her enemies for however long she pledged. The end result is either she will die, or her targets will;

either way her deeds bring much greatness to her family. They'll be given a seat of power in the elders' chambers, and will become quite wealthy. A lot of families take it as a chance to start afresh. If Udthulo makes it back, she'll be a hero."

"I saw a few people in Sanctuary with similar face markings," I said.

"They will be the few who completed their task and returned. They are revered by our people. Songs are sung about them, tales are told; their deeds will be remembered down the ages."

"And some dwarves are just crazy and want to kill things," Birik said, and he laughed so hard that it turned into a weird choking noise. Malib had to slap him on the back to help him— immediately after which, they both began laughing.

"How much further?" Irkalla asked.

"A few hours," Zamek told us. "This is the last place we'll be able to rest. After this the elves get more numerous, and more dangerous."

"So the elves we've been fighting *haven't* been dangerous?" Remy asked. "That's good to know."

Zamek smiled. "They send their young and inexperienced out to fight in the areas they know dwarves inhabit. It's to test themselves. Either they kill a dwarf—or something equally valuable, like a troll—or they get killed, and no one mourns them. Blood elves care little for emotion."

"And once these were your friends?" Remy asked.

"A long time ago, yes. We welcomed the shadow elves here."

Udthulo re-entered the shop, and whispered, "Patrol. Eight elves, coming up this way. One's a commander."

I remembered the last commander I'd seen, and had little interest in getting any closer to one without the full use of my magic.

"I saw one earlier," I whispered as we hid ourselves by the window, glancing out into the dark street before us.

"They are exceptionally dangerous," Zamek said. "I don't know how the blood elves get them so big, but something sets them apart from normal elves."

As if on cue, the sound of marching feet drifted toward the shop, carrying with it an energy of dread.

"Do we go or stay?" Udthulo asked.

"Stay," Zamek commanded. "The library is not far, but there are many elves between here and there. Let's not draw attention to ourselves. We don't need to fight every elven patrol we come across."

Udthulo nodded, and although she was clearly unhappy about the decision, she went back to looking out of the window.

The elves marched by us, only ten feet from where we were hiding. We had our weapons at the ready, but remained silent and still. The smell of blood and death lingered even once they were gone.

The commander was several dozen feet behind the rest of the group, pushing a blood elf along. The elf was either injured or exhausted, and couldn't keep up with his brethren, so had slipped behind. The commander took a swipe at the elf, who hurried his pace, tripped and fell.

"Useless!" the commander shouted. He wasn't the same blood elf Mordred and I had seen earlier; this one was slightly broader and had dozens of scars all across his bare chest and stomach. Some looked to have been made from weapons, and some from a claw of an animal. Whatever had caused the scar across his stomach could have disemboweled him. The commander had been fortunate to live.

He kicked the wounded blood elf over onto his back, then stomped, punched, and kicked him to death in the middle of the street. When he was done, he drove his saber into the throat of the blood elf. The commander removed the blade, stepped over the corpse, and left it there to bleed out. The blood elves who'd marched on stopped and cheered for their commander as he rejoined them.

"Apparently, blood elves take their marching seriously," Remy said, when the street was once again devoid of life. "What the hell was that all about?"

"The commanders are there to instill discipline," Udthulo told us. "That's almost their entire role. If someone is flagging behind because they're injured, they're eliminated. It's for the betterment of the rest of the group."

We left the building and sprinted to the other side of the street, taking refuge in the alleys that crisscrossed the entire area. We ran into four more patrols on the way to the library but were fortunate enough to escape detection. We only had to fight twice more, and both times we had superior numbers and the advantage of surprise.

"I thought there would be more elves," Irkalla said.

"Yeah, a lot more," Diane agreed. "What gives?"

"I don't know," Zamek said looking to his dwarven subordinates for explanation. They shrugged, just as clueless. "Something has to be happening. There should be more patrols, more lookouts. We're close to the library, and I can't imagine the elves making things easy for us. Besides, if this way is so clear, why didn't those in the library leave? Something feels wrong."

A few hours later, we came to a low, crumbling wall. I peered over the top and immediately moved back.

"You okay?" Remy asked.

"Don't like heights," I told him. "That's a shocker."

Remy looked over the wall and turned back to me. "Well, that's unexpected."

Beyond the wall was a sheer drop hundreds of feet into the darkness below. A huge chasm just a few feet away from us stretched as far as I could see. A few hundred feet to the left of where we were and about thirty feet up was a large stone bridge that stretched several hundred feet over the chasm.

"How do we get over that bridge?" Diane asked.

"Good question," Irkalla said. "I assume any blood elves on it will probably notice us when we walk past them."

"We're not going to," Zamek told us. "There's a pathway that goes down and around the side of the cliff just below us. It leads to the supports under the bridge. We can walk across the supports to get to the other side."

"There's no other way?" Remy asked. "Like a catapult, for example? Because I'd probably prefer that."

"There used to be a higher tunnel far to the north that cut through the mountain, going around the bridge, but it was blocked when most of Brigg's people escaped. The library is over that bridge. And the bridge is now our only way in—unless you want to wait a few weeks while we dig out the tunnel, attracting every blood elf in a dozen miles to our location?"

"I'd rather do that," Remy said. "Seriously, give me a spade."

"Let's get this over with," I said, really not enthusiastic about making this climb.

Zamek and his dwarves had to use their alchemy to reveal the path, quickly pushing aside the rocks that hid it from view. More than once I thought the sound of rocks being moved around would make someone come investigate, but it was soon over, and the path down to the bridge was revealed.

Alchemists can change one thing into something else so long as they're touching the object they're manipulating, and what they want to change has the same components as the original material. So a rock can become a set of stairs or a shield, but it can't turn into a moving tank with a missile launcher, which would be a lot more useful.

Despite the fact that we all had abilities that allowed us to see in near pitch-darkness, the journey down the path went slowly. We had to go quietly or else the blood elves would have heard the sound of us sprinting down the path, and surprise was pretty much our only advantage.

When we reached the end of the path, I looked up at the bridge's underside. There were thin mesh walkways along either side and a crisscrossing of metal floor beams that ran up the center. Posts sat every few dozen feet, with handholds easily visible on them. It didn't exactly look like it would be a barrel of laughs, but it looked sturdy, and so long as I didn't look down—or think about looking down, or think about anything involving heights—I should be okay. You weren't going to get a second chance with it.

"How do we do this?" Remy asked.

Zamek motioned with his hands. "Straight up either side. The side columns have enough space for a dwarf to step around with ease, so it should be okay for you lot. We take it slow and easy. Make a mistake and you're done."

While it was nice to have someone agree with my mental assessment of this death trap, I could have done with a slightly more upbeat talk.

The metal frame of the bridge was easy to climb for the first few struts, although it got considerably more difficult the further up we went, as the incline became steeper and steeper, until the only way to continue on was to get on all fours and climb like a chimpanzee.

By the time I'd almost reached the halfway point, I was hot, sticky, and liked Remy's catapult idea better than my current position. When I made it to the halfway mark, I took a deep breath. The way down was steep, and probably more dangerous than the way up, but at least there was light at the end of the proverbial tunnel.

"How are you doing?" Remy asked from the strut behind me. "Because this sucks a monstrous amount of ass."

"Let's just get it finished."

"Wait," Diane almost growled from the strut in front of me. She lifted the bow from her back and notched an arrow. She remained that way for several seconds, her arm never wavering, until she released the arrow. "Elf down."

I half expected her to have to deal with several more of the elves before we'd reached the other side, but I needn't have been concerned. We made it, sweaty and less than thrilled about the journey, but we made it.

"If we have to do that again on the way back," Remy said, ruining my good mood, "I may just move into the library and live there."

"We're not out of the woods yet," Zamek told us. "We need to go up this side of the chasm and around a corner at the top. We should be out of sight of the elves for most of the ascent, but it's still dangerous."

"What happens at the top?" Irkalla asked.

"There's an old tunnel up there, long abandoned, but it'll take us up above the library. Once we've found the right path, we can just move the rock around and drop onto the top of the library. Any questions?"

No one asked anything more, and we were soon climbing the thin walkway up the side of the chasm. There were a few times when we had to wait behind an overhang or be spotted by the elves. We reached the peak pretty quickly, and hurried across the exposed area to an alcove.

"Where's the tunnel?" I whispered.

Zamek ignored me and began searching the alcove.

"You know if they decide to come this way, we have no means to escape," Remy pointed out.

"Very helpful, Remy. Thanks," Diane said, using as much sarcasm as possible.

Zamek rejoined us and didn't look very happy. "We have a problem. The tunnel was caved in. We're going to have to clear out a lot more rock than we'd anticipated."

I sighed. It was going to be one of those days/weeks/months. "Meaning, we need to buy you time."

"That's about the short of it. The second we start moving rock around, those things are going to hear, and they're going to come and investigate."

Remy removed the twin daggers from his belt. "We get it: kill anything that comes this way. How long?"

"Long enough to get the job done," Zamek said matter-of-factly.

"Plenty of time to get killed," Irkalla said. She removed the claymore from her back. "Ready when you are."

The sounds of tons of rock being shifted could probably be heard all the way back in Sanctuary, so it was hardly a great surprise when most of the blood elves on the bridge began to run toward us.

I stepped out from the alcove flanked by Irkalla and Remy. We started off down the path, followed by Diane, who let loose three arrows unhindered by the distance to the bridge, killing a blood elf with each hit. She was going to run out of arrows well before she ran out of targets.

Either there had been a lot more elves on the bridge than I'd first seen, or there was a camp nearby, but there were nearly a hundred of them by the time they reached the bottom of the walkway. They paused for a few seconds, snarling and shouting insults about how they'd defile our corpses. An elven commander, eerily similar to the one we'd seen on our way here, barged to the front of the crowd and screamed something about feasting on our skins. Then the group charged.

Four against a hundred wasn't exactly great odds, and Diane did her best to thin out their ranks, killing a dozen as they ran toward us, but it didn't take long for them to reach us. I parried a sword thrust from one blood elf as they swarmed around us, and returned the parry with a slice through the elf's throat, using my momentum to spin toward the next, catching it in the chest. Another two went down with cuts to their exposed legs, then decapitation.

The killing of each elf brought a new one into the fight, and I was soon covered in blood. I blocked a hammer, stepped under the weapon, and thrust my spare sword up into the elf's chin and out the top of his head. I kicked the body away just as a knife flew past my head and into the eye of a nearby blood elf.

I turned toward the thrower and saw Irkalla, surrounded by corpses. An elf charged into her, and she used her necromancy to pick it up by the throat and toss it aside, kicking it in the head as it landed. Remy was like a whirlwind of movement, constantly cutting and stabbing at anything taller than he was. His speed and agility made it impossible for any one elf to get close.

The second I'd taken to scan the battlefield, an arrow flew toward me, but I stepped aside and used my air magic to send it into the back of the head of a nearby elf. My magic might not have been overly powerful when used on organic matter, but that didn't mean it was useless. One of the elven commanders charged at me, whipping his two-handed maul at my head with staggering speed. I used air magic to send the maul sailing comfortably over my head, using the elf's own momentum to send him past me. He spun around, swinging the maul toward my pelvis. He kept moving toward me, forcing me further and further back, as he stepped over the corpses of his own men to get to me, swinging the maul from side to side with barely any effort on his part.

He roared in rage as he swung the weapon up and toward me in the blink of an eye. I reacted without thinking, activating my shadow magic. The shadows in front of me instantly grabbed the maul and dragged it into the ground so fast that the elf had no time to let go of his weapon. His arms were buried up to their pits in the rock. Strips of shadow leapt up, wrapping around the commander as he struggled to get free. The other blood elves backed away, shocked and afraid. The shadow continued to drag the commander down into the darkness, vanishing from view. I removed my magic, unsure of what I'd actually managed to achieve.

Many of the elves turned and ran, and to be honest, I felt like doing the same. I had no idea how I'd managed to drag a blood elf into magical shadow, especially considering magic wasn't meant to work on them. But I had bigger problems. The fleeing elves quickly found their resolve when they were joined by hundreds of their friends, who had heard the fight and charged over to see what was happening.

"We need to leave," I said. "Now!"

The four of us ran back to Zamek, who, along with the other three dwarves, was finishing up the tunnel.

"Hundreds of the bastards have turned up," I said. "No idea where from."

"The front of the library is swamped with them," Udthulo told us. "It's why we're going this way."

"Everyone get in," Zamek ordered, and no one needed to be told twice when the first of the blood elves reached the alcove and spotted us.

Malib, the last into the tunnel, began to collapse the walls and mouth, giving us protection from the mob. Once done, several tons of rock covered the entrance, and the blood elves would have a considerably longer and more difficult time of removing it than the dwarves.

The tunnel was big enough for us to stand up in and wide enough to walk two by two, but it was full of stale air and darkness. Sounds of rage came from the elves on the other side of the entrance, but I did my best to ignore them. I applied my night vision and turned back to make sure everyone had made it through.

"Good work. Let's go," Zamek said. But he stopped when Malib collapsed to his knees, showing the arrow that had caught him in the throat.

Zamek was beside his friend in an instant, but it was too late. Malib died making sure all of us were able to continue. And as much as I didn't want to think about it, I doubted very much that he would be the last.

CHAPTER 29

The tunnel was lengthy, and no one spoke for the entire time we walked through its darkness. Malib's body had been left where he'd fallen, something none of the dwarves were happy about, because bringing home the fallen was part of their creed. But we had no idea what was going to happen next, so he had to be left behind.

After some time in the tunnel we reached a part that forked off into three more tunnels. We paused, while Zamek tried to figure out where we were.

"So, you used your new magic to kill an elf," Remy said. I was surprised he'd managed to stay quiet as long as he had; it must have been torturous for him. "I thought Mordred said that your magic wouldn't be as powerful on them. That looked pretty powerful to me."

"I don't know what I did," I said.

"We saw the elf get sucked into those shadows," Irkalla said, taking a swig from her water skin.

Diane sat down beside me. "Whatever it was, it scared those elves. I don't think they're used to seeing magic that works on them here."

"Wait, you used magic that worked on the elves?" Birik asked. "Why didn't you use it on those who murdered my friend? Why didn't you stop them?"

He took a step toward me, his hands gripped tightly around the hilt of his two-handed sword.

"It's not Nate's fault!" Remy snapped. "It's not anyone's fault but the people who actually killed him."

"Shut your mouth, fox!" Birik said. "If you hadn't come here, Malib would still be alive, and we wouldn't be here."

"We didn't ask to come here," Irkalla told him, stepping between Birik and an angry-looking Remy. "We're just trying to save our friend."

"What about *my* friend?" Birik screamed. "Why didn't you use your magic to save *him*? It's always the way with you earth-realmers: you come here demanding help, telling tales of how awful it is that you have to be away from your precious friends and family, never caring about what impact *being here* actually has on *us*!"

"The only earth-realmers sent here are those who were torn from their families and sent here against their will," Remy pointed out. "And most of those probably never even see a dwarf before the blood elves get them."

Birik stared at Remy for several seconds. "I meant before the elves. When we *allowed* earth-realmers to come and go—a policy that was short-sighted in its stupidity."

"Enough, Birik." Udthulo hadn't moved from her seated position close to the tunnel Zamek had continued down. "It's not their fault, or anyone else's from the earth realms. Malib died. Dwarves die in war."

"What do *you* know about war?" Birik's face was full of rage as he turned on the female dwarf. "You're only here because your mother died. You're only here because you decided you might like to actually do something to help for a change."

Udthulo exploded from the floor and was at Birik in a heart-beat, grabbing the larger dwarf around the throat and planting him on the ground.

"Tell me how I don't know war again, Birik," Udthulo demanded, her voice calm and terrifying.

Irkalla took a step toward the pair, ready to separate them, but it wasn't needed. "That's enough!" Zamek ordered as he returned to us.

Udthulo was on her feet within a second, and Birik slowly got up, trying to hide the hurt and anger in his face as he kept his eyes on the ground.

"I don't care about the reason," Zamek said, "but I will not have my people fighting here. We need everyone we can to complete this mission. Fighting among yourselves is pointless."

Both dwarves nodded.

Udthulo walked off and Zamek remained beside Birik, placing a hand on his friend's shoulder. "None of this is their fault. None of it is anyone's but the elves' fault. If you want to be angry with someone, be angry with the right someone. If you lash out like that again, I'll leave you here. I won't carry a liability around."

Birik nodded once.

"I found the entrance to the library."

We all followed Zamek until we reached a part of the tunnel that looked exactly like every other part of the tunnel. Zamek placed his hand on the dirt and it shifted slightly, exposing a trapdoor he levered open with the hilt of his battle-ax.

Zamek motioned for me to take a look inside. I lay on my front and put my head in the hole, looking at the room upside down. It was a vast room, with row after row of books, all on shelves. Hundreds more books and scrolls lay littered across the floor, and some were piled haphazardly in large stacks. It was a bibliophile's worst nightmare and dream all at once: more books than you could read in a lifetime, and most of them badly taken care of.

I got back to my feet and dusted myself down. "There's no one in there. Lots of books, huge windows down one side, several doors, too. No idea where any of it goes."

We all climbed down into the hole using the rope Udthulo tied around the trapdoor handle so that we could actually get back up to the tunnel when we needed to.

I picked up several of the scrolls and books, each one instantly translated as I read part of it. "Most of these are actually about agriculture. This one is about keeping cows. I'm going to guess they're not why we're here."

"We traded cows, sheep, and pigs for weapons once," Zamek said, picking up a hefty scroll and tossing it aside after looking at the first line. "The humans who lived on the surface tended to the animals," Zamek said. "Long time ago, though. I assume the humans are long gone."

I nodded. "I didn't see any. My guess is they didn't last long against the blood elves."

Zamek nodded sadly. "Shame. There were plenty of good people up there. I'm hoping one day we'll take back this mountain and go across the realm, where we'll find pockets of humans and dwarves still free."

"You're not in contact with the other dwarven cities?" Irkalla asked.

"They all fell at once," Zamek said. "If there are any still out there, we haven't heard from them."

"So where would Brigg be?" Diane asked.

"Um, everyone should come see this," Remy called out from the far side of the room.

"We're in the center of the library, so Brigg should be in the west wing," Zamek explained as we all moved over to Remy. "That's where the tracker is flickering."

I was about to ask a question when I reached the window and looked down. A hundred feet below and across several hundred feet of open courtyard were the destroyed gates to the library, beside a partially ruined wall which, if the remaining parts were any indication, had once stood fifty feet high. The bridge was a few hundred feet beyond the gates, the flickering of torches in the darkness telling me that the elves were still there. Still ready to fight.

I went back to looking at the architecture of the library building. It had been made in a horseshoe fashion and was a stunning structure, made of white stone. The building and grounds together would put something like the Houses of Parliament to shame. But how nice the building looked wasn't why Remy had called us over. The blood elves were.

There were thousands of them, all camped out in the courtyard, and spilling out through the ruined front wall and gate of the library, their camp torches shining in the darkness for as far as I could see.

"So that's where those elves came from," Diane said. "I'd really like it if we didn't go down there."

"I'd really like it if we had a big bomb," Remy said. "Several of them. How do we get out of here when the front door looks like Woodstock, but with more psychopaths, and the caved-in tunnel we came down is now probably getting attacked by several hundred angry elves? Asking for a friend."

"We'll find a way," Diane assured him. "We always do."

"I await the fabulous plan, then." Remy rolled his eyes. "I bet it's going to be a great one."

"Are you always like this?" Irkalla asked.

"Yes," Diane and I said in unison.

With the closest we'd come to frivolity for several hours out of the way, Zamek brought us all over to a table, where he unfurled a scroll he'd removed from his pack. It was a map of this floor of the library.

"There are fifty floors in this building, and that's not counting the ones that stretch underground. We can pretty much take those as being firmly in the elves' control, as are the lower levels of this building. The dwarf who returned to us from Brigg's group confirmed the number of blood elves."

"They really want those locations," I said.

"And the spirit scrolls," Remy continued.

Zamek nodded. "We won't have long to find Brigg and any of his people, find the scrolls and destination addresses, and get out of here. I think the blood elves would very much like the head of a prince, even one no longer given that title. And they will certainly all know you're here, and what you did with your magic."

"So I painted a big bullseye on me."

Zamek nodded. "Pretty much, yes. I wouldn't be surprised that if we all manage to get out of here in one piece, they'll put a large bounty on your head. I meant to ask how you used your shadow magic to kill that elf. Either you used a huge amount of magic to do what you did, or shadow magic affects the elves more than other types. We'll need to talk to the elders when we return. They might know more."

"I don't know," I reiterated. "I wish I did, but I have no clue."

"So, where are we on this map?" Diane asked.

Zamek picked up a piece of rock from the floor and placed it in front of him, next to several small marks that I assumed were meant to be Zamek and his team's trackers. He removed a small compass-sized item from his pack and tapped the glass screen. "The tracker is twelve floors below us, in the east wing. The tracker says he's in the far room, over here." Zamek placed a second piece of rock. "It's going to take a few hours to get there, so I hope no one is interested in resting. We do this quick and quiet. No fuss; any necessary kills must be done without any alarms being raised."

No one had a problem with that. We all took a few minutes to get a drink and eat some of our supplies before we were trudging through the library in search of Brigg.

The library appeared to me to consist of one long corridor with hundreds of doors down one side. Each floor had the same layout, but we often found the stairwells partially collapsed and had to break through the floor of one room to drop down onto the level below. The dwarves couldn't move the debris without causing an avalanche—something that would be dangerous, even for alchemists. It was quicker and easier to just destroy a separate part of the floor.

I was surprised to find that the entire place wasn't overrun with blood elves, as we only came across a few, and they were easily dispatched, most of them looking tired and weak.

"Their numbers aren't as big as I assumed," I told Zamek.

"Agreed. I'd expected more resistance." Zamek replied as he removed his battle-ax from the skull of one elf. "For hundreds of years the blood elves only pilfered from certain parts of the library where they thought the spirit scrolls were. It allowed us to create expeditions to search in the least infected parts of the building. But now that the elves are looking for the addresses for the tablets, too, they've swamped the lower floors. Something is making them more cohesive than it has before."

"Or someone?" I suggested.

"Or that. This hooded figure."

"How many humans do they have?" Diane asked.

"Unknown. If they took those from the human villages above, a few hundred thousand, but that would have been centuries ago, and humans don't live that long. My guess is, a lot more of them have been stolen from other realms over the last few years. We've found people in military uniforms, earth-realm people, and those from other realms where humans live. Mostly earth, though. Jinayca didn't mention it earlier, but we've seen an increase in human slaves. Whatever the elves are doing, they're quickening their timetable."

"Well, if the witches did create the tablets that sent us, it makes sense. A lot of them love Hera and will happily do whatever she asks, no matter how awful it is," Diane said. "I imagine she'll have gotten a lot of those to help out."

"Mara," I said softly. "She's got to be involved in this."

"Chloe's mum?" Diane asked. "I remember her. I wanted to punt her head off."

"She's such a sparkling human being," I admitted. "I hope I'm wrong, but it doesn't feel that way."

"How many witches are in your realm?" Udthulo asked.

I shared a look with Diane and Irkalla. "I have no idea."

"A metric shitload?" Remy guessed. "I remember taking a

census for Elaine a few decades ago. She wanted to know exactly how much support Hera was getting from the witches. I can't remember the exact figure, but it was around a hundred thousand. And forty thousand of those are in a coven that is very pro-Hera. Hera might not trust all of those who help her, but that still gives Hera a sizable figure to work with. In theory they could be sending a lot of innocent people here every year. That also means we have a lot of witches murdering people. Shit, if that gets out, Avalon will want a cull."

Diane stopped walking. "That would be dangerous. Tarring all witches with the same brush and going after them for what a few are doing would prove that Hera was right all along. Witches will be killed: a lot of them."

"It could start a war," Irkalla said. "And at the very least, it would drive a lot more witches into Hera's arms. I guarantee she's thought about that. If anyone ever finds out the witches are behind sending people here, she'd probably start the purge herself, and then claim the witches could come to her for sanctuary."

"This is still that hypothetical situation you were talking about?" Remy asked. "Because it sounds pretty close to what could actually be happening."

We went back to silence as we continued down the levels until Zamek stopped us one floor above where we needed to be.

"This is it. Brigg should be down these stairs, and about two hundred feet north of here." He removed the tracker again and tapped it before nodding to himself. "Let's go."

We walked slowly down the stairwell until we'd reached our target level, then hurried along the corridor until we came to a room at the far end. Zamek tried to push the door—there was no handle, and didn't look like there ever had been—but found that it wouldn't move. Runes had been carved into the frame, spelling out *locked* over and over again. In smaller runes along the top of the frame was the word *blaze*. Brigg had set a rather unpleasant trap for anyone trying to get in.

"We're not getting in through that door," I said. "How about the wall?"

"If Brigg booby-trapped the door, then the wall will be too," Birik told everyone. "He's . . . careful like that."

"He has to have a way in and out," Diane said.

"His own alchemy, I imagine," Birik said. "Anyone else tries it and they get a nasty surprise."

Zamek hammered on the door. "Brigg, it's me, Zamek. Open the damn door." He hammered a second time.

"Prove it," a voice said from inside the room.

"Open the fucking door, you lunatic!" Zamek snapped.

The door slid out toward us and then to one side, revealing an elderly dwarf with a long red beard and a nasty cut across his forehead. The cut was recent, and would leave an equally nasty scar.

"Get in, you fools," he snapped, and he ushered us all into the room before closing the door and resetting the trap.

The room looked like every other room in the building, full of books and shelves, although this one curved around to the side. A small fireplace sat off in a corner, and it appeared to be in good use. Three dwarves lay on a pile of old clothes and cloth, using them as makeshift mattresses, weapons close to hand even as they slept.

"Why are you here?" he asked once he was done with the door.

"We came for you," Zamek said.

"Bollocks," Brigg said. "I sent someone back expressly telling you to stay away. I can't go back to the city and leave all of this in elven hands. I'll die first. And seeing how the elders have sent exactly zero people to help, I assume that's exactly the way they like it. You didn't come here to help, my old pupil. So, why are you here?"

"Our friend was poisoned," I said. "She needs a spirit scroll or she'll die."

"And who are you?" Brigg asked.

The others introduced themselves first, and when I said my name, Brigg's eyebrows shot up.

"Brynhildr's boy?" he asked. "I haven't seen you since you were . . . well, that doesn't matter."

I finally recognized his face. "You were the dwarf at the temple. The one who performed the ritual." I hadn't meant to let my anger infect my tone.

"You want to save your friend, or give me shit about something I did sixteen hundred years ago?" he snapped.

"Both," I snapped back.

Brigg and I glared at one another for several seconds while no one else spoke. Eventually, he sighed. "Fine. Let's just make sure the last of my team is back here, and then we'll talk. I promise."

There was another bang on the door. "Wait," Brigg said, and he went to open the door.

"Nate, calm yourself," Zamek whispered. "Brigg is not a man to be forced into answering questions. If you want to help your friend, do not anger him. We will never get back in time to save her."

I nodded. I understood how important saving Chloe was. But Brigg was my chance at getting answers, and the fact that he'd told me we would talk meant that we *would* talk. Whether he wanted to or not.

Two more dwarves rushed into the room, followed by a human. "Ambush on the sixteenth floor," the human said. "We lost Yami."

"Fucking bastards!" Brigg shouted. He closed the door once again. "At this rate, we'll lose too many to keep them back."

The human walked over to us, while Zamek and Brigg spoke in hushed tones. "You're from the earth realm?" he asked.

I nodded. "We got sent here by someone who wants us out of the way."

"Join the club," he said, offering his hand. "You're not human, though."

"Sorcerer." I pointed over to my companions as I introduced them. "Trying to find spirit scrolls."

"Well, that could be a problem," the human said. "The spirit scrolls are on the eighteenth floor, in a hidden room in the west wing."

"Of course they are," Remy said.

"So apart from a bit of a walk, what's the problem?" Irkalla asked.

"The blood elves took the eighteenth floor about twelve months ago. We're trying to drive them back, but not having a lot of luck. They have a new commander, someone who wears a hood. He's got some serious power; he tore the front gates off the wall by himself. That's why the blood elves were able to swarm this place."

"Well, this sounds like a problem."

"It could be, yes," the human agreed. "Oh, I'm sorry, I haven't introduced myself. I'm Adam. Adam Range."

"You're Chloe's dad?" I asked.

His face lit up at hearing Chloe's name, confirming my suspicion, but his expression was quickly replaced with fear and worry. "Yes. You know Chloe? How is she?"

I wasn't really sure how to start the sentence that needed to be said. "She's the reason we're here. She needs the scroll."

For a second I thought Chloe's dad was going to break down, but he held it together. "Brigg, we're getting these people to those spirit scrolls if I have to blow up half of this building to do it."

"Don't even think—" Brigg began, and then he turned back to Adam. Something in the human's face made him pause. "We'll help her."

"Or I'll die trying," Adam said with utter conviction.

CHAPTER 30

The meeting that followed the revelation of Adam's identity was short and to the point. We needed to get to the eighteenth floor, and do so without attracting the hundreds of blood elves that lived inside the building from floor twenty down.

The blood elves were slowly encroaching floor by floor. Whoever this new person in charge was, he'd certainly given them the incentive they needed to dominate the library. Brigg, Adam, and his people had tried their best, but it was like trying to push back the ocean with a spoon.

Adam left at the end of the meeting, and I went to find him, hoping to give him some comfort that Chloe would be okay. I found him sitting next to a pile of books with his eyes closed.

"My wife, Mara, sent me here," he said. "Used a tablet she was working on for months. Always told me it was witch stuff and none of my business. Turns out, I really should have been more interested in whatever *witch stuff* was."

"I think she sent us here too. She coated one of the tablets in the venom of a creature called an ekimmu. My friend was meant to be the person to touch it; Chloe was in the wrong place at the wrong time."

"To your knowledge, has my wife put Chloe's life in danger before?"

"A few times, yes. Chloe lives with her friend, Kasey, who is the daughter of my best friend. Chloe and Mara haven't talked since . . . well, they had a row." It was Chloe's job to tell her dad about her sexuality, not mine.

"I'm going to kill Mara if I ever get out of here. I never thought I was capable of murdering anyone until the first day I turned up here and a blood elf grabbed me. I fought back, killed one, and escaped into the city. Six months I lived in this city, with no idea where I should go, until the dwarves found me. That was, I assume, many years ago. Time is funny under the mountain."

"Probably about three or four years ago, I think. Chloe mentioned that you vanished."

"Yep, that's one way of putting it. We're going to save my daughter. You know that, right?"

I nodded. "How have you survived out here for so long?"

"I found one of the scrolls. Turns out bonding with a bunch of spirits will give you some serious power. In my case, it's the ability to track an item. I think about the item I want and it lets me hone in on it—a bit like using GPS in my head. It doesn't always work, though; I need to have the *exact* item in mind. It's hard to explain."

"So the scroll's power is random?"

He shook his head. "I don't think so. When I came here, I wanted more than anything to get home. And when I found a scroll, all I could think of was getting back to Chloe. To be honest, I'm not sure; I would have thought it would have just let me create realm-gate portals so I could go home, but the scrolls don't work like that. They don't let you just pick what you want; they sort of look deep down into you and pick an ability based on your own soul. So maybe in my soul, being able to find anything

I wanted was what I needed the most. I don't really know, and I've spent almost the entire time I've been here either trying to find a way home, or trying to help the dwarves stay alive."

"Is that why you came here? To try and find a way home?"

Adam nodded. "I wanted an item that would help me get home, but I need to know the exact item for my power to work. So I came here hoping to find something useful."

"Would location addresses to use on a tablet so we can get home help?"

"What?"

"The blood elves have allies who used a portable realm gate." I explained more about the tablets. "We need to find the addresses for the earth realm. Once we've got them, maybe we can figure out how to create our own tablet and get home."

Adam's face lit up with genuine hope. "Tell me more about these tablets."

I told him everything I knew.

He listened attentively, not speaking until I'd finished. "When the dwarves found me, I told them about the tablet that had sent me here, and for the most part, they had no idea what I was talking about. Jinayca suggested that I come on this expedition so that I might be able to find some sort of Rosetta Stone and figure out how to create my own, but no matter how much I want to find it, it doesn't seem to exist. I've tried thinking of every permutation the dwarves here have suggested—nothing. Those addresses are gone." Adam sounded defeated.

It was a tough blow to take, but I refused to just give in. "Any chance there could be something here blocking your power?"

Adam thought for a second. "It's possible."

"Can you search for power blockers instead? Maybe we can

figure out how to find these addresses if they're hidden from view. The dwarves didn't want anyone finding them. Maybe they're in a rune-scribed vault or something."

"That's possible," Adam admitted, brightening up. "So if we can get the scrolls and the addresses before the blood elves, we can save Chloe and stop these assholes from creating super-powered monsters. The dwarves might actually have a chance to win. Then I can go home. It's a long game, but there's no other choice.

"Unfortunately, most of the librarians were killed during the war," he continued, "and the thing about the dwarves back then was that they really didn't like sharing their knowledge with one another. It's different now—it's a matter of survival—but back then the librarians who lived here either died here, or fled, and there are none left—no one they taught the language to. So, even if we find the addresses, how do we create the tablet?"

"One of the people back at Sanctuary said that if we can rune-scribe the knowledge of the languages onto a human, then they could create the tablet."

There was a sparkle in his eyes. "That could work."

"I'll leave you alone to work on it."

"Thank you."

I went back to the others and explained what Adam was trying to accomplish. The three dwarves who I'd seen asleep when I'd arrived were now up, preparing their gear for a fight.

"I don't think he'll find anything," Brigg said sadly. "All he's wanted to do since the day I met him is get back to his daughter. I can't imagine anything worse than knowing she needs you and knowing there's nothing you can do."

"We can find her those scrolls," I told him.

Brigg nodded, and pointed to a part on a map that had

been laid out on the huge table next to one wall. "The blood elves are looking for the scrolls, but they have no idea where to look. We do. Unfortunately, it's right under their noses. Before the blood elves defiled this place, I found where they're hidden. Unfortunately, they're in a room that's completely sealed, and I have no idea how to get in. I found nothing that would suggest an entrance or exit. Whoever created it was very keen to keep it locked. I saw no runes or markings, but when I tried to use alchemy, it blew me back forty feet."

"That where you got the cut?" Zamek asked.

"No, this was from a blood-elf sword. I didn't duck quickly enough. Still killed it, though, so it's not all bad."

The whole situation was beginning to sound worse and worse. "So we have a room that we can't get into, and there's a whole lot of really nasty elves between us and it? That sound about right?"

There were several nods from people around the table.

"In that case, how do we get into the room?" Irkalla asked. "Because otherwise, this whole thing is a giant waste of time."

"We tried going through the floor above, but that's rune-marked, so it's out. We tried from the floor below, but the same problem. The only way into that room would be if you could get outside the library and go through the outside wall. I've checked; there are no rune marks. The problem with that is the huge number of blood elves in the yard below."

"So one of us has to make some sort of mad dash outside, or distract thousands of blood elves so that we can get in without them being there."

"Or teleport into it," Diane said.

Several eyes looked at me.

"Shadow magic," I said. "I'm not exactly practiced with it."

"It could work, although I have no idea *how* it would work. I also have no idea if you'd be able to bring all of the scrolls back. There are several hundred."

"Can I take someone with me into the room?"

"I could go," Brigg said. "It would give me a chance to see if I could unlock it from the inside."

"A few hundred scrolls can't be that heavy," Remy said. "Can they?"

"Depends on the scroll," Brigg countered. "I have no idea what condition they'll be in. A thousand years is a long time to be locked in a room, but in theory it's a sealed room, so they should be fine. Besides, they're impervious to most things that would destroy a scroll, so as likely as not they'll be in one piece. The main thing is, they cannot fall into enemy hands. The elves already have too many of these scrolls, and there are enough in the earth realm without adding to them."

"Wait: these things are already in our realm?" Remy asked. "I think this is something we should have been told more about."

"They've been there for millennia. We know that people stole the scrolls in the past, especially before the blood elves came. We know that scrolls were given as gifts to earth-realm dignitaries: a token of the pact that we made with Avalon to supply them with dwarven weapons. That was before we realized how dangerous they were, but it was long enough to put more than a few scrolls out there. Combine that with those that were stolen and there are probably five or six hundred in your realm already."

"There could be five hundred super-powered scroll-users in our world right now?" Diane asked. "How do we not know about this?"

"Well, apparently Avalon knows," Remy said. "Or at least some of the people working for them do. I wonder how many of those scrolls actually were given to Avalon, and how many fell off the back of the first cart they were put on?"

"That sounds like Avalon," I said. I thought about it for a moment. Over the years I'd fought a lot of people whose power I couldn't put into one species category or another, and I've fought people who turned into monsters more than I care to remember. "I'll just add it to the list of things Merlin kept from me."

"This is one of those things that Merlin would probably like to forget," Remy said. "The last person who investigated the dwarves was Mordred, and that didn't turn out so well. Not the nice chap who likes to talk about *Mario*—and seriously, what the hell is *that* about?—but the psychopath who liked to cut people into tiny pieces and make them vanish. No one wants a re-creation of that particular man. Maybe Merlin thought it better to be out of sight, out of mind. The dwarves have vanished: no longer my problem."

"That also sounds like Merlin," I admitted. "Mordred was framed because he came here to investigate weapons he found." I was talking mostly to myself. "He came here because he found one of the scrolls, or the person using it. We were investigating a bunch of murders, and we'd found dwarven blades and armor, but no scrolls. I was sent away soon after, but he continued looking into it. That's when he found a scroll. Someone in Avalon set him up. Who in Avalon kept this all secret?"

"Kay, Arthur, Elaine, Merlin: take your pick," Zamek said. "All would have had a vested interest in keeping this quiet. And if one of them was the one smuggling weapons and spirit scrolls out of the city, they'd *really* want to keep that quiet. Whoever stole the scrolls could have sold them to Avalon's enemies, flooding the world with humans who have the power of sorcerers. An enemy of Avalon's with an army of powerful spirit-scroll users— it's not a nice thought."

"I spoke to Mordred before I came here," I said. "He was sacrificed to help someone save face. He was framed for the king's murder because he found something he shouldn't have. Someone in Avalon set him up. And according to Morgan, there were more than enough people in Avalon who wanted him out of the way. Mordred was meant to become the king, not Arthur. His abduction was beneficial to a lot of people. It's not difficult to link the smugglers of the scrolls with the same people behind what happened to Mordred: Hera, Kay, and the like. They were the ones who came here when it was under blood-elf rule; they were the ones who wanted him dead. I'd put money that they were also the ones stockpiling stolen spirit scrolls, and wanting Mordred out of the way. And by the time we realized he was innocent, it was too late."

"Let's get these damn scrolls, and let's do it quickly," Irkalla said. "Later, we can deal with who got Mordred almost killed. One problem at a time."

Adam rejoined us, looking intrigued. "I found something. There's a second rune-warded room one floor up from here. I don't know if the addresses would be in there, but that whole area was where the research into the tablets was done, so it's a good bet."

I kept looking at the map for a second longer, and felt eyes on me. "Scrolls first, then the addresses. We'll need to go up to get out, unless you all want to fight the horde on your front lawn. The addresses can be done after." I looked around the table at everyone who was going to take part. "I want us all back here in one piece. So, let's get this done."

Everyone took a few minutes to get ready before two of the dwarves left the room to scout ahead and ensure we weren't going to be walking into a platoon of blood elves. Our destination was over a dozen floors down and on the other side of the building, so we plotted a course to avoid as many blood elves as possible.

"I hear you used your magic to kill an elf," Brigg said as he sidled up beside me.

"Looks that way," I admitted. "Wish I knew how."

"I have a theory."

"A theory?"

"Yes, it's a collection of ideas intended to explain something, but not necessarily ideas that have been proven to be correct."

I rolled my eyes. Apparently I was starring in an episode of *The Naked Gun* and no one had told me. "I know what the word *theory* means, Brigg. I want to know what *your* theory is."

"Oh, I wasn't sure. Anyway, my theory is that it's only elemental magic that the elves, and other creatures in the realm, are immune to. The crystals that affected their immunity to magic only ever reacted to elemental stimulus, not your omega magics. I found several scrolls about the subject in one of the rooms about six hundred years ago. Haven't met a sorcerer to test it out on, though."

"I'm sure I'll get a chance to test it again."

Brigg ignored my sarcasm. "I hope so."

When he didn't leave, I spoke, "Got something else to say?"

"We need to talk. Before we do this. I wasn't going to; I was going to try and ignore you before you left, but Adam made me see that maybe I owed you a few answers."

We walked off to the far end of the room and took a seat on the floor. I felt apprehensive about what I would learn, and wondered if maybe Brigg would spoon-feed me what he thought I wanted to hear just to get out of a situation he didn't want to be in.

"I don't know who your father is," were the first words out of his mouth about it. "The only person who knew that was your mother. Or maybe Merlin. But my point is the number is small, so don't ask."

"I learned who my mother was the day I ended up here. Three days I've been here. And then when they tried to rune-scribe me, my brain went nuts and showed me the ritual you put me through. I literally know nothing else about my mother or why I was dunked into a pool of blood. Oh, that's not true. I know that Merlin knows who my mother was, and has kept it from me for the last sixteen hundred years."

Brigg nodded, and his expression softened. "Your mother, Brynhildr, was a good woman. Smart, fearsome, and more than capable of holding her own. She was one of the few associated with the Norse pantheon that I actually liked."

"She was a valkyrie."

"Her people gave their allegiance to Odin because it was a mutually beneficial idea. The Valkyrie were exceptionally powerful warriors, and Odin didn't want that power slipping into anyone's hands but his. He offered them *a lot* for their help. We're talking giving them money, power, their own realm if they needed it."

"The valkyrie have their own realm?"

"I'm not sure if that part was ever finalized before the Norse cut off all contact with the outside realms, but last I heard, yes.

Your mother and the rest of the valkyries worked for the Norse gods for centuries, maybe even longer, and then out of the blue your mother was banished. She was pregnant at the time, with you. I don't know who your father is, Nate, but whoever it is pissed off Odin enough to jeopardize his entire pact with the valkyries. Your mother had to smooth everything over and almost make them swear to continue to serve the Norse." He paused for a moment and sighed. "I'm sure you have lots of questions, so go right ahead."

I had more questions than time to ask them, but a few sprang to the front of my mind. "Who was my mother hiding me from?"

"People who *really* didn't want you around. Hera wasn't meant to be there; that was something your mother was less than happy about. Hera was one of the people you were being hidden from. But then, Merlin made sure you were kept safe, so it all worked out. Besides, Hera only knew that you were there for the memory-erase, not anything else."

"Why take my memories?"

"Well, we had to make sure that you couldn't remember who you were. Your mother was insistent. She had people who would have liked to use you to get to her, so she did the thing she never wanted to do: made you forget her."

"What are the blood-curse marks for?"

"To keep your powers in check. I don't know what they do, or what they block; those marks were handed to me by your mother. But I know she was worried that the vast amount of power inside of you would cause people to hunt you. It had to be released slowly. I performed the ritual, but I didn't perform the blood magic that bound those marks to you; that was someone else. I have no idea who. Sorry."

"Those marks still aren't gone. Sixteen hundred years and counting."

"Blood magic isn't an exact science. They'll leave when they're good and ready."

"What war was coming?"

"The Norse were on the brink of a civil war. That's why they vanished and shut their borders. Your mother didn't want you involved. As it turned out, it's a war that lasted a long time. No one really knows what happened once they shut their gates."

"Why you? Why did my mother bring me to you? And why have people such as Zeus, Thor, and the like at the ceremony?"

"You saw all of that blood in the pool? Well, we needed power to add to it. Zeus, Thor, Merlin: they all bled into that pool, just enough to ensure the marks bonded quickly. They added their power to your blood-curse marks. Your mother asked each of them individually to attend before you were even born, but when push came to shove, she just didn't want to go through with it. Understandable, really. She was losing her child."

"She told me that my father was dead. I guess giving me up wasn't as easy as she'd hoped."

Anger flashed across Brigg's face. "Don't do that. Don't talk about it as if you have any idea what she went through. She hated having to give you up. She did it to save your life. As for your father, I never heard he was dead. In fact, I heard she saw him just before the ritual. Again, I don't know who he is, nor did I ever care to find out. Some secrets are best left staying that way."

"So he could be alive?"

"Could be. Could be anything for all I know. Can't say I know what happened to your mother, either. You stayed for a few days after the ritual, and she left. She sat with you while you were semiconscious, but we needed her to go before you fully woke. I learned that you were ambushed on the way to Camelot."

I nodded.

"You ever find out who?"

I shook my head.

"Yeah, well, I'll leave you with this. Name one person off the top of your head who would risk doing something *in* Avalon itself, outside of the city of Camelot, just to try and kill a possible rival."

One name came to mind first. "Hera."

Brigg stood and placed his hand on my shoulder. "Good guess."

"If she wanted me dead, why stop there? Why not keep trying?"

"Ah, Nate. Hera always liked to think she was the top of the pile, but she never was."

"She is now. Zeus vanished a few hundred years ago."

Brigg shook his head. "No. She might be in control of whatever Zeus and she achieved together, but she's still working for someone else. How many times has she tried to kill you, personally?"

"She tried to have me killed several times over the years. I can't prove anything, but I'm pretty sure she has. Every time I get in her way, she sends some people after me."

"And there's your problem." He leaned closer and whispered, "If Hera *really* wanted you dead, she'd do it herself. She's not above it. Which means they're token efforts by someone who doesn't want to be seen to be trying to kill you. Who is so powerful that they scare Hera? Someone who has enough power to make sure that she leaves you alone. For centuries. You understand?

Someone out there scares her so much that she never tried to make a concentrated effort to kill you again."

He stood up straight.

"It's not Kay, that's for sure."

"No, it's not."

"Merlin?"

"If it were Merlin, you'd have been killed a thousand times over."

"Then who?"

Brigg shrugged. "I have no idea. I've been stuck in here. They've separated the dwarves from the earth realm, the Norse gods from everyone, and from what I've heard from your companions, fractured Avalon. They've spent a long time plotting and planning and moving figures around. And while I have no idea who it is, I hope like hell I'm dead when they decide to make themselves known."

CHAPTER 31

I was thankful when we reached the west wing staircase, where the two scouts waited for us.

"Lots of elves after floor twenty-one," one of them told us. "There are a few scouts up above it, but they haven't been able to get past the rune-scribed parts of floor twenty-five, so that's holding them."

"You set a trap?" Diane asked.

"The entire floor is inscribed with runes," Adam said. "If anything resembling an elf walks on it, the whole floor becomes an inferno, as do the next five floors above."

"That would burn this whole place down," Zamek said. "I'm pretty certain the elders wouldn't like that."

"If they come that far up, we have no chance anyway," Brigg told him. "Better to burn this place to cinders than let it fall into their grubby hands."

"I thought dwarves really hated to destroy anything written," Remy pointed out.

"And now you see why it's so important that we drive them back," Brigg said. "We can't lose the library. It still has plenty of secrets to give up, and I have no intention of going down without a fight. There were always a few stragglers on higher floors, but if those creatures get to floor twenty-five en masse, that's half of this library. The only reason they'll make it that far up is because we're dead."

We followed the scouts down the stairwell, moving slower and with more caution the closer we got to our destination. When we hit floor twenty-five I peered around the corner at the hallway and found all of the doors open and runes etched onto every surface. They glowed golden with power, standing starkly against the library's white stone.

The runes had been etched into the stairwell for another four floors. On one landing there were bloodstains, old and brown, on the floor and walls, and pieces of dwarven armor scattered across the floor. There had been a lot of fighting here at one point, maybe when the elves first invaded; it was hard to tell.

Brigg placed his hand against a gouge on the wall that looked as if it had been made from a bladed weapon.

"During the original elven uprising, the fighting here was ferocious," he said wistfully. "We lost a lot of good dwarves when the elves first came, but we drove them off, locked the gates, and had some semblance of freedom here. But then they came back with that hooded bastard."

He walked off without another word.

"He's been through a lot," Adam said. "Lost his son and wife in the first war with the blood elves, his three daughters over the years too. It's just him and his scrolls now. This place is all he really cares about."

"He was a soldier once," Zamek said. "A general, a warrior. He fought the blood elves beside me in the citadel, giving so many time to flee. He was beside me when the citadel fell, when we had to retreat into the city, and after all of his losses, I know for a fact that he wouldn't hesitate to save these scrolls over a dwarf. He thinks we failed as a species, but he hates the blood elves more. Just be careful with any plans he suggests. It's almost guaranteed that he wants the blood elves to die a lot more than he wants to live."

As we reached the nineteenth floor, I mentally readied myself for whatever was coming up, and hoped my shadow magic would be able to get me into the room in one piece. Brigg sent his people down one end of the hallway to watch for elves, while Diane, Irkalla, Udthulo, and Birik went to the other end.

"Do you know what you're doing?" Remy asked.

I ignited my shadow magic and widened the shadows made by the crystal lights on the ceiling. The shadow stretched out beneath my feet and I sank into it, noticing Remy and Brigg's looks of concern as I did. I was about to tell them it was fine, when a second later we were all inside the shadow realm I'd last been to with Chloe when we were escaping the panthers.

"What is this place?" Remy asked, glancing around. The nerves in his voice were easy to hear, and even easier to understand.

"It's where my magic takes me," I explained. "I can bring a shadow toward us to use as an exit. I just need to find the right one."

I began searching for the shadows when we heard a defiant roar. Out of the darkness charged the commander I'd sent here during the attack on the walkway. Both Remy and Brigg unsheathed their weapons, but I raised a hand toward the commander creating gray shadows that wrapped around the elf until there was nothing but shadow, and then it vanished.

I dragged the correct exit shadow over to us, and a second later we found ourselves out of the shadow realm and inside a small room.

"What did you do?" Remy asked as soon as his feet touched normal stone, an expression of relief on his face.

"I wrapped the commander in several different shadows and sent him back to this realm." I explained. "When my curse marks unlock a new power, they don't unlock the how-to guide to go with it. I'll need to figure out how everything works in time, but I've been using magic for a long time, and natural instinct counts for a lot where magic is concerned."

"What happened to the commander?" Brigg asked.

"A guess? A different part of him arrived at a different shadow. I won't know for sure until we get out of this room, but if that's what happened it's probably not pretty."

"Yeah, well it worked, and we don't have to deal with it," Remy said. "Right now, I'll take any small victory we can get."

I looked around at the hundreds of scrolls that littered the benches and floor inside the room. There were dozens of runes on the wall too.

"Any clues how to open the door so we don't have to go back through that realm?" Remy asked.

"I'll look into it," Brigg said, and he set about trying to decipher the runes while Remy and I found an old trunk and began loading the scrolls into it.

"I hope one of these things works," Remy said, opening a scroll. "None of it means a damn thing to me."

I took it from him and started reading. "This is a spirit scroll," I told him. "This writing says nothing in particular; it's just a bunch of words for power, contract, spirit, and then names. Three names, to be exact: Aelia, Hiram, and Ninsun. Two male, one female. A Roman, a Carthaginian, and a Sumerian name."

"What bar did they walk into?" Remy asked.

I ignored him. "And below those names is one I can't even begin to pronounce."

"It's the name of the demon," Brigg said without looking over at us, totally ignoring Remy's comment.

I put the scroll into the trunk. "I think the rest of it's probably best left unread, then."

As we finished, Brigg was drawing runes on the wall in charcoal. "I know what they did to seal the room. I'm going to unseal it, which will cause the wall to open. They actually used alchemy to create this room, so I'm going to use the same method to destroy it."

"Just do it," I said.

Brigg placed his hand on the wall and it shimmered golden before parting to show the hallway beyond.

"Simple," Brigg said with a level of smug satisfaction.

I dragged the trunk out of the room and dropped it on the floor.

"An elf exploded," Diane said. "It just appeared out of nowhere, spread all over the place. I assume you did that."

I noticed the fresh blood spray and lumps of unpleasant-looking meat that had once been an elven commander spattered all over. I guess my assumption had been correct.

"Sorry about that. Not quite used to the new magic."

"Do you want to call the rest of your troops back?" I said to Brigg. "We can get going."

Brigg walked off without another word.

"What's wrong with him?" Remy asked.

"He was expecting more fighting," Adam explained. "I think he's disappointed that there hasn't been more bloodshed."

"He'll get his chance, I'm sure of that," Diane told him. "So how do we get out of here with a trunk full of scrolls? The way we came in through the top of the building isn't exactly friendly anymore."

"We need to get those addresses first," Adam said. "And then we'll figure something out, I guess."

"There's another way," Brigg said as he returned with the dwarves. "On the floor below us, part of the floor is built into the mountain itself. We could use our alchemy to tunnel through it, creating a way to escape, but there's going to be a lot of noise, and that means a lot of blood elves to clear out first. There's a good reason we haven't done this before."

"I'd better go for those addresses then," Adam said.

"We'll wait here for you," I told him. "But be quick: we can't afford to hang around."

Irkalla, Zamek, and Adam ran off together, and I was pretty certain that whatever they ran into they'd be able to deal with. The remainder of us took a few moments to rest before the eventual fighting. If Brigg wanted more elves to kill, I was certain he was about to get his wish.

CHAPTER 32

Adam, Zamek, and Irkalla returned after only a few minutes. "There was nothing there," Adam told us. "The runes were on a locked room. Zamek managed to disarm the runes, but we got inside and it was all gone. At some point there might have been something, but the runes had been created to destroy whatever was inside."

"Whoever had done it really hadn't wanted those addresses in elven hands," Zamek said. "There's no way to salvage anything."

"Any chance there are more elsewhere?" Remy asked.

"If there are, they're either hidden from my power somehow, or it's not a scroll. Something outside of what I've been thinking those realm-gate tablet addresses would be on."

It was a crushing blow, but something to work on when we were safely back in the city.

We dragged the trunk all the way across to the east wing. The few blood elves we saw ran rather than fought, something everyone who had been around them for a lot longer than I had found strange.

I placed the trunk near to where the dwarves were going to work, in a quickly emptied room. Brigg wasn't thrilled about being separated from the scrolls, but it was either that or risk the possibility of them being destroyed by the shifting walls and rock beyond.

The sound was deafening, and those who weren't helping to tunnel out of the library quickly left the room and prepared for whatever might come our way. Diane, Irkalla, Remy, Zamek, Birik, Udthulo, and I made quite the dangerous team. Even Adam stood alongside us, and while I didn't think finding an item was going to come in too handy in a fight, I was grateful for any help we could get.

When the blood elves came, it started with a rumble of the ground that intensified, and I rolled my shoulders in preparation. The rumble grew in strength, and I noticed everyone else in the group flexing their shoulders or bouncing from foot to foot. Armored boots landed on the stairs, and I was ready for what was about to happen. The elves spilled out of the stairwell like soldier ants leaving their nest.

I ducked a spear slash and drove one of my swords up into the blood elf's gut, twisting it and pulling the sword out, then taking the elf's head before he hit the floor. A second and third elf tried to pin me in the stairwell, so I turned and leapt down the first part of the stairs to the landing just below. The elves followed me, but one of them got reckless and tried to leap for me. He was dead before he'd hit the floor. Another used my diverted attention to throw a hatchet at me, which I only just avoided in time. But I couldn't avoid the third elf's sword as it cut across my arm.

I sliced through the elf's leg just above the knee and stabbed him in the neck as he fell. I was about to run back up the stairs when three more elves appeared at the mouth of the stairwell. Two came up from below. I was trapped, and really didn't want to fight so many elves in such a small place, so I jumped down on the two below me, surprising them and knocking them to the ground, a sword in each of their chests.

I rolled off the elves, dodging a knife that whistled past my head, and kept moving until I was around the corner of the stairwell. I waited until I saw the first elf and rammed my sword into his throat, killing him instantly, then kicked him back into his two comrades. They pushed the body aside and came toward me.

I parried the first attack with ease, punching the elf in the face and pushing him into a group of his allies. Two more elves took his place to fight me, the attacks flowing quickly, forcing me to block and parry between them. I jumped back, swirling the shadows beneath their feet, then impaling the two elves with hundreds of spikes.

I removed the magic and the two bodies fell back to the ground with a dull thud. I took a moment to rest against a nearby pillar before heading for the stairs.

"Funny seeing you here."

I turned and sprinted at the voice, the need to kill enraging me. "Kay!" I screamed as I closed the gap between us.

A sword of blood magic appeared in Kay's hand, and he parried my strike, then punched me in the ribs with his free hand.

The blood magic that encased his fist caused me to cry out in pain.

"Did you miss me, Nate?" He smiled. "I knew you'd survived, and that you'd been transported here. Shame that, unlike me, you don't have a means to get home. I'll think about your death occasionally when I need to smile."

"Think on this!" Shadow poured out of the ground, slamming into Kay, and threw him back against the nearest wall. I stood and looked over at one of the men responsible for my being here.

"How long have you been working with Mara?" I asked.

"You know about the witch?" Kay said. He spat blood onto

the floor. "I'm impressed. You should have died back at the house. I got into trouble for failing that task."

"Who are you working for?"

"If you want that information, you'll have to catch me."

He turned to run, but I tripped him with shadow. "Yeah, I don't see the problem there."

"I see you've learned some new tricks."

"I'll tell you what I've learned, Kay. I've learned that you are a nasty, traitorous piece of filth. I've learned that you've allied yourself with Hera." I took a shot at the last sentence, wondering if I was right.

His laughter told me I wasn't.

"Hera? Oh, Nate, I don't work for Hera. Nice try, though. You really think Hera, of all people, is the top of the food chain? She would have tried to crush Avalon a thousand times over if she'd been in charge."

His words just confirmed what Brigg had told me. Hera was working for someone else. Someone even more powerful, with even more influence.

"Why are you here?"

"I'm not about to tell you anything, Nathan."

I wrapped shadows around Kay and tried pulling him down into my shadow realm, but my magic wouldn't take him. "You don't even understand how your magic works, do you?" he mocked. "You can't take a sorcerer into a shadow realm, Nathan. You really should learn how to use it before trying things like that."

I wrapped the shadows tighter squeezing the life out of Kay. "That works, though."

"I'm just the go-between," he wheezed, struggling for a

second, a look of panic in his eyes. "I bring messages from Hera here to this realm, and take them back to her. That's it."

"How do you jump between realms? By tablet, by any chance?"

He nodded.

"I thought you don't work for Hera?"

"I don't, but after you managed to disrupt our plans in Avalon, I was punished for my failure. You can gloat now."

"I'll gloat when you're dead. Which will be in about thirty seconds." I removed the shadow magic and stepped away. "You think you have the guts to fight me, Kay?"

"I am unarmed."

"You're a sorcerer; you're never unarmed. But if you really need to feel better—" I picked up one of the blood-elf swords and tossed it over to him. "—pick it up."

"You trust me not to use magic? How sporting."

"Not really, but here's the thing: I'm more powerful than you. We both know it, especially now, with my shadow magic. You can use your blood magic, or try to use anything else you've learned, but I'll still kill you. At least with a sword you have a chance. Even a slim one."

"You hate me so much that you want to watch me die, don't you?"

"Yes." It was an easy thing to admit. "I hate you, Kay. I've always disliked you, but you threatened my friends and those I love. And for that I'm going to cut you into tiny pieces and nail the rest of you to the wall."

Kay picked up the sword and threw a fireball at my face at the same time, followed by a plume of flame that I didn't even bother to avoid. I just wrapped myself in the shadows, and walked through the shadow realm. A second later I came out just a few feet behind Kay. The bolt of lightning that left my hand skewered him through the back, sending him flying across the room.

He hit the floor and spun, throwing lumps of rock at me, collapsing the wall beside me. My air magic caused the rock to fall away and I dove back into the shadows again. But this time I felt sluggish, as if walking at half-speed, and I came out of a shadow nowhere near where I wanted to be, only a foot away from where I'd entered. Apparently there was a finite amount of times I could access the realm without causing myself serious problems.

"Interesting fighting technique," Kay taunted as he threw blades of blood magic at me.

I deflected them with a shield of air, and created a sphere of air in my hand. I ran toward Kay, who used the stone of the library to put up his own shield. At the last second, I ignited the lightning magic, and poured it into the sphere, causing it to crackle as I drove it into the rock. The rock shield exploded.

At the same moment, I wrapped myself in air, ignoring the shards of rock that bounced off it, and kept on moving forward, creating a second sphere, this one of pure air, and slammed it into Kay as the dust and debris rained around us.

Kay flew back into the window, which splintered, the sounds of the blood elves far below streaming through the small cracks in the glass. I wrapped air around Kay and squeezed it tightly, before throwing him behind me. He bounced along the ground, until he collided with one of the pillars. The dark-blue shirt he'd been wearing was torn to pieces, and his chest was one large, bloody, open wound. It was a shame I hadn't been able to hit him with the lightning sphere as it probably would have torn him in half.

I stalked over to Kay as he threw out weak blood-magic blades again, easily avoided, and countered with a whip of lightning that tore across his back and legs.

Kay screamed out in pain, and rolled onto his back. "Please!"

I created a blade of fire and stood above him. "'Please?' How many times have you heard that word and still killed? Still hurt people? How many people have begged you to stop?"

His eyes moved slightly to look at something behind me, but the fear remained. I turned to fight the newcomer, but was struck in the chest by an open palm. I had never been hit so hard in my life. A few ribs broke from the blow as my feet left the floor and I flew back into the furthest wall, my head striking the brick and causing me to see spots.

"Kay, get up," the hooded man said.

"You're the one the dwarves have been talking about," I said. I tried to stand up, but he kicked me in the chest, and almost broke every bone in there. "Who are you?" I eventually managed to gasp, while my magic tried to knit my bones back together.

Kay launched himself toward me, and the hooded man grabbed him by the neck and lifted him from the ground. "I can see why you don't like Kay," he said to me, barely acknowledging that he was one-handedly holding a fully grown human male two feet off the ground.

"He's . . . an . . . asshole," I eventually managed. Just breathing hurt; speaking wasn't something I could do a lot of.

"Can't stay—sorry." He tossed Kay to the floor. "Get going, Kay."

Kay stared at me for several seconds, seemingly overflowing with unbridled rage, but he left anyway. The hooded man pulled back the hood to reveal a bald head and sharp features. He had a long, almost golden beard, and blue eyes that reminded me of a Siberian husky.

"I was told that Kay and some of his friends had taken it upon themselves to kill you. Clearly they weren't up to the task. But, if I let you live, you're going to come after me, disrupt my plans, and generally be a pain. So, while I have nothing against you, you need to die."

He took a few steps toward me when Brigg charged out of the stairwell, his ax raised high. The mystery man dodged the blow, grabbed hold of Brigg by the top of his head, and crushed it like a grape. He picked up the ax as Brigg's body fell and threw it at the next dwarf to leave the stairwell. The dwarf crumpled to the floor, and I wondered how many more this murderer would kill before he was stopped.

I channeled everything I had, putting every last bit of the soul I'd taken from the blood elf into it, and blasted Brigg's murderer with enough air to take him off his feet and out of the window. I managed to limp to the broken window despite the pain, and watched him hit the ground far below. I doubted I could have survived a headfirst drop from this high, but he was soon on his feet, albeit swaying from side to side.

Diane, Irkalla, and Remy ran down the stairwell, all three covered in blood and nursing wounds. Diane stood beside me and allowed me to lean on her.

"I'm sorry about your friend," I told Adam and Zamek, the latter of whom was nursing a nasty cut across one eye.

"He wasn't my friend," Zamek said. "He was just an old man who tried to do the right thing. He deserved better."

"The tunnel is done," Adam told us.

"And I doubt the blood elves will let us rest for long," Diane said. "We've lost a lot of people here. Let's not add to it."

Udthulo stood at the foot of the stairs. "I've finished with the wounded. Birik is hurt badly."

Zamek closed his eyes and breathed deeply. "Let's go look at him."

We all walked back up the stairs, Diane helping me. "Thanks," I said when we got to the top.

"I thought we'd lost you," she whispered.

"Not here. Not to these creatures." I managed to force a smile, but it was soon erased when I saw the carnage. Body parts and blood saturated the whole area. One of Brigg's dwarves sat slumped against a pillar, over a dozen blades in his body, and a litter of bodies at his feet. He'd gone down swinging.

Birik was laying on the floor of the room where the new tunnel had been created. He'd been hit in the chest with something heavy. His armor was badly dented, and part of it had pierced his skin. He was slipping into unconsciousness, and would die without help.

"Commander with a maul," Udthulo said by way of explanation.

Adam kneeled beside him. "Most of his ribs are broken, but his lungs are still inflated. Chalk one up for the dwarven physiology. He's not going to be able to walk anywhere, though."

"We'll carry him," Udthulo said and after a lot of maneuvering, we managed to get Birik carried piggyback-style.

"Let's go," I said after feeling the ground shudder beneath my feet.

Even with the wounded, we made good time through the

new tunnel, then Zamek collapsed it behind us. My magic had managed to heal my ribs enough so that I could walk and breathe without feeling like I was on fire.

We came out close to the bridge, which was empty, allowing us to cross without incident. Irkalla carried the trunk the whole way. We were all determined to get back to Sanctuary as quickly as possible. We'd lost a lot of good people in the library. I was damned if we were going to lose anyone who was already depending on us.

CHAPTER 33

We hadn't the time for me to take the soul of any dead blood elves, so I was unable to use my necromancy to heal up. On the plus side, I heal fast, even for a sorcerer, so by the time we'd made it back to Sanctuary, my ribs were almost back to normal. They didn't cause agony anymore, but they were sore to the touch, and would probably be that way for several hours.

Birik made it back to Sanctuary alive, but it was a close call, and as the gates were opened, there were still large numbers of dwarves at the top, just like there had been when we'd left. We saw no evidence of fighting, but from the expressions on several of the dwarves' faces, and their inability to meet my eyes, I immediately wondered what had happened.

"What's going on?" Remy asked me.

"I have no idea, but it feels off," I said.

We dropped Birik off at the medical center. Irkalla and I went to Chloe's room, hoping that whatever was wrong had nothing to do with her condition.

"What happened here?" I asked Jinayca as she left Chloe's room.

"We were betrayed."

"Chloe?"

"She's fine. She needs a scroll, though."

Irkalla dropped the trunk at her feet. "Pick one."

Jinayca nodded to Grundelwy, who dragged the trunk into the room and closed the door. "They'll find the right scroll, I promise."

"So what happened here?"

"Jurg was murdered, and we were betrayed," Jinayca explained. "Kasey."

I swore I felt my heart stop beating. "Where is Kasey?"

"She was abducted by Stel: the one who put the runes on you all. We don't know why he took Kasey, but it happened not long ago. He drugged her, and took her through a freshly built tunnel, collapsing it afterward. He killed Jurg on the way out for trying to stop him."

"Why would Stel do that?" Irkalla asked.

"We don't know. The rest of the earth-realmers and our guards are searching the city for answers. Stel's home has been turned inside out; the room in the temple too. It was rune-marked with defensive runes. It took a long time to get inside, but there's nothing there."

"I want to help," I said, making it sound like she had no choice in the matter. "How long has Stel lived here?"

"Since we lost the war. He's been a studious and helpful member of the community. There was no indication that he would ever be involved in something like that."

A thought occurred to me. "Kasey was half elemental, and Zamek said that some dwarves don't like elementals. Could that be something to do with it?"

Jinayca paused. "It's possible, I guess. We didn't consider that as a theory because we didn't know what she was."

"Can you take me to Stel's house?" I asked. "I'd like to have a look around myself, if that's okay?"

Jinayca nodded and led me down toward the temple. She'd told me that Stel's room returned nothing of interest, but that it was still rune-marked. It was an odd thing to do: protect your room from people snooping around but keep nothing incriminating there. Maybe it was just a place for whatever research he was conducting. Once we'd arrived, I decided to check for myself and entered the temple while Jinayca spoke to the guard outside before leaving me to my investigation.

I asked the dwarf on guard where Stel's room was and he gave me directions. When I'd reached the room on the second floor, there were several more dwarves, none of whom asked me why I was there and just accepted it as I entered the room and began looking around.

"I'm sorry for your friend," Morgan said from the corner of the room. "We will find her."

"Where's Mordred?" I asked.

"Running laps."

"Why?"

She shrugged. "He was in here and started humming something, so I told him to go outside as the noise was somewhat disturbing while we were searching. He couldn't stop doing it, so he went for a run. I think he's trying to get his head clear. He'll be back soon enough, though."

I nodded. "You find anything, by chance?"

She shook her head. "It's weird. Stel went to a lot of effort to hide absolutely nothing. Well, nothing except his weird obsession with the blood elves."

"There's a new player with the blood elves," I told Morgan. "That hooded guy the dwarves spoke about? He threw me around like a rag doll, crushed a dwarf's head with one hand. He's like nothing I've ever come across. His power is insane."

"Sorcerer?"

"Couldn't tell. His hands and arms were covered. Oh, and Kay's here, too. I almost killed him, but got interrupted."

"Wait: *Kay* is *here*?" Morgan asked.

"He's sort of working for Hera, although she's not in charge. There's someone above her. No idea who it is, but I can't imagine it'll be anyone nice."

"So Kay can jump from here to the earth realm and back again?" Morgan asked.

"I have no idea. I'm hoping Nabu will be able to shed some light on it. Where is he, by the way?"

"He went off to search closer to the tunnel they found."

I dropped a bunch of empty scrolls onto the floor. "I'm going to go walk the tunnel they found in case they missed something."

I left Morgan to continue her search and exited the temple, spotting Mordred doing laps around the building while he loudly hummed the theme tune to *Super Mario*. And yes, that's as weird as it sounds.

I found the mouth of the tunnel by following the sounds of dwarves arguing.

Stel had put the tunnel behind a small shack, partially blocking it from view with the use of large boulders. You could only find it if you actually walked around to the back of the shack and behind the boulders.

"Who owned the shack?" I asked the dwarves.

There was a lot of shrugging, but no one seemed to know. I tried the door and found it unlocked, and the interior to be completely empty. It was just a big empty box.

"Weird, isn't it?" Nabu said as he left the tunnel and walked toward me. "He went to a lot of effort to hide the tunnel behind an empty shell."

"It must have belonged to Stel, then."

"Maybe."

He didn't sound convinced, and I took a few minutes to update him with what had happened in the library.

"So it looks like Kay has the ability to jump between realms with the use of a tablet," Nabu said when I'd finished, latching on to the one thing I knew he'd find interesting. "And from what he said about being the go-between with Hera and this realm, I get the feeling he can come and go as he pleases."

"Any idea how?" I didn't bother mentioning that he'd helped create the damn tablets in the first place, and should shoulder some of the responsibility for their use, mostly because it was pointless. I couldn't blame Nabu for their creation, anymore than I could blame ancient man for the creation of the bladed weapon. It might not have turned out very well, but I doubt Nabu envisioned this particular circumstance when he helped make them.

"It was the problem we had when we created them," he said. "It's why we gave up on the project."

"Not everyone, apparently. Who else was involved in their creation? Non-dwarves, I mean?"

Nabu paused, and for a split-second I thought he was going to lie to me or fob me off. "Siris was there. She knows how the tablets work."

I sat on the steps of the shack. I really wanted to punch Nabu, but it wouldn't have helped very much. "Of course she was. And obviously Siris is alive and well."

"We never found her, Nate. Not even a glimpse of where she might have fled. But my guess is she's involved in this somehow."

"How long have you had those concerns? Because they might have been helpful to share, Nabu."

"Sharing information is not in my nature. I find the idea of people knowing more, or as much as I do, disconcerting. Several of our pantheon have expressed irritation with my methods over the years."

"You mean you got punched a lot?"

"On occasion, yes. Irkalla is usually very quick to show her displeasure at any secrets I've kept from her." He sat beside me. "In the interests of cooperation, I believe that Siris has had help from within our pantheon. In fact, I think several people within Avalon are working with her. Not including Kay, Hera, and whoever this hooded man is. I've been trying to get information on them for the better part of a thousand years, and have gotten exactly nowhere. Whoever they are, they went very deep underground after the Acre incident, and are only now showing their true colors again."

"You know, I've wondered before about all the plots I've managed to stop over the years, and just how many I might have missed—small pieces of a larger plan being moved around without anyone ever finding out about it until it's too late."

"Avalon is corrupt. You know that."

"I know that Elaine, and the people she trusts, are doing their best to stop that from spreading."

"Yes, and they should be commended for it, but you can't stop this kind of disease; you can only operate and remove the part causing the problems. The thing is, everyone knows that Hera would like more power. Everyone has known that for centuries, but Zeus managed to keep her in check until he vanished. For the better part of five centuries, she's had free rein to plot against Avalon."

"She's not in charge. Kay all but confirmed that."

"I never assumed she was, but to whom would Hera report? Who is so powerful that she would allow them to take control? And whoever that is, we should not want to confront them. Not without being prepared."

"Okay, those are future problems. Let's deal with the one at hand. Kasey has been taken by Stel, presumably to the citadel. Why?"

"She's an oddity." He quickly raised his hands when I shot him a look of anger. "I didn't mean that in the way it sounded. I, too, am an oddity. I am a rare species, an *och*, and there are very few of us. Some consider us spirits of creation, and more than once someone called us 'Olympian Spirits', a term I despise, as there is more than one person who is each kind of spirit. I am immortal to the best of my knowledge, and can understand any language I've ever read. I remember everything. I knew the world was round thousands of years before it was deemed a fact. I understood our place in the cosmos before humans were even capable of writing their own name in something other than dirt. I am an oddity: an anomaly. And Kasey is the same: an elemental werewolf. That is something people would want to study."

"Wouldn't it have been easier to study her without drugging her and taking her to wherever Stel took her? Surely that's a lot more complicated than just studying her."

"True, but you're thinking with logic, and it appears that Stel made the decision hastily. Maybe Kasey discovered something he was doing, or interrupted him. I don't know."

I stood and entered the shack. "If you were going to hide something, where would you do it? A sealed room, or somewhere out of the way?"

"Out of the way. A sealed room is a giant red flag."

"Exactly. But you can't just leave stuff lying around; that would defeat the purpose of your little hidey-hole. So, where would you keep it?"

"You believe that Stel kept his secrets in here?" Nabu looked around. "There's no writing on the wall or floor. The room is devoid of everything—there's not even a bed or table. Why would he keep things here? And where?"

I stared at the shack's floor; something wasn't right about it. The grain in several of the wooden boards looked peculiar and didn't quite match the rest of the floorboards. I searched, but found no mechanism or handle to lift a trapdoor.

"The answer is in here somewhere, I'm sure of it."

Nabu walked around the room, which didn't take long, and then paused. "Do me a favor," he said. "Go outside and throw a ball of fire under this shack. The building is at least two feet off the ground, so it should clear across to the other side."

I did as he asked and crouched outside, readying a small fireball, before throwing it under the shack. It hit something halfway and extinguished. So I threw a second and the same thing happened. I walked to the next side and did the same thing, with the same results.

"There are polished mirrors under here, to make it look like there's nothing there," I told Nabu.

"Yes. I imagine that Stel picked this place because of that.

This shack is far too old to have been created recently. It's probably a throwback from when this whole place was used by the dwarven priests. Everyone has secrets they'd like to hide, and if memory serves me correctly—and it always does—the ground under here would have been a small stream a thousand years ago. It was diverted so that it didn't come down this far when Sanctuary was created. Now it goes to several wells that litter the main living area above. It's a wonderful piece of construction."

"You know this how?"

"I did some light reading on the city while you were all gone. I wanted to know how things worked. Looks like it was useful after all."

"You think it's safe to punch a hole into the floor?"

"I assume so. Stel probably used his alchemy to move the wooden boards aside."

I used my air magic to cut a hole in the floor roughly where the mirrors were and found a hole below.

"I'm going to see where it goes. Care to join me?"

Nabu nodded and I allowed myself to drop down into the hole, falling only a few feet before landing in a much larger, and darker, space below. I ignited my shadow magic and my vision became perfect. It was much better than using my fire magic.

The hole beneath the house was essentially an entire room. There were tables made from the rock, and after I looked around, I found a rune that had stopped the crystals on the ceiling from glowing, and wiped it out, bathing the room in a more natural light. I removed the magic eyesight as Nabu read scroll after scroll from the rock table.

There was a small bed in the corner, and I wondered why anyone would want to sleep here.

"Okay, so how would he communicate with anyone outside of the city?"

"With this." Nabu passed me a small mirror. On the back were several runes that essentially turned it into a phone.

"A magic mirror?" I asked. "Isn't that a bit . . . Disney?"

"Where do you think those stories of magic mirrors came from? While I've been here, I've been looking into several dwarven inventions that have fallen out of use. According to the records I found, the dwarves had been using them as communication devices for years, although after the fall of the city, they were used less and less. They're easy to . . . I guess the word is 'hack'. The blood elves already have an advantage, so the dwarves stopped carrying them whenever they left Sanctuary. If the elves got hold of them, it wouldn't take much for them to listen to whomever was on the other end."

"How?"

"The mirrors are only capable of connecting with one other mirror elsewhere. They would have been made together, and then given to the people who wanted to communicate." He took the mirror from me and tapped it in each corner, and then once in the middle. It shimmered, and the mirror turned into the view of a room somewhere I'd never been.

"Can they hear us?" I asked.

Nabu nodded.

"Nathaniel Garrett." The hooded man came into view. "You found Stel's hiding place. I knew someone would, but he didn't have time to destroy everything. I apologize for the mess he made in bringing me the girl. A friend of yours, no doubt."

I clenched my jaw shut.

"Don't bother threatening me; I'm not going to kill her. I didn't even want her; she's here on Kay's request. He's pretty angry that you nearly killed him. He wants to punish you, so he took her. You come here, and you get her back."

"And you kill us both the second I arrive."

"Actually, the girl can go about her own life the second you arrive. She was never a threat to our organization, and certainly not to me. She's fun, though, isn't she? Tore the throat of one blood elf right out. Funniest damn thing I've seen in ages. Oh, and when you come—and we both know you will so don't bother arguing— bring Mordred. I'd really like to kill him. It's been so long, and I've got so many ideas on how I'd like to prolong his agony."

"Who are you?" I asked.

"Nabu there will tell you." He waved. "Hi, Nabu. Miss me? How's the wife? Still dead? Shame; she really was in the wrong place at the wrong time. I know it's a bit of a trek to the citadel, so I won't give you a time limit, Nathaniel, but the longer you delay, the more likely it is that Kasey will turn into a very dead werewolf half-breed."

The mirror went dark.

"I've got to go to the citadel."

"He'll kill you. We'll come up with a plan. And then we will all go and get Kasey. I won't leave you to his whim. There's no one on any realm who deserves that."

"Who is he?"

"That's Baldr, son of Odin. And one of the most dangerous people I've ever had the misfortune to meet."

CHAPTER 34

After talking to Nabu, we both left the temple area and I got everyone together to discuss future plans in the elders' building we'd been using since we arrived.

Chloe had insisted on joining us—her recovery was nothing short of remarkable. She was still weak, and looked pale, but it had taken a few hours for her to be up and around, and it appeared as if she was getting healthier by the minute. It was a big weight off my mind. And even more so knowing that Jinayca was the person keeping an eye on her.

"Baldr is *here*?" Morgan asked, her voice unable to hide the fear.

The group had reassembled in the elders' meeting room, along with Zamek, who still looked worse for wear: his face bruised, with several healing cuts on his forehead.

"Where's Nabu?" Jinayca asked as Chloe sat down beside me, placing her hand on mine and squeezing slightly.

"Baldr mentioned his wife, so he decided to take some time to himself," I told them. "He seemed pretty shaken up by it. Wasn't his wife killed before I was born?"

Irkalla nodded. "Murdered in her home while he was away, along with every single one of her guards. A human was caught and punished, but there was always a suspicion that there was more to it. Nabu and Baldr had never gotten on, and Baldr had made vague threats against Nabu for investigating something Nabu was keeping pretty close to his chest. This was a few hundred years before the Norse pantheon vanished. So although Nabu suspected Baldr's involvement, once everyone went missing, Nabu couldn't find any concrete answers from him."

"Why are you afraid of Baldr, Morgan?" I asked.

"That's something for Mordred to tell you if he wants to. But from my point of view, Baldr might be one of the most evil people I've ever heard of. I spent some time looking into him for Mordred a few centuries ago, and the things I uncovered—the number and method of those he killed—made my skin crawl. He's not someone I'd want to go up against."

I looked over to Mordred. "You want to share?"

"Baldr was one of the people who spent a great deal of time and effort destroying me during my stay here. I won't allow him to do those things again. If I go there, it's to kill him. It's what he deserves."

"I never heard anything about him," I said. "Nothing like that, anyway."

"He didn't have a lot to do with the outside world," Mordred explained. "He stuck to the Norse realms."

"He was not a pleasant man," Jinayca interjected. "I personally didn't like dealing with him when he arrived. He liked to go out of the mountain into the forest to hunt creatures there. He liked to hurt them before they died. He'd purposefully wound the creature, but let it live so he could hunt it down again."

"So are all of the Norse pantheon as pleasant?" Remy asked. "Do they all want Avalon destroyed?"

"There was a civil war between parts of the Norse pantheon," Jinayca said. "Baldr was on one side, Odin on the other. I have no idea who joined which side after that, but Odin had nothing but respect for Avalon from the times I'd spoken to him. So to answer your question, I doubt it. It looks like it's just Baldr and whoever is helping him."

"Is Baldr the leader of the side fighting Odin?" I asked.

"Not sure," Zamek said. "If he's not, then he's pretty high up in that side. He's not someone who likes taking too many orders."

"And Kasey is his prisoner," I said with a sigh. "She's in the citadel. Baldr said she'll be released if Mordred and I give ourselves up."

"Do you have a plan?" Mordred asked me.

"Basically, we're going to give ourselves up, and the rest of you are going to infiltrate the citadel and wait until Kasey gets out. Then we're going to kill them all. Anyone got any arguments with that?"

No one did. Even Morgan didn't argue about being split up from Mordred.

"I'm coming with you two," Chloe said. "And before anyone argues, someone has to be there to take Kasey; they'd expect it. And I'm only a little old witch, so they won't see me as much of a threat. Besides, my mother helped put me here, and I'd like to help screw up whatever plan she and her insane friends have come up with."

"If you think you're up to it, you're welcome," I told her.

"You know they're never going to let Kasey go," Irkalla said. "Ever."

"I know," I said. "They'll make a big song and dance about it, and then just keep us all there anyway. Or try to kill her in front of us. Chloe's going to make sure that doesn't happen. And she's right; she's the least threatening, and most unknown, of everyone here. I'm not sure if they even know she took the spirit scroll, but even if they do, these people are arrogant and won't much care."

"If she goes, I'm going!" Adam shouted from the head of the table, gaining a nod of appreciation from Chloe in response.

"Fine," I said. "Humans galore."

"So where do we go?" Diane asked.

I unfurled a map of the entire mountain on the table. "I've been told that several of the dwarves have been working on getting the tunnel unblocked. Jinayca, any updates on that?"

Jinayca stood. "It should take a few hours, but from what they've figured out, the tunnel that Stel created goes to this point here." She touched the map. "The citadel is here, which is some way after that. You just need to figure out how to get from there to there without starting a war."

"The old guard tunnels," Zamek said. "It's how we all escaped when the elves first attacked. We collapsed most of them behind us as we fled, but there are a few left. It was decided to leave them be, just in case we needed to re-enter the tower for any reason. It's single-file, though, which is why we haven't used it. Once you're in that tunnel, the only way is forward; there's no escape or room to fight down there. And there's one other problem."

"It takes you into a sewer?" Remy guessed.

"The barracks," Zamek corrected.

"So the second we gain entry, we're getting into a fight," Morgan said.

"Well, yes and no," Zamek interjected. "If we can get into the barracks and do it quickly, we could overrun whoever is in there and kill them all before a fight starts."

"That's a big if," Irkalla said, "but possible."

"When does this all go ahead?" Diane asked.

"Soon. But there's one other thing. Kay has a tablet that allows travel between realms without leaving the tablet behind. I don't know how, but we need it. It's the only way home, and also I'd really rather not have something that dangerous in their hands."

"So we need Kay alive?" Morgan asked.

"God, no. I'm going to tear his head off and shove it up his ass. No, we need that tablet. If he doesn't have it on him, we'll need to find it."

"Are we sure it exists?" Diane asked.

"He confirmed as much to me. I'll try to get him to talk, but I might not have time, and this is a one-time trip into the citadel. We don't get another shot at this. Those blood elves are going to outnumber us ten thousand to one. But most of them are going to be outside the building so we can lock it down and get what we need."

"So we gain entry, kill the guards, lock the citadel down, find a tablet, and get home?" Mordred summarized. "Sounds easy. Let's do it."

"What happens to this city once we've done this?" Chloe asked. "Are the elves going to attack it?"

Jinayca nodded. "More than likely, yes. It'll take them some time, however. We can prepare the surrounding area to make it more difficult, too."

"How about we give them something else to think about?" I asked.

"Like what?"

"The bridge that connects the citadel to the rest of the elven-controlled territory. There are a lot of elves on that bridge."

"A lot under it too," she said.

"How many problems would destroying it cost them?"

"They'd still be able to get in and out of the citadel, but it would cause problems getting large amounts of supplies in. They'd have to go through the bottom levels, and they're not designed for it. It would give us time."

"Then we'll see what we can do about the bridge."

"None of the dwarven elders will like it." She stood. "They'll say it's destroying our ancestry. And the possibility of not telling them is out. Give me some time; I might be able to convince them, and if I can't make them listen to reason, well, in that case I'll figure out a way to get anything you might need without their help."

Everyone filtered out of the room, leaving me alone with the Fates, who I hadn't even noticed had entered the room.

"You're very stealthy," I said. "Like big cats or something."

"Do you know why we're here?" Cassandra asked.

"Because you told Mordred he had to kill me?" I took a guess, and let just enough annoyance into my voice to make it known I was less than thrilled about their prophecy.

"We didn't lie," Ivy said.

"Did you really need to tell him at all?" I asked. "And exactly why does he need to know that he has to kill me? He's trying to convince people he's changed—that he's not a psychopath who wants to murder me every ten seconds, and then he tells me he has to kill me. How quickly do you think I'm going to trust someone who tells me they're going to be responsible for my murder?"

"You both need to understand what's at stake here."

"For you or me?" I asked Cassandra. "Because if I remember correctly, you held stuff back from me the last time I went to see you and people died. Good people. So are you lying to Mordred now? Is he going to try and kill me, but I kill him first? Is that the game you're playing?"

"No games here, Nate," Grace said. "Just the truth."

"Yeah, 'just the truth?' Because I don't believe that."

"We may have abridged the truth," Ivy said.

I threw my arms in the air. "What a complete shock. So, what's the *actual* truth? I have to die, or thousands more will? Is that it?"

"It's not that simple."

"It never is with you people." I took a moment and counted to ten.

Ivy came over and placed her hand on mine. "If you survive the coming years, there's a chance you'll become the thing you hate the most. You'll become a monster: a cruel, vicious beast who thinks nothing of following the plans of those he works for. I've seen it. I've seen the bodies in your wake; I've seen the deaths of your friends and loved ones. I've seen it twist and break you. You'll become Mordred, but there will be no turning back for you. I don't want that. That's why we told Mordred: because we knew he'd tell you, and we knew you'd end up here."

"So essentially I need to stop whoever is pulling my strings? What do you think I've been doing? I'm not playing games here. I've made sure to try and stop anyone who manipulates me, or tries to hurt the people I care about. And you tell me I'm *still* going to be manipulated into turning into a monster?"

Ivy nodded. "The manipulation started long ago."

"Who's doing the string-pulling?"

"We don't know," Cassandra admitted. "It's like a swirl of darkness and has been that way for a long time. We saw it cover Mordred, and now it covers you. Mordred is free from it, but you're not. And if you don't become free from it, Mordred will have no choice but to kill you. It's the only way to save the lives of so many."

"So I either free myself from a manipulator or turn into an evil version of myself? And if it's the latter, the only thing that can stop it is Mordred. Brilliant. That's excellent help, thanks. How is what you want me to do any different to what I've been doing? I'm not going to just lie down and let someone manipulate me."

"What if the manipulator is someone you care about?" Ivy asked. "What if it's a friend of yours: someone you think of warmly? What if, while you're fighting against everyone who tries to hurt you or your friends, it's *one of your friends* who's slowly taking you into the darkness we see in your future?"

I opened my mouth to speak and quickly closed it, choosing my words carefully before I spoke again. "I trust my friends. I have to. If I think for one second that one of them is out to get me, to turn me into something I'm not, then I might as well just go live at the top of a mountain alone for the rest of my life."

Ivy took a deep breath, slowly letting it out before she began talking. "The next few years are crucial for you. Things are going to change in your life; your resolve will be tested. Yes, we told Mordred he had to kill you, because in his future that's true. He will have to kill you to stop you. He's the only one who can. But if you can fight it—if you can stop this manipulation, stop the erosion of your soul—then maybe there's a chance for you."

"Are you lying now?" I asked. "Did you know that Mordred would become cured? That me shooting him would eventually cure him?"

Ivy shook her head. "I saw his death and nothing more. There was nothing beyond that."

"So it's possible that he could kill me, and I still survive. My heart could stop, but I live. And after that I could still turn into a monster, or be free from the manipulation?"

Ivy nodded. "Is that a risk you want to take? It would be better to find another way."

I shrugged. "I don't put much stock in the odds. I've made a life of beating them at every available opportunity. Mordred isn't going to kill me, and I'm not going to allow myself to be manipulated by some unknown force. I will do what I think is right, but if Mordred comes for me, I'm not just going to let it happen."

"We will be staying here, in this realm," Cassandra told me. "Either you'll successfully take Kay's tablet and return to the earth realm, leaving us safe, or you'll all be dead. Going with you would put us in Baldr's hands anyway."

I understood why they were doing it. It certainly made sense to stay away from those who would use them.

"And when we're not in the same realm, I can't see your future," Ivy admitted.

"Good." I didn't want to be annoyed; after all, they were only trying to warn me. But it felt like an invasion of privacy nonetheless. They'd told Mordred he would have to kill me, and then told me that essentially I either allow it to happen or I murder people in some crazed mission of vengeance. I didn't want to believe them; they'd certainly held information back from me before, but it was still something I had to consider. Was Mordred right? Would he have to kill me to stop me? Would he be able to? The whole thing made my head hurt and I left the room without another word.

"Did the Fates talk to you?" Mordred asked me as I exited the building.

"You are exactly the last person I want to talk to."

"They told you what they told me, yes?"

I sighed and nodded. "Either you kill me, or I become a raving psychopath hell-bent on killing a lot of people. Yep. It was a fun conversation."

"Did it make your head hurt?"

I nodded. "All of this fate stuff makes me feel nauseous. They lied to you, or they manipulated the truth. Apparently one of my friends is going to turn me to the dark side or something, and if I don't give in, I don't go full evil. So you're off the hook. Frankly, my head does hurt."

I rubbed my temples.

"I hope you're right," he said. He waited a few seconds before continuing. "You know the second I see Baldr I'm going to try and kill him."

"Yeah, I figured as much. You think you can hold it together long enough to do it when we're not surrounded by blood elves?"

"Don't know. I've wanted him dead for a long time. He's powerful, Nate—unbearably powerful—and in all honesty I'm not sure if I even *can* kill him. Or if he can be killed."

"He's a sorcerer?"

"Yes. And he's more dangerous than anyone you've ever met. He hates Odin for some reason, and Zeus, and pretty much anyone of the old guard. I think he killed Thor, too."

"'*Think?*'"

"Just a rumor I'd heard. As you know, the Norse gods are all hidden in one realm or another, so getting reliable intel is difficult."

"So exactly how, and why, is he here?"

"I don't have the answer to either of those. Do you think

Chloe is okay? You think she'll be able to cope with what she might see in that place?"

"I don't think she has much of a choice. She'll be okay, though. She's stronger than most her age. And that scroll gives her a whole new set of powers: a set I'm somewhat concerned about."

Mordred slapped me on the shoulder. "She's in the temple if you happened to want to talk to her before we leave."

I found Chloe by the side of the temple with her father, Adam, as he tried to teach her to use the powers of the scroll she'd taken in.

"Can you hear the spirits?" he asked as I stood and watched, not wanting to ruin her concentration.

"Hearing them isn't the problem," she snapped. "Getting them to shut up is!"

"There should be one spirit more than the others that you like, that you feel good about. You need to accept that spirit as your guide. It will make things easier."

"They've been telling me that for the last few hours, but frankly they're all very irritating."

"Don't pick with your mind; pick with your heart."

Chloe didn't look impressed. "That's the single biggest crock of shit I've heard anyone say. 'Pick with your heart?' *Really*? And then I'll make a bag out of hemp and call myself Jewel."

I tried not to laugh, but it came out anyway. "Sorry," I said. "I didn't mean to interrupt."

Adam didn't look thrilled about it, but his expression of annoyance soon eased away. "Actually, we could use a break.

Chloe is having trouble accessing the power inside of her scroll. She's yet to pick a spirit, and until she does, the power she's been given will be hit-and-miss. And she'll be unable to fight off any of the demon's advances."

"So, she has to accept a spirit to be her guide, and then accept them all, including the demon?" I asked, hoping I had the right idea.

Adam nodded. "She will be able to use a modicum of power until then, but once she's accepted the demon, she'll be able to access that extra reserve whenever she wishes. And until she does, the demon will be able to influence her, try to get her to just accept him and ignore the other spirits."

"So what's the problem?" I asked. "Just pick a spirit and crack on."

"It's not that easy," she said. "There are three spirits in this scroll, and frankly, they're all somewhat know-it-all."

"I'm going to get some water," Adam said. "See if you can help."

He walked off and I sat on the stone beside Chloe. "How's your dad?"

"I never thought I'd see him again. It's been awesome having him help me train."

"Is that why you're not picking a spirit: because it means he needs to stick around and help you more?"

She opened her mouth and closed it. "He wants to stay here. He says I have a good life back in the earth realm, and that now he knows I'm safe, he doesn't need to come with me. He says he can do real good here. But I need him. He's my dad."

"I know. Have you told him that?"

She shook her head, and wiped away some tears. "I don't know how."

"Just tell him. You'll find things a lot easier after that."

She nodded to herself, and for a moment I thought the conversation was over. "What if we don't get Kase back?"

"We will."

"I . . . I want to kill my mum."

"Really? Because I don't think you do. Taking a life isn't easy. So you might say you want to kill your mum, but you don't. You're not a killer, Chloe. You might have to be, one day; that's the world we live in. But not at seventeen. And not your mum."

"I know," she admitted. "It's just, I'm done with her. She's insane, and psychotic, and clearly only thinks of herself. I want no part of that."

"She's a bad person, Chloe. You're better off as far away from her and her insane coven as possible."

"What's going to happen to them when we get back through to our realm?"

I paused. "I don't know. Arrest is the most probable action, although if they mess around or resist, they're likely to find themselves executed instead. What your mum and her coven have done, creating a krampus a few years back—they got away with that by the skin of their teeth. Sending us here is an abuse of magic. It's an abuse of a lot of things. They'll need to be punished for it."

"I honestly can't believe she would go so far: to try and get us trapped and murdered by these elves." She took a deep breath. "Let's discuss something else. Like how I pick the spirit to guide me, or how I don't let the demon inside my head out. I'm not sure if the medicine was worse than the illness this time around."

"You're alive. That's all that matters right now."

She nodded. "When we get back, I'm going to take some

time away from all of this. If my dad stays here, my mum goes to jail, and who knows what else, I need to do something for me. Maybe go to university, or just feel like someone who's almost eighteen. At least for a while."

"Sounds like a good plan to me."

"In the meantime, I get to try and figure out which spirit is the least annoying of the three in my head."

"You want a hand with that?"

She nodded.

"Sit down, close your eyes and take a deep breath."

She did as I asked.

"Just concentrate on breathing—ignore everything else. Ignore where we are, or what you're feeling. Just concentrate on breathing in and out. In and out, over and over, as your mind relaxes."

She sat that way for sixty seconds, the tension in her shoulders slowly ebbing away.

"I'm going to count to three. On three open your eyes."

She sat a little straighter.

"One. Two." I leaned down to her ear. "Pick a spirit. Three."

She opened her eyes.

"Which spirit came to you first?"

"The Roman woman, Aelia," she said. "She was an archer, a hunter."

"Go with her then." I straightened up. "I'll let you get used to your new powers."

"Thanks, Nate."

"Just make sure you keep that demon in check. I don't really want to have to deal with you rampaging across the battlefield at the wrong moment."

"You and me both, Nate. You and me both."

I walked away and found Adam beside a large carving of a dwarven warrior. "She trusts you," he said.

"She's a good person," I told him. "She's been through a lot. I think trust is important to her."

"Thank you for all you did for her."

"It was my pleasure."

"If the demon gets out, we'll need to stop it."

"We'll cross that bridge when we come to it."

"I've been out of her life for so long, I need to find a way to be there for her. Originally, I wanted to stay here and help the dwarves, but maybe Chloe needs me more. I'd like to make up for lost time. And I'd like to see Mara get the punishment that's coming to her."

"Trust me when I tell you, we *all* want that."

Adam laughed. "She used to be a good person. But she started dealing more and more with that coven of hers, and then when Hera entered the picture she just went full crazy. That was after Chloe was born. I thought about running away with Chloe, starting over, but Mara would have used her witch contacts to find us. And I couldn't risk losing Chloe. And now that I've found her, I don't want to lose her again."

"Don't talk like that. We're all getting out of here."

He nodded solemnly and walked off toward Chloe.

"Have you got a moment?" Jinayca asked as I was just about to make my way back up to the rest of the group.

"You spoke to the elders?" I asked.

She nodded. "They don't like your plan. They don't want to agree to your plan. They'd really like to send me with you, but that's not an option either. Instead, I'm going to be sending a group of twelve dwarves to the area to help you collapse the bridge. I just need you and your group to cause a big distraction. They'll need about an hour."

"You said earlier that there were other ways into the citadel."

"There are tunnels that lead down to the level under the bridge. It's how the elves move about so freely. There are entrances into the citadel from there. They used to be for servants and those who didn't wish to be seen."

"So it would be helpful if those tunnels were no longer usable."

"It would," Jinayca agreed. "But the bridge is capable of bringing more elves across in one go than the tunnels. The tunnels are a dozen dwarves wide; the bridge is twenty or thirty. They could have an army across it in a lot shorter time."

"Use your people to destroy some of the tunnels. We'll deal with the bridge."

"How?"

I had no idea. "I'll improvise. But we'll ensure that the bridge gets out of commission. Just make sure some of the tunnels closest to here are collapsed. If they're going to come attack you, let's give them a longer journey."

"Okay. I'll leave the bridge to you." She held out her hand, which I shook. "It's been a pleasure, Nate. I'm sorry you didn't find out more about all that happened to you here. Brigg's death left a lot of things unanswered."

I looked over at the temple. "There were plenty of other people there who can tell me. I'll learn why they did it one day, why they had to take my memories and put these marks on me. That's the thing with secrets this big: eventually they come out. And then it's just a case of cleaning up the mess they leave behind."

CHAPTER 35

It took several frustrating hours to get everything ready, and even then it was another few hours before we actually left Sanctuary. Jinayca wished us all good luck, and Zamek led us out of the city.

We were soon trekking through parts of the mountain that had seen no dwarven visitors in a very long time. The dwarves Jinayca had sent ahead a few hours earlier lay in wait to collapse the tunnels on my signal. I still wasn't sure what the signal would be, but I told them it would be impressive, so I guess I had to come up with something. And fast.

The occasional blood-elf patrol was nothing to the group, and I for one felt pretty good about our chances. That feeling went away when the citadel loomed above us.

We'd hidden behind a large mound of stones that allowed us to look down on the massive structure and surrounding area. The bridge that connected the citadel to the road was several hundred feet long. Thousands of blood elves were camped in large areas to either side of the road. More were on the bridge, and even more than that far below the bridge, their campfires making it look almost serene from this distance. Some of the closer elves were resting by open fires, some practicing combat, and others beating human slaves.

"The elf camp goes to the south," Zamek said. "What used to be a barracks and training areas is now completely held by the elves and their slaves. A lot more of them will be in that tower."

"How many dwarves lived in the citadel?" Chloe asked.

"Thousands," Zamek said. "Royalty, members of staff, lords and ladies of court, elders. And now it's held by blood-elf filth."

"We're not here to take it back," Nabu reminded him. "Where do we go from here?"

"We need to take a tunnel to the east of here. It curves down and around a second set of tunnels: ones we stopped using due to the possibility of cave-ins. They were sturdy enough when I was last sent through, but that was a thousand years ago, so I'm hoping they're still the same."

"Chloe, Adam, you're with Mordred and me." I scanned the bridge, and the elves upon it. "The rest of you, good luck getting into the citadel. Remind any dwarves you see to wait for my signal before they start blowing tunnels."

"You figured out how to destroy that bridge yet?" Diane asked.

"Not even slightly," I told her. "It'll come to me."

"Do not die," Remy said. "And if you get out, I may kiss you on the lips, you lucky devil."

"I'd rather you didn't," I said with a smile.

Remy chuckled. "Well, I just don't know if our friendship can take that kind of rejection."

After everyone had said their goodbyes, we watched the rest of the group go until they vanished behind a large, partially collapsed building.

"You ready?" Mordred asked.

I nodded, and thought about how much had happened

between us since I lay trapped in the Fates' back garden. I'd gone from hating him to attacking him to not trusting him to something I couldn't quite understand. It wasn't trust, or acceptance, but it felt like there was something I could begin to look past, that I could start to move past the last thousand years of lies and death, and look toward those who had turned Mordred into the walking bundle of mayhem he'd become. Those people were going to find I was less than pleased about what they'd done. I just hoped that when Mordred and Baldr met again that Mordred wasn't going to snap and kill everyone trying to get to Baldr.

We made our way to the main road that led to the bridge and followed it down. The feeling of more and more elven eyes boring into me grew the further we went. We were all fully armed, although I doubted it would have made much difference if we'd gone naked. We were outnumbered by such a degree that I'm pretty certain it could be classified as royally fucked.

Elven archers sat on the higher parts of the camps beside us, but there were no attacks, no threats. They just sat and watched. Silently. It was the creepiest thing I'd encountered in a long time.

Unfortunately that ended when we made it to the bridge. A number of elves began beating their weapons against nearby stone or their own shields, causing a huge din that washed over us. We began crossing the bridge, staying in the middle to avoid the elves on either side. The smell of cooked meat made me wonder what exactly it was the elves were cooking, and then I quickly realized I didn't even slightly want to know the answer.

We were just over halfway when the thirty-foot-high black, steel doors of the citadel slowly opened.

"Really went for the whole fantasy cliché thing with those, didn't they?" Chloe said. "They might as well have written *We're the bad guys* in six-foot-high, bright-red letters."

"I'm not sure it was a cliché when they were first made," I suggested.

"Ominously dark doors have always been a cliché, since the very first one ever used," Mordred said.

"Why aren't you all more terrified?" Adam asked.

I shrugged. "Oh, I'm scared. I'm just not going to let them know that."

Several blood elves filed out of the citadel, taking up residence on either side of the bridge while Kay left the comfort of the mighty building to walk toward us. He was smiling, and that made me want to punch him in the face. Repeatedly.

"Good to see you again, Nathan," he said with far too much cheer to be normal.

"Nice to see your face has gone back to its usual smug-prick appearance," I said with a grin. "I was worried my footprint might stay on it." I laughed in an exaggerated manner, ignoring the fact that Kay was clearly angered by my comments.

"I'm going to flay you alive," he said. "I'm going to enjoy it."

I leaned in close to him, and six blood elves behind him dropped their hands to their swords. "Well, I figure that instead of doing that, I'd just kill you, take your tablet and go home. Or kill you once I get home. To be honest, I'm pretty flexible on that point."

The look on Kay's face was almost worth the punch to the ribs. I wouldn't bend over, though. I wasn't about to let him see he'd hurt me in any way.

"Enough!" Baldr shouted as he left the confines of the citadel just as Kay stepped forward to hit me again.

Kay stepped back like the good little lapdog he was.

"Your brother would be so proud," I whispered.

"You really should save your breath," Kay said. "You're going to need it."

Baldr stopped six feet away, his hand resting on the pommel of his sheathed sword. "Mordred, it's so good to see you again."

Mordred just stared ahead for several seconds, until Chloe placed a hand on his arm pulling his attention over to us, the expression of hatred softening.

"Where's Kasey?" he asked.

"Are this girl and man here to take Kasey back to the dwarven Sanctuary? That's what they call that pathetic little town they've created. A town we could obliterate within seconds, should we so choose."

"Why haven't you, then?" I asked.

"Because it's not worth the time and effort. We have bigger things to consider."

"The addresses and spirit scrolls," I said. "They're the bigger things, aren't they?"

Baldr laughed. "The addresses? Oh, we copied those years ago and destroyed them. It's how we managed to make Kay's tablet that lets him jump between realms. We would like those scrolls, though. We know they're in Sanctuary. But don't worry about that; we have plenty of scrolls here—plenty more on the earth realm, too. We'll turn that dwarven town to rubble soon enough, and then we'll have new little powerhouses all over the globe. All of them ready to lose their minds to a demon, all of them ready to cause havoc at our command."

"You can't command a demon," I said. "Pandora didn't work out so well."

"Actually, you can," Baldr said. "But we'll discuss it more inside the citadel." He turned to the elves. "Bring the bitch."

"Don't call her that!" Chloe said, her voice rigid iron.

"She's a female werewolf; what else should I call her?"

"*Kasey*," Chloe said. "Her name is Kasey. You can call her Miss Carpenter though."

Baldr's face lit up. "'Miss Carpenter?' Is that a fact?" He turned to the blood elves again. "Bring out *Miss Carpenter*."

Kasey was marched out by two blood-elf commanders holding an arm each. Her face was a little bloody, and the anger inside of me ignited. "Are you okay?" I asked as she was pushed toward Chloe, who caught her, lowering her to a seated position.

Kasey nodded. "I wouldn't behave; they thought they could make me. Didn't turn out so well, did it?" She shouted the last sentence and spat on the ground beside Kay's feet.

"Filth, just like your mother and father," Kay said, disgusted.

"Bring Mordred and Nathan up to my residence in the citadel," Baldr said. "They may say goodbye to their friends. I would be very wary about giving the archers above you any reason to fire. Their arrows aren't silver, but they are tipped with spider venom. I assure you, no magic will help heal it." He walked away, back into the citadel, and I helped steady Kasey who had gotten back to her feet.

"You're going to go with Chloe and her dad," I told her.

"Can't leave you alone in there," she whispered. "They'll kill you."

"I'll be fine," I promised her. "I just need you to get out of here before they change their minds."

"The archers are going to kill us anyway," she said. "I heard them say it."

I nodded. "I'm staying here and waiting for them to reach the end of the bridge, and walk to that tunnel over there."

"You're coming with us," Kay said and went to grab my arm, but paused at my expression.

"If you touch me, you die first. If anything happens to them, you die first. You might kill us all, Kay, but your corpse is going to be the first one to hit the floor."

Kay clenched his jaw, but nodded, so I stood and waited while the three of them crossed the bridge as a few hundred blood elves bayed for their blood. I'd told Chloe what she needed to do. Get into the tunnel closest to the bridge and destroy it. She assured me she could use her new power to do it, and I hoped she was right. If not, they'd be inside a tunnel with a large number of blood elves. And there would be nothing anyone could do to help them.

My heart beat faster as they reached the tunnel, Kasey no longer needing help to walk, and entered the mouth.

"They're safe. Now come with me, or we go hunt them down."

I ignored Kay and counted to ten. I got to seven when the mouth of the tunnel exploded, raining down chunks of rock onto the blood elves closest to it.

"A trick?" Kay screamed.

"Insurance," I told him. "Now we'll come with you."

Kay visibly seethed, but there was little he could do about it. Chloe and Adam had been given instructions to run halfway down the tunnel where they'd meet several of the dwarves from

Sanctuary. They'd used the few hours' head start to create a new tunnel directly under the original escape route. The tunnel would be collapsed behind them, and Chloe, Adam, and Kasey would meet up with the rest of the group.

Mordred and I allowed ourselves to be marched into the citadel, and waited while the doors swung shut behind us as the smell of blood and death filled our noses. It made me cough.

"It takes a bit of getting used to, doesn't it?" Kay said with a laugh. "The smell wafts up here from the cells below. They're down those stairs over there." He pointed to a curving staircase that vanished somewhere beneath us. "They didn't used to be cells, of course. When the dwarves lived here, they were guard rooms, but the elves like people to know what awaits them when they first enter. And frankly no one wants to tell them to stop."

Any of the old furnishings were long gone, replaced with stained walls and floors. I doubted they had a cleaner come in on anything close to a regular schedule. We followed Kay through the dark corridors, hearing the screams of whatever victims they had somewhere in the mass of hallways and rooms.

"Do you remember those screams, Mordred?" Kay asked. He paused and raised a finger. The scream was followed by a plea to be allowed to die. "These rooms make wonderful dungeons: all private and the like. You used to have to go to the dungeon to be *questioned*, but now, it's just a short walk."

We walked past a staircase and stopped next to what had presumably at one point been a window. Now there was just a hole in the side of the citadel, with a wooden lift just outside it. A piece of rope hung down one side of the lift. A pulley system sat attached to either side of the lift, the metal chains vanishing high above us.

"It's as close as this place gets to a lift," he told us, stepping on, and pulling on the piece of rope. "It's a bell. This lift only goes from here to the floor we want. It's a bit of a long walk, and honestly just as long of a trip, but you get much nicer views."

As the rickety makeshift lift began its crawl upward, it took a lot of effort not to look down and maintain an outward appearance of not caring. By the time it stopped, we were several hundred feet above the ground, and I was grateful when we stepped back into the citadel.

"If I remember correctly, you don't like heights," Kay said to me. "I'm so sorry; that must have been awful. You should have said something. I just remembered there's a lift inside the citadel. We could have taken the old dwarven lift; it's a lot less problematic."

"The view was nice—lots of death and torment. You've really made the place your own."

"You took your time. You'll have to excuse the decor," Baldr said from in front of a set of open double doors. "The blood elves definitely take after their name. Never met creatures quite like them. They're savage, bloodthirsty, and utterly without remorse. They really are an impressive creation."

"'Creation?'" I asked. "Someone *created* them? I thought the crystals did that."

He motioned for us to be taken into the room behind him where we were both roughly pushed into chairs. They didn't bother binding our hands, but they did finally remove our weapons, placing them on a nearby table.

"Oh, they did," Baldr said when the elves had left the room, leaving us with him and Kay. I liked those odds. "Those crystals were a wonderful find. When the elves were having their silly little civil war, we discovered that the crystals had a tendency to make them more hostile, aggressive, and willing to go that step further to hurt people. It's why we suggested the dwarves looked after the elven prisoners. We made sure that no one knew the effect the crystals had and then sat back to watch the fireworks. Fun time for everyone."

"Except the dwarves," Mordred pointed out. "And me."

"The dwarves weren't thrilled, no, but they had their own problem when the king refused to cooperate with our group. It's why he had to go, and why the elves were allowed to destroy so many dwarves. We didn't expect them to leave en masse, though. Or that we couldn't find them after they'd fled." Baldr walked over to Mordred and flicked him in the forehead. To his credit, Mordred did nothing in response. I wasn't sure I would have been so calm.

"You were just in the wrong place, Mordred," Baldr told him. "You and your little friends were all looking a bit too closely at those dwarven weapons you'd found. And then you discovered those people with the spirit scrolls. Fortunately, by that time Nate had been sent away, and we were able to distract your other allies with new missions and jobs. But you couldn't let it go. You were going to be king, and a king doesn't just drop something because it's uncomfortable. Didn't turn out so well for you. We were just going to kill you, but then you came here and met with the king and he started investigating. It was easier to kill two birds with one stone. Didn't expect you to escape; that was on us. Didn't expect you to go against the programming we'd tried so hard to instill on you, although you did still try to kill Nate over and over again, so some of it worked."

"Why me?" I asked.

"You were looking to become a problem," Baldr told me. "That's it. But Merlin sent you to China for the better part of a century, and then orders changed and we were to leave you be. Did you think you went all this time without Hera, or someone else killing you, because they were worried you'd defeat them? We were told not to kill you—to let you just be Merlin's hound, pissing us off on occasion, but never doing anything of any real long-term damage. I know you think you were the big, bad Hellequin, but in reality you never went up against anyone of our caliber.

"Actually, that's not true. You did test several of our group on a few occasions. Most recently with Hera's plan to take over Tartarus. She was furious about it." Baldr started to laugh.

He turned to Mordred. "Oh, and with what you did to Mars Warfare. She was pissed off about that too. That would have been a nice little earner: weaponizing children for future use. She was more angry at Ares, however, for the fact that he'd allowed Mordred to be employed, and obviously Hera knew that Mordred was there, and that he wanted to kill her. That's why she was never in the country at the same time, and why she never put herself in a position of danger. She was going to kill him, but it was nice having him in one place, knowing where he was at all times, so it was allowed to continue. But those times are at an end. We've now had the okay to murder you, Nate. Mordred was always going to die, but we've been waiting a while to finally get you. Before now, it was only as a last resort. Now, it's for fun. Looking forward to it."

"So who's in charge?" I asked. "You said 'new orders.' Who's ordering you about? You and your group: you're all known as 'my liege,' but do you have a liege too?"

Baldr looked over at Kay. "I'll whisper their name to you as you die, Nate. Would that make it better?"

"What about Merlin? Is he on your side?"

"You ask a lot of questions for someone in your situation," Kay said.

"I was always told it's better to ask a lot of questions than to go ignorant. Besides, I've never been in a position to ask about your group before. Or, how Baldr killed Thor."

"You heard about that one?" Baldr asked, with a chuckle. "I cut his head clean off while our father watched. The great Thor, a headless corpse. I think my father is still crying about it. You should be happy about it, Nate. My father banished your mother from the realm of Asgard, did you know that? Banished to the earth realm, just for going against his wishes. And she still refused to join our cause. She said that starting a war in Asgard was pointless, that Odin would never allow himself to lose. And she was right: the war is still ongoing. It's still almost impossible for anyone to get out of there and go to the earth realm."

"That must put a damper on your plans to run the earth realm," Mordred said. "Shame."

"It is a shame, actually," Baldr snapped. "My father had the realm gates destroyed by the dwarves who resided in Asgard. I got here through one of those fucking tablets, and now I can't get home. And you want to know why? Because no one knows the address for Asgard in that stupid made-up language. No one. The address was in the library, and we still can't find it. My entire reason for coming here has turned into my own prison. Even now, my blood elves are scouring the building for it, tearing it apart, and nothing. So, I'm stuck here with my thumb up my ass."

"How do you know your side hasn't already lost?" Mordred

asked and received a punch to the face that knocked him to the ground.

"Because after a thousand years of fighting, we wouldn't hand Odin a victory after only five years."

"You've been here five years?" I asked. "That has got to suck. Blood elves aren't exactly chatty."

"It's been . . . testing, yes," Baldr admitted. "At first I was just going to kill all of the dwarves in that town, but over the centuries since the blood elves took this place, they formed lots of little groups, and it's taken me this long to get them all working in unison again. I can't go home without those scrolls, but once I have them all, and we've figured out how to bring the blood elves with us, we'll cut across Asgard, and anyone else who stands in our way."

Kay walked over and hoisted me up. "Oh, are we going on another trip?" I asked, as half a dozen blood elves entered the room and began marching me out.

"You are," Baldr told me. "Mordred is staying with me."

"I for one couldn't be happier," Mordred said. "It'll give us time to catch up."

"I'll see you soon, Mordred," I told him.

"Oh, are you two friends now?" Baldr asked in as patronizing a tone as possible. "It's so good to see you both back in one another's good graces. I was worried you'd always hate each other."

"Can I ask you something?" I said just as I reached the door.

Baldr raised his hand, and the elves stopped. "Go on."

"Bring him to the room when you're done," Kay told the blood elves and then left the room.

"Did you really kill Nabu's wife? Did you really arrange it?"

Baldr laughed. "That's it? Yes. He was an affront to me, and was investigating a number of crimes that could have been traced back to me. I gave him something more interesting to search for. You must have felt the same way when Jane died, yes?"

I stared at Baldr. My wife, Jane, had been murdered centuries ago by a human in the English army. I'd found him and tortured him to death, but he'd sworn that he had been given the task, that he'd been working for someone. It was information that I couldn't verify, even after an extensive search.

"*You* did that?" I asked, my words coming out slowly.

Baldr shook his head. "I was in Asgard. But it's funny how similar it was to what I did. I wonder if someone you knew was behind it, someone who really didn't like you? Maybe you should have a conversation with Kay when you get the chance. He might know more."

CHAPTER 36

The blood elves brought me to a large room several floors down, using the stairs instead of any of the lifts. I didn't fight or struggle; there was no need. They were taking me exactly where I wanted to go.

The large room was bare-floored and wet, as if someone had recently sloshed out the blood and muck that had been spilled across it. Chains hung from the ceiling, and a bench with straps sat in one corner, while the other corner held a table and various implements hanging from hooks above it.

Apart from a few dim lights situated around the room, the entire place was bathed in darkness. Kay sat beside a smaller table next to the ceiling chains. A collection of knives lay on the table, and he was lovingly polishing one as we walked in.

I was shackled to the chains, which were made from silver, and the elves left the room.

"You can't escape now," Kay said.

I looked at my wrists. The shackles were pretty heavy-duty, and it would be more than a little difficult for me to burn or cut through them. Silver didn't stop my magic, but it was partially immune to it, and if I got cut with it, it would do considerable damage. Silver blades were dangerous to sorcerers for a very good reason.

When I didn't respond to Kay's obvious taunt he stood up and shoved me. I swayed from side to side, and stared at him.

"Why aren't you trying to get me angry?" he asked. "Why aren't you trying to get me to bite?"

"You murdered my wife." I said my words slowly, making sure to put no emotion into them.

"Ah, you figured that out? Took you long enough. I didn't actually *do* anything; I just hired a few people to ensure you were treated to her demise when you finally came home. I was outside the house when the soldiers arrived. A few of them went inside while the rest went down to the village. If it makes you feel better, it's a trick Baldr used first, and we appropriated it on a few occasions. Husbands, wives, children: it didn't really matter; some people just need to be sent a message, or given something more important to attend to. I bet you don't even remember what you were investigating."

"I was looking into the murder of a vampire lord. He was an ally of Avalon's, specifically Elaine's. By the time I went back to Merlin after Jane's death, he told me the crime had been solved. I never looked into it again."

"So it worked. You were no longer a problem for us in that matter, and you gained some humility at the same time. Also, I did it because I hate you. I've always hated you, and I will always hate you. You're so self-righteous, and you manage to get all of these idiotic people to trust you, to like you, and you were a threat to our plans because of it. How many of those people would have gone for us had we gone after you? Tommy, Hades, Diane, and countless others. You gave us no choice."

"No choice." My voice sounded detached, as if it wasn't really me speaking.

"You know, in a way I'm glad you discovered it. You should die knowing that I was better than you throughout your life. Better in every single way. You just never saw it before."

I breathed out slowly. "Who do you work for, Kay? Apart from Hera, and Siris, and Baldr, who's in charge of it all? Merlin?"

Kay laughed. "No. Merlin isn't in charge of anything."

"So who?"

Kay stood before me. "Baldr told you: he'll whisper it into your ear as you die. You want to know something funny about when Jane died? Before she went, before she finally submitted to death, I went to her. You should have seen the surprise in her eyes. I whispered in her ear that you would never know the truth of what had happened. I guess I was wrong." He brandished a scalpel. "How silly of me."

"It's quite dark in here."

He looked around. "I guess it is. You see, I know a little something about shadow magic. And that is that it doesn't like the darkness. The darker it is, the weaker your power. So you can keep trying to grab the shadows, but it's going to be difficult." He sliced across my stomach, only a tiny incision, but enough to cause pain. "Also, it doesn't help when I do that."

He turned away and placed the scalpel down, picking up one of the swords that Zamek had given me. "I think I'm going to use this to cut your head off at the end."

He turned away for a second, and when he turned back, his jaw dropped open as the shackles unlocked and I fell to the floor. I'd drawn one of the dwarven runes on the palm of each hand. It meant lock and unlock. It's one of the twenty-one original dwarven runes. Takes a little out of you, but all I had to do was press my palm to the shackle. Unfortunately, I didn't expect it to take so long for me to get my hand just right; I should have drawn them on my wrists. Hindsight and all that.

I punched Kay in the jaw hard enough to send him staggering back toward the table. A blast of air magic toppled him over it, pulling all of the blades with him. Kay got back to his feet brandishing one of the swords that Zamek had given me.

"You should put that down," I told him. "It's dangerous."

Kay's arm wavered slightly, and he looked at the door.

"You murdered my wife. Would you like to guess what I'm going to do to you?"

"You can't beat me; a hundred thousand blood elves are right outside the citadel. You're never leaving."

I threw a ball of flame at the overturned table, which quickly caught fire. "Will you look at that. Light."

The shadows wrapped around Kay before he could scream and dragged him down onto the floor in the blink of an eye just as his glyphs lit up to defend himself.

I grabbed the Zamek sword from the floor after Kay had dropped it, and placed the point against his throat. "You murdered my wife. I'd stay very still."

One of the shadows leapt at Kay's leg, wrapping itself around the limb, tighter and tighter.

He cried out and tried to kick it away with his free leg, but it was useless.

"Did you tell her not to struggle?" I asked. "Did you tell her that it was because of me that she died? Did you enjoy listening to her screams?"

"It was centuries ago!" he screeched. "She was human! She was nothing!"

I balled my fists and the shadow began to increase the

pressure around Kay's leg. The sound of tearing and his accompanying screams—quickly cut off as more shadow wrapped around his mouth—were when I knew that he was going to lose a limb if I continued. I stopped.

"The pain you're going through must make it difficult to use your magic. That and the fact your arms and legs are covered in shadow must be quite terrifying. I wish I could take you to my shadow realm and keep you there to make this slower. I want to stay here for a long time and watch you beg me as I tear you apart," I told him. "That's what I want. But Mordred will need my help, and I'm not going to let him die for my vengeance. Where is the tablet you used to jump between realms?"

I released the shadow on his arms, and he reached inside his jacket and passed it to me. The tablet was smaller than the ones that had been sent out: no more than the size of a pocket notebook.

"How does it work?" I rewrapped the shadows around his arms, tightening them when he tried to move.

"Anyone who wants to travel needs to have placed their blood on the tablet. Only someone who can use magic can actually activate it though."

"Why not use it to take the blood elves to the earth realm?" I tightened the shadows again.

"Their blood doesn't allow it—something to do with the crystals. They need a realm gate. Baldr was trying to get the one in the citadel to operate again. But it hasn't worked yet; they can't create a guardian from the humans they have."

"Where are the human slaves?"

"All over the place. Mostly in the camps away from here," he said quickly. "You going to save them all? There are thousands of them; most have been here for generations. They don't know anything else except death and pain."

I removed the shadow that had been wrapped around Kay's arm, and as he moved it, I severed it at the elbow with the sword, rewrapping it in shadow to stop him from bleeding out. I gagged him once more and crouched beside him. I couldn't save all of those people, but I could tell Olivia and her people, and maybe they could help. It didn't feel very heroic, but I didn't have a lot of other options. Taking them all back would be impossible, primarily because if they were in the camps it would require us to fight our way through tens of thousands of blood elves to get there. And that was *if* they even wanted to leave.

Kay stopped hyperventilating and stared at me with hatred. I removed the shadows from across his face. "Jane died because of you, Nate."

"No, Kay. She died because of *you*. And you're going to die because of you too. There's no one else to blame here. No one else." I punched him in the face. "And don't ever utter her name again."

"Arthur will kill you when he wakes up. If you kill me, he'll hunt you down and deliver vengeance."

I shrugged. "*If* he wakes up, I'll deal with that problem. If there's a true afterlife, I hope you burn in it."

I tightened the shadows around Kay's neck until he couldn't breathe, wrapping them around his jaw and mouth. I didn't want to hear him speak ever again. I wanted him to suffer, but Mordred would need me. The shadow forced Kay up to a kneeling position, and I brought the blade down across his neck, the shadow moving aside as it touched. Kay's head rolled away. I thought about taking his soul, but there was no way to know exactly what effect the power he possessed would have on me. I wouldn't have time to try and acclimate myself to that much power, memories, and evil. Instead, I took a moment for Jane before leaving the room.

Outside in the hallway, I came face-to-face with the half-dozen blood elves who had led me to Kay. I stabbed the closest in the neck and threw the second sword at the blood elf the furthest from me. The sword's blade slammed into his chest, taking him off his feet.

I disarmed the third blood elf as he drew his sword and severed his arm at the elbow with it. I pushed him into the next blood elf, driving the blade into the chest of the fourth, then kicked him to the floor. The fifth came at me with his sword, but I impaled him with a spear of shadow. The sixth remained alone, a mixture of fear and hate on his face. He screamed and charged at me. I avoided the swipe of his sword, and used my air magic to pick a dagger from the floor and drive it up into his skull. He fell to the floor dead a second later. I removed the heads of the third and fourth elves so that none remained alive.

I walked over to the huge window looking out at the bridge far below, and used the blood of the slain elves to draw the original dwarven rune for collapse onto it in several places around the base and side of the window. Or at least as much as I could reach.

Then I ignited the runes.

The effect was spectacular, as the entire wall just collapsed, taking the window, and a massive amount of rock above, with it. Several dozen tons of rock fell at high speed into the bridge below, making a terrifying noise. I stood as close as possible to the jagged edge of what had once been the floor, and could see only a huge plume of smoke and dust. Then I ran up the stairs toward the fight between Baldr and Mordred.

As I reached Baldr's room, the Norse god crashed through the far wall with a very determined-looking Mordred stalking him.

"Need help?" I asked.

"He's mine," Mordred told me and charged into Baldr, taking him off his feet, and driving a blade of air into his chest.

Baldr broke Mordred's arm and tossed him aside into the nearest wall. Mordred vanished from view in a cloud of dust.

"Do you want to try?" he asked me.

I used the shadows around him to take hold, and he walked through them as if I'd used string.

He removed his jacket and threw it on the floor, revealing the purple glyphs adorning his arms. Matter magic.

"Doesn't work on me," he said. "I'm too powerful to be stopped by shadows. You'll need to do better."

I threw a fireball at him, which he allowed to burst against his chest.

"Do better," he repeated as he closed the gap between us, and I narrowly avoided being punched. He hit the wall instead, which disintegrated from the blow.

I rolled to my feet and ignited a sphere of air in my hand, spinning it faster and faster as I dumped lightning into it.

"Not going to kill me, little Nathan," he said. "You're welcome to try, though."

The glyphs turned yellow and I managed to close my eyes as bright, blinding light poured out of him. I slammed the sphere into the ground just in front of me, which tore the floor apart.

The light dimmed and I opened my eyes.

"You should have been burned," he said. "I guess the shadow magic does have some uses after all."

A blast of air smashed into Baldr, flinging him back into the other room, as a wounded Mordred staggered out of the hole in the wall he'd created.

"Be careful: he hits like a charging rhino," Mordred said.

We both entered the room and found Baldr by the window at the far end. "I wonder if I could kill you both? Let's find out."

He moved quicker than anything I'd ever seen, charging toward me as I threw lightning at him, and dodging at the last minute to hit Mordred, who had been trying to slow him down with liberal use of air magic.

As Mordred went flying into the wall behind him, Baldr used his own momentum to bounce toward me, and the only thing that saved me from being seriously hurt was a shield of lightning hastily raised in front of me.

Baldr screamed in pain as his bare skin touched the shield, and he skipped back, the skin on his hand red and raw from where he'd touched the lightning.

"Just like Thor," he snapped. "Lightning didn't stop me from killing him, though."

I dashed forward, creating a sphere of lightning and attempted to tag him with it, but he moved too fast, so I just detonated the magic inside the sphere. Baldr couldn't avoid the wave of electricity as it crashed into him, forcing him off his feet. The wave smashed into the wall behind him, destroying the windows.

"You don't really think that's it, do you?" he asked, coming toward me, the purple glyphs blaring brightly across his arms.

I avoided a punch I was certain would have taken my head

off, and hit him in the chest with another electrical shock, sending him back a few feet again. Mordred took that opportunity to wrap tendrils of blood magic around Baldr's arm, which caused him to yell. He threw a ball of light that exploded in Mordred's face. He screamed and dropped to his knees.

Baldr ignored him, and turned his attention to me once more. "I hear you can't use blood magic," he said with a chuckle, as his own blood magic trickled over his fingers, forming a blade. "It's a real shame; you'll never know the joy of using it to take someone's life."

I hadn't had the time to take any souls before I'd come upstairs to face Baldr; I hadn't wanted to leave Mordred alone for a second longer than necessary. But it meant that my necromancy wasn't as strong as it might have been otherwise. Baldr was stronger, faster, and much more powerful than I was, even with my new upgrades. I wished that I'd taken Kay's spirit. The extra power could have really come in handy.

So I did the only thing I could, and, keeping an eye on Baldr, who didn't seem that concerned about us, walked over to Mordred.

"Are you okay?"

Baldr looked at his nails and scratched his jaw a little, but was in no hurry to fight us.

"My light magic lets me heal much quicker than most sorcerers. I'll be back to normal in a few seconds. Didn't realize light magic could hurt *me* though. That's new."

"I need time," I whispered.

"How much?"

"I need to take Kay's spirit, but I have no idea what it'll do to me. It's the only way, though. I need the power. We can't beat him like this."

Mordred got to his feet. "I'll give you time, Nate. Just hurry."

I sank down into the shadows around me, landing in my shadow realm. I moved the gray world around until I found the shadows that left the room, and tried to go further, but it was too difficult, and I couldn't quite figure out how to make those shadows come to me.

"You can only emerge from shadows that are within a certain area of you," Erebus told me as he stepped out of the gray. "Hello, Nate."

"Are we in the shadow realm or my head?" I asked.

"Both. We're still in your head, but you're physically in the shadow realm. I can't go into that realm; I'm not actually a real person."

"Then why are you here?"

"To stop you from making a huge mistake."

CHAPTER 37

"I really don't have time for this. Mordred is going to die if I don't help." I snapped.

"We are in your mind," Erebus said, his voice calm. He looked exactly like me except with longer hair. "Time doesn't pass here in the same way. A few seconds there, a few minutes here. We have time."

I crossed my arms over my chest. "Go."

"Do you really want to take Kay's soul? You know what you'll see?"

"Jane's death. I'm aware. But I need the power. We can't beat Baldr; he's too strong. I need something, and if that means putting myself through whatever awful shit sits inside Kay's soul, then so be it. I'll deal. Besides, maybe it'll show me who these *my liege* are."

"You don't believe that for one second. You know full well that whoever manipulated the minds of these people isn't about to let you figure it out just by taking their souls. You know there will be traps and things planted inside his memories for an occasion such as this. Besides, can you even take Kay's soul? He didn't die fighting; he died kneeling on the floor, gagged so he couldn't beg for his life."

"So what do I do?" A thought occurred to me. "The blood

elves. I can take *their* souls, use them instead. Some of them fought back."

"You can, yes. And then what?"

"Is there a point asking me?" I snapped. "And then I go kill Baldr."

"Even with added power, killing him won't be easy. He's much older than you or Mordred and considerably more powerful. He walked through your magic; only lightning had any effect. And we're not outside, so using natural lightning is impossible."

"Okay, so what do I do?"

"When those curse marks were added to you, when they stopped you from accessing your magic, they also planted the knowledge of how to use them inside you. I am that knowledge. I taught you how to use your lightning, didn't I?"

I nodded. "So you tap me on the head, and I know how to use my shadow magic?"

He shook his head. "Shadow magic is powerful—more powerful than most realize. And while it's true you can't bring sorcerers into your shadow realm, and anyone you do bring in here will start to weaken quickly, there's another reason you shouldn't bring people down here."

"And what's that?" I asked.

Erebus pointed behind me. "That's the reason why."

I turned and almost jumped out of my skin. A few feet away was a floating mass of darkness. The shrouded figure wore long, dark robes that rippled along the floor, seemingly with a life of their own. It wore gray armor over its chest, visible under the robes, and its hands were little more than claws. Two orbs of blue light bobbed inside the shadow where the creature's face should be.

"What is *that*?" I asked.

"A wraith. Don't worry; we're still in your head. I'm just showing you what's currently happening in your shadow realm."

"They live in my shadow realm?"

"This one does. Every sorcerer who uses shadow magic has his own realm. The realms are a part of you; you are linked to it by more than just the ability to go there. Should it be damaged, that damage will happen to you. It's your own little place to tend and take care of."

"And the wraith does what?"

"Well, the wraith feeds on anyone you bring in here. It's why you really shouldn't bring anyone in here. They don't distinguish between friend and foe. They distinguish between you, and not-you. And the not-yous are to be eliminated as quickly as possible."

"So this realm is dangerous to anyone I bring in here?"

Erebus nodded. "There's an upside, though. The wraith feeds on the bodies of those you bring here. It literally folds that person's power into you. It increases your power without having to take a soul to do it. It isn't as powerful as your necromancy, but it's quicker, and it means you don't have to learn everything of the person from the souls you take."

"Will it help strengthen my necromancy?"

Erebus shrugged. "The number of sorcerer necromancers can be counted on both hands and feet. Those of you who use shadow magic, too—probably on one hand; I have no idea. When those blood-curse marks were put on you, so was some knowledge of how to use your magic: knowledge that's still inside your subconscious mind, inside *me*. You need to know how to use it. You need to confront your wraith. It won't hurt you. You're its master, its reason for existing. A little bit like me."

"You want to take control of me, though."

"True. Although not for the reasons you think. I'm hoping once those other marks are gone, I'll be able to explain why. You'll be able to understand what I truly am, and why you need me. And then I'll vanish forever."

I whipped around toward him. "*You'll vanish?*"

"Once you have no more marks, and I've done what needs to be done, yes. I have no interest in keeping control of you forever. That's not what a sorcerer's magic does. You have been lied to about us, about the power a sorcerer possesses. All of you, all sorcerers, have been lied to. We are not your enemy. I know you don't believe that, not truly. And I understand why. But you will. Like I said before, we are your birthright, not your enemy."

"So every single sorcerer under two thousand years old has been lied to?"

"That's my guess, yes. At some point, you'll have to find out why, and who arranged it, but they are problems for another time. Less immediate than your current situation."

The idea of not having Erebus there, to have him leave—it didn't feel good. I didn't know what he was, or why my magic felt the need to create someone for me to talk to, and I had no idea if it happened to every sorcerer, but the thought that we'd been lied to about what the magic was, about what nightmares were . . . That was something I would not allow to continue, and would need to be investigated further.

"Good luck," Erebus said. "Your power is greater than it ever was before. Calling me to help will be much harder, the amount of power you'd need to use to bring me to the surface, incredible. But we'll see one another again, soon. Until then."

He vanished and the wraith began to move toward me, the

robes trailing it. It stopped just in front of me and looked down. It was over seven feet tall, and the robes brushed against the bare skin on my arms. It wasn't scary, or worrying. I felt no malice or anger from the being.

"So you're like my gardener in here?" I said.

The wraith's voice echoed all around me. *I am here to protect you. I am here to feed you power. I am a wraith. I will sustain you.*

"'Sustain?' I don't need food and water?"

Sustain your power. You should probably continue to eat and drink.

I wasn't sure, but I thought I noticed a hint of sarcasm in its voice. "Wait there." I moved the shadow realm around me until I found the exit I needed and emerged on the staircase outside of the room where Mordred was fighting Baldr. I wished Mordred luck and sprinted down the stairs until I saw the bodies of the elves. I enveloped them in shadow and dropped them into the shadow realm, where I followed a second later.

The six elves were lying in the middle of the realm as the wraith hovered nearby. *You should not watch this.*

"I have questions," I said as it hovered close to the bodies.

Be quick; their presence causes me pain.

That was information I hadn't been expecting. "Can you leave this realm?"

It turned back to me, and regarded me with its eyes. *Yes. If you wish it. I am strong, fast, and magic cannot harm me. But light will harm me, and I cannot feed in your realm. My time there is fleeting. I would not be able to recognize friend from foe for long, either. I advise against bringing me out of this realm.*

I removed the tablet from my armor. "Can I leave this here?"

Anything you leave in this realm will be here when you return.

The exits might change for you, depending on the shadows around you, but this is your realm, your creation. Go help your friend.

"Thank you." I placed the tablet on the ground before leaving the shadow realm. I ran back up the staircase to Mordred and Baldr and reached the floor as Baldr stepped out of the room.

"You ran off," he said. "Mordred didn't fare so well by himself."

I looked behind Baldr and saw Mordred lying on the floor, his face a mask of blood. His chest rose and fell steadily, though, so he wasn't dead. He turned my way, opened one eye and smiled as the cuts on his face began to heal in front of my eyes.

I nodded.

"So what's the plan here?" Baldr asked. "Going to use your shadow magic a bit more? Maybe you're going to try to electrocute me. That worked well for you last time, but it's not likely to kill me. You're not even as powerful as Thor."

"You like talking about him," I said as the feeling of power swept through me. I placed a hand against the nearby wall to steady myself.

"Weakening already?" Baldr joked. "And I like talking about it because it's the single greatest thing I've ever done. Murdering that unbearable asshole was my pleasure. But killing you and Mordred: that might just be even more fun."

The feeling of gathering power had stopped, and I moved away from the wall, noticing the cracked rock where my hand had been. I wondered just how much I had after the wraith had taken all six of the blood elves. Time to find out.

A blast of lightning left my hands, smashed into Baldr and lifted him off his feet, throwing him back into the room behind.

"That it?" Baldr asked, sprinting toward me.

He was moving as fast as he had the last time, but for some

reason I was able to track him with greater ease. I dodged the punch and hit him square in the jaw, which forced him to step aside. The shock on his face was easy to read, but he wouldn't leave himself open like that again.

I motioned for him to come fight me. And winked.

He kicked out, and I wrapped his leg in air, throwing him across the hallway to the wall behind us, but he absorbed the impact and came racing back, punching me in the jaw before grabbing my arm and throwing me up into the air.

I hit the ceiling high above and immediately created a sphere of lightning in my hand, making it bigger and bigger, until it was a few feet in diameter. I fell back toward Baldr, who hastily moved aside, as I detonated the magic, tearing the floor beneath me to shreds. Baldr backed into the room with Mordred. A small blast of air magic changed my trajectory and I landed on the crumbling hallway floor, only to be met with a flash of light that forced me to turn away for a second. A second was all Baldr needed.

The blow lifted me off my feet and forced me back into the hallway, over the destroyed portion and into the wall on the far side, just as I used the shadows around it to cushion the blow. Shadows exploded up from the floor all around me and streaked toward Baldr, who dodged most of them. A few grabbed hold, but he tore his arm free, his strength greater than that of the shadows. But it kept him busy as I jumped over the hole, creating a second sphere, this one of fire, before I landed.

I drove the fire sphere into Baldr's chest. The flames and air engulfed him, wrapping all over his body. But a second later the fire was turned into steam as water tore through the maelstrom, forcing me to dive aside.

The sound of footsteps on the stairs beside us took Baldr's attention, and he walked back into the room, putting some distance between himself and whatever was coming to join the fight. Kasey, in her werewolf beast form, ran toward me, stopping as a low growl escaped her throat. She glanced over at Mordred and me as we got back to our feet, and then turned to Baldr, opened her mouth, and sprayed ice at him. He jumped out the window.

I ran over and watched Baldr fall the hundreds of feet, losing sight of him well before he hit the bottom.

"You think he's dead?" Kasey asked, changing back into her human form.

I shook my head.

"He'll survive it," Mordred said. "If nothing else, his matter magic makes him almost impossible to kill. But it'll be a while before he's even close to full strength again. Thanks for the save."

Chloe ran into the room and hugged me. "I'm glad you're okay," she said, passing Kasey her leather armor to put on.

"Me too," I told her. "Did everyone make it?"

I got my answer quickly as everyone else walked into the room. "So far we're all here," Diane told me. "I'd quite like to go, though. I think we may have pissed off a lot of blood elves."

"Also, we blew some up," Remy said. "And part of the citadel fell off and destroyed the bridge. It was so cool. The elves were all, 'Nooooo!' and then they got squished. But they were colossal assholes, so I don't exactly feel bad about it. Did you do that?"

I nodded.

"We found Stel. He's dead too."

"Did *you* do that?" I asked him.

"Actually no. He ran away and got squashed by part of the falling bridge. I'll admit, I chuckled for a good solid minute."

"He laughed so hard, I thought he was going to have an asthma attack," Chloe told me.

Remy shrugged. "Stel threatened Kasey, kidnapped her, and almost got us all killed rescuing her. Fuck the pancake-shaped prick. So, how'd you break the citadel?"

"Another time. I know how the tablet works." I explained about the blood use, and why the blood elves had been unable to use it to go through to the earth realm. Before everyone asked questions at once, I dropped into my shadow realm, and retrieved the tablet. I looked around for the wraith, but it was nowhere to be found, so I left.

"I figured Baldr would have gone through to the earth realm too," Irkalla said, as I emerged. "Surprised he didn't."

"Wasn't allowed to," Mordred said. "He's not the top of the tree. He's close, but he's not up there. And once we're back in the earth realm, we're going to have to deal with Mara, and her reason for sending us here. This isn't over, Nate."

"Everyone place your blood on the tablet," I said, passing it around. Once everyone had bled on it, Kasey passed it back to me.

Blood elves began climbing the stairs, forcing Morgan and Zamek to defend the entrance to the room. Fortunately, getting from the stairs to the room had been made more difficult by the partially destroyed hallway floor, so they had to stand across the hall and fire arrow after arrow through the doorway.

"Zamek, we can't leave you here!" I shouted, and ran over to him, forcing the tablet into his hand. "Use it. We can always send you back."

He paused but then nodded and slammed his bloody hand onto the stone.

"Any time now!" Morgan shouted as her golems blocked the arrows that came through.

I turned at Morgan's shout and realized her golem was in the wrong place to stop an arrow from flying past toward Chloe, who was oblivious to it all. Adam dove at Chloe, pushing her aside, and took the arrow in his chest. Chloe screamed when she saw her father hit the ground. The others in the group immediately turned to help as Kasey had turned once again into her wolf-beast form and blocked the entrance to the room with blasts of ice.

"It won't hold forever," she said.

I ran over to Adam, who was coughing up blood, while Mordred knelt beside him and tried to heal the wound with his light magic. The arrow had been pulled out, and I picked it up.

I remembered what Baldr had told us before we'd entered the citadel. "Spider venom. The arrow heads are coated in it."

"The people who take the scrolls are still human," Nabu explained as he dragged me away. "They have a higher ability to heal, but he took an arrow to the heart. He's going to die, and there's nothing we can do to stop it. All Mordred is doing is slowing down the inevitable. Let them say their goodbyes. He won't survive the trip."

"My dad will not die!" Chloe snapped.

Adam raised his hand and stroked his daughter's chin, leaving a bloody smear. "I love you, little girl. I'm so glad I got to see you again."

"No, no, no, no," she repeated over and over. "Please."

Adam forced a smile. "Mordred is keeping me alive, but he can't do it forever."

"I can try," Mordred said. "I'm not going to let anyone else die in this shithole. Not without a fight."

"The venom will kill me," Adam said. "Magic won't stop it."

"I've just found you," Chloe said as tears fell freely.

"I'll always be here," Adam said, and he tapped her head. "And here." Placing the tip of his finger against her heart. "No one can take that away."

"I love you, Dad," she said. "I love you. Please stay. Please."

"Nate, you take care of my little girl."

"She's pretty good at taking care of herself," I told him. "But I'll always be around."

Adam nodded and smiled. "She's made her daddy proud. Now run, all of you. Get out of here. It was an honor to meet you, to know that Chloe's friends love her. To know that she's surrounded by good people."

Mordred looked over at me and shook his head.

"It's okay," Adam said, and he weakly took Chloe's hand in his. "Your daddy loves you. He'll never stop loving you." And then he died.

Chloe's howls of pain and hurt were muffled as Diane and several others surrounded her, hugging her tight, but even their presence couldn't completely drown out the torment.

The ice at the door began to crack, and I activated the realm-gate tablet, taking us all home.

CHAPTER 38

Now. Earth realm.

I landed in a field. I wondered why Kay's tablet was designed to take him back to this particular location. The middle of a field wasn't exactly what I was expecting. It wasn't muddy, thankfully, but it was a bit disorienting, and it took me a few seconds to remember what had happened just before we shot through the realm gate.

I staggered to my feet and looked around at the rest of the group.

"So this is the earth realm?" Zamek asked. "Smells funny."

The howl of pain from Chloe caught my attention, and I spun to find her no longer looking like the Chloe I knew. She knelt over the body of her father, her face contorted, full of rage, and no longer human in color. It was a dark red and orange, with ridges protruding around the eyes and cheeks. Her eyes appeared more like those of a wolf than a human; she was a predator, and one with a power we were unaware of.

"She's let the demon out!" Nabu shouted as he ran toward her.

Chloe raised her hand in his direction and a blast of bright-yellow power exploded from it, smashing into Nabu and throwing him back over the field.

"Kinetic energy," the demon that used to be Chloe growled. "I absorb it. Redirect it. Fun, yes?"

"How do we stop her without killing her?" I asked.

"Chloe!" Kasey shouted. "It's me: come on, you know me. Please don't do this."

Demon-Chloe roared something and charged her best friend, but Diane got between them, taking the demon off its feet and planting her face-first on the ground.

"Get off her!" Kasey screamed. "Just let her be, please! She won't hurt me."

"She's been taken over by a demon," I told her. "Chloe needs to take control back, or this could turn very bad, very quickly. And that demon doesn't care about you or any of us."

Kasey stared at me. "Please let me try."

Demon-Chloe continued to struggle in Diane's iron grip, but I nodded to her, and she released the younger woman, stepping back a few paces.

"Chloe," Kasey said, edging closer. "Please. It's me. It's all of us. We're your friends."

"Friends?" Demon-Chloe spat. "Friends couldn't save him. Didn't do anything to try."

"That's not true, and you know it's not," Kasey said, her voice always soft. "We did everything we could to save him. It's no one here's fault. It's the elves' fault. It's the fault of the people who sent us there."

"Mara," the Demon-Chloe said, and she sprinted away so fast few of us could keep up with her.

We followed Demon-Chloe out of the field and over a small bridge until we reached a house nearby. The Demon-Chloe screamed for her mum to leave the house, but as the rest of us reached her, Asag was the only thing to leave the building.

"Thought you'd all be dead!" he shouted while several of the little mini versions of him stood around, ready to fight.

I didn't stop running when I saw him. I poured power into a sphere on my hand and sprinted past the Demon-Chloe. Asag recognized me and began to laugh.

"Sure, you go first!" he roared.

Just before I drove the sphere into him, I changed its shape, making it drill-like, then slammed it into Asag's chest with every bit of force I could manage.

The magic literally tore him in half, from the top of his shoulder down across his chest and through the top of his hip. There was no blood, just a silver tar-like substance, as the smaller versions of him collapsed into piles of rock.

Mordred walked over to the corpse of Asag and with a blade of blood magic, cut the monster's head off. It took him a few hacks to get through the rock, but when he did, he kicked the head aside. "Just wanted to make sure," he said.

I turned and stepped in front of Demon-Chloe. "See? We're all on the same side."

"Kill my mother," the demon said.

"Not yet," I told her. "Come on, Chloe: fight this. I know you want—"

A window shattered at the rear of the property.

"Make sure she doesn't kill anyone," I said as I charged around the side of the building, catching a glimpse of Jerry as he escaped the sun, and ran into the dark woods behind the house. I moved the shadows around in front of where he was running, and he tripped headfirst into a tree. More shadows wrapped around him, holding him in place.

"You're not even a master vampire," I said as I got closer. "You're nothing: a waste of breath. Where's your girlfriend?"

"Basement of the house," he said. "She's alive."

"Why'd you do this: join Kay? Was it really because I didn't stop you when I promised I would? Is that what this is all about?"

"I found that I enjoyed hurting people, hunting people. Humans are ever so easy to kill. I found Kay by accident. He introduced me to Asag, and the rest is history."

"Kay is dead. Asag is in several pieces. Who else?"

"Her name is Siris."

To hear her name spoken, to have it confirmed that she was involved, made me wonder what her plans were. And how many more had to die before she achieved them. "What does she want?"

"She's going to kill Brutus. We were meant to get certain people out of the way before we started. You've been gone a week now. The attack has already begun."

I increased the pressure of the shadows. "When did it start?"

"A few hours ago. An explosive in Brutus's building. They took Brutus. He's going to be used in some sort of ceremony. I don't know all the details. I was just here to make sure Mara was kept safe. She knows how to make those tablets."

"You shouldn't have killed Francis, shouldn't have tried to kill me. Certainly shouldn't have done any of this."

"Francis was no friend of yours. He lied to you. He knew who you were. Brutus did, too."

I nodded, remembering the video on the mini SD card. "I know. He told me. And you know what? I'm not angry with him. Not with

Brutus, either. I'm going to save my anger for people who *really* deserve it."

Jerry's expression was one of utter shock. "But he betrayed you!"

"And he's dead. And you betrayed me, and you're still alive. Guess which one of those I'm going to rectify?"

Jerry spat at me. "I turned some humans into vampires. They're going to be waiting for you and your friends, Nate."

"I'm so sick and tired of you lower-level pieces-of-crap vampires thinking you can just create an army. You can't. The only ones of you with any real power are the masters and lords, and frankly none of them would just randomly start creating vampires. It shows how pathetic you are. You might as well not even be the same species as them."

"They're going to kill you anyway. It only takes one."

"Goodbye, Jerry," I said and forced him down into the shadow realm. The wraith could use him as food to power my magic. At least that way he'd finally have a use.

I walked back to the house and discovered the door had been torn off and tossed aside. Mara was outside in the garden, flat on her face with Diane kneeling on her back. Chloe was sitting on the ground crying, while Kasey held on to her. They'd managed to get Chloe back to her non-demon self, and I hoped she stayed that way.

Remy left the house with several tablets and dumped them on the ground. "I called Olivia and Tommy too," he said. "They won't be long."

"Jerry confirmed it. Brutus is in trouble," I told Diane, explaining what Jerry had told me.

Remy dashed back into the building and returned with a

laptop. He used the Internet to find a news channel, which had a breaking story about an explosion at Brutus's building.

"I need to go," Diane said.

"I'm going too," Nabu and Irkalla said in unison.

Remy threw them a pair of car keys. "I think it's the least she can do."

Mara cursed something as Diane got off her, but before she could spit out more of the grass, Chloe was up and punched her in the jaw, knocking her mother to the ground.

"*You murdered him!*" Chloe screamed. "You nearly murdered me, my friends, people I love. And for what? Power? You murdered my dad!"

"I thought he'd died long ago," Mara said with no hint of emotion as she got back to her feet.

Chloe didn't have time to hit her again, because Irkalla did it for her, although without using anywhere near enough power as she could have. Mara slumped back to the ground, rubbing the side of her face.

"We'll go," Diane said. "Be careful. We didn't see anyone else, but that doesn't mean they're not here."

"We'll be up in London as soon as Avalon turns up here. I don't want to leave Mara alone with anyone here. I don't think they'd be held responsible for their actions."

"I am alone," Mara said, rubbing her jaw. "And you have turned into the daughter I never wanted to have. More like your father than a witch."

Remy removed his sword and held it against Mara's neck. "Speak again without being asked to, and I *will* kill you."

Mara glared at him, but said nothing.

We dragged Mara into the house and tied her hands with

some zip ties before I went down to the basement and freed Jerry's girlfriend, Laurel.

"He's dead," I told her after removing the silver manacles around her wrists and ankles.

"Good," she said. "He was . . . not the man I fell for."

"I'm sorry."

She nodded. "Me too."

She let me help her back upstairs and sat on the sofa. She wasn't injured, at least not physically, and it appeared that Jerry had only drugged her and kept her here until she'd decided he was in the right. She'd been there a few weeks, surviving on the rats that Jerry or Asag had given her for food. I was really glad Jerry was dead.

I went into my shadow realm to see if Jerry was finally gone from everyone's life, and found the wraith hovering around.

"Thank you for your help," I said.

The wraith regarded me for a second. *The vampire was delicious. If such things matter to you, alive is preferable to dead.*

"Do I need to keep feeding you to keep you strong?"

Not at all. The more I eat, the stronger you become. There's a limit. I can only eat so many corpses in one day, or in one sitting. But a regular enough stream would be advisable to see your power levels up.

I wasn't really sure how I felt about feeding my enemies to the wraith.

You would kill them anyway, yes? he asked, as if able to read my thoughts.

It had a point, but that didn't mean I liked it.

I left the shadow realm and went outside, where I found Morgan and Mordred. "Avalon will not be as accepting of me as you all are," Mordred said. "I do not think they'll believe me."

"I think that's a fair assessment," I admitted. "Run. Both of you. Get as far from here as you can."

Morgan nodded a thank you.

"You should know that if there's any doubt in you about who you are, today made all doubts in me vanish. I saw you try to save a life today. I saw the pain on your face when Adam died. Now go: get somewhere safe. Because this is far from over, and when we stop whatever is happening in London they're going to come for us all. You two included."

"Nate, I need to tell you something. It's important."

"Mordred, you *need* to go. Whatever it is, it'll wait."

"Thank you," Morgan said, and I watched as Morgan began to drag Mordred away. Then they both ran off into the woods.

I went to find Chloe and Kasey, both of whom were sitting against a nearby tree, taking a well-earned moment of rest.

"Mordred and Morgan gone?" Kasey asked. "My mum isn't going to be happy about that."

"I'll explain everything to her. Somehow. I haven't quite figured out how yet, but I will, I'm good at explaining things."

"Can I watch that? Because she's going to shout and it'll be funny."

"Thanks, Kase. Nice to have you as backup."

Kasey laughed and the tension eased a little.

"How are you holding up?" I asked Chloe. "I know it's a stupid question, but I don't know how else to ask it."

She nodded. "I can't do this anymore. I need to get away. I need to do something normal."

"You said that before. I assume this has all confirmed it."

"Yes. I just want to do something that isn't fighting demons, or monsters, or having my mum try to murder those I love." She stared at me for a short time. "I can't use my witch magic. I can't access it. The scrolls took it away from me."

"I'm sorry." I wasn't really sure what else to say.

"It feels like part of me is missing. I don't know how I'll cope not being able to use it anymore. It feels strange. This whole thing is going to take some time to get used to. I need to learn how to control the demon. I allowed all of the spirits and the demon to merge with me, but I had no idea how much power me losing control gives the demon. It's scary."

"Take as long as you need."

Olivia and Tommy arrived ten minutes later, and both of them hugged Chloe and Kasey so tightly I wasn't sure they'd ever let go. Eventually Tommy relinquished his hold and grabbed me in a bear hug, kissing me on the cheek.

"Thank you for bringing them back," he said.

"Chloe lost her dad," I told him, and then explained to both him and Olivia everything that had happened as more and more Avalon agents showed up. They began cordoning off the area and started their search for even more evidence against Mara.

Mara was dragged out in handcuffs, a sorcerer's band on her wrist, and I motioned for the agent to stop so I could speak to her.

"Your coven will be disbanded. Your allies arrested or executed. We know Hera, Siris, and the rest of their group were behind it all, and we will find proof of that. You're done here. You're done ever seeing the light of day. I'm going to make sure they find the deepest pit in the most awful realm imaginable, and I'm going to put you in it."

"Filthy sorcerer. Knows nothing," she snarled.

"I know that Kay's tablet went from your house to the

dwarven realm and back again. Always the exact same spot. I assume you and Kay were friends, so you might like to know that he's not going to be around again. Mostly because his head is no longer attached to the rest of him. Enjoy prison."

Mara glared at me.

"You're never going to see Chloe again," Olivia told her. "Not ever. Unless she wants to see you, you are officially out of her life. You're an evil witch who lives in a house in the woods, the only way you could be more of a pathetic cliché is if your house was made of gingerbread."

"You can't keep her from me."

Olivia punched Mara in the face, putting some serious power behind the blow and crushing the witch's nose. "Get her gone," she snapped at the agent, who wisely did as he was told.

"London is under attack," I said to Olivia.

"I know. We heard a few hours ago. Only just discovered it was Brutus, though. There's a helicopter in the nearby field waiting to take you to London. I'm going to stay here and clear things up. Besides, I'm Avalon, so I probably wouldn't be welcomed. Tommy, Remy: I assume you're both going with him?"

"Try and stop me," Tommy said.

"Us too," Kasey and Chloe said in unison.

I shook my head. "Right now, Chloe, you only just got a handle on that demon inside of you. I can't have it rearing its head again when you get upset. And, Kasey, your friend needs you more than anything else in the world right now. We'll be fine, but you need to stay here."

Kasey and Chloe accepted my words, although they clearly didn't like them.

"I was about to say no myself," Olivia said. "It's your turn to be the bad guy, rather than me or Tommy. I quite like that idea on occasion."

"Thanks," I said and gave her a hug.

"Thank you for bringing them both back. I'll make sure they're looked after here."

I passed Olivia the tablet. "Put it somewhere safe—far away from everything else. Then when you figure out how to get a fucking battalion into that realm, go take it back from the blood elves and Baldr. The dwarves deserve to have their kingdom back."

"I spoke to Zamek," she said. "He's already at the helicopter waiting for you. He's upset he had to leave everything. Tommy wants to offer him a job. See if you can get him to accept it; it would give him purpose. And purpose is sometimes all we need when we've found that everything we've ever loved or known has crashed around us. I want him kept away from Avalon, too. They'll question him on everything, and there are still elements there I don't trust."

"You don't trust Avalon?" I asked. "That's new."

"I've spent the last year finding traitors, and people who want to destroy our way of life. A lot of them had hidden but powerful backing. If we find evidence to prove that Hera has been involved with Kay and Baldr, then we could uncover a lot of bad people within Avalon."

"You ready?" Tommy asked as he left the house.

I nodded.

"Oh, and when you get back, we need to talk about Mordred, and why he isn't here right now," Olivia said. "A long talk. In a locked room."

I was already walking away at that point. "Sorry, can't hear you," I called out. "The wind here is dreadful." I whipped up some air magic to make my point and Olivia scowled.

"You know she's not kidding," Tommy said.

"Yeah, but how do I tell her that Mordred is one of the good guys now?"

Tommy opened his mouth to speak. "You sure?"

"One-hundred-percent yes."

"Well, who'd have thought it: Mordred on our side?"

"I never said that."

"You don't think we're the good guys?"

I didn't respond for a few seconds. "All I know is, we're in the middle of a storm, and I really have no idea which way is the right way to turn. And until I do, I'm not sure who our allies or enemies are."

"We know that some of them just attacked Brutus," Tommy said as we reached the helicopter. Zamek and Remy were already on board.

"And right now that means I have someone to go hit. Repeatedly. And after the last few days, frankly, I don't think they're going to find me in the mood to play nice guy."

CHAPTER 39

Smoke and fire. They were the main things visible from the building long before we got close enough to make out any of the details. The closer we got, the more the black, tar-like smoke billowed up into the sky. The sounds of sirens blared all around. The pilot landed on the roof of a building downwind from the smoke, and it didn't take us long to get to the ground floor and out onto the busy streets.

Police were everywhere: human police. Human fire brigade. Human paramedics. All helping, all trying not to show the public how scared they were. I walked past a policeman, who put his hand out to stop me, saw Remy, the walking fox, and blinked.

"My name is Nate Garrett," I told him, regaining his attention. "What happened here?"

"Sorry, sir, we're not at liberty to say."

Tommy walked over to the police officer and showed some ID. The officer immediately stood straighter and nodded, pointing down the street, past the cordon and people who were still trying to get a look at what had happened despite the danger.

"What did you say to him?"

"I have my old SOA ID," he said.

"You left working for Avalon a century ago," I pointed out.

"My ID is still valid. Olivia made sure of it after the Reavers attacked. Apparently, I'm trustworthy."

As we turned the corner, I looked up at the damage to the building that used to belong to Brutus. The Aeneid was five hundred feet tall, and designed to look imposing and inviting at the same time. It was Brutus's living quarters and main headquarters; hundreds of others called this home, too. The last time I was here, it had been under attack from enemies who'd been working within Brutus's own staff. I hoped that wasn't the case again. Unfortunately, even with eyes as good as mine, I couldn't quite tell what damage had been done to the building. Tommy walked away and found several official-looking people and began talking to them.

Zamek was still carrying the swords that'd he'd retrieved from the dwarven citadel, and wearing his armor. Along with Remy, a heavily weaponized three-and-a-half-foot-tall fox, they stood out a little bit, and received the occasional glance from the humans around us. I wondered just how many of them were aware of Avalon and its people.

Tommy returned before anyone came over to enquire about who we were and what we were doing.

"The explosion happened on the twenty-seventh floor. It took out three floors on either side of it, so whatever they used was potent. It happened a few hours ago, and the fire brigade tried to get up there, but part of the staircase has collapsed, and the lifts are ballsed up."

"So how do we figure out what's going on?" Remy asked.

"How did you get here so quickly?" Diane asked from behind me.

"Avalon perks," Tommy told her and then explained what he'd been told.

"We need to get up there," Remy said from beside her.

"Diane, where the fucking hell have you been?" Licinius shouted as he crossed the road. "And get out of the road—people are going to start taking photos of you." He pushed us all through the doorway behind us, which led into a small, empty shop.

"Why is there a dwarf here?" he asked.

"No time. What happened?" Diane asked, getting the conversation back to more important matters.

"The fucking building blew up," Licinius said.

"We got that," Remy said slowly, as if he were explaining something to a particularly difficult child. "Tell us *how*."

Licinius clearly didn't appreciate the condescension, but held his tongue. "A few hours ago, the cleaning lady arrived, as she has every day for the last ten years, but something was off. Her movement was weird, as if she hadn't done the job before. But it was clearly her; I'd seen her hundreds, if not thousands, of times. I followed her when she left the floor before her shift was over, so I was three floors down when the explosions began. At least four bombs, all placed around the floor. I do know that the cleaning lady wasn't who I thought she was."

"Changeling?" I asked. Changelings could become other people by physically taking their appearance and leaving the original a smooth sack of skin and organs. They were rare and dangerous.

Licinius nodded. "He or she—I don't know—tried to change into me, but I killed them before they could manage it."

"How many are hurt?"

"The targeted floors were mostly empty today; a lot of those who live there are off at a retreat: team building. Thankfully, the injury count aside from those floors is low: only a few dozen. But no one has been able to get up above the damaged floors to check for more. The police here are mostly hand-picked by us, and like most in London are aware of who and what we are. Same with the fire brigade, but that doesn't mean everyone here knows it. The civilians in the crowds certainly don't, although now they probably have a few pictures of a dwarf and a walking fox."

"Most foxes walk already," Remy pointed out helpfully. "And I think dwarves exist in this realm: just not Zamek's kind."

"What about Brutus?" Diane asked, moving the conversation off Remy's mocking.

"He was in his penthouse: thirty-sixth floor. No one has seen him since, but he should be safe. The building is in no danger of collapse, and the damage appears to be contained to six floors. I have people working to move the debris, but it's slow going."

"I can help," Zamek said. "Rock, brick, any kind of building material: moving is a dwarven specialty."

"Let him," Diane said before Licinius opened his mouth. "It's been a long few days."

"You can tell me all about them later. Right now, let's save some people."

We left the shop at the sound of a helicopter overhead, which was flying toward the smoke that continued to pour out of the building. At first, I thought it was a news crew or someone equally insane to be that close to a burning building, but the helicopter wasn't anything the news companies use.

"That's a Black Hawk," Remy said.

We all watched as the Black Hawk landed on top of the Aeneid.

"Anyone else find that odd?" Tommy asked.

"Brutus doesn't own a Black Hawk," Diane said.

"I didn't order a Black Hawk," Licinius said. "We've been in contact with Brutus; he's on the top floor, and appears to be fine. There's no need to risk a helicopter landing."

"He could have contacted someone in Avalon to rescue him, but that's not exactly what I'd expect from the man," Diane said. "I'd expect him to pour himself a vodka, sit back, and wait for us to get up there. Calling anyone for help, especially Avalon, isn't really his style."

"Then who is up there?"

The explosion at the side of the building confirmed that it was no one good. Glass and concrete began to rain down on the people closest to the building, and they ran for cover under the overhangs of the buildings nearby. I blasted a few pieces with air magic, but my involvement was thankfully minimal.

It didn't take long before the Black Hawk was on its way again. And all of us were helpless to stop it.

"We need to track it. Any idea how?" I asked. I looked around for someone with a radio I could nab.

Diane figured out what I was suggesting and called over some people, who, from their uniforms and badges, were clearly part of Brutus's security staff. Or former staff, depending on how much trouble they were in. She took the radios from them and passed one to me and one to Tommy.

Tommy nodded and set off toward the helicopter, changing into his wolf-beast form as he went. He was faster than any of us, and probably more equipped to track people—or at least the exhaust smell of the helicopter.

"You know humans are watching us right now?" Licinius said, reminding us all about something we really didn't care about.

"It's dark. The lights are far enough away to shield Tommy

and the rest of us, and any civilians or press are far enough back that we're not exactly in their line of sight. We're good."

"Why don't you do something constructive?" Remy asked. "Somewhere other than here?"

"Diane, what are *you* going to do?" Licinius demanded to know, anger coming off him in waves. "You weren't here when this happened. You're meant to be in charge of his security. This is your screw-up."

For a second I thought Diane was going to punch him, as her hands balled into fists, but she relaxed before speaking. "I'm going to find Brutus."

"We don't even know he was on board when it flew away," Licinius pointed out.

"True, but we will once Tommy lets us know. If Brutus isn't on that helicopter, we'll help you get up to his floor, but if he is aboard the Black Hawk, we're going to go and save him. Sound okay to you?" Her tone suggested she didn't really care if it sounded okay or not.

The radio crackled. "Guys, are you there? I think we have a big problem."

"Bigger than a blown-up building and a possibly kidnapped Brutus?" I answered.

"They brought him to the British Museum. I've just watched them march him out of the Black Hawk. I don't think they can see me, but they've taken him inside."

"We'll be there soon as we can."

"There are a hundred soldiers in front of this museum. And they look like they're armed with swords and stuff. A few of them have guns, but most don't. I guess a hundred soldiers in London with guns would catch someone's attention a lot quicker than without."

"Anything else?" Irkalla asked as she joined us, along with Nabu.

"I saw Siris. She was on the Black Hawk. She's with Gilgamesh. He's helping her."

"Son-of-a . . ." Irkalla started and walked off muttering to herself.

"We'll be there soon. Stay safe," I told him and ended the chat. "So that whole hunting Siris down thing that Gilgamesh said he was doing?"

"I had no idea he'd be working with her," Nabu said. He looked genuinely shocked by the news, and judging from Irkalla's punching of a car window, she wasn't pleased, either.

"How do we stop them?" Diane asked. "Gilgamesh is a walking powder keg, and Siris isn't far off Baldr in terms of power, and easily his equal if you're talking ruthlessness."

"I don't know," I said, honestly, "but we'll figure it out on the way."

"Well, this couldn't be worse then," Nabu said. "They are going to use a tablet to open a portal. They could be bringing anything or anyone through that gate."

"Use the Mercedes G-Class at the end of the street," Licinius said. He fished some keys from his pocket, tossing them over to me.

"Nate, this is bad news," Remy whispered as we went to the Mercedes. The others went over to the car they'd arrived in.

I climbed into the driver's seat and breathed out slowly. Driving angry wouldn't do me any good.

"How are we meant to get to Brutus with Gilgamesh, Siris, and who knows who else helping them?" Remy asked. "I don't have a nuke. Can I get a nuke?"

"Remy, I barely trust you with the weapons you do have," I pointed out.

"Spoilsport." He chuckled. "We're so screwed, aren't we?"

I looked at my fox friend. "We'll be fine," I said. "It's only a small army. You managed to get through one in the dwarf realm."

"We managed to avoid most of the army, though," Remy told me. "It's a bit harder when you have to go through the army to get to the thing you want." His face became solemn. "You've got a plan, though, right?"

I nodded, but all I could think about was how useful Remy's nuke would be right now.

CHAPTER 40

We stopped the car a few blocks over from the museum and ran through deserted streets to where Tommy said he'd meet us.

"The police have told people to stay off the streets," Tommy explained after he dropped down from the balcony of the building he'd been using to spy on the museum. He was back in his human form, although I didn't want to know where he'd picked up the jeans and T-shirt he was wearing.

Diane, Irkalla, and Nabu arrived soon after.

"What's the plan?" Diane asked.

Tommy led us into the building and up the stairs to a door that led to a roof terrace. It would have been a lovely view, if it wasn't for the fact that you could see the collection of people outside the British Museum behind the closed gates and high walls.

"We don't have a plan, do we?" Diane said.

"Not so much, no," Tommy said. "Brutus is in there, but I have no idea how to get to him."

"Are they human?" Nabu asked.

"No," Diane and Irkalla said in unison.

"Vampires," Tommy said. "I can smell the death on them. Where did a few hundred vampires come from?"

"Jerry," I said. "He told me he'd turned a bunch of people. Jerry was no master, though, so none of them there will have that kind of power. But they're still going to be stronger and faster than humans. And they outnumber us ten to one."

"Not the worst odds ever," Irkalla said. "And there are no giant snakes this time."

I looked her way. "Don't jinx it."

She smiled.

"To make this even worse," Tommy said, and pointed to toward the museum, "you see that there?"

I followed his direction and my heart sank when I saw what he was pointing at. "That's an M134 Minigun."

"Where?" Remy asked, sounding a lot happier about it than I would have.

"Between the columns. It's slightly hidden by darkness, and under a roof. It fires 7.62 NATO rounds—lots of them. As in several thousand per minute. We need to figure out a way to get past that without being shot."

"If we rush them, we're going to get cut to shreds," Diane said.

"I have a plan," Tommy said, "but Nate isn't going to like it."

"The last time you had a plan, I ended up jumping out of a helicopter."

"Funny you should say that."

"I'm not jumping out of a helicopter, Tommy. Besides, do you see one that we could get in?"

Tommy told me his plan. It was stupid. It was dangerous. And it wasn't like our options were overly brilliant without it. Charging through the front gate would be insane, time-consuming, and result in the injury or death of people I cared about. Neither of those was acceptable. We needed to make our mark, and do it quickly. We needed to crush the opposition without giving them time to regroup, but more importantly, we needed to get that machine gun out of commission. We needed our equivalent of a nuclear bomb.

Me, apparently.

"We'll be ready," Tommy said. "Just be careful."

"I hate you," I told him. "I'd like that on record. I hate you so much."

"You love me and you know it. Just get those gates open, stop the machine gun, and don't die."

"Fuck their shit right up," Remy said, patting me on the arm.

I climbed back into the Mercedes, and drove as fast as possible back toward the building we'd landed on when first arriving. I sprinted up the stairs and found the pilot waiting for me, the rotors already spinning.

"Tommy called; said you needed me," she told me as I climbed in and put my earpiece in, before fastening my harness.

"My best friend is an asshole," I told her, as the helicopter lifted.

"You ready?" the pilot asked, and we quickly accelerated off the rooftop and up into the night sky. "I heard a rumor you don't like heights. That true?" she asked.

"No, my eyes are closed because I really enjoy hanging out of helicopters that are high in the air," I muttered.

"How high do you need to be?"

"A hundred feet should do it," I said. "I'm not sure just how much impact I'll be able to stop. I've managed to slow myself from a fall of about sixty or seventy feet before, but even so, this isn't going to feel great."

"If you don't think you can do this, say now. Because I can't hang around. This needs to look like a passing flight—not anything stopping."

"I *can* do it," I said, unsure if I was convincing her or me. "I just don't *want* to do it."

"Get into position," she said.

I pushed open the helicopter door and lowered myself onto the grab rail. This was a bad idea. "When you get back to Avalon, please feel free to punch Tommy in his stupid face."

The pilot smiled. "Go. Destroy." She winked, making me smile, and I pushed myself off.

I knew I needed to slow myself down so that I didn't pancake into the ground at high speed, but that wasn't going to be enough. I held my hands out in front of me and created a sphere of air, pouring more and more magic into it, growing it larger and larger until it was the size of my torso. Only when I'd stabilized it, when the lightning, fire, and wind inside were no longer in danger of exploding before I hit the ground, did I remove one hand from the sphere and use it to wrap myself in air magic. Slowing down would have been a mistake, a mistake I didn't realize fully until I was maybe fifty feet from impact.

Some of the vampires looked up. Several pointed or shouted, although I couldn't hear their words, and it was too late to stop me anyway. I couldn't see the machine gunner under the roof of the museum, but it didn't really matter. I was moving faster than the vampires could have possibly reacted.

I detonated the magic at the exact moment it touched the concrete. The power softened the landing, but only a little, as the explosion tore into the vampires all around me. I tried to direct the blast out in front of me, but the shockwave of magic smashed into everything unlucky enough to be within ten feet and continued spreading through the crowd of vampires, tearing apart those who were too close to the initial detonation and flinging away those further back.

The machine gunner fired once before the magic hit him like a truck, smashing him back into the wall with a crunch, and turning the machine gun into scrap metal.

After the noise in my ears had died down, and my body had decided that I was capable of movement again, I got back to my feet as the surviving vampires swarmed toward me, only to be met by my friends, which gave me time to recover.

"That was crazy," Irkalla said. "Utterly crazy."

"I ache," I told her, as the fighting raged around us.

"Get to Brutus!" Tommy shouted, in his werewolf beast form once again, as he tore the arm from one vampire and threw it at another one.

Irkalla and I avoided most of the vampires and reached the museum entrance, where she used an errant vampire as a door knocker. She stepped through the shattered entry, grabbed the vampire and removed his soul, killing him before he could get to his feet.

"So where do we go from here?" I asked as we entered the Great Court. A circular structure sat in the center of the massive main hall showing various signs pointing to exhibits to either side.

"This way," Irkalla said, pointing to a sign that said *Mesopotamia*, and I followed her for a few steps before Gilgamesh walked out from a doorway to the left of us. He carried a huge sword in both hands. He wore an oversized red and white tunic that came down to his ankles and looked a little ridiculous.

"I didn't want it to come to this!" he shouted.

"You betrayed us," Irkalla said. "How could you?"

"I can't betray what I don't believe in. You were all so keen to join Avalon, to become a small cog in that machine, that you never stopped to think about what really needed to happen. Avalon will be rebuilt with true power. You can't stop that."

"We can bloody well try!" I snapped.

"You should leave," he told us. "I don't want to have to kill you; I never did. Siris was wrong about that. She shouldn't have sought your deaths back in Acre. But you left me to hunt the woman I love, and I was never going to kill her."

"You helped her hide?" I shouted.

He nodded. "Took her back to the realm she'd been using as a base of operations. Hid her there for a long time: long enough to start again. Word reached us that we were to do nothing until we received orders."

"Who do you work for?" Irkalla asked. "Who's behind all of this?"

"That doesn't matter. You're never going to meet them. You either leave, or die. There's no third option here."

"Siris has twisted your brain!" Irkalla shouted, her voice echoing around the massive hall.

"Siris is the only one who knows what she's doing. You can't turn me against her."

"Where's Brutus?" I asked. "Why Brutus, of all people?"

"We're going to take London," Gilgamesh said, taking a step toward us. "It's the first part of the plan. Take London, establish a new, better place for us to show our power, and then move from there. Brutus is a relic: someone who should have been destroyed centuries ago. He revels in his own opulence. He sees himself as leader, but does nothing to help those less fortunate. He only helps himself, and those he deems worthy."

"And that means he should die?" I asked, drawing the two dwarven swords.

Gilgamesh paused. "He'll die because the only thing he's good for is being a symbol: a symbol of the new guard crushing the old. A symbol for the transfer of power."

"That's it? There's nothing personal in all of this?" I asked. "Even though Brutus is the one who helped kill the giants who lived here when he first arrived all those centuries ago?"

"He hunted my kind to extinction in this country. I've wanted to kill him for a long time for what he did." Gilgamesh grew in front of me, going from seven to ten feet tall in seconds. His bulk increased in size, and by the time he was done, the massive claymore he was carrying looked more like a gladius. The tunic no longer appeared oversized, instead fitting his frame perfectly. He reached behind a marble pillar and removed a blue and silver shield. It was the size of a car bonnet.

"Well, shit," I said.

"Who holds London when this is all done?" Irkalla asked, pulling a dagger from a sheath at the small of her back.

"I don't care for politics. Hera, Siris, and the others can decide that. Maybe Kay. He likes power."

"Kay is dead," I told him.

"He was told to leave you alone. He never did like the fact that he simply wasn't as powerful as he liked to believe. I guess he won't be doing much of anything now." He held the sword out in front of him. "You can't beat me, Nathan. Not with all your power. And certainly not with a woman like Irkalla as your backup."

He swung the sword toward me and I threw myself to the ground, rolling under the blow and coming up running as I tried to put some distance between us.

"A woman like *me*?" Irkalla asked as she stepped toward Gilgamesh. "Let me show you what a woman like me can do."

She ran toward Gilgamesh. It was the single craziest thing I've ever seen. A five-and-a-half foot, 112-pound person against a ten-foot-tall giant, who probably weighed the better part of half a ton.

Gilgamesh laughed, but raised his shield in defense. I ran back toward the pair, hoping to help Irkalla, but she didn't need my help. She punched the shield head on, and it just vaporized in front of her. Gilgamesh flew back into a nearby pillar, hitting it with a crunch.

"This is on me!" Irkalla shouted. "Go find Siris!"

I did as she said, just as Gilgamesh charged toward Irkalla, who ducked his attack, and hit him in the stomach hard enough to stagger him as an explosion rocked the building.

CHAPTER 41

I found the stairs and took them two at a time, leaving Irkalla and Gilgamesh to fight. I had no doubts that it would be a close thing, but I was certain that Irkalla would be able to defeat the giant.

I reached the top and a blast of air opened the two doors, allowing me to run through them without stopping just as another tremor shook the building. I followed the signs to the Mesopotamian exhibit, running down a long corridor before barreling into a massive room that overlooked the main hall below. Brutus was tied up against a suit of armor, a sorcerer's band around his wrist.

The room was adorned with various artifacts from medieval Europe. Swords hung on the walls and I could spot the old coins and pottery in the glass cases along the side of the room. A huge window sat on one side, overlooking where I'd left Gilgamesh and Irkalla.

Siris stood in the center of the room. She was laughing. Several stone tablets sat on the floor in a circle at her feet with one in the center. The center table glowed a brilliant gold. It hovered slightly before flinging itself through the window and vanishing into the main area of the museum where Irkalla and Gilgamesh were still fighting. Trails of golden particles, starting from the remaining tablets and showing the trajectory of the one that had left, hung in the air.

She turned to me. "You will not stop me!" she snapped.

"That's sort of why I'm here," I pointed out. "Just give in, let it go, and we'll get you whatever help you need."

"Stick me in a cell in The Hole? I don't think so."

The Hole was a prison run by Avalon. It was ideally the perfect place for someone like Siris, but I wasn't sure if even The Hole would be able to contain her anger and hate.

The building shook again, more powerful than before. "What is that?" I asked.

"Ah, it's the tablets. This requires a lot of power."

"What are you trying to do?"

"You'll see."

I walked over to Brutus, and removed the gag around his mouth. Siris didn't try to stop me. "She's not quite all there," he said.

"I noticed."

There was another tremor and the glass window beside me exploded as the tablets crashed through it.

"They broke her tablets up," Siris said, almost giddy. "They broke them up and we found them. It took so long to piece them back together. Now you get to reap the benefits."

I turned to throw a blast of air at her, but she was already running off, so I unfastened the ties holding Brutus and helped him down from where they'd put him.

"They really did a number on me," he said after sitting on the floor. "That Gilgamesh can really throw a punch."

"Yeah, we might need to go help Irkalla. She's probably still fighting him."

Brutus nodded. "I killed his ancestors, or relatives—I can't remember which ones."

"Pretty much."

"I thought I was done paying for my actions all those years ago. A different time, and a different man. They wanted me dead, Nate. They want my city for themselves. I can't let them have it."

"You won't. Don't worry."

I walked over to the window but could find no trace of Irkalla or Gilgamesh, although there was a lot of blood on the marble floor. I turned back to warn Brutus that Gilgamesh might not be dead, when the tablets on the ground that had been there moments earlier disintegrated. And the tablet outside in the main hall lifted up into the air as a rift opened between our realm and another.

"How do we stop that?" Brutus asked.

I turned back to the window. "I have no idea. Let's just get you out of here." I helped Brutus to his feet as Siris reappeared and blasted me in the back with her earth-elemental power, knocking me through the window to the hall below. I managed to slow my descent, and only hit the floor with a slight jolt. But before I could launch myself the fifty feet back up to Brutus, a roar of a creature I'd never heard before came from the rift, which continued to grow, a kaleidoscope of colors bouncing all around the tear in our realm. The creature inside roared again, and it took everything I had not to run as far and fast as possible.

The creature's massive taloned foot was the first thing I saw. Each talon was the length of a man, attached to a foot that could crush a car with ease. A second foot appeared soon after, and then the head, and before I knew what was happening, a dragon climbed through the portal.

The creature was gargantuan: larger than any living thing I'd ever seen. Its body was completely black, save for the yellow and orange of its eyes. It looked down at me as Irkalla ran out, grabbed me and quickly pulled me behind a huge column. One of her arms was bleeding, but now was not the time for an update.

The dragon roared.

"Tiamat," Irkalla hissed. "The stupid fool brought her back."

"I thought she was dead."

"She doesn't look very dead now, does she?"

Tiamat opened her mouth and purple flame burst forth from it, destroying everything it touched in the main hall.

"Oh, Tiamat," Siris called out from somewhere above us. "Take this gift. Take it and be free. Burn this world so we might remake it in your image. Oh, great and powerful Tiamat, help us rebuild this accursed world. Help us cleanse it of the taint of corruption."

I saw Brutus fall through from the floor above, but he never hit the floor. Tiamat caught him in mid-air and bit him in half before my eyes. She allowed the top half of his body to hit the floor with a splat while she swallowed the bottom in one bite, then finished him off as if he were nothing more than a doggy treat.

"How do we kill a dragon?" I asked.

"I don't even know if you can," Irkalla replied.

"Go forth, oh, great Tiamat. Cleanse this city of its corruption," Siris said.

"She needs to shut the fuck up!" I snapped and spun around the corner, sprinting toward Tiamat as she beat her wings and released her terrible purple flame, destroying the dome directly above her in seconds. She beat her wings again, and I wrapped myself in a shield of air, before throwing a loop of it around the closest wing.

Tiamat took off out of the museum, high into the air, as I climbed the black scales along her back, looping the air magic around her to hold me steady as she reveled in her newfound freedom. More purple flame burst from her mouth, leveling a building and tearing through several cars outside the museum. We were about as high as when the helicopter dropped me when I looped the air around Tiamat's neck and pulled tight. She bucked and took off high above, moving several hundred feet in seconds as the city of London became a blip below me.

I held on with everything I had. To do otherwise meant my death, and frankly, that was one thing I really wasn't keen on. I didn't even have a plan beyond climbing on the dragon, and if I was being honest, that was a pretty stupid plan. Leaping onto the back of a dragon and riding it high into the air doesn't normally come under the heading of well-thought-out ideas.

When it became obvious that she was going to keep going until I died or let go, I tightened the air loop around Tiamat's neck and twisted my body, forcing her to turn back down toward the city.

"Release me!" Tiamat said, her voice booming in my ears, despite the speed of the wind whipping around me.

"Not a chance," I snapped, and she spewed purple flame again, ripping apart several floors of an office block as we flew further and further into London's heart.

I wrapped air around Tiamat's muzzle, forcing it closed. I figured it was probably designed like a crocodile's, and once you keep the bottom jaw shut, they can't open the top one. I vaguely remembered reading that somewhere, or I was talking shite and had no idea, but it was better than sitting there and hoping for the best.

Tiamat skimmed the tops of buildings and shook her head from side to side, eventually forcing me to release the muzzle I'd employed.

"Why don't you just stop?" I eventually shouted as we neared St. Paul's Cathedral.

"What a good idea," Tiamat said, and she landed on top of the cathedral, her claws punching through the brick, and her wings enveloping a structure that was never really meant to hold a dragon. People had gathered in the streets below and I really wanted to tell them how stupid they were, but Tiamat's purple blaze did that for me. I had no idea how many she'd killed since arriving in our realm, but I had to stop her.

"Humans always think they can tell me what to do," she snarled, then blasted more purple flame at innocents below.

"Stop being a dick!" I shouted, changing the chain of air around her throat to include spikes. I pulled it back as hard as I could, and Tiamat roared in pain, thrashing around until I replaced the spikes with normal air magic.

"I will feast on your organs for that!" she cursed.

"Good for you, but while I'm sat here, we're both in a stalemate."

A low rumble started in her belly, traveling up just below me before bursting forth from her mouth as an almost missile-like object that streaked its purple flame along the street in front until it hit a truck. The truck vanished in a ball of flame, which also engulfed a few cars that were nearby.

"Do not presume to threaten me again, human."

"Sorcerer," I corrected, not wanting to think how many innocents would die if I couldn't stop Tiamat. "And you need to stop doing that." I removed the air magic and poured lightning into the back of Tiamat's head, keeping the pressure on until she bucked, throwing me back along her spine. I was just able to grab hold of her wing as she took off once again.

The movement of the wing was like being on the world's most evil bucking bull—a bull that really wanted to tear me in half. I used one hand to wrap air magic around Tiamat's back leg, and as I swung down, I created a blade of lightning and carved through the thin membrane that covered the wing.

Warm blood poured out of the wound, drenching me. Tiamat fell toward the River Thames, crashing into and over the Millennium Bridge, tearing most of it apart. I was thrown free over the remains of the bridge, close to the Tate Modern Museum. I managed to ignite my air magic to cushion my fall, before rolling several feet onto a small patch of grass. It felt like years had passed since I'd saved the young girl here only a few days earlier.

People had already been sprinting for their lives off the bridge before Tiamat crashed into it. A fire-breathing dragon had that effect on people. But I saw that more than a few had fallen into the water. Tiamat was some distance from the bridge now, but was thrashing around after being caught up in the bridge cables.

The bridge itself was now mostly in two large pieces; about a hundred and fifty yards had been torn apart, most of it ending up in the Thames. The middle section still attached to the struts was bent at a ninety-degree angle, but the parts on either side were still mostly intact. Although from the way some of the support struts were bent, I doubted they would stay that way.

I wrapped air around the struts, helping to keep them upright as people rushed off the bridge until it was empty. Then

I released the air and began helping people out of the water just as the bridge collapsed.

I looked up as the sound of a horn broke through the cries and screams in the air, and saw a familiar-looking Mercedes driving along the other side of the river, stopping just short of the ruined bridge. Diane got out, along with everyone else who'd fought at the museum.

Diane saw people in the water and dove straight in, swimming over to them as Tiamat finally managed to free herself and turn toward me. I turned and ran, hoping to put some distance between her and me, but a jet of purple flame barred my exit and I stopped running just outside the Tate Modern. The purple flame set fire to the nearby trees, the heat easily felt from several feet away.

"I'm going to kill you, little sorcerer!" she seethed, as she climbed over the bridge remains toward me. "You have ruined my wing!"

"Going to ruin a lot more than that," I told her.

She opened her mouth to breathe more purple flame, and I wrapped myself in air, channeling every ounce of power I had into it as something landed on Tiamat's head. It was Remy, who immediately started stabbing his sword into her skull.

"Like irritating bugs!" Tiamat shouted, swiping Remy off her head. He bounced along the ground before smashing through the Tate Modern's windows.

"Now, where were we?" Tiamat asked.

The earth around me erupted directly into the dragon's maw as Morgan walked toward it.

"Go check on Remy," she said. "I'll keep this one busy."

I was halfway to Remy when the earth that surrounded Tiamat

was torn apart by Morgan's magic. Tiamat batted most of it aside, and some of it smashed into me, knocking the air out of me.

"More little sorcerers!" the dragon roared. "You will not hurt me!"

Morgan fired more earth at her, but Tiamat replied with her purple flame, and it soon overwhelmed Morgan, forcing her back too close to Tiamat's massive talons. The dragon flicked Morgan aside with one such talon, her body rag-dolling across the floor until she smashed into and through several trees, vanishing from view. I had no idea if those who had been hurt were alive or dead. And a rage, the likes of which I'd barely felt before, ignited inside of me.

I got to my feet and walked over to Tiamat as I pulled bolts of lightning down onto her, forcing her to retreat to the sky, hovering just above the River Thames. She couldn't fly too high; her damaged wing made sure of that.

I kept redirecting the lightning through my body, aiming the bolts at Tiamat, who moved closer to land, until she was only a few dozen feet from me. I stopped and watched as she made a noise akin to laughter.

"Is that it?" she bellowed. "Is it my turn now?"

The sound of a rifle-shot tore through the night, followed by a second, and a third. The last of the three struck Tiamat in the eye and she was forced to land back on the relatively solid ground of the bridge remains. I looked across the river to where I thought the shots had originated and saw Mordred on the far bank, rifle in hand. Tiamat turned on him and began pelting the riverside with flame. Mordred disappeared from view behind a large building, and Tiamat turned back to me, putting herself in the middle of where the bridge had once been.

"I have grown weary," she said, moving ever closer. "I am going to kill you now."

Behind her Mordred rode a motorcycle toward the bridge. When he reached the part of the bridge closest to him, he used air magic to propel himself and the bike over it, landing on Tiamat's back, where Mordred lost his balance, but I didn't see where he ended up.

The riderless bike skidded up Tiamat's back, impacting with the rear of the dragon's head before bouncing off onto the ground nearby, where it touched the purple flame that had been smoldering away, and exploded. The light from the fire made the shadows flicker and appear as if they were alive. I made them shoot up from the ground, wrapping around the dragon's head and neck, tighter and tighter, like reeling in a large fish. She used her flame once, but she couldn't quite get the aim, so it sailed harmlessly over my head, missing the museum too.

"I am a god!" she screamed, and began moving closer to me.

"Not anymore!" I shouted as she came only a few feet from me. "You hurt my friends!"

Her eye was no more and blood trickled from dozens of wounds she'd sustained, but still she fought, as she got closer and closer until she towered over me.

"You cannot kill me with your shadow magic, sorcerer!" she snapped.

"I wasn't planning on it," I explained and removed the shadows. She reared back, which was exactly what I was expecting and I instantly created a soul weapon, driving the jian up into her exposed chest.

From above, Mordred wrapped blood magic around her

mouth before using his light magic to blind her other eye. He dropped down beside me and we both ran until we were directly under the dragon. Mordred used his own air magic and sliced open her belly. He looked over at me and nodded. In a heartbeat, I removed my jian, put everything I had into two spheres of magic, and forced them both up into the sliced underbelly of Tiamat.

The magic tore her apart from the inside out. As my elemental magic destroyed her from underneath, we sprinted out from under the dragon, and I collapsed to my knees. Mordred knelt beside me, breathing rapidly. He was as spent as I was. But Tiamat still wasn't dead.

I pushed myself off the ground, creating a sphere of power between both hands, pouring air, lightning, fire, and shadow into it. I ran toward Tiamat, who opened her mouth, the purple magic pulsating far inside her body.

I avoided the open maw, and drove the sphere toward her ruined eye. At the very last second, I changed it into a blade of brilliant white, crackling energy, and shot the merged energy into her eye. Once inside her skull the magic exploded, tearing the back of her head apart, and continuing on through the top of her spine, as if she'd been hit by a barrage of missiles. Magic continued to pour out of me, and for a heartbeat I wasn't sure if I could stop it, but within seconds Tiamat's entire body shuddered from the power I was pouring into her.

I collapsed to the ground, every ounce of magic inside of me spent. My body screamed at me in pain to let it rest. I put my head on the cool grass and concentrated on my breathing. It was then that I looked over at where Morgan had been thrown and forced myself to my feet. I needn't have worried as she dragged herself onto the grass, looked over at me and winked.

"I'm not certain, but I think being hit by a dragon really hurts," she said.

"I'm glad you're alive!" I shouted back. "I need to check on Remy."

I turned and watched as my fox friend walked out of the Tate Modern like nothing had happened. He brushed some dirt from his tail and waved.

"How is that possible?" I asked as he stood beside me. "You should be broken."

"Yeah, thanks, Nate. Nice to see you too."

I grabbed him and hugged him.

"You hug me any longer, you'll need to buy me food," he said. "Also, I got a bunch of lives from the witches who did this to me. I think I used a few up, but I'll be good."

Tommy walked over. He was drenched and had probably been dragging people out of the river. He was also only wearing a pair of red boxers.

"Mordred wants to talk to you," he said, his voice tense. "He's . . . different, isn't he?"

I nodded. "I don't exactly know how. He's not the Mordred I grew up with, but he's not the insane criminal, either."

"Are you going to put some clothes on?" Remy asked Tommy. "You're giving me envious thoughts here."

"Hey, I'm proud of my body," Tommy said.

"No shit. You're wearing silk boxer shorts. Where did you even find boxer shorts out here?"

Morgan laughed and then yelped, before telling them both not to make her laugh.

I left them to their argument and joined Mordred, who was sitting beside Tiamat's massive jaw. "We just killed a dragon-god. A dragon so old, and so powerful, that other dragons would have looked and gone, 'Shit, dude. I'm not going near her.' I think that makes us badasses."

"That we did. I think the badass motherfuckery was in abundance today."

He nodded slightly. "Let's never do that again."

"Agreed."

"When we got back, there was something I wanted to tell you. Something I felt you deserved to know."

I motioned for him to continue.

"Back in Acre: Isabel was my daughter. That's why Siris went after her. She knew once I found out, I'd never really be on her side. I'd never allow Siris to use my daughter in the attack, so she killed Isabel before I could kill her."

I'd considered the idea that she was Mordred's daughter for many years after Acre. "I'm sorry, Mordred. I really am. Thank you for telling me."

"I'm telling you for two reasons. One, it's time you knew the truth. And two, I'm going to kill Siris. I'm going to tear her in half. I'm not going to stop until it's done. So if you need me, that's where I'll be: hunting her down and killing everything between me and her. I owe Isabel that much. I wasn't exactly much of a father. Her mother had been human and had no idea who I was. I liked her, though, genuinely liked her, even in the haze of insanity." He turned his hand over to show me he'd created a truth rune on his hand. "Just so you know."

"Can I ask you something while you have that on your hand?"

He nodded.

"How'd you survive the shot to the head?"

"My magic healed me. There was a blood-magic curse mark on me that activated when my heart stopped beating. It used my nightmare, or whatever you want to call it, to keep me alive. The nightmare is gone now, and my magical power has increased in the process. I don't think the nightmares were ever meant to be something we should be afraid of."

"My nightmare said the same thing. He said that the magic is our birthright, not our enemy."

"That's the impression I got. All I know is that my nightmare cocooned me in magic for the better part of three months while my injuries healed. Physically healed, anyway. And I doubt I'm lucky enough to have the only beneficial nightmare."

"It's a lot to think on."

"This whole thing is a lot to think on. I think I'm going to buy a bottle of Scotch, the world's biggest bag of fish-and-chips and drink and eat myself into a coma." He hummed the *Mario* tune again. "I'm not sure if I want to stop having these little brain things. I quite like having my mind always on the move." He smiled.

"Good luck, Mordred."

"To you too, Nate. We'll be seeing one another soon enough."

"I'm not going to let the Fates' prophecy come true. Whoever is pulling my strings, they're not going to get me to become someone I'm not."

Mordred shrugged and got to his feet. "Maybe the Fates were wrong, Nate. Either way, I don't feel like killing you these days. I feel like making things right, you know?"

I did.

"The Fates aren't always right, and frankly they tell you what they want to tell you half the time."

"That's very true."

"I really hope it doesn't come to that, Nate. I really would like to see if we could be friends instead."

I stood and offered him my hand. He shook it without hesitation. "It's been so long since I've been able to call you a friend, Nate. I'm sorry for all I wronged you."

He turned and walked away, humming the *Mario* theme tune to himself.

"Mordred," I called after him, and he stopped, looking back at me. "Don't be a stranger."

He smiled, it was warm and reminded me of simpler days. "You too, Nate. You too."

And then he was gone, leaving me to deal with several dozen tons of dead dragon.

CHAPTER 42

Turns out getting rid of a dead dragon was a lot easier than I'd expected. Mostly because it soon became apparent that it wasn't our problem.

The entire group had gathered together outside the Tate Modern, comparing war wounds and trying to figure out where to go from there, when a helicopter buzzed overhead, landing just beyond the nearby wall.

"Anyone else notice it was a Black Hawk?" Irkalla asked. Like everyone else who'd arrived with Diane, she'd gotten drenched saving lives.

No one said anything.

Licinius was the first person I saw, wearing a clean suit and looking like he'd spent more time getting ready than he had pulling people out of a partially destroyed building. Zamek, covered in dirt, stared at the dragon then walked over to us.

"That's a dead dragon," he said.

"We're thinking of keeping it as an ornament," Tommy said. "It'll make the nice beginnings of a flower bed."

"A shrubbery," Remy corrected. "Gotta have a shrubbery."

"You need to talk to Licinius," Zamek said. "And I don't think you're going to be happy with what he has to say."

"What do you have to say, Licinius?" I called out to him.

The sorcerer walked over to us. He didn't look thrilled to be here, but then it had been a rough night for everyone. "Hera has taken control of the city."

"*What?*" Diane shouted. "She's in control of the city? She helped murder Brutus!"

Licinius nodded. "I know."

Hera was the kind of woman who, while beautiful on the outside, was so utterly poisonous and vile on the inside, that it made you think you needed a wash any time you met her. With bleach. Time spent with Hera would be only slightly less preferable than having my limbs sawn off with a rusty bayonet.

"She couldn't have waited a few days to step in and throw her weight around?" I asked. "At least try to make it look like she cared?"

Licinius removed a piece of paper from his pocket. "The official answer to why she's involved is: *I graciously stepped in to help oversee the transition of power from Brutus, who was a long-time power in the region, and his death will be keenly felt. While his loss is great, we cannot allow this great city to fall to ruin without a hand to steady it.*"

"Why are you working for this harpy?" Diane asked Licinius, barely keeping her anger in check.

Licinius took a deep breath, but with no immediate answer, Diane's anger flared. "You traitorous little shit!" she snarled and started toward Licinius, but I stepped between her and her would-be victim.

"Explain quickly," I told him.

"Hera, Ares, and several of her . . . friends arrived at the building about an hour ago. It was explained in no uncertain terms that I either work for her as the new king of London, or she would replace Brutus with one of her close friends."

"You could have had her marched out by her ears," Diane snapped.

"I made some calls after she arrived, talked to a few friends in Avalon. It took every favor I've ever managed to acquire, but I found out that this takeover was signed off by Merlin. It's not official, and there's no paper trail, but he's definitely involved. I was also given a very strong sense that if I didn't agree to this, everyone in Brutus's employ would be dead. After some checking, I found out that several of the higher-ups in Brutus's organization had already made deals with Hera for her to take over. This might be Hera doing it, but it's Avalon-backed."

"You're sure?" I asked.

Licinius nodded. "Merlin's hands are unofficially in this. I don't know what game he's playing, but he's helping Hera play it. When Brutus allowed Ares to put Mars Warfare in London, Avalon used it to keep an eye on him. I'm hoping that by taking this role, I can do the same with the rest of them."

"If they find out, they'll kill you," Diane told him.

"I know. But the alternative is to allow them to destroy everything Brutus worked for. I can't allow that. That tablet Siris sent you; I had one just like it, but after you used it and vanished, I decided that I probably didn't want to use mine. I started looking into them, and then Brutus got killed and Hera turned up. She told me that I was lucky not to have gone with you. It meant she could offer me a job."

"I couldn't work there," Diane told him, her anger all but gone. "I'd do something stupid, like tearing her arms off."

"Hera has told me to tell you that she'll give you twenty-four hours to get out of London." Licinius removed a USB drive from his pocket and passed it to Diane. "This holds Brutus's entire files on everyone he ever had dealings with in Avalon. Also, your files are on there. I scrubbed them clean afterwards."

"Twenty-four hours is quite reasonable for Hera," I pointed out.

"That's officially. Unofficially, she has jack-booted assholes ready to start roaming the city looking for you in the next hour. You all need to leave—now. Something is happening, and this is the first part. You need to get out of London and not come back. She doesn't care about legalities: not now. And whatever Merlin or Avalon once offered in terms of protection, I'd say those days are over. They went for you before and screwed it up, and you managed to hurt them. Badly. Next time, it won't be some stupid plan led by an arrogant Kay. It'll be Hera herself. And she'll just go straight to the nuclear option."

"She's working for whoever is in control of this group," I told him. "A group that apparently involves Merlin after all. You need to be careful."

Licinius turned and walked away.

"Why would Merlin want to help take Brutus down?" Diane asked. "Why would he want to ally himself with people who want to overthrow Avalon?"

I honestly had no idea.

"Brutus has several files on prominent members of Avalon," she continued, holding up the USB drive. "I have no idea how long his encryption will take to get through, but when I've cracked it, I'll send them over, Nate. Maybe it explains why Merlin is involved."

I turned to the group. "I just wanted to say thank you. None of us would be here today without us all working together. Get out of London and watch your backs. This isn't over."

The group separated, with Remy, Tommy, Diane, and Zamek coming with me back to my hotel room.

"I'm going to talk to Avalon," Remy said. "I want a transfer."

"To where?" I asked.

"Your house. You've just painted a big target on your head, and they're going to come for you. You're going to need protecting."

I opened my mouth to argue.

"He's right," Diane said. "Anyone who was watching all of this knows you and Mordred were able to talk without killing one another, knows you killed Kay, a dragon, and helped the dwarves."

"About that," Zamek said. "I'm staying. I know I could go back, but you need me here, and Jinayca would be perpetually angry with me if I just left you here. Although if we can use the tablet to let her know I'm okay, that would be good. I know we'll have to figure out how to change the runes so we don't end up in the citadel again, but I'd be appreciative."

"I'm sure we can manage that," Tommy told him.

"We'll figure out a way," I promised, "even if we have to send Remy back."

"That's right, pick on the little fox guy. It's not like I'm small and quiet and can turn up in unexpected places with a knife or anything."

"Have I ever told you how much you worry me?" Diane asked.

"Probably. Everyone else has."

There was laughter in the air as we walked through London toward the hotel room I'd rented. I hoped my car was still there. Then we all had to leave. London was Hera's. And at some point whoever she worked for was going to make sure I was the target they put the most effort into. I'd managed, with help, to screw up their plans this time. Next time I might not be so lucky.

I would have to explain Mordred to Olivia—probably several times. And I would certainly have to deal with Elaine and tell her of Merlin's unofficial endorsement of Hera. Neither were going to be fun chats, but for all the horror and evil I'd witnessed over the last few days, I'd also seen a lot of hope. A lot of goodness.

We hadn't stopped the cabal, or whatever they wanted to be called, but we had hurt them. I wondered how long it would take before they decided to return the favor.

CHAPTER 43

Six Months Later. Canada.

I'd arrived in the North Shore Mountains after spending the better part of the last few months hunting for those who wanted to plot against me and my friends. I'd coerced Tommy into accompanying me on the trip so that we could track our enemies together.

A lot had changed in six months. Chloe had gone off to try and have some semblance of a normal life. Mara Range had been placed in a deep, dark pit somewhere; I cared little about where. And London had outwardly changed not one bit. There were rumors that Hera was culling those who lived there and disagreed with her, but nothing concrete.

"It's cold, Nate," Tommy said from beside me in the Ford pickup we'd hired from a rental place; it was a truck without a working heater. "Even for a werewolf."

"It's winter in Canada. It's meant to be cold," I said, using my fire magic to warm myself.

"I thought we might have gone to one of those nice non-freezing parts of the country." He paused for a second. "You're using magic right now, aren't you?"

"The very thought!"

Tommy couldn't look at me because he was driving and needed to concentrate, but I knew he wanted to glare at me.

The tires on the pickup crunched under the fresh snow, and even though the forest and mountains around us were picturesque, I was grateful it had stopped snowing a few days earlier. Despite being on an ordinary highway, the journey was treacherous enough without freshly fallen snow adding to the danger of driving into the mountains.

"How far up this road do we need to go?" Tommy asked.

"There's a spot to park not far from here. We'll need to hike the rest of the way. He's about an hour from Lion's Bay."

"He lives in the middle of nowhere is what you're saying?"

"Pretty much. It took me six months to find Gilgamesh. I'm not going to let him go easily."

"I don't think he's going to let you take him easily, either."

Tommy had a fair point, but I went back to looking out of the window, hoping that I wouldn't have to take Gilgamesh by force.

After half an hour, Tommy parked the pickup close to the lake and got out. "Looks beautiful," he said. "Any wolves in this part?"

I shook my head, and grabbed a small bag from the back of the vehicle. Real wolves and werewolves rarely got along, with the real wolves seeing their were-counterparts as a threat. "Bears, cougars, and coyote are about as dangerous as it gets here, but I doubt we'll see any of them."

"What's in the bag?" Tommy asked.

"Provisions. Some water, fruit bars: that kind of thing. And some beer."

"Beer?"

"I'm hoping this won't turn violent, Tommy."

"Is that why I'm going in a different direction?" he asked, removing a shotgun bag from the pickup and slinging it over his shoulder.

"You're my plan C."

"C?" he asked, with a raised eyebrow. "If A is peaceful, and C is a gunshot, what's B?"

"I kick his ass all over this mountain. I don't want him dead. Plan C is a dead giant. I'd rather save that for no other choice."

We set off at a good pace, using a trail that had already been created over the years, until we were an hour away from the lake. We stopped walking, the path leading higher into the forest, and went off the trail into the trees.

"Do you actually know where you're going?" he mocked.

"No. I figured we'd just walk around for a bit until a bear finds us," I told him sarcastically. We climbed higher and higher, until the trees broke, turning into bare, and mostly flat, rock.

"This is me." Tommy glanced off toward his destination. "Best of luck, Nate."

I watched him walk to the north, across the rock, and drop down at the end. We'd used Google Earth to check the best spot for him, and he was certain that he would have a good line of sight from that location to Gilgamesh's cabin. I just hoped he wouldn't be necessary.

I headed west, and it took me another twenty minutes to find the cabin. It had been built in a large clearing, maybe a hundred feet in diameter, with trees surrounding two-thirds of it. I looked through the bare spot, somewhere in that direction among the Rocky Mountains, toward a waiting Tommy with a rifle. Probably looking right at me. He would only have a small window to take a shot, but it was better than nothing.

The cabin looked like it had been there a long time, and I wondered if Gilgamesh had made it himself, or if he had appropriated it. It was a small building, probably only suitable for one, maybe two at a push, and made of dark wood. A small window sat near the front door, which was painted a dark green. There was a fire pit out front in the clearing, and two wooden chairs sat beside it. A stack of wood sat beside the cabin, presumably partly for the fire pit, and if the brick chimney on the roof was any indication, partly for the fireplace inside.

The snow had been cleared away from the whole area, leaving the green grass free from its freezing touch. I removed two bottles of beer from my bag and planted them both in a nearby snowdrift before starting the fire pit and taking a seat in one of the chairs.

I wasn't worried that Gilgamesh would see me and run; he wasn't the kind of person to do that. He'd confront me. He might have hidden for the last year, but from what I'd deduced he had come straight here and hadn't moved around.

It took ten minutes for Gilgamesh to emerge through the trees, holding a deer carcass against one shoulder.

"Nate," Gilgamesh said, his tone friendly and conversational. He wasn't surprised to see me.

"Gilgamesh. Nice cabin."

"Thanks. I didn't build it, but it's made for a pleasant home. There's a town not too far, so I get most of what I need from there. And anything else—" He dropped the deer on the ground. "—I take from the area."

He shrank down from a ten-foot-high version to his normal size, which was still incredibly tall. His T-shirt and jeans looked baggy on him, and he was barefoot. "I'm going to change. You okay out here?"

I nodded and let Gilgamesh enter the cabin. He emerged a few minutes later in better-fitting clothing, including some boots.

"They don't make clothes in giant size," he said. "So I had to make them myself. I'm not good enough to make my own giant shoes, though. And I was traveling light, so could only bring with me what I desperately needed."

"You want a beer?" I asked, picking a bottle out of the snowdrift.

"The other one," he said.

I sighed and removed the other bottle, throwing it over to him.

"It's not poisoned," I assured him, and used my air magic to pop the cap on my own beer, before taking a long swig.

He removed the cap with his fingers and took a drink, before looking at the bottle. "Japanese? You couldn't have just brought cheap stuff?"

"I like it," I told him. "And most beer is awful, so you get what you're given."

He drank some more of the alcohol. "It's nice."

"Told you."

"So, are we just going to be all civilized about this? I tried to kill you and Irkalla last time I saw you."

"Didn't work out too well for you, did it?"

"Irkalla was stronger than I'd expected. I only just managed to flee."

"Well, I figured we could do round two, and batter one another around a bit, or we could have a beer, and talk, and then you come with me."

Gilgamesh finished his beer and put the bottle down. "I can't do that last bit, Nate."

I nodded. "I'd hoped you'd see reason. I don't want to hurt you."

Gilgamesh stared at me and laughed. "The last time we fought, just me and you, I beat you. Easily."

It hadn't been easily at all, but I let him have his ego-polishing moment.

I placed the bottle of beer on the ground. "It's been a long six months, Gilgamesh. Siris is still missing, Hera is in control of London, and Merlin allowed it. Nothing feels like it's going to have a happy ending."

"You won't find Siris unless she wants to be found."

"I found you."

"I had no intention of leaving this realm."

"You should have kept running."

"There's no one Avalon would send that concerns me. I'm surprised they sent you."

"They didn't send me," I confirmed. "I'm here because I want to find Siris and her people and have them stopped. I want Hera out of London, too. And you can tell me where Siris is, and who she's working with."

"I don't know a damn thing. I made sure of that."

"In that case, you're still going to be going to prison for helping Siris murder Brutus and a bunch of other people. Hera might have Merlin in her pocket, or maybe it's vice versa, but no one will be able to stop Olivia from sending you to The Hole."

Gilgamesh darted across the clearing, increasing in size as he went. He grabbed the deer carcass and threw it at where I'd been sitting. Unfortunately for him, I'd already moved into the shadow realm.

I came out behind him, a sphere of lightning in my hand, and unleashed the magic an inch from his back. He flew through the air, and smashed into several trees, tearing more than one of them apart with the force.

"Stay down," I told him.

He ignored me and got back to his feet, roaring in anger before charging forward. He grabbed hold of one of the tree trunks beside him and flung it in my direction. A second sphere turned it into pulp. I didn't want to keep going in and out of my shadow realm; I'd have gotten too exhausted. There was no way to beat Gilgamesh if I wasn't at my best.

I gathered the thousands of pieces of wood all around me in a bubble of air and flung them back toward Gilgamesh at high speed. He'd started running toward me the second he'd thrown the trunk, and couldn't avoid the incoming wooden shrapnel. Instead, he raised his arm to protect his face. Pieces of wood were embedded in his arm, but he showed no outward pain at it, and continued on, unabated.

I dodged aside at the last possible second, throwing a torrent of air at Gilgamesh's legs, hoping to trip him. But he managed to turn toward me faster than I'd anticipated and grabbed hold of my leg, lifting me off the ground and flinging me toward the trees.

A blast of air stopped me from breaking bones when I struck the huge trees, but it still hurt, and Gilgamesh was already charging toward me once more.

"Last chance!" I shouted.

He ignored me until the shadows burst out of the ground, wrapping around him and stopping him in his tracks.

He tore himself free from several of the tendrils of shadow, but I was adding more and more with every second, faster than he could destroy them.

"Don't fight it," I told him.

He roared in fury and lurched forward, growing in size again, ripping the shadows apart, enough to gain momentum. I removed the shadows, which surprised Gilgamesh and he stumbled forward, catching his feet just as I drove a three-foot-wide sphere of lightning into his chest. The magic exploded all around him, tearing at the earth, and throwing him back.

Gilgamesh found himself on the floor, his chest a mass of bloody, raw flesh. He bared his teeth and used a nearby tree to get back to his feet. I raised one hand toward the sky and the rumble of thunder sounded above us. Lightning flashed down from above toward my finger and then traveled through my body out of the other finger that was pointed directly at Gilgamesh. The bolt had absorbed my magical power as it had traveled through, increasing its already considerable power.

It hit Gilgamesh in the torso and drove him back into and through several large trees. The earth beneath me shook as they hit the ground, along with Gilgamesh a moment later. The old king, covered in branches and leaves, pushed them aside with anger as he clawed himself back to an upright position. Blood poured from multiple wounds on his body, but he would not quit.

The hand that the lightning had left had become charred and painful; it would take some time to heal. I'd hoped the use of real lightning, mixed with my own power, would stop him, but I hadn't been that lucky. He pushed several tons of trees aside as if it were a garden fence and began striding toward me once again.

"That it?" he demanded and ran forward, screaming the whole time. I used my air magic to try and slow him down, but fighting one-handed hadn't been my first choice. And the pain from using my magic with a busted hand was excruciating. He grabbed hold of me, picked me off the floor and dumped me on the ground.

"You think I'm going to let you take me in, Nate?"

"Unfortunately, no," I said. "I wish it had been different, though."

Gilgamesh reared back to strike the killing blow, not paying attention to the shadows moving beneath me, until we both began sinking into the shadow realm. He released me and tried to grab hold of something, anything, to claw his way to freedom, but it was too late, and soon we were both standing in my shadow realm.

Gilgamesh's power faded to nothing, and he dropped back to his normal size.

"What is this?" he demanded to know as I got to my feet.

"Shadow realm. It's where my wraith lives."

"A wraith?" Fear crept into his voice for the first time.

"Want to meet him?"

Gilgamesh shook his head.

"You have no power here, Gilgamesh. You can either surrender, or die. Pick one."

"Don't leave me in here," he almost shouted. "I'll come with you."

I could feel the wraith gliding about in the darkness beyond, just waiting for an opportunity to feed on the new arrival. It was disconcerting.

I took Gilgamesh out of the shadow realm and left him lying on the dirt as I retrieved a sorcerer's band from my bag. He allowed me to put it on him, and got to his feet.

"You're a monster," he said.

"I've been called worse."

We marched forward, Gilgamesh in front, until there was a crack of a rifle and Gilgamesh fell to the side with considerable force. A second crack, and another round hit him before he'd struck the ground. I dove back, putting the trees between me and the rifle. Tommy wouldn't have taken the shot; he'd have known better.

I fished out my radio. "Tommy?"

"Nate, we've got a shooter. They're a few hundred yards south of me. I can't see them."

I looked over at Gilgamesh, who was lying on his back. He'd been hit twice: once in the heart, once in the head.

"You there, Nate?" Tommy asked.

"You see the shooter?"

"I saw someone take off; I can follow them if you like. I'm not sure how much help it would be, though. They've got a hell of a head start."

"Male or female?"

"Female. Although I didn't recognize her scent."

"Leave it. Come over to the cabin. We'll go from there."

I searched the cabin, Gilgamesh, and the surrounding area, but found nothing. Both bullets had been powerful enough to leave exit wounds, and both had probably been silver. Like most species the substance can kill, silver is also toxic to giants.

Tommy arrived and helped me bury Gilgamesh before we headed back to the pickup, where we found a transponder and tracker on the underside of the vehicle.

Tommy sighed. "We've been followed this whole way. They must have already scouted the area well in advance in preparation for our arrival. So, what now?"

"Now we go home, tell Olivia and Elaine what we know, and try to figure out who the shooter was."

"She was good Nate. I didn't even smell her until she'd fired. Not sure how that's possible."

"Magic," I said, taking a wild guess.

We were about to get into the pickup when Tommy said, "Remember a few years back with those witches in Germany? One of those killed a bunch of professionals, and she didn't leave a scent."

"Her name was Emily; she was the coven's enforcer. You think that maybe she did this?"

"We took in Mara, disbanded their coven, and arrested several members. I don't think the ones who remained free and still worked for Hera were just going to go quietly into the night."

He had a good point. "Worth looking into."

We got into the pickup and I took a deep breath. "This didn't go as planned."

"Nope. But then things rarely do."

"There's a war coming, Tommy. I don't think we can stop it."

"Well, we only have one choice, then." He started up the vehicle.

"Win?"

"Win hard."

I looked at my friend.

"Nate, we'll either win, or we'll damn well make sure the enemy knows they've been in a fight to end all fights."

I smiled. "Too fucking right we will. Too fucking right."

Tommy started the car at the same time as a call came through on his mobile. He switched the engine off and answered it, his expression growing more shocked with every second.

"What happened, Tommy?" I asked, concerned.

Tommy passed the phone to me. "It's Olivia. You're going to want to hear this."

"Olivia, what's going on?" I asked, feeling a tightness in my chest.

"Elaine just called me," Olivia said. "It's going around Avalon like wildfire and I wanted you to know. It's about Arthur."

The bad feeling intensified. "Okay, what is it?" I snapped, probably before Olivia could actually continue.

"He's awake."

E P I L O G U E

Mordred

A year after helping to kill a dragon and going back into hiding, and six months after Arthur woke, Mordred sat outside the building humming to himself. He'd been humming the same tune over and over since he'd agreed to do the job he was about to undertake. It was a song he hadn't been able to get out of his head, but he was okay with that. He liked it and he found it calming, even if it was beginning to drive Morgan up the nearest wall.

He'd picked the spot himself, simply because it was far enough away from the main complex that no one would suspect him, but close enough that he could get over the ten-foot barbed-wire fence without much difficulty when the time came. He was waiting for night because he intended to wear a mask, and frankly people wearing masks in the daylight were usually a cause for concern. At night, you wouldn't notice until it's too late.

The mask was of a wolf, for no other reason than he liked it. He'd made the eyeholes a little larger, but thought it looked pretty interesting. The mask didn't cover his mouth, which left him free to speak to the people in his ear.

"Any chance you could pick a different song to hum?" a woman asked through the earpiece he wore.

Mordred smiled. "Morgan, my dear friend. No."

"It's very annoying."

"It's from *Final Fantasy Nine*. I like it."

"It's the same thirty seconds over and over again."

"You could say the same thing about modern music. At least mine comes from an interesting place."

"A video game."

Mordred didn't care for Morgan's mocking tone, and he began humming the tune again.

"Seriously, enough!" a second female voice snapped. "You know the deal here, Mordred."

"No killing," Mordred reiterated. He was beginning to get fed up of explaining over and over how he was no longer a psychopath. He thought about making up business cards.

Mordred
Was a Murderous Psychopath
Cured
Mostly

He had to admit, it needed some work.

"Are you listening to me?" Morgan asked.

"Completely," Mordred lied.

He ran toward the fence and threw tiny blades of air magic at it, slicing through the chain-link with ease, which collapsed as he barreled into and through it. He knew where he needed to go, and made short work of the parking area at the front of the complex, quickly reaching the side of the massive building. It belonged to Avalon, and the interior had been rune-marked so that no magic or abilities could be used once inside. Mordred didn't have a problem with that; he was more than capable of using his fists and feet and head, and on occasion his knees and elbows. He repeated the word *elbow* over and over in his head. It sounded funny. He chuckled.

"Mordred, you okay?" Morgan asked.

Mordred nodded, and then paused for several seconds. "You didn't see me nod then, did you?"

There was a sigh somewhere to the side of Morgan.

"I'm fine," he said. He really did feel okay, too. After returning from the dwarven realm, his head had started to retain more stable thoughts. His focus had improved, and he felt less of a need to go off on a tangent. It's amazing what having people try to kill you will make you achieve. But on occasion his head was still a jumble, especially when doing something with a high-intensity factor. And breaking into an Avalon building staffed by armed Avalon members to steal back the tablet that they'd brought back with them from the dwarven realm was probably considered a high-stress situation.

"I'm gonna go be a ninja now. Speak to you soon."

He waited to see if anyone would reply, and when they didn't, he used air magic to help him scale the side of the building. Climbing it was much easier when you can wrap tendrils of air around any holds and use them to pull yourself up. At the tenth floor, he paused by a window and placed his hand against it. Light cascaded from his fingers, melting the glass, allowing him easy access to the dark building.

Those he was working with had scouted the building well. After all, they knew Avalon better than most, and had explained that the night shift would be light, even if they would also be armed. The second he stepped into the building, Mordred felt his magic stop. It was a horrible sensation: the idea that a part of you couldn't be accessed. He wanted to get this done as quickly as possible.

He moved through the small office and opened the door a crack, looking out into the corridor beyond. There were several doors leading to offices and rooms he had no interest in. He wanted to get up to the next floor—the top floor of the building, and one only accessible from the floor below.

Avoiding the guards turned out to be quite straightforward, and Mordred found himself enjoying hiding in the shadows until they'd walked past him, before continuing on again.

"I really should have gotten you guys to give me a cardboard box," he said as he reached the stairwell to the floor above.

"What?" Morgan asked.

"Don't worry." He removed the card from his pocket and swiped it against the card reader before punching in the key on the numerical pad. The door popped open, and Mordred stepped inside, closing it softly just as the sound of footsteps began to echo in the corridor behind him. He remained behind the door, crouched down, as the footsteps grew nearer. Fortunately, the guard only paused before resuming his duties.

Mordred crept up the short staircase, then along a lengthy hallway. He paused on occasion to stare through the glass panels that adorned either side, trying to figure out what was done inside each of the rooms, but he knew he didn't have long. Besides, all he could really make out were some shapes in the darkness.

At the end of the corridor was another numerical pad and card swipe, and he used the second number he'd memorized and swiped his ID once again. He stared at the ID card, which belonged to someone who didn't exist: a person added to the internal database for this express purpose. Mordred had asked to be called Mario Bros, but they hadn't found that as amusing as he had. After refusing to be called anything he didn't like, they'd finally settled on Yoshi Hino. Mordred had been pleased with that one. It was a small victory, but you took what you could get when Avalon was involved.

Something inside the metal door hissed and unseen locks moved before it slowly swung open. Mordred stepped inside—and came face-to-face with half a dozen guards.

"I don't know who you are," one of the guards said, a large man with a shaved head and bushy eyebrows, "but you shouldn't be here."

"I got lost," Mordred said. "Needed to take a leak, and I've been wandering about for ages trying to find a toilet."

"You can come with us quietly, or . . . Well, personally I'd prefer the other option."

"What's the other option?" Mordred asked, sounding genuinely curious.

"We beat you into a coma," the man told him, sounding unnerved that Mordred hadn't figured out his meaning without needing it spelled out.

"Oh, you were being all clever and subtle," Mordred said. "Sorry, I'm not good with subtle these days. Do you want to try again?"

The six men shared confused glances.

"Um, do you all need a moment?" Mordred asked. "I'm just here for the one thing, and then I'm done."

"Don't chat with them, Mordred," Morgan almost screamed into the earpiece.

Mordred shrugged and darted toward the closest man, kicking him between the legs and shoving him into the man behind. Mordred pivoted and planted a kick in the chest of the third man, who fell back just as the fourth and fifth grabbed Mordred's arms. The sixth punched him in the kidney and went for a second blow when Mordred used his captors' arms to lift himself up and planted his heel on the incoming guard's nose, crushing it.

He kicked the knee of the fourth guard, dislocating it, and broke two of the fifth guard's fingers when he refused to let go. A knee to the faces of guards four and five rendered them both unconscious.

Mordred's mind was calm; there were no thoughts to distract him. Fighting was one of the few times his brain shut off, giving him time to himself.

Guards one and two were soon back on their feet, but Mordred was faster, grabbing the hand of one and breaking the wrist as he threw him into the third guard. The second guard managed to land a punch on Mordred's jaw, which angered him, and he snapped his foot out at the side of the guard's knee, breaking the joint, and then punched him over and over in the face until he felt the nose and jaw give. Only then, when blood flowed through Mordred's fist, did he stop, stepping back as the third, and final, guard looked on in horror.

"None of you guys have guns, then," Mordred said. "Why not in here, but out there?"

"Too sensitive in here," the third guard stammered. "Are you going to kill me?"

Mordred was actually slightly offended. "No. Why would I do that?" He looked down at the badly beaten guard on the floor.

"Yeah, about him. He'll be fine. The problem is, if I just tie you up, they're going to know you didn't fight back. So, I can either knock you out, or you can try to hit me and I'll knock you out. It all really depends on whether or not you can handle the fact that you got knocked out without fighting back. To be honest, the end result will be the same."

The guard kicked out at Mordred, forcing him back.

"Nice technique," Mordred said, smiling under the mask. "Good snap, too. Human, yes?"

He nodded.

"I figured all you guys would be. Can't trust a nonhuman with all these artifacts. That's what you're guarding. Old weapons, supposed lost manuscripts, and the occasional piece of jewelry. Nothing you need to get someone with actual power to guard."

The guard threw a punch, but Mordred ducked under it, punching the guard in the jaw with an uppercut. The guard staggered back. Mordred caught his shirt and slammed his forearm into the guard's face. He let the unconscious guard drop, then began humming again.

"Will you cut it out?" Morgan snapped. "Are they all alive?"

"I was told not to kill them, and no one is dead," Mordred told her. "Hurt, though."

"The item you seek is in the room to the far left of your position," the second female said.

Mordred nodded and made his way there, where he opened the door and stood in wonder at the contents. There were row after row of shelves, all with metal trays, each one labeled with several numbers.

"You want six-four-nine-nine-one," the woman told him.

It took Mordred thirty seconds to find it, open the tray, and remove the tablet from inside. He placed it inside his jacket and left the floor the way he'd arrived, avoiding the guards once again on the level below until he could climb back out of the window and, with his magic restored, lower himself to the ground.

It took him three minutes from grabbing the tablet to sprinting toward the pickup area: a small nearby car park.

Morgan was leaning on a red Nissan Navara, a smile on her face. "You enjoyed yourself."

"You know what? You're right. I did," Mordred told her, as a second woman left the truck and held out her hand for the tablet.

"You think that doing this job will finally convince certain people that you're no longer insane?"

"It's a start," the second woman told her as she left the pickup.

"Olivia," Mordred said. "I forgot to ask earlier, but I assume Nate doesn't know of our meeting here?"

"I don't want Nate involved in this," Olivia told him. "Not until we know who is and isn't coming after us. Arthur's revival has changed things. Things that shouldn't necessarily be changed."

"You don't trust Arthur."

"I don't *know* Arthur. People keep telling me he's the second coming, that he's going to fix things, but so far, I have no evidence to back that up."

"He's not the man everyone thinks," Mordred said.

"You've said that before. Care to elaborate?"

Mordred shook his head. He was certain no one in Avalon would believe him, certain that people would think he was crazy. And maybe he was; maybe his addled brain had made him see things that weren't real. But something bothered him, and it bothered Morgan, too, so maybe it wasn't just Mordred's brain.

Either way, he wasn't saying anything until he knew more. He wouldn't make that mistake again.

"You don't trust Avalon?" Morgan asked Olivia. "You work for them. Shouldn't you be slightly more trusting?"

"Olivia doesn't trust anyone," Tommy said, leaving the pickup, and nodding thank you to Mordred. "And no, Nate must not know that we stole this back. Those people in there were experimenting on it, trying to figure out how to make more. Hera was seen leaving this facility on several occasions."

"Couldn't you have just taken it yourself?" Mordred asked.

"Not without a paper trail, or tipping off someone that we're looking into their activities. This had to be done quietly. That's more your territory, Mordred."

He beamed. "You want me to go steal more of her stuff?"

Tommy shook his head. "I'm surprised you got in and out of there so easily. It's meant to be high-security. I thought the tablet would be better protected."

"Hera doesn't think anyone will ever go after her," Morgan said. "She's always been that way."

"We'll contact you if we need you again," Olivia said.

Mordred bowed his head. "Of course. But I'm not an assassin for hire. Don't ever think I will kill for you. If you do, we're done."

Olivia climbed back into the pickup, and Tommy waited outside. "Mordred. Stay safe."

Mordred gave the thumbs up, but inside his mind was racing. Avalon was breaking apart, just like he always knew it would. Hera and her people would take control one piece at a time, and Arthur's appearance would only speed that up. The war was going to start, too; he could feel it. And then everything about himself and about Nate would come out in the open, exposing those who had a hand in the misery that had befallen them both. The people responsible for what had been done to them both would feel their wrath, even if it meant sacrificing himself to achieve it.

ACKNOWLEDGEMENTS

So, here we are at the end of another book, and it's time to thank all of those people who helped make this possible.

As always, a big thank you to my wife, Vanessa, and our children, who continue to support and inspire me in equal measure. I wouldn't be finishing my sixth book without their backing, or Vanessa keeping the children busy so I can work. There's not enough wine and coffee in the world that I can give her in gratitude.

To my parents, for always believing in me, and telling me to hurry up and finish the book.

My friends and family, who have always stood beside me (and in some cases behind me giving me a shove to get on with it): you have my unending gratitude.

A lot of people say they have the best agent, but they're wrong, because I do. Thanks to Paul Lucas for his help and friendship.

To Jenni Gaynor, my editor, who sifted through the book to help make it gleam. Without her, this book wouldn't be close to what it currently is. Also it's nice to have a fellow geek as an editor who gets all of the video-game references I made in the book.

Eamon O'Donoghue, cover artist extraordinaire: Thanks, dude. It means a lot that you've done all of my Hellequin covers to date.

D.B. Reynolds and Michelle Muto. Two of the finest people I know, and both amazing writers. They've beta-read my stuff for years now and have always been nothing but amazing.

A big thanks to everyone at 47North who helped put this book together. There are too many people to list here, but each and every one of them knows how awesome they are.

And last, but by no means least, you guys who read this book and then decided to read the acknowledgements too. You get a special mention. Thank you so much for giving me any kind of success I've had, and for any I might have in the future. Thank you for taking time out of your day to leave amazing reviews, or email me to tell me what you thought about the books. Without you, I'm still writing for myself. You're awesome.

ABOUT THE AUTHOR

Steve McHugh is the author of the popular Hellequin Chronicles. He lives in Southampton on the south coast of England with his wife and three young daughters. When not writing or spending time with his kids, he enjoys watching movies, reading books and comics, and playing video games.